CLOSE QUARTERS

As I heaved myself upright again, I checked to make sure that I had penetrated far enough that my background was clear, and I wasn't about to accidentally put a bullet into one of my teammates. There was the chance that something would over-penetrate and hit the house across the street, but there really are only so many angles that can be called "safe" when you're opening fire in a residential neighborhood.

The subgun came out of my jacket, hitting the end of the sling, the fiber-optic sights gleaming even in the dark. I was only a step away from the car, and while they had been watching me and laughing, neither of the *sicarios* had gotten out, though their windows were rolled down to let the smoke out. I could see just enough to see the surprise on the closest *sicario*'s face, just before I obliterated it with a four-round burst of 9mm hollow points.

His companion didn't even have time to register shock as the contents of the first guy's skull splattered all over him. The other advantage of my position was that, instead of having to traverse the width of the car, as I would have if I'd opened fire through the windshield, I only had to move the muzzle a little over an inch to give Number Two the same treatment. Dark, glistening liquid splashed out the open window and his cigarette fell to the street as his lifeless corpse sagged against the door column.

The entire assassination had taken about three seconds, and the only sound had been the clicking of the action and the faint tinkle of the brass hitting the rocks.

D1522709

LEX TALIONIS

PETER NEALEN

This is a work of fiction. Characters and incidents are products of the author's imagination. Real locations are used fictitiously. This book is not autobiographical. It is not a true story presented as fiction. It is more exciting than anything 99% of real gunfighters ever experience.

Copyright 2017 Peter Nealen

Printed in the United States of America

http://americanpraetorians.com

Also By Peter Nealen

The Brannigan's Blackhearts Universe

Kill Yuan

The Colonel Has A Plan (Online Short)

Fury in the Gulf

Burmese Crossfire

Enemy Unidentified

Frozen Conflict

High Desert Vengeance

The American Praetorians Series

Drawing the Line: An American Praetorians Story (Novella)

Task Force Desperate

Hunting in the Shadows

Alone and Unafraid

The Devil You Don't Know

Lex Talionis

The Jed Horn Supernatural Thriller Series

Nightmares

A Silver Cross and a Winchester

The Walker on the Hills

The Canyon of the Lost (Novelette)

Older and Fouler Things

And in the councils of all the states of Etruria the leading men openly stated, "that the Roman power was eternal, unless they were distracted by disturbances among themselves. That this was the only poison, this the bane discovered for powerful states, to render great empires mortal. That this evil, a long time retarded, partly by the wise measures of the patricians, partly by the forbearance of the commons, had now proceeded to extremities. That two states were now formed out of one: that each party had its own magistrates, its own laws. That though at first they were accustomed to be turbulent during the levies, still that these same individuals had ever been obedient to their commanders during war; that military discipline being still retained, no matter what might be the state of the city, it had been possible to withstand the evil; that now the custom of not obeying their superior followed the Roman soldier even to the camp. That in the last war in the very field, in the very heat of battle, by consent of the army the victory was voluntarily surrendered to the vanquished Aequi: that the standards were deserted, the general abandoned on the field, and that the army returned to the camp without orders. That without doubt, if perseverance were used, Rome might be conquered by her own soldiery. That nothing else was necessary than to declare and make a show of war: that the fates and the gods would of themselves manage the rest.

-Livy

CHAPTER 1

You know, a normal person, upon stepping out of a grocery store in a small town in Wyoming might not even have seen the dark red Crown Vic and the four young men in it. It wasn't sitting in the small parking lot, but across the street, in the shade of a big elm tree. There wasn't much about it to make it stand out, aside from the tint in the windows.

If they had noticed it, and picked up on the fact that the four young Hispanic men sitting inside were watching them intently, like these four were watching me, a normal person still might not see it as an immediate threat. Uncomfortable, certainly, and slightly out of place; *vatos*, as these definitely were, just going by their appearance and attitudes, were not exactly common in northern Wyoming, and nobody likes to be watched by a pack of young men like that. But they might still see them as only a threat to be avoided, and try to ignore them long enough to get out of their line of sight.

But I am by no means a normal person anymore. Haven't been for a lot of years. Most "normal" people would probably call me "paranoid" if they could see inside my head. I would probably correct them, pointing out that I am, in fact, "professionally paranoid." It's kept me alive in some very, very unpleasant places. I noticed the car immediately, and one look at the gangsters inside told me all I needed to know. These sons of bitches were dangerous, they were hunting, and they were specifically hunting *me*.

I didn't look directly at them as I walked across the street toward my beat-up old pickup, but kept them within my peripheral vision, watching them without focusing on anything in particular. I'd learned a long time ago that if you keep your eyes slightly unfocused, you can actually *see* a lot more around you. Details get fuzzy, but any movement will be instantly visible, and you can keep track of your quarry spacially all the time. It also keeps people from getting that hackle-raising feeling of being watched, since you're not staring at them.

Let these fuckers think I was oblivious.

I made a show of looking both ways before crossing the street, even though there is usually very little traffic in Powell, and crossed to the truck. My .45 was on my hip under my jacket, but I had a *lot* more firepower in the

1

cab. Part of me was hoping not to have to use it in town; Powell had a very low crime rate, and committing the first killing in decades was not going to help us stay low-profile. We might have a good relationship with the county sheriff, but word of a shooting was going to get around.

I got in and started the truck up, making sure my SOCOM 16 was next to my leg and easily accessible. Meanwhile, I reached into my pocket, pulled out my latest burner phone, and sent a quick text back to Jim and the rest of the team. It was only one word: "Wildfire." It was a duress code that we'd used clear back to Djibouti. It meant that things were getting hairy, and the guy who sent it was in trouble. The guys back at The Ranch knew where I'd been going, so they'd have a starting point. Still, it was a long enough drive that I couldn't afford to wait around for support. I'd have to deal with this myself.

To my complete lack of surprise, the car followed me as I pulled away from the curb and headed west, out of town. They weren't terribly good at this; they were following too close, and trying to pull this off in a small town was never a good plan in the first place. Outsiders were noticed, especially Hispanics in a place where most people were pretty white.

I was driving through town partially on autopilot, already thinking ahead, trying to remember good ambush sites. There was no way I was going all the way back to The Ranch with these clowns in tow, and if they were who I thought they were, shaking them was going to require some applied violence. Outnumbered four to one, I wanted a terrain advantage.

Unfortunately, Powell sits on pretty flat ground. Surrounded by fields, there aren't a lot of good choke points or covered and concealed positions that provided enough standoff close to town. I'd have to head north, up toward Polecat Bench. There were hills and ravines up there where I could set up, though I needed to open up that time-distance gap so that I could park the truck and move away to find a shooting position.

I was studiously avoiding thinking about the wider implications of a car full of possible *sicarios* in our backyard. There would be time for that later, provided I got out of this with my head still attached to my shoulders. I needed to concentrate on the fight at hand.

I wove through the outer neighborhoods, moving just over the speed limit. I'd made sure a long time ago that I knew Powell, Ralston, and Cody like the back of my hand, just in case. I don't think that, at the time, any of us had figured that we would actually be E&Eing through ranchland Wyoming, but here I was, and the worst-case scenario appeared to be coming true.

I took a dogleg south and turned onto Highway 14, heading southwest toward Ralston. The Crown Vic was still following; I'd been moving quickly, but there was too little traffic to be able to lose them, particularly in the middle of the morning. Most of the locals were working the fields or the range at that time of day. That was okay, though; I hadn't expected to shake them off in town.

I ran through the gears as I accelerated down the highway, the Crown Vic keeping pace behind me. They hadn't started shooting, which was good, but I didn't want to give them a straight line of sight any longer than I absolutely had to. They were bound to get impatient sooner or later.

I'd thought about going through Ralston and hitting the 294 north; there were several turnoffs into the foothills of Polecat Bench up there. But with them following so close, I realized that I didn't want to stay on one road that long. So, as soon as a turnoff presented itself, heading out into the fields to the north, I suddenly stomped on the clutch and the brake and twisted the wheel, turning off the highway with a squeal of tires and onto the side road. Working the clutch and accelerator faster than I think I ever have before or since, I ran back through the transfer case, roaring past two farmhouses before taking another left.

The Crown Vic had almost spun out when I made that turn off the highway. They'd swerved hard to avoid slamming into my tailgate, then back to follow me through the turn, and almost flipped over. I was briefly disappointed that it hadn't happened; that would have solved my problem, and possibly left one or more of them alive to work over for information.

I kept taking turns, avoiding staying on a straight line for very long. They had to be getting pissed by now, but they still hadn't opened fire. Eventually, I was going to have to stay on the straight and narrow a little longer, put on some speed, and see if I couldn't open that gap up a little farther.

Hitting the next major road, I banged a hard left and raced over the creek, heading up into the hills. I was pushing the truck as hard as I dared; I didn't want to flip on a curve or lose control on a bump, but I knew the road and I knew the old Dodge's capabilities well enough. I kept my speed right at the edge of what both the truck and I could handle, roaring up into the foothills.

I glanced in the mirror behind me. The Crown Vic was falling back a little. I grinned tightly. Tough guys they might think themselves, but my *chollo* buddies back there were flatlanders. They weren't comfortable driving at high speed in the hills. I was opening that gap.

My next turn was a risky one. The first violent turn off of Highway 14 had been onto a paved road; this one was onto dirt and gravel. And I waited until the very last moment to stomp on the clutch and wrench the wheel over.

I damned near broke the rear end loose as I hit the gravel road. The truck definitely fishtailed a little, and it took a good hundred yards before I was confident that I was fully in control again. Then I was bouncing and roaring up the road and over a ditch, leaving a cloud of dust between me and my pursuers. They could easily see where I had gone, but they wouldn't be able to spot me well enough to hit me for the time being, and if they were driving like flatlanders on the paved road, this gravel track was going to give them fits.

I had to slow down a little as the track headed into the next draw, but I was relying on that dust cloud to provide some concealment. I bounced back over the dry wash and turned off the dirt road onto a barely defined vehicle track going up the side of the finger.

After trundling another three hundred yards, just around the curve of the draw, I found my spot. I threw the truck in neutral, set the brake, and killed the engine. I didn't have much time.

My chest rig was on the floor under my seat. A yank brought it out as I kicked the door open, then I swapped hands, grabbed my rifle, and bailed out of the cab. I had to move fast, before the dust settled.

I ran uphill, my boots slipping slightly on the bunchgrass as I went. I was aiming for a rocky outcrop at the top of the hill, hoping to get there before the gangbangers could get around the curve of the draw and spot me. I hoped they'd get focused on the truck and not notice me, even though the slope was open ground covered in sagebrush and bunchgrass.

My heart was pounding by the time I got to the top and flung myself behind the boulders. I leaned my rifle against the rocks, lifting one eye over the edge to watch the draw as I shouldered into my chest rig. I only had four mags in it, plus one in the gun, but a hundred rounds of 7.62 would be more than enough for this situation.

As soon as the fast-tech was snapped around my waist, I grabbed the rifle, bringing it to my shoulder and pointing the muzzle past the side of the boulder, my eye finding the scope as I scanned for targets. The dust was settling around the parked truck. There was still no sign of my pursuers, yet.

The draw stayed still and silent. Even what little traffic there was out on the highway was all but inaudible. The only sound was the whisper of the wind in the grass and the faint creak of my boot as I shifted my position ever so slightly.

I was suddenly struck by the impression that, if not for the old Dodge sitting down there on the slope below me, and the modernity of my rifle and chest rig, this wasn't all that different from what some frontiersman might have experienced out there a hundred fifty years before.

Time dragged on, or at least it seemed to. The draw stayed empty. I was starting to think that the bad guys had given up. Or maybe they'd buried the grill of that low-slung car in the ditch only a few dozen yards from the road.

Then movement caught my eye. A voice echoed down the draw. Rendered unintelligible by distance, it nonetheless had the unmistakable tone of a curse.

I eased out just far enough to get the dark figure in my scope. It was one of the bald ones, wearing a black jacket buttoned at the collar and baggy jeans. He was struggling up the draw, a pistol in his hand. He didn't look like he was dressed for walking in the badlands. And he really didn't look happy about being out there, either.

I placed the stadia line on his upper chest and rested my finger on the trigger.

Then I hesitated. I knew what this was; those men were there to kill me, or, failing that, to kidnap me for torture and later murder. I didn't know for certain who they were, but we'd killed enough MS-13 thugs in Arizona and Mexico that I had little doubt that those guys were there in some connection to the mountain range of corpses we'd left behind us in Mexico and Central America.

But we were Stateside. I'd willingly ignored and blatantly violated a lot of laws downrange, particularly in Latin America. I'd killed a lot of people. But for some reason, being in the US gave me pause. Technically speaking, if I dropped the hammer on that guy, from far outside the range of his dinky little 9mm, it would be a homicide, not self-defense.

But I knew, in that pause, that these dogfuckers wouldn't hesitate. Giving them a chance would be suicide. My finger tightened on the trigger.

The rifle *boomed* loudly, the report echoing and rolling down the draw. The bald guy staggered, then fell on his face.

I quickly transitioned to the next one, a baby-faced little fat fuck with longish hair and a white t-shirt. He was momentarily frozen with shock; they must have been expecting to catch me unawares and helpless. Not only did that suggest that they had no idea who they were fucking with, but they must not have been familiar with the Mountain States. While not everyone was armed up there, a lot of people were, and not just with little subcompacts for CCW. Truck guns were pretty ubiquitous, especially with the hard times that had marked the last few years.

His hesitation didn't last long, though. These guys hadn't come up here to pop their violence cherry; they'd traded shots with other gangbangers before. He dove for the dirt, holding his pistol up uselessly, searching for a target.

I eased off a little of the tension on the trigger and adjusted. It wasn't an easy shot at two hundred, but I was in a good position with good glass. I let out most of the air in my lungs, paused, let the reticle settle as best it could, and squeezed. The trigger broke just as the stadia line crossed the bridge of his nose.

Another rolling *boom* echoed down the draw, and he jerked as the bullet passed through his face and cored out his heart.

Satisfied that he wasn't getting up again, I kept scanning, looking for the other two. There was no sign of the car; I assumed they'd gotten stuck and continued on foot. It was probably a pretty safe assumption. That was not terrain for a Crown Vic.

5

But after five minutes, they still hadn't appeared. I came off the scope and eased away from the boulder, careful not to skyline myself. I scanned the slope behind me, then started working my way around to the western side of the hill. I *should* have been able to see them if they were trying to come around to my flank, but I was in combat paranoid mode at that point, and wasn't going to leave anything to chance. Besides, it's never a good idea to stay in one place for long, especially when you've just smoked two of the bad guys from that position. Mobility is security for a sniper, and for all intents and purposes, that was my role at that moment. I was alone, and couldn't rely on anyone else to watch my back.

The far side of the hill was as empty as the draw, and while *I* might have been able to find some microterrain to conceal my approach, even in the sage and bunchgrass that provided all the ground cover there was to see, it was doubtful that my adversaries could. I figured I could be fairly confident that whatever military training was seeping into the world of the Latino gangbanger, through the likes of MS-13 and *Los Zetas*, open-ground infiltration was not one of the skills being taught.

I paused behind another outcrop, taking a second to plan my next move. I needed to get back to The Ranch. First priority had to be getting to a secure location, and that was the only truly secure location for Praetorians in the world.

I needed my truck; it would be a long haul on foot. I carefully moved back around the hill to my previous vantage point, stopping and waiting to watch and listen. I didn't want to run to the truck only to go barreling into the last two gangsters' fire. They had some ground to cover before they could do anything with their pistols, presuming they hadn't gone back to get more firepower out of the car, but since I was by myself, I had to err on the side of caution.

But as I scanned the draw, I saw nothing but the two corpses lying where they'd fallen. Somebody out at the nearby farm had to have heard the shots, but unlike a lot of urban areas, the sound of gunshots out in the open wasn't a terribly significant thing out there. I could have been somebody out plinking or shooting coyotes.

In a way, that was just what I'd done.

There was still no sign of their buddies. I waited for a few minutes, my eyes skimming over the slopes opposite and craning my head out just enough to see below me. Nothing. The draw was just as empty as before. They must have scrammed as soon as they saw the first two catch it.

I held my position a little while longer, then started back down toward the truck. They may have run, but I wasn't putting money on them making their retreat permanent. Not only was I already a target that they'd been paid for, unless I missed my guess, but I'd just smoked two of their homies. They'd want revenge, if nothing else.

6

I half-ran, half-slid down the slope, coming to a halt against the cab of my truck in a small cloud of dust. I hadn't shut the door, so I tossed my rifle in on the seat and followed it without bothering to strip off my chest rig. I pulled the door shut with a *bang* as I jammed the key in the ignition, stomped on the clutch and brake, and twisted.

That old, faithful truck started with a roar, and in moments I was moving again, bouncing and swaying toward the far end of the draw, watching the mirrors for any sign of my attackers.

My rear view stayed empty even as I rounded the hill to the west, passing an abandoned farmer's shed. I spotted the dirt road through the fields and made for it as fast as I dared. It was a bumpy ride, and I about knocked my head against the ceiling of the cab a couple of times.

Once I got on the road, it got easier. I turned north through the fields, and headed up to the top of Polecat Bench. I'd have to be careful on my route back, and make sure I wasn't dragging anyone along with me.

It did occur to me, as I planned my route, that evasive driving might be pointless. If they could find me in Powell, they had to know where The Ranch was.

I shouldn't have been surprised. While I had been assured that steps had been taken to discipline the members of the Network (or the Cicero Group, as the more dramatic members liked to call it) who had leaked our information to the bad guys while we were in Mexico in the hopes of using us as bait, I still didn't know just how much had been leaked in the first place, or even if the leak had been entirely plugged. We knew where a *lot* of the bodies were buried, and we had demonstrated a willingness to violently stomp all over cunning plans hatched in back rooms and restaurants, far from where the bleeding and the dying was happening. There were definitely people we had worked for who considered us a liability.

That said, we had plenty of enemies outside the Network, as well. We'd spent the last several years leaving a growing swathe of dead jihadists, rogue operators, and narcos behind us. For the most part, until Mexico, we'd kept our profile low, at least outside of certain circles. But sooner or later, the butcher's bill comes due, no matter how righteous the killings.

I was afraid of what I was going to find as I drove north.

***

The Ranch sat on about two thousand acres, backed up on the Beartooth Mountains. It had once been a genuine cattle ranch, up until a combination of the economic downturn, the ever-increasing costs of ranching, and the younger generation's lack of enthusiasm for raising cows forced the aging owner to sell. He hadn't been running cattle for some time before he sold the land. Some of us felt a little bad about buying his land and *not* actually ranching on it, as he evidently had hoped that somebody would take up the torch when he was gone, since his kids wouldn't.

7

But we'd turned it into our base of operations and training center. While we might have been sneaky and underhanded when it came to getting the job done overseas, for this place we'd crossed our t's and dotted our i's. All the requisite paperwork was filled out for a tactical training facility, not unlike Blackwater's old one at Moyock. In the interests of increasing our security and being neighborly, we had even actively cultivated a close relationship with the local sheriff, having the department out to train and shoot with us regularly.

The entry gate was closed and appeared abandoned as I pulled up. I knew better. I'd helped put the concealed, hardened guard posts in myself, so I knew where to look. Even then, I couldn't see anyone, which was kind of the whole point.

I was already on the phone. "I'm here," I said, holding the phone with two fingers in my wheel hand.

"Roger," the voice came from the speaker. "I see you. You sure you're clean?"

"As a whistle," I replied. I had been very careful and very watchful on the way back. That was actually putting it mildly. I had been on edge, poised to go into aggressive evasive driving, while ready to draw my .45 and dump the mag into any vehicle I saw that looked remotely suspicious. None of us who had deployed as Praetorian Security (I'm sorry, *Solutions*) shooters ever quite turned it off, anymore. But even so, this had been a nastier shock than I'd expected.

One of the younger guys stepped out onto the road. He was wearing plates and carrying an AR-10 slung in front of him. He peered at me until I waved, then unbarred and swung the gate open. I rolled through, pausing just inside with my window down.

After he secured the gate, he walked up to my window. "Sorry, Mr. Stone," he said. "I didn't recognize you at first."

"Don't apologize," I told him. "You did what you were supposed to." I glanced at the glorified pillboxes set in the brush beside the road. From inside, I could see the men with rifles watching through the firing slits. "Has there been any activity out this way? Any probes, or anything suspicious?"

The kid shook his head. Holy hell, he barely looked old enough to shave, much less be a vet who had done his four years in the mil and gotten out. Or was I just getting that damned old? "We haven't seen anything but you guys who were out coming back in in a hell of a hurry," he said. "What's going on? All I've heard is that something's happened and we had to go to stand-to."

"You know about as much as I do at the moment," I told him. "Somebody tried to jump me out in town, and it sounds like I wasn't the only one. I'll make sure the word gets passed down once we know more. Just keep your eyes peeled."

8

"Roger that," he said. I waved vaguely at him and put the truck back in gear, heading up the gravel road toward the main house.

Larry and Nick were on the porch as I pulled up, both kitted up and armed. Larry was a bald giant of a man with a dark beard that showed streaks of gray these days. He'd trimmed it down from his "scary murder hobo" beard to a goatee, but that didn't make the six-foot-five mountain of a man any less intimidating. He looked like a monster, which, conveniently enough, was his callsign. Of course, his love of B-grade monster movies and action-horror novels had gotten him the callsign, but most people outside the team wouldn't realize that.

Nick was not a small man, but next to Larry, he looked like he was. Almost half a head shorter, he was still heavily built, though his brown hair and beard were also starting to show a little gray. His eyes were set in a semi-permanent squint that still saw a lot more than it seemed.

Nick blew out a relieved breath as I pulled up and piled out. "Have we got everybody?" I asked, even as I dragged my rifle out of the cab with me.

Larry shook his head, his mouth tightening to a thin line inside his goatee. "Hal's on the way back, but we've had no contact with Jim or Little Bob," he said. "They're the only ones still out."

I fought back the sinking, hollow feeling in my gut. Jim had been my assistant team lead for years now. Little Bob had been with us since we'd first gone into Kurdistan. Both were solid professionals and good friends. If they were out of contact, it could only be because things had gone very, very bad.

"How many of us actually got hit?" I asked as I mounted the steps to the porch.

"Hal's running as far behind as he is because he had to lose a couple of bad guys who started shooting at him," Nick told me. "Apparently, there was a sheriff's deputy only a half mile away, and he got involved. Jack had a narrow scrape, and a couple of the newer guys got a bad feeling down in Cody and came running back up here. Not sure about anyone else."

"I left two corpses and a couple of scared gangbangers on the west slope of Polecat Bench," I said, as I headed inside, looking for Tom Heinrich. If anyone was going to have a more complete picture of what was happening, it would be him. The retired Colonel and I didn't see eye to eye all the time, but he'd been hired to run training and turned into a pretty good mastermind at turning the company into the de facto private special operations command that it was.

Tom was in the command center in what had been the master bedroom. Nobody lived in the main ranch house anymore. It had been entirely converted into a headquarters building, though one that could be used for meetings with clients and outsiders as well. Most of us had our own cabins scattered across the northernmost corner of the two thousand acres of the ranch, away from the ranges.

9

Tom was standing in the middle of a room covered in maps and whiteboards. We had a few laptops up, too, but most of us had become rather minimalist when it came to having monitors everywhere. Whiteboards and paper maps are simple, cheap, and don't require power and working internet connections.

Tom looked up as I walked in, my rifle still in my off hand and chest rig over my jacket. He was smoking, which was rare indoors, but given the day I'd had already, I imagined that Tom no longer gave a shit about filling the room with smoke. The crow's feet around his icy blue eyes looked deeper than normal, and his already gray hair seemed to be going whiter by the day.

"Jeff, good," he said. "Glad you made it back in one piece. What's the score?"

"Two dead gomers, two in the wind," I replied. "How many incidents so far?"

He pointed to the map of Wyoming spread on the north wall with the hand holding his cigarette. There were several red pins in it. "You make six, including James and Robert. I'm counting them both as 'incidents' until we get some contact and/or confirmation otherwise."

I studied the spread, which covered nearly a hundred miles. "All within the last couple of hours?" I asked.

He nodded, taking another drag. "Tighter than that," he said, checking his watch. "The first incident was…seventy-four minutes ago."

I shook my head. "Well, if there was any doubt that this was coordinated…"

"There is certainly none now," Tom finished for me. "The only question is which one of our admittedly myriad enemies has finally caught up with us?"

"After Mexico, I'd be willing to say that it won't be just one," I said. "Let any one of them get wind of us, and all kinds of assholes will be dropping their feuds just long enough to put us in the ground. It's the way of the world." I stepped closer to the map. There were little notes attached to the red pins with callsigns, indicating who had been involved. The only two that were missing were "Kemosabe" and "Sasquatch." "Do we have last known positions for Jim and Little Bob?"

He shook his head. "Not precise enough," he replied. "They were both heading into town this morning, but we haven't exactly been doing five-point contingency plans while Stateside." He frowned. "That's probably my mistake, but I imagine that it wouldn't have gone over well."

I grimaced. No, it wouldn't have. I would have chafed at it, myself. Stateside had become much less stable in the last few years since the beginnings of the Greater Depression, but it was still Stateside, and most of us, if unconsciously, associated it with safety. We still went everywhere armed, but I don't think any of us had *really* anticipated a situation that would have required downrange levels of security and contingency planning to present itself, particularly not in rural Wyoming.

"I'm going to get reset, grab some more ammo, and go find 'em," I said. "Powell's not that big; we shouldn't have too much trouble." *Especially if they've run into something they can't handle*, I didn't say.

No sooner were the words out of my mouth, then a sudden roar of gunfire sounded from the direction of the gate.

CHAPTER 2

I hadn't put my rifle down. Tom grabbed his M1A from where it had been leaning in the corner as we both turned and ran out of the ops room.

Larry and Nick were already in Nick's big diesel, and Tom and I hauled ourselves into the bed. It wasn't quite the leap that it might have been a few years before, but we got ourselves situated and braced in a few seconds, before I banged on the roof of the cab with my off hand. Nick threw the truck in gear and we roared down the long driveway toward the gate.

It was more of a road than a driveway; the gate was almost a mile from the ranch house. Tom and I held on for dear life as the pickup raced over the unfinished gravel track, leaving a cloud of dust behind us. I could hear the shooting even over the roar of the engine and the buffeting wind of our passage. Those boys at the gate were getting some.

It took only a bruising couple of minutes to get there, but by the time we skidded to a halt in a cloud of dust and bailed out, rifles in hand, it was all over but the screaming.

Three bullet-riddled cars sat at angles across the entrance, one only a few feet from the barred gate, which, while it looked like any other ranch gate at first glance, was actually reinforced enough to withstand the impact of a Level 7 armored vehicle without moving. Several bodies lay motionless in the dust below opened doors, and at least one bloodied head was lying on the dashboard below a shattered windshield.

I had a sudden flashback to the ambush in Arizona, just before we'd crossed into Mexico and into the shadowy world of El Duque. The remains of the MS-13 ambush had looked very similar, especially after I'd shot three gangbangers over the hood of our Expedition with a shotgun. I'd stared at the same mélange of blood and broken glass then, too.

I shook it off as I stepped toward the gate. The kid who'd let me in only a few minutes before was coming out of the pillbox on the south side of the gate, his rifle in his shoulder. There were moans coming from somewhere in the wreckage of the attacking vehicles; somebody back there was still alive.

The kid hesitated as he looked at us, as if unsure what to do next. After all, he was new, and here were four of the company's plank-owners, three of whom had been in the middle of some of the nastiest ops we'd ever run. He looked slightly intimidated.

It was a strange feeling, realizing that I was now one of the old hardasses that the younger guys looked up to. It didn't seem like all that long ago I had still been trying to make my own mark.

That was not the time or the place for such ruminations, though. I just made brief eye contact with the kid, then nodded toward the gate. "Don't just stand there, son," I said. "Let's go see what we've got. We don't own the objective until we've gone through it."

The kid started a little, then stepped forward, unbarred the gate, and pulled it open before falling in behind us. I led, with Larry and Nick on my flanks and Tom following a step behind, on Larry's flank. The kid fell in behind Nick.

"Let's try to secure at least one alive," Tom said. "Raoul should be able to get something out of him."

"We don't always kill *everybody*, Tom," Larry said, a note of unaccustomed asperity in his voice. For all his intimidating size and great skill with a gun, Larry is ordinarily one of the nicest guys I'd ever met in this business. But Tom's comment had just pissed him off.

I held my peace. That was another conversation for another time.

Keeping at least a yard away from the first car, I stepped carefully around the open door, my rifle up and trained on the cab, my eyes scanning the wreckage over the sights. I had the rifle canted to use the offset irons; while I could—and had—used the scope at close ranges, I much preferred iron sights at that range.

The car had been *hammered*. If I'd been counting bullet holes, I would have had to give up pretty quickly. Those boys at the gate hadn't fucked around. The gangbanger lying half in the car, half on the ground had been turned to hamburger. If my brain hadn't gone cold and calm, as it usually does in a combat situation, I might have sneered at the Hi Point lying in the dirt under the nearly shredded car door.

The guy in the passenger seat hadn't even made it as far as the driver. He was slumped against the dash, blood and brains leaking out of what was left of his skull.

A quick glance toward the back of the car confirmed that neither of the two who had been riding in the back seat were going anywhere. Both had managed to bail out, but had been cut down barely a step away from the car, and were lying in the road, their blood soaking into the dust.

Nick and Larry had fanned out as we passed through the gate, and were closing in on the other two vehicles. One of them was smoking, sitting on two flat tires, just as bullet-riddled as the first. I circled around the first car and closed in on the Ford sedan, Nick on my right.

The driver and one of the passengers in the back were obviously dead. The driver had a gaping hole in his neck, and the guy in back was lying half in the road, staring up at the sky, a fly alighting on his motionless eyeball. I started to ease to my right, intending to circle around behind the car. I didn't want to get in between the vehicles until I knew that everyone in them was dead or secured.

There was some groaning and cussing in Spanish coming from the far side of the car. I circled around, keeping my muzzle trained on the car, my eyes flicking back and forth between it and the far vehicle. Larry, Tom, and the kid had stayed with us, rather than split up and cut off each other's fields of fire.

There had only been three guys in the car. The passenger door was open, and a youngish-looking man with long hair and a sallow face, wearing baggy shorts and a soccer jersey with a telltale "13" on the back, was trying to crawl away, toward the ditch on the far side of the road. He looked like he'd been gut-shot.

As I came around the car, he turned and glared at me, sheer hate in his eyes. It was the look of a wounded animal, not a man. He rolled over and tried to point his cheap 9mm machine pistol at me.

Maybe I should have tried to warn him not to. I didn't. Instead, I just smoothly lifted my rifle, put the front sight post on his forehead, and squeezed the trigger. The rifle bucked smoothly, flame spat from the muzzle, and his head jerked backward with a spray of blood and bone fragments before flopping messily to the dirt.

His death hadn't silenced the moaning. So, there was at least one still alive. Fortunately, Tom hadn't said anything about me smoking the crawler. He might have occasionally let his background as an officer get the better of him, but he wasn't a second-guesser when it came to battlefield decisions. I was pretty sure he'd seen the gun, too. That had been a cut-and-dried shoot.

Together, we advanced on the last car. Steam was coming from the radiator, and the engine was still running, though it was starting to sound pretty fucked up, grinding and rattling. There had to be quite a few bullets interfering with its functionality. It must still have been in gear, too, because it was nosed into the ditch, with the rear wheels still spinning. I suspected the driver was dead, his foot still wedged on the accelerator.

My suspicions were confirmed a couple of steps later. Most of the driver's brains were splashed across the headrest and the door column. It looked like he'd taken a tight burst to the face. There wasn't a great deal left of the top of his skull.

The passenger and one in the back were similarly fucked. The moaning was coming from the far side of the car.

I moved around the back again; it put me across from the northern pillbox, but I wasn't climbing down into that ditch in front of a still-revving car. We could worry about shutting the engine off once we were sure there weren't any more gangbangers lurking around with guns.

15

The last thug was lying in the ditch, where he'd apparently crawled after the car got lit up. His white t-shirt was mostly red; it looked like he'd taken a couple of bullets, though they weren't immediately fatal hits. As Larry, Nick, and I came around the trunk of the car, rifles up and trained on him, he shoved his Beretta weakly away from him and raised his shaking hands. He must have heard the gunshot a few moments before, and realized what it meant.

Nick stepped forward, unslinging his rifle and handing it off to the kid. "I've got him," he said. I moved up with him, keeping my rifle trained on the scared gangster's face.

Nick didn't waste time, but jumped down, stepping on the gangster's extended hand before kicking the Beretta a good four feet away. Then he reached down, grabbed the young man by the wrist, twisted it so that he had to either roll over or risk having his arm broken, and propelled him, screaming in pain, up out of the ditch and facedown onto the road.

He wasn't gentle, but thoroughly, and rather invasively, searched our captive, turning up a knife, a couple spare mags, and two cell phones. The gangster, a skinny, beak-nosed kid, was screaming and crying in pain, in between cussing us out and demanding that we had to take him to a doctor.

He wasn't getting any sympathy from us. You come to our house and try to shoot up the place, you get what's coming to you.

Nick was just about finished when Tom's phone rang. He lowered his rifle and stepped back to answer it, while the rest of us watched Nick and the wounded gangbanger. I couldn't hear much of the following conversation, but Tom's normally grim voice got even more grave than usual, and I felt that sickening feeling in my guts again, even as I was careful not to show anything in my expression.

He hung up and put his phone back in his pocket. "Jeff," he called. His tone wasn't encouraging.

I lowered my rifle and stepped over to him, Larry moving up to take my place covering the captive gunman.

Tom's face was drawn, and he was searching in his pocket for a cigarette. He was a habitual chain smoker, but I could tell that this was something more. "That was Sheriff Eaton," he said, his voice slightly hollow. "He didn't want to say much over the phone; he's aware of our...difficulties today, and I think he's figured out some of the implications. But he did confirm that Robert is in the hospital, in critical condition. And, he wants one of us to come into town to identify a body."

That faint feeling of nausea became a heavy, leaden ball of dread in my stomach. "I'll go." I already knew what I was going to find, but it was my team, and I had to handle this myself.

Tom opened his mouth, then shut it tightly. I looked him in the eye. "What?"

16

He shook his head. "Nothing," he said ruefully. "I was about to turn into a mother hen, and caught myself."

I just nodded and headed for my truck. Tom had been about to voice his concern that nobody go out alone, which was just common sense at that point. He'd thought better of it because he knew that, as pissed as we all were, we were still professionals, and didn't need the reminder.

Most of the rest of the team had pulled up to the gate by the time I got back to my truck. "Bryan," I called out to the tall, dark-haired, lanky man who had just gotten out of his Tacoma, his OBR in his hands and murder in his eyes. I pointed to my truck. "Get in. We've got to go meet Brett Eaton."

Something must have been in my voice, because Bryan's expression changed as he searched my face. "Oh, fuck," he muttered, but he got in the cab without another word. I shoved my SOCOM-16 next to my leg, slammed the door, and put the truck in gear, easing it through the narrow gap between two of the wrecked cars.

"Is it Jim or Little Bob?" he asked as we got on the road.

"Pretty sure it's Jim," I replied grimly, my eyes on the road and my knuckles white around the steering wheel. "Little Bob's in the hospital."

"Fuck," was all he said.

***

I've seen a lot of dead bodies over the years. I've made quite a few of 'em. And I've seen more than a few teammates and brothers-in-arms go down. Even been a pallbearer at a few of their funerals.

But looking down at Jim Morgan's mutilated corpse, I thought it was probably one of the worst things I'd ever seen.

The local cops had circled the scene with yellow police tape. Both county sheriff and Powell PD cars were parked on the street, lights still flashing. The corpse had been dropped in the parking lot of a local lumberyard on the edge of town, apparently before the yard had opened. There were chalk marks and little placards everywhere, indicating every detail of the crime scene that had already been painstakingly documented. They were just waiting for us.

Jim had been shot four times, before he'd been decapitated and his hands cut off. His body had been stripped naked, and his head and hands had been placed in his lap. His genitals had been cut off and stuffed in his mouth.

A copy of the same wetwork ad that we'd turned into death cards in Mexico had been stapled to his chest.

A couple of the cops standing nearby looked a little green. They'd seen plenty of horrific accidental deaths, whether from traffic accidents or farm machinery, but they hadn't seen this kind of violence before. I pegged the couple of hard-eyed mothers who seemed relatively unfazed by the carnage in front of them as vets. There might not have been much violence in Powell in a long time, but there was plenty in the world outside, and a lot of infantrymen found their way into law enforcement after getting out.

I was flanked by Sheriff Eaton and Chief Mays. Ordinarily, this should have been entirely a Powell PD show, but I got the distinct impression that the crime was so horrific that Mays had called in everybody he could to deal with it.

A vaguely disturbing thought occurred to me. As horrified, grieved, and monumentally, volcanically pissed as I was, this gruesome horror that was threatening to make a few of the cops lose their lunches—those who hadn't already—was actually rather *mild* compared to some of the shit I'd witnessed over the last few years.

"When did he come into town, do you know?" Sheriff Brett Eaton was trying to stay strictly professional, though I knew he was just as affected as the cops and deputies. He'd spent a *lot* of hours on our ranges, and had become a friend more than a client. It had been, initially, a purely pragmatic move on our part. If you want to survive in the environments we routinely worked in overseas, you have to either go as completely unnoticed as possible, or make friends of the locals. Since a two thousand-acre ranch with a shoot house and 1000-yard ranges wasn't exactly going to go unnoticed, we'd gone for making friends.

Working with the local sheriff's department wasn't like working with, say, Hussein Ali's al Khazraji militia. While enough of a bond had been built in Basra that pretty much the entirety of the crusty old commander's extended family had insisted on joining up with the company, they were still Arabs, and we weren't. The sheriff and his deputies were a lot closer to us than the Arabs ever would be, regardless of how much blood we had shed together with Hussein Ali and his boys. What had begun as a strategic move to secure our position in northern Wyoming had turned into a genuine friendship and partnership.

"I don't know for sure when he left," I replied, "but Jim was always an early riser, especially Stateside. When was the body found?"

"When the manager showed up for work, about seven-thirty," he answered. "We've been trying to get in touch with you for a while. The boys were ready to pack the body up a couple hours ago, but I thought you needed to see it; this looks like a message, and I thought you might know just what it says."

I shook my head, still staring down at my friend and assistant team lead's corpse. "We've been a little busy," I said. That got a look from him, and a frown.

"Are we going to find more bodies cropping up?" he asked.

"Not of ours," I replied grimly. "A few of theirs. About a dozen out by the ranch gate."

"Son of a..." He ran a hand over his face. "What the hell is going on?"

"Trust me, you don't want the whole story," I told him. "But this is definitely coordinated, and I'm fairly certain that it's connected to some of our past operations."

"Terrorism?" he asked, a faint hush entering his voice. That had become the magic word over the last couple of decades, the invocation of ultimate evil that presaged awful things to come, even though it had, ultimately, become routine in the brave new world since the '70s.

I grimaced. "It's a bit more complicated than that," I told him. "You'll find most of the bodies are Hispanic. Given the predominance of the number thirteen on their clothes and their tattoos, I'm pretty sure I know who they are. I'm just not sure who sent them yet."

Eaton gave me a hard look. He was getting older and going to fat, and his hard look wasn't nearly as intimidating to me as he might have liked. "I might not want to hear the whole story," he said, when I appeared completely unfazed by his glare, "but I think I need to. If we're looking at a shooting war in northern Wyoming, my people and I need to know what we're in for."

I looked him in the eye for a moment, then let out a breath and nodded. He had a fair point. I could hope that this attack was the only one coming, at least for the moment, but as has been said by many, "Hope is not a plan." That death card stapled to Jim's chest was a clear enough message that these shitheads hadn't planned and executed this operation by themselves, or in a vacuum. We might have a little breathing room while whoever had sent them reset and adjusted their plans and tactics, but this was far from over, and Brett and his people were going to have to deal with the consequences just as much as we were.

"Let's get Jim's body taken care of, then I'll tell you what you need to know on the way to the hospital," I said. He stared at me for a second, his eyes narrowed. I knew he'd picked up on the phrase "need to know," even though I hadn't meant it precisely that way. But he kept his thoughts to himself, and just nodded his assent.

Bryan and I lifted Jim's body into the body bag and then onto the gurney for the trip to the morgue. He was our guy, and Brett and Mays had enough respect for us to allow us that courtesy, though a couple of the paramedics looked like they wanted to object.

I tossed Bryan the keys to my truck. "I'll ride with Brett," I told him. He just caught the keys and nodded. There wasn't much to say.

Brett got into his car, and I slid into the back seat. Brett might have made a crack about riding in the back seat of a sheriff's car, but refrained. Even as grim as the day already was, I was sure that Bryan wouldn't have, and would probably have something cooked up in his twisted mind by the time we got back to The Ranch. He'd have time to perfect it on the way.

19

As Brett hit the lights and put the car in gear, I started in on the story. I was as brief as possible, leaving out a lot of the gory details that he didn't need to know, but I outlined the initial op in Kurdistan, which had led us to Basra in search of the Qods Force command cell. I told him how we'd found out about the Project, a rogue group of American special operations contractors who had embarked on aiding Salafist jihadis in Iraq to act as a counter to the Iranians, and how that had led us into contact with the Network, or the Cicero Group. I told him what our contact with the Group, Renton, had told me about the backroom factionalism and manipulation of national and international politics to personal and group ends that had nothing whatsoever to do with patriotism or ideology, and everything to do with money, power, and influence.

That contact had led to our operations in Mexico and Central America, where the hunt for an elusive HVT known only as El Duque had led us further down the rabbit hole into the tangled web that was the true face of the new international order. He listened carefully as I briefly ran down the blurred lines between politics, espionage, terrorism, and organized crime, and some of the backstabbing we'd endured as we had hunted for a ghost in Latin America, leaving a bloody swathe of corpses and upset political and financial apple carts behind us.

"So," he said, after mulling over my words for a few minutes, "you're telling me that you guys have pissed off a lot of powerful and unscrupulous people here in the States, a lot of Islamic terrorists, just about every cartel south of the border, and the Chinese on top of it? Is that about right?"

"Pretty fair assessment, yeah," I replied.

"Holy shit."

"No kidding."

He didn't say anything more until we got to the hospital, apparently digesting the horror story I'd just told him. When we got there, he parked right in front of the Emergency Room and got out, then let me out of the back.

"What are you going to do?" he asked quietly, as I climbed out. "If this is only the first move?"

I looked him in the eye. "We're going to do what we've been doing for years now, Brett," I told him. "We're going to find them and we're going to fucking bury them."

He looked down for a moment, his lips pursed. When he looked up again, I could see the conflict in his eyes. "You know, given the oath I swore, and given what I suspect you're actually saying, I should try to stop you. I'm an officer of the law. I can't just stand aside and let you guys run around like vigilantes with machine guns."

I smiled coldly. "I didn't say we were going to be vigilantes, Brett," I pointed out. "I only said we were going to bury them. I never mentioned how."

20

He searched my face for a moment, reading what I wasn't saying. I was giving him an out, a way to say that he hadn't know what was coming. Finally, tight-lipped, he just nodded fractionally and jerked his head toward the ER doors. "We'll have to discuss this in greater detail later."

"No," I answered as I walked past him. "We won't."

A flicker of irritation crossed his face, but he composed himself. I hoped he was reminding himself that I was trying to keep him out of trouble. Brett was a friend, and one I would regret losing.

The Powell Hospital ER wasn't big, and it was easy to pick out Little Bob's room by the pair of uniformed Powell cops sitting outside. They both looked up as Brett and I walked past the nurse's station. Technically, I was supposed to have left my gun in the car, but since Brett was with me, and still armed, I wasn't worried about it. There was no way in hell I was going anywhere in the near future without being within arm's reach of a weapon.

Little Bob was unconscious under the sheets, with both IV and oxygen lines going into him, along with all kinds of monitors and electrodes. They'd cleaned him up, but there was a bandage alongside his head, and his chest was partially exposed, to reveal the bandages over at least three wounds.

"He was shot four times and stabbed at least once," Brett explained as I went to the bedside. "He gave as good as he got; we found his pistol with the slide locked back, and enough bloodstains on the ground to suggest that he got at least three of them."

I looked down at him. Bob Sampson had joined the team just before Kurdistan, and had gotten the nickname "Little Bob" because the team had had two Bobs, Bob Fagin having been one of the original Praetorians, and we'd needed some kind of differentiation between them. Also, unlike Bob Fagin, Little Bob was a giant of a man. Bob Fagin had been dead for years, but Little Bob was still Little Bob. He tended to surprise people when he talked, since his voice was soft and high; he wasn't feminine, but he could have been a schoolteacher, just to hear him talk. It had made his callsign of "Sasquatch," given his size and hairiness, that much funnier.

I shook my head. "Dammit, Little Bob," I muttered. "Still getting your ass shot off. I thought you'd learned to duck since Iraq." Little Bob had caught a round in the side during our final confrontation with the survivors of the Project.

I turned to Brett, and nodded toward the two cops outside. "I'm sure he's in good hands here, though I'd suggest getting some more firepower out front. These assholes aren't fucking around, and if they make another try for him, they'll bring the hate."

He nodded, his expression hooded. "We'll have two deputies out in the parking lot twenty-four hours a day," he promised, "with patrol rifles and shotguns." He squinted at me for a second. "I'm tempted to ask you guys for

21

some backup, knowing what kind of hardware you've got on that ranch, but somehow I suspect you're going to be busy."

"Ask me no questions, Brett, and I'll tell you no lies," I told him. "Trust me, it's better this way."

He sighed. "Dammit, Jeff, my job's to enforce the law. And you're not exactly setting my mind at ease that I'm going to be doing that properly if I leave you guys be."

I looked back at Little Bob for a second. "I'll make you a deal, Brett," I said. "If the FBI and half a dozen organized crime and terrorism task forces descend on this place in the next twenty-four hours, *and* go after the bad guys instead of trying to lock us up for shooting a bunch of poor, oppressed brown guys with automatic weapons, then we'll hold our peace and let the justice system do its thing. If not, then we'll handle things the best way we know how."

He looked pained at that. The truth was, I think he knew that no such thing was going to happen. The Mountain States had been left nearly autonomous for several years now, especially as several of the major cities had descended into near-anarchy following the dollar's collapse and the subsequent disintegration of the welfare system. Even assuming that none of the string-pullers Stateside were involved, Federal law enforcement just didn't have the manpower to deal with everything on its plate.

I could feel the rift opening as Brett composed himself. He was caught between a rock and a hard place. We were friends, and one of us had been murdered, another at death's door. But his duty was to the law, not to his friends. Conversely, he didn't have nearly the manpower or the firepower to keep us from doing much of anything, and he knew it. It had to stick in his craw.

Unfortunately, as much as we really wanted to maintain the relationship we had built with local law enforcement, we knew enough about the reality of the situation to know that going through the system was no longer an option. The war had just come home, and we were going to have to fight it or lie down and die.

I clapped him on the shoulder as I left the room. "Thanks for keeping an eye on Little Bob, Brett," I said. "I promise we'll do what we can to keep as much of the trouble to come as possible away from here." He just nodded stiffly, probably thinking that it was a little too late for that.

I felt my shoulders start to slump as I stepped out into the parking lot, where Bryan was waiting with my truck. Dammit. I had hoped that Brett would be on our side, and losing that support hurt on a personal level, not just because of the strategic pragmatism involved in befriending the department.

That thought was all that the horror needed to start getting past my otherwise ironclad self-control that had kept me from being overwhelmed by what had happened. I was shaking a little, my eyes stinging, as I climbed behind the wheel. For a second, I just sat there, my hands on the wheel, staring at nothing. Bryan glanced at me once, then looked out the window, giving me some space, at least for a moment.

Jim was dead. That cantankerous old bastard had become a fixture of life since before I'd taken over the team from Alek, several years before. He'd been an older, retired Special Forces NCO, who had joined up ostensibly because there weren't any other jobs available for a guy who'd been in the gun club for twenty-two years, though I'd gotten to know him well enough to know that most of that claim was bluster. Jim could have done just about anything he'd put his mind to. He could even have been in Brett's place, easily. He'd wanted to stay in the game, and he'd been damned good at it. He'd been a stolid, quiet professional, who'd had a way of tempering my own hot-headed violent streak without ever saying very much.

And now he was gone, murdered in the night by a bunch of vicious little fuckstains for standing against some very, very bad people. I felt the familiar spark of rage start to glimmer through the roaring blackness of grief and despair, and fed it. It was the only way I knew how to cope, to keep my head above water.

My phone buzzed in my pocket, yanking me out of my reverie. I hauled it out and stared at the screen for a moment before the number registered.

I almost didn't answer it. But I finally hit the "Accept" button and lifted it to my ear.

"Yeah."

"Oh, thank God," Mia said. "Are you all right?"

Mia had been the Cicero Group intel specialist that Renton had sent down to support us in Mexico. She was a pro. She was also very pretty, knew it, and used it to her advantage at all times. We'd shared a weekend at a high-end hotel in Veracruz on surveillance. She'd done a good job of convincing everyone around that we were a couple, which had made it a little awkward for me and the rest of the team. I will admit, she made me a little nervous. I was never entirely sure what her angle was.

"I am," I replied after clearing my throat. "Though not everybody else is." I paused a second. "Wait a minute. How do you know what happened?"

"I don't," she replied. "Or, I didn't until you just confirmed it. I just avoided getting snatched by three gangbangers in a van half an hour ago. I put two and two together."

"We got hit this morning," I confirmed, somewhat back on solid ground. Hearing her voice and the note of stark relief in it when I'd answered the phone had thrown me a little. "Most of us are secure, but Jim's dead and Little Bob's critical."

"Oh, dammit," she said. She paused for a moment. "I'm on my way to you. I've got some territory to cover, so it's probably going to be a day or

23

two, but I think we've got a better chance if we stay close." I couldn't object. "I'll see you soon. And Jeff? Stay safe? Please?"

"I will," I replied, somewhat by rote. I had no intention of "safe" having much to do with our actions over the next days or weeks. "I might not be here by the time you get in, but Tom will know to expect you."

She didn't reply right away. I could almost see the look on her face as she once again put two and two together. "Make sure you let him know where you're going," she said finally. "I'll see you soon." She hung up.

I looked down at the phone and sighed. I was pretty sure that meant she intended to link up as soon as possible, and even lend a hand. Trouble was, I still didn't know if she was being sincere, or still running whatever agenda the Network had laid out for her. We were all pretty sure she'd been put with us in Mexico as a watchdog, and we still couldn't be sure that that role wasn't continuing.

I started the truck up and put it in gear. There was a gangbanger back at the ranch who had some questions to answer.

CHAPTER 3

The wrecked, bullet-riddled cars had been dragged away from the gate by the time we got back. With the uproar in town, the sheriff's department hadn't showed up yet, though I was sure they were on their way. It was going to take them a while, though.

I pulled the truck up in front of the porch and got out. Tom was waiting in the doorway.

"Where's shithead?" I asked. The fury was burning pretty hot by then; I'd been feeding the flames most of the way back from town. It might not have been the healthiest way of coping, but as long as it kept me from breaking down, I was going to stick with it. I had so damned much bottled up grief and fucked-up shit in my head by then that I didn't dare open that floodgate. That way lay madness and fatal alcohol poisoning.

Tom jerked a thumb toward the back. "In the barn." I just nodded tightly and started around the side of the house. "Jeff," he called. I stopped and turned back to look at him. "Try to leave him mostly intact," he said. "We're probably going to be making local law enforcement plenty uncomfortable in the near future as it is. Let's not make matters any more tense than we have to."

I just nodded, keeping my teeth together. Tom and I had clashed in the past over similar admonishments. He'd done a good job running things back at home, but those of us out on the pointy end tended to bristle at "suggestions" about how we should run ops. I had to remind myself that Tom was right here with us on the chopping block, and that he hadn't hesitated to grab his own rifle and join us at the gate.

The barn was about a hundred yards behind the house. There were actually three of them; two hay barns and a horse barn. The hay barns had been converted into team rooms and temporary barracks. We'd considered keeping the horse barn as it was; there had been some talk about keeping a few mules and horses for training, in the event that we found ourselves in a situation like the SF guys in Afghanistan back in the early '00s. The idea had been scrapped once we'd found out how much it would have cost in time and money to keep the animals.

So, the barn had been turned into a gym. Given that it was big enough that even we couldn't fill the entire thing with weights and racks, about a quarter of it had been turned into storage and the other quarter into a dojo, with pads on the floor and walls and heavy bags hanging from the rafters.

I headed for the storage area, where a sort of cubicle of lockers had been built. Inside that little cubicle, hidden from the rest of the barn, the captured gangbanger was sitting, zip-tied to a chair with a burlap sandbag over his head. Two shop lights were standing in the corners, aimed at him.

His wounds had been hastily bandaged. He wasn't at any risk of bleeding out, not yet. It also didn't look like anyone had been in there since he'd been strapped to the chair. Tom had left him to stew and think about what was coming.

Tom had a vicious streak of his own.

I walked up to him and yanked the sandbag off his head. "Nap time's over, fucker," I snarled.

He winced at the sudden brightness and squinted up at me. "Hey, what the fuck man?" he said, feebly jerking his hands against the zip ties. "You can't do this. I got rights!"

I laughed without humor. It was an ugly sound, even to my own ears. "Rights. Sure. Keep telling yourself that, asshole," I said. I took a step in front of him, momentarily blocking the work light that had been shining in his eyes. I must have been little more than a looming silhouette, but this kid still didn't understand just what kind of trouble he was in. He didn't get it, not yet. "It's only going to make this last longer."

"Man, fuck you, *puto*," he said, trying to spit at me. He'd lost a good deal of blood, though, and he was dehydrated. He managed to almost reach me with a pathetic spray. I kept my face carefully impassive. "You can't do shit to me."

I let him eyeball me for a moment, letting him start to bow up, get some of his confidence up. As long as he could stare me down without my reacting, the more he'd start to think he really was as tough as he wanted to be, the bullet wounds in his body notwithstanding.

Then I hit him.

It was a good punch, a hard right hook that took him right in the cheekbone and popped his head around so hard he might have gotten whiplash from it. I followed it up with a vicious left and then another right, then hooked an uppercut to his chin that snapped his head back hard enough that the chair tipped over and he landed heavily on his back on the dirt floor.

I stepped over him, grabbed him by the hair, and hauled him upright again. Holding him up with my right, I punched him three times in the groin, my teeth gritted with the sheer, killing fury that was driving my fist into his body. Right at that moment, I didn't give a fuck about information. I wanted to punish this son of a bitch, and I was relishing doing it with my bare hands.

I let go of his hair and stepped back. He doubled over and retched violently, puking what little was left in his guts on his shoes. When he had nothing left, and was just dry heaving, I grabbed him by the hair again, twisted his head back, and pulled my folder out of my pocket. Snapping it open with a flick of my wrist, I held the point less than an inch from his eyeball.

"Rights?" I gritted. "You'd have rights if the cops had you. You'd have rights if the Feds had you. But I'm not a cop, and I'm sure as hell not a Fed. I'm a fucking *mercenary*. And considering you fucks just murdered and mutilated a very good friend of mine, I'm off the clock. So, I don't even have an employer to make the rules about what I do to you. Think that over very, very carefully before one more word comes out of your fucking sewer."

There was real fear in his eyes, though one was swelling shut where I'd hit him. He wasn't looking at me, but going cross-eyed looking at the point of the knife that was poised to put one of his eyes out. He didn't say anything.

"I didn't say you could take forever at it, cockbag," I told him. "Either you start talking, or I start cutting pieces off you, starting with your eye."

I hadn't meant to, but the knife blade must have moved fractionally closer to his cornea as I spoke, because he squeezed his eyes shut, as if his eyelids could block the razor-sharp steel.

"I don't know anything, man!" he all but screamed.

"Bullshit," I replied relentlessly. "Say goodbye to your fucking eyeball."

I am not by nature a sadistic individual. But right at that moment, it didn't matter. Nothing did, only the hate roaring in my ears and turning my vision red, and the vision of Jim's butchered corpse.

The sudden acrid stink of piss filled the small space, competing with the stench of his vomit, even as he tried to squirm away from the threat of my knife. Between the zip ties and my iron grip in his hair, though, he couldn't move. The point touched his eyelid.

"Stop, *stop!*" he screamed. "*Madre de Dios, stop!*" He squeezed his eyelids tighter shut. Tears of terror leaked out. "I'll tell you anything, man, anything! Just don't cut me!"

I eased back the knife ever so slightly, but tightened my grip on his hair. "Well, then," I said, "start talking."

"What do you want to know?" he sobbed.

"Everything," I rasped. "Who sent you? Where are they? What was the job?"

"I don't know who they are, man." I tightened my grip fractionally as a warning, and he tried to shake his head frantically. "I swear, man, I don't know! They were Mexicans, that's all I can tell you!" He paused a moment. "They were important; they must have been, if they could even get a meet with us, much less hire us. They might have been *narcos*, I don't know."

"How many? Did they have bodyguards?"

"Six, maybe? I don't know." He shrieked as I jerked his head back again. "Six! There were six of them, six of the important *pendejos*."

27

"How much security did they have?" I asked.

"I didn't count 'em," he said. Tears were still leaking from the corners of his eyes. He was terrified, and the pain of the blows I'd given him had to really be setting in by then. "But yeah, yeah, there were guards!" I barely had to move even a little to elicit a response from him. Any shift in my stance or my grip was a threat.

"Give me a ballpark figure," I pressed.

"I don't know...thirty, forty?" He sobbed. "Please, man, I don't know!"

"What did they tell you?"

"I just got what Miguel told us; I wasn't in the meeting itself," he said. He looked up at me through streaming eyes and saw me tilt my own head warningly. "They said that you guys had killed a bunch of their friends down in Mexico, and that we needed to send a message for them, you know? A message that it's a bad idea to fuck with them. They didn't have to tell us anything else, except where to find you."

I could believe that. *Mara Salvatrucha* had a well-earned reputation for brutality going back years. They used guns, but they also had a taste for using machetes. They would have taken any suggestions as an insult, and anyone dealing with MS-13 would be wise not to insult them.

Of course, we'd killed quite a few of theirs in Arizona, Mexico, and Central America, too, though it was anyone's guess if this cell had heard about it. MS-13 wasn't exactly a hierarchical organization with a well-established intel apparatus. They were more of a franchise.

They must have gotten paid a lot to venture this far north, though. I'd heard of some *narco* activity in Billings, but for the most part, the Mountain States weren't a hotbed for cartels. Maybe because the local "habit" of choice was homemade meth, and there just wasn't a large Hispanic population for the Mexican and Central American gangsters to blend in with.

Which led me to my next, and most important, question. "Where?"

He hesitated for the briefest moment before he sobbed, "They're in Pueblo." He had to have pretty well despaired by then. He had to know that if we let him go, he was a dead man. He probably figured that he was a dead man, anyway.

And I was tempted. Between Jim lying in the parking lot, naked and dismembered, and Little Bob all shot up in the hospital, I wanted to ram my knife to the hilt in his eye socket and wrench it around until he stopped squirming.

But then, as I looked down at him, his trousers soaked in urine, blood, and puke, tears mingling with the blood and bruises on his face, one eye swelling shut, something changed. I didn't feel sorry for him, not quite. He was still a scumbag and a murderer, who had been party to the sadistic murder of one of my best friends. But at the same time, he was a sniveling, terrified kid, zip-tied to a chair and utterly helpless.

And I'd damned near murdered him myself out of rage. I almost felt sick. I took a step back, folded my knife, stuffed it in my pocket, then turned on my heel and left him there, his chin on his chest.

I stepped out of the barn and looked at the sky, taking a deep, shuddering breath. I liked to think that I'd only ever killed people who were trying to kill me, though that wasn't actually true. That Qods Force Colonel in Kurdistan suddenly nagged at me. I'd shot him in the back of the head after Haas had been done with him, and buried him in a shallow grave.

Now, having come so close to killing another captive in cold blood, I suddenly realized how much time and energy I'd spent since either trying to justify that killing or just to forget it.

"Well, is he still alive?" Tom asked, forcing me to compose myself and shelve my reverie for another time. He was smoking what had to be his tenth cigarette of the day, at least.

"He's still alive," I replied tiredly. "I didn't even carve anything off him. So, you can get off my ass about it."

He didn't say anything, but just nodded and took a deep drag on the cancer stick. I got the sudden impression that he was giving me a moment. "Did he talk?"

"Yeah." I turned back toward the house. "It sounds like some of the cartels didn't like our interference down south. They sent some reps north to hire these assholes to deal with us. Shithead back there tells me that they met in Pueblo."

"It's certainly enough of a shithole for a bunch of cartel types to blend in there," Tom mused as we walked back toward the house. "Are you sure he was telling the truth, or telling you what he thought you wanted to hear?"

The truth is that information extracted under duress is always somewhat suspect. I was fairly sure the kid had spilled his guts; he wasn't trained, he wasn't nearly as hard as he thought he was, and I'd sufficiently terrified him that unless he was a damned good actor, he hadn't had the time or the mental acuity to just make stuff up, especially after I'd rattled his brains with those punches. But confirmation of the truth of anything extracted during any interrogation took time, time that we really didn't have.

"He was convincing enough," I said, after a moment's consideration. "That's no steely-eyed operative in there. That's a scared, wounded kid who thought he was a lot tougher than he is. I'm sure he didn't tell me everything, but he wasn't ready to get the hell beat out of him when he started bowing up. I think I shocked him hard enough that he wasn't holding anything back. Might have forgotten a few things, but not deliberately holding it back."

"Hmm." He glanced sideways at me, and while I didn't meet his eyes, I could still see the wheels turning. I was calm now, at least outwardly, but

Tom had seen me walk back there brimming with fury. I was waiting for him to say something about whether or not I was justifying my own rage-induced violence as some kind of calculated interrogation technique, which it wasn't. But he didn't. Maybe he bought my façade. Maybe he knew that he didn't *have* to say anything.

"Pueblo, then," he said, dropping the burnt-out cigarette to the dirt and grinding it out with his boot. "Nothing more specific than that?"

"No, I didn't get the impression that he was much more than outer cordon security for the meet that set up the hit," I answered. "We still need to see if we can get some descriptions, but I don't think he knows much. He just knows they were Mexicans, and they had security."

"We'll get Raoul on him, but we aren't going to have much time. We're going to have to turn this guy over to the sheriff's department once they get here."

I nodded, grimacing. "And they're not too far behind us, either." I was momentarily tempted to say fuck it, and hide the kid from Brett until we'd wrung him dry. But that would ultimately mean we'd have to dispose of him later, and after what I'd just almost done, I wasn't ready to do that again. And if Brett found out we were withholding a prisoner from him, and were interrogating him, there'd be hell to pay.

"I hope you didn't mark him up too much," Tom murmured quietly. Anyone else, I would have figured they were being a bit squeamish, but with Tom, I knew that he was thinking about long-term consequences for the company. He was a ruthless, cold-hearted motherfucker when it came to looking after the company's interests, and if bad guys got hurt, as long as it didn't adversely affect the company, he generally didn't give a shit. But this was a dicey situation, to put it mildly.

"He's hurting," I admitted, "aside from the holes we already shot in him. And I'm sure he'll tell Brett and the rest that I beat him up. I'll fess up to it. Call it heat of the moment."

"I'd rather you weren't around," Tom answered. "Brett can't make things awkward about hauling you in for assault and battery if you're not here."

"Brett's already nervous about what we're going to do," I told him. "If I don't own up to shitstain's bruises, it's going to further damage what little relationship we've got left with him. He's already afraid we're going to go behind his back and start killing people." Which was precisely what we were going to do; this was out of Brett's league. "Besides, I wouldn't worry too much about Brett trying to throw me in jail. You haven't seen Jim's remains, yet. I have, and so has Brett. I think he'd be more suspicious if I *hadn't* worked the kid over."

"I hope you're right," Tom said, as we stepped up onto the porch. "I don't want to have to bail you out and then have you break bail to go narco hunting a state and a half away."

Even as he was speaking, two sheriff's department cars pulled up to the gate, one of them stopping next to the shot-up cars, the other easing through the gate to approach the house.

"Well, I guess we're about to find out, aren't we?" I said.

***

I was true to my word, and took Brett to see the captured gangbanger myself. The kid was conscious when we walked into the barn, though one eye had swollen shut. He looked like he'd been through the meat grinder.

As I had rather expected, when he saw the badge, he first froze, then immediately started babbling. "That guy tortured me!" he yelled thickly.

"Shut the hell up," Brett cut him off before he could really get going. "I saw what you and your buddies did in town. You're in a lot more trouble for that than he will be for hitting you a couple times." He stepped forward, pulling his handcuffs off his belt. "You got something to cut these zip ties?" he asked me.

Without a word, I stepped forward and pulled my knife out. The gangbanger flinched a little as I did, and Brett's eyes flickered. He noticed. But he didn't say anything as I cut the captive free.

If the kid had had any ideas about making a run for it, they were quickly dashed, as Brett had ahold of one of his arms as soon as I cut it free, and slapped the handcuffs on quickly, reciting the kid's Miranda rights in a dead, robotic tone that suggested that his heart really wasn't in it.

He hauled the gangbanger out of the barn to the car, and stuffed him into the back seat. The kid seemed to have decided that *omerta* was the better part of valor under the circumstances, though I had no doubt that as soon as he got in front of a lawyer, he'd be telling a hugely embellished version of the beating I'd given him. It wouldn't be entirely inaccurate. It also probably wouldn't get him off, though it might get me in trouble. He couldn't claim police brutality, since I was a private citizen, but wrongful imprisonment and assault and battery were possible.

With the prisoner safely in the car, Brett turned and looked me in the eye. "You should have told me you had a live one when we were in town," he said.

I just shrugged. I couldn't think of anything in particular to say that would reassure him that I hadn't been holding a prisoner illegally for the sake of interrogating him using violence and the threat of worse violence. In large part, because if I tried to say that, it would be a bald-faced lie.

He sighed. "Given everything else, I think I can arrange for no charges to be pressed, even if this little turd makes a big deal out of it. I'm sure Tom knows some good lawyers, too, in case it does become a problem. It should be an open and shut case of self-defense, and anything that might or might not have happened after can be fairly easily put down to severe emotional distress.

I can't say I wouldn't have worked him over even worse, after seeing what they did to Jim."

"You probably shouldn't be saying stuff like that," I pointed out. "Prejudicial, or some such."

He laughed hollowly. "I won't tell anybody if you don't," he said. He looked down at the dirt for a moment. "I probably should tell you not to leave town for a while, in case we need you to come in, but I'd probably be wasting my breath, wouldn't I?"

I nodded. "We've got some work to do. And the less you know about it, the better."

He sighed again, shaking his head, as he looked back at the car and the gangbanger in the back. "Just promise me one thing," he said. "If whatever you're going to do is likely to lead to more stacks of dead bodies in my county, you'll let me know."

"I'll do the best I can," I told him. "Although—and I never said this— if we play our cards right, this should be taken care of far away from your jurisdiction."

He gave me a bit of a rueful look. "I'll believe that when I see it," he said, as he went to get back in the car. "After all, this happened here. I'm not convinced this little dustup is all over."

I couldn't disagree with him, either.

***

The deputies stayed on-site for hours, carefully documenting everything, even the skid marks from where we'd moved the shattered car away from the gate so that we could get out. Every piece of brass, every bloodstain, every impression of a body, every piece of bloodied, shattered glass was carefully marked and photographed. Each of the gunfighters on the gate was interviewed, though their statements were as bare-bones as possible, and the self-defense aspect of shooting the wounded gangsters who had tried to point weapons at us was always stressed. After seeing the spectacle of Jim's mutilated body, I didn't think any of the deputies were terribly interested in finding reasons to go after any of us. It was still a delicate balancing act.

No sooner were the sheriff's department vehicles out of sight down the road than my remaining team and I were packing to head to Colorado. If they thought we'd hurt them in Mexico, they hadn't seen anything yet.

32

CHAPTER 4

"Damn, these guys ain't even trying to blend in, are they?" Jack muttered.

"No, they aren't," I replied from the back of the van, where I was already snapping pictures. We'd done a few recon passes just by driving through the neighborhood, with the passenger looking like he was texting while he took pictures with his phone, but the bigger Nikon provided better quality, and the van meant that we could get better pictures in general. Trying to be discreet with the phone usually meant that the angles were poor. Sitting in the back seat of the panel van, I had a lot more freedom of movement.

Right at the moment, my viewfinder was filled with a relatively fit young man with a pencil mustache and immaculately gelled hair, wearing shiny pants, an equally shiny black shirt open nearly to his sternum, and a short, white jacket. A thick gold chain around his neck and mirrored aviator sunglasses completed the image. I couldn't see from our vantage point, but I was sure there was a pistol in his waistband. The handful of other young men around him weren't as fancily dressed, though they were still wearing that sort of northern Mexican, garish, semi-formal attire that, to someone looking closely, screamed "*sicario.*" These guys weren't the baggy-clothed local hoods, any more than the other groups we'd picked out over the last few days.

We'd been in Pueblo for a week. It had been a week of long days, longer nights, and not much sleep.

We'd had very little to go on, initially. I knew a few guys who had done some work down around Pueblo in the past, and they'd offered a little bit of general atmospheric information, the most useful being the fact that the gangs were mostly centered on the East Side. They hadn't been kidding; it hadn't taken long to see that the East Side was essentially a no-go zone for anyone who wanted to avoid trouble. Even the local cops steered clear.

As we had cautiously ventured into the East Side, generally either driving through in the beater vehicles we'd bought with cash up in Wyoming, or shuffling through on foot, disguised as one of the numerous derelicts haunting the town's street corners, we'd started to build a picture. It was, necessarily, incomplete. There's only so much you can put together by observation over the course of only a week. Really getting down into the nitty-gritty of an area's human terrain takes months. We didn't figure we had months.

Every city has gangs. They're part of the wildlife of any urban area, regardless of ethnic makeup. Even the Middle East has gangs, though with the way that part of the world has been going for the last few decades, it's often hard to pick them out from the Islamist insurgents—often because they're the same people.

Different cities, of course, depending on local culture and law enforcement, have differing levels of gang problems. Pueblo had a bad one. There were dozens of local gangs, apparently into all sorts of narco trafficking, extortion, car theft, or just plain young, belligerent assholes being violent for the sake of being violent.

But the landscape had changed recently. The out-of-towners, who, even those less flashy than White Jacket out there, stood out if you were paying attention, were only part of the equation.

It was becoming harder, at least in the States, to pick out who was *Mara Salvatrucha*. The leadership network of MS-13 had, in recent years, started to urge their cells to downplay the extensive tattooing and distinctive clothing—usually with the number "13" plastered all over it—in favor of a lower profile. It was a matter of practicality and an expanding capability. *Mara Salvatrucha* wasn't just a gang. It was an international criminal empire, though more of a cellular, corporate one than a hierarchical one. There was still plenty of room for violence and intimidation, but they were finding that the violence was, if anything, more effective when the victims couldn't see it coming from a mile away.

There were still indicators, though. And if we were reading them right, MS-13 was taking over Pueblo. Big time.

They were everywhere, and we had observed numerous examples of local gangs taking their orders and offering a cut of their take to the MS-13 guys. It was subtle enough to probably be invisible to anyone who wasn't looking—and a lot of the locals didn't want to look—but after a while you could pick out the tax collectors and enforcers making their rounds. Sometimes there was some posturing, but it was usually violently quashed by the MS-13 enforcers. There had been five shootings and six stabbings that we knew of within a half-mile radius of where Jack and I were presently parked, just in the last few days.

But if MS-13 was enforcing its rule in Pueblo, even they appeared to defer to the outsiders. We didn't know exactly which cartels were represented, though I had a feeling that White Jacket was tied in with Guzman-Loera. He had that northern Mexico hilljack flashiness about him. The Sinaloans had been poor Mexican rednecks until they had gotten filthy rich off a combination of narcotics, extortion, and bloody violence, and it still showed.

White Jacket and his entourage piled into a shiny, gold-chased Hummer and the equally garish Escalade parked beside it. They pulled out of the driveway and headed down the street. Jack didn't turn around, but asked, "Do you want to follow 'em?"

I scanned the house that they'd come out of. A one-story, orange stucco job with an open porch and a relatively large yard, it looked no different from any of a dozen residential homes. But there were faces in the windows, and though they were too far away and it was too dark inside to tell, I was sure that there were guns there, too.

"Nah," I answered. "I think we've got our target house. This wasn't just a meet; this is their safehouse. We'll want to confirm that White Jacket and his buddies are on-site when we hit it, but if not, we can move on to another target. It's not like we've got a shortage."

Jack snorted. "True enough." Jack was relatively new to the team; he'd joined up just before Mexico. The sandy-haired former Ranger and SF Weapons Sergeant didn't talk all that much, and when he did, he tended to be rather acerbic. He was plenty competent, if a bit of a belligerent son of a bitch.

"I'm calling everybody in," I said. "Time to get this show on the road." Putting the camera down, I pulled out my phone, a burner pre-paid job, and banged out a quick mass-text. *Salt Creek House. 2300. Everyone.*

Jack just sat there behind the wheel, leaning back so that he wasn't that visible, shaded by the sun visor in the windshield. We wouldn't move for a while; if we drove away too close to White Jacket, it might raise suspicions. We didn't want our targets to be suspicious. We wanted them fat and happy, ready for the slaughter.

I took a few more snapshots, then pulled out my notebook and got back to planning. The book was already crammed with notes, sketches, and checklists. I kept my eyes roving outside the van's heavily tinted windows, but my focus was on what was to come.

Some of that was a self-defense mechanism. I'd had far too much time to think on the drive south, and had found my mind going down some very, very dark paths. Burying myself in the preparations, planning, and reconnaissance had helped keep me focused and somewhat even-keeled.

It would have been a little worrying, if I'd let myself think about it. What the hell was I going to do when I didn't have a mission to focus on and an enemy to hate?

I just told myself that the way the world was going, that eventuality wasn't likely to happen anytime soon, and shoved it to the back of my mind. Again, probably not the healthiest coping mechanism, but after decades as a gunslinger, I didn't really have much else.

The Salt Creek safe house wasn't much to look at, which was why we'd picked it. None of us were staying there on a long-term basis; most of us had been sleeping in cars or in a trailer just outside of town for the last week.

Bryan and Derek had each spent a couple nights sleeping in the open, as part of their bum disguises.

The white walls were as dingy as anything I'd seen in the Middle East, and the roof was sagging. It looked like the front porch was about to fall off the face of the house. The front yard was nothing but bare dirt with a bent, mangled cyclone fence around it.

Most of us had parked several blocks away, and worked our way in on foot. Jack and I had actually come in the back way, past piles of junk and beater cars, to jump the fence and enter through the back door, which was barely hanging on its hinges anymore.

Some of our safe houses in the Middle East and even Mexico had been turned into op centers, with maps, laptops, and tracking boards arranged in a central room. We weren't playing this one that way. We wanted to be able to break contact and get the hell out of Dodge at a moment's notice, without leaving anything behind. A large part of that was because none of us really wanted to cross swords with American law enforcement, and regardless of how evil the scumbags we were planning to put in the ground were, the cops were going to have to try to look into it.

So instead, we had a couple of tablets, notebooks, and reams of photos printed out at the local Kinkos spread out on the floor. All of it would be packed up and go with us when we left the safe house.

It was a dirty, grungy-looking bunch of peckerwoods that was gathered in the living room in the sickly light of a fluorescent Coleman lantern at midnight, and I'm including Ben, the sole black guy on the team, in that description. We called him "Carleton" for being "the whitest black man," which never ceased to get a rise out of him, but when the dude dressed more cowboy than any of the rest of us and listened to bluegrass all the time, it was going to happen.

"All right," I said, getting things going, "we've got four major targets. Any MS-13 that gets taken out in the process is an added bonus." We had our target packages laid out on the floor in four vague groups. I pointed to the first one. "Here's number one; Fat Boy. We don't know for sure who this guy is, but Raoul's fairly confident that a couple of his buddies are former *Los Zetas* shooters. They've networked with several of the local gangs, and recon has identified several possible spotter groups loitering around his safe house. At least one of those is going to need to get taken out before we make the main assault. Preferably, we'll nail two of them; hitting one a couple minutes before the other should hopefully provide enough of a distraction to have everybody looking the wrong way when the real hit goes down."

I pulled out the tablet with our overhead imagery on it, and got it centered on the target neighborhood. I pointed to the known spotter locations. "These kids are usually hanging out on these corners, and stay until about midnight. Groups of five or so. They do the usual gangbanger stuff, too, including intimidation, the occasional robbery, and drug dealing, but they're definitely staying there as lookouts. This one on the north is probably going to be the easiest to hit first, so, Bryan, you've got that one. You've got the special present?"

Bryan nodded, lifting the ratty backpack packed with explosives and nails. "Right here," he said. "And I've got the detonator, too, just to make sure none of you fuckers get any ideas." It wasn't much of a joke, but it got dark chuckles anyway. We were in that kind of mood.

"Just make sure you look pathetic enough that they can't resist robbing you," Ben said, "though that shouldn't be too hard for you." Bryan flipped him off.

The banter was a good sign. The rest of the team wasn't any better balanced after what had happened than I was, and the drive south had been a quiet one, overshadowed by a simmering, murderous anger. The fact that we could still fuck with each other meant that we hadn't gone all the way over the edge. Once things got quiet and the "dead face" started to be seen, then it would be time to worry.

And yes, there's a difference between "dead face" and "game face." I'd been around long enough to recognize it, though I probably wasn't so well qualified as to judge properly which one I was wearing.

"All right, knock it off," I said. It might have been a good sign, but we needed to get this brief done and scatter before too many people noticed that there was a light on in this house. "Coordination is going to suck, since we can't be on comms all the time. A vagrant on a cell phone…well, it's not impossible these days, but it's still a possible compromise that we can't really risk. So, Bryan, you'll stay out of sight until we've confirmed that the target is there. I'll contact you by cell, then you can move on your targets." He nodded, his game face back on.

"Derek is going to be Drive-by Bum. He'll be with the main strike force until it's time to move. Again, as far as coordination goes, once I've given Bryan the go-ahead, Derek will close on his target group. Going hot is on Bryan. Once he gets 'mugged,' he'll run away and clack off the backpack. We'll be close enough to hear it. The boom is your go signal, Derek." The hatchet-faced, dark-haired, former SF guy nodded. Derek was our resident computer geek, but he wasn't your ordinary pencil-necked, soft-as-baby-shit image of a geek. The guy was just as much of a killer as any of the rest of us; he wouldn't have been on a team if he wasn't. That didn't stop him from being the team's resident oddball, but for once he didn't decide to add one of his quips in the middle of the brief.

I traced the road up to the house we'd fingered as Fat Boy's safe house. "Once we've got our hole, we roll up and execute. The plan is still to make it look like a drive-by, though we won't be fucking around; no 9mms on this job." More nods. We already had the two M60E4s loaded in the van. "At the risk of making it look more professional, Larry, Eric, and Jack will be flankers. As soon as we pull up, you guys are going to bail out and sprint your asses off to the back of the house to make sure we get any squirters.

"Nobody gets out of that fucking house alive," I stressed. I didn't need to reiterate it, either. There was a deadly glint in every eye that was looking back at me.

These assholes had fucked with the wrong guys.

"After the initial fires, we'll have no more than five minutes to sweep the house and clean up anybody still breathing," I went on. "There won't be any SSE; at this point I don't give a shit about additional intel, and we don't want to get caught in Blackhawk Down in Pueblo at one in the morning. We'll sweep the house, make sure the job's done, and get the fuck out. Questions?" Nobody raised a hand. We had, after all, been hashing out the vague outline of this plan all the way south from The Ranch. We'd just needed the specifics to fill in the blanks.

"While the East Side is apparently a no-go zone for the cops, we don't want to take chances on crossing them. I don't want any dead cops on our hands. So, Derek's going to set up a rash of 911 calls to draw just about every cop in the city off to the west."

"Already done," Derek put in. "It's just waiting for me to send the command. And there might be a couple other nasty little surprises built in." He grinned evilly, though when I raised an eyebrow at him—the "extra surprises" had not been in the plan—he spread his hands innocently. "Nothing too destructive," he said, "but they need to stay tied up for a while. I've got a couple contingencies worked up for it. Their comms are going to be fucked for a while, and I've got several bots that should have them chasing 'assault in progress' for a couple of hours."

"At least until they figure out that they're chasing ghosts, while there's audible gunfire and explosions coming from the East Side," Eric pointed out, rubbing his shaved head.

"But there's *always* gunfire coming from the East Side," Derek pointed out. As if to punctuate his statement, we heard three pistol shots in the distance. "The cops are already wary about investigating any of it. If they do come in after us, they'll be inclined to come in force, and that's going to take time to organize. All I've got to buy us is a few minutes."

"Fine," I said. "It sounds like a good idea. We'll roll with it." I'd learned a while ago to let Derek do his magic when it came to computers. I wasn't a Luddite, but I wasn't any kind of code geek, either. Derek knew that sorcery and I didn't. I deferred to his expertise. "Make sure you take one of Logan's party favors," I added, "just in case you've got to drop it and run."

"Already planning on it," he replied. Logan Try was our aging, thoroughly cantankerous gear guy. He hadn't deployed since East Africa, but had instead ensconced himself in the machine shop in another of the Ranch's outbuildings. He'd sent a duffel bag full of scratch-built 9mm bullet-hose submachine guns with us. They were of considerably higher quality than most of the homemade firearms that cropped up on gun blogs every once in a while, and more durable than the polymer 3D printed jobs. They were also completely without serial numbers, and completely untraceable if we had to dump them.

"All right," I said, checking my watch. "I've got 2320. Let's aim for Time on Target of 0100. Final go time is situation dependent." I looked around the dim room. "Last chance. Did I forget anything?"

A few guys shook their heads. We gathered up what we'd brought and slipped out in ones and twos, careful to leave the house looking as dilapidated and abandoned as it had been when we'd arrived.

***

Even with the back seats all stripped out, the van was crowded. None of us were especially small guys, and we'd brought a lot of firepower. And since the flanker team was poised to go out the back doors as soon as we stopped, they weren't exactly sitting comfortably. They were all crouched in the back, weapons held ready, holding on to the walls as best they could as the van swayed down the street. Ben was braced across from the sliding door, one of the 60s across his knees. Nick was driving, and I was in the right seat. I'd considered using one of Logan's toys, but had stuck with my SOCOM 16. Derek had one of the cheap little bullet hoses because he was closing to bad-breath distance with his targets, and might have to break off in a hurry and try to blend back in with the underbelly of Pueblo. I had wheels, and was probably going to be shooting through walls and windows. I wanted a rifle.

We were waiting in the shadows, under a burned-out streetlight, a few blocks from the target house. We could actually see Derek's targets, a group of four *vatos* lounging under another streetlight on the corner a couple blocks ahead. Derek was already out and shuffling toward them. I'd just gotten off the phone with Bryan, and we were going hot.

At least, we were supposed to be. Derek had needed to slow his roll, stumbling and sitting down in the gutter for a moment, because the expected boom hadn't come yet.

Then we heard a series of four loud *pops* to the north. Nick and I looked at each other. That wasn't good.

CHAPTER 5

The sound of pistol shots could only mean that things had just gone very, very bad. Of course, being the East Side, we heard sporadic gunfire all the time. If I had been inclined to wishful thinking, I might have been able to put it down to just another couple of gangbangers removing themselves from the gene pool. But the timing, the direction, and the fact that the explosion we'd been waiting to hear hadn't gone off yet, disinclined me to such hopes. Bryan was probably dead, and our first diversion was a bust.

Strangely enough, I didn't feel the surge of rage and frustration that I probably should have. I was in the zone, game face on, and I just did what came naturally anymore when things inevitably fell apart.

I attacked.

"Go, go, go!" I yelled out the window. Derek was close enough that he surged to his feet, though he had the presence of mind to lend the movement a drunken sway. He didn't rush the gangbangers down the street, either, though they turned toward us, having heard my shout without necessarily understanding what I'd said, or even where the sound had come from.

Nick started slow-rolling the van, keeping us to just under a walking pace, creeping up to our imaginary line of departure. He kept the lights off; we didn't want to otherwise draw attention to ourselves until either Derek dealt with the pickets or we had to intervene.

Derek was doing a workman's job of looking and acting like one of the numerous derelicts wandering the streets of Pueblo, keeping his head bowed as he shuffled and swayed like he was crazy, smashed, high, or some combination of the three.

He'd almost made it another block, eliciting only the vaguest interest from the gangbangers, before a bone-rattling explosion rocked the night. A bright flash lit the sky to the north, and all four gangsters suddenly turned to look.

Derek didn't waste any time. He suddenly abandoned his addled shuffle and sprinted forward, bringing his weapon out of his jacket as he went.

He covered the ground quickly; Derek was no slouch when it came to cardio. Lean and hungry-looking, he ran a lot, and it paid off. Before the confused gangbangers knew it, the bum who had been swaying and staggering along the sidewalk far enough away to not even be worth picking on was right on top of them, pointing what looked like a pipe with a handgrip at them.

41

In fact, that was essentially what it was. Logan hadn't wasted time or materials making the little subguns aesthetically pleasing. They were essentially mutant crosses between Uzis and Sten guns, only slightly longer to allow for the integral suppressors.

Those suppressors were *good*, too. Almost good enough to mourn ditching them, though Logan would just look at you funny and say it wouldn't be that hard to make new ones if you said so.

There was hardly any noise as Derek brought the little bullet hose to bear and opened fire. We just watched the four young men stagger under the impacts of the bullets, dark fluid splashing from exit wounds as they fell to the street beneath the streetlight.

It was a fast, professional shooting, as much as it might have looked at first blush like a gangland spray and pray. Derek had punched the gun out to the end of its sling and held it tightly controlled, sweeping the stream of bullets across the targets' centers of mass. All four had taken at least two to three fatal hits in a single burst.

Nick didn't wait to admire Derek's shooting. He just floored the accelerator, threatening to throw the flanker team in the back against the rear doors, and sent us roaring down the street toward the target house. I heard Ben rack the 60's charging handle, getting ready to lay the hate, and I brought my rifle up to my lap.

We could see the front door of the target house already. There were a couple of people out on the porch, looking in the direction of the explosion. Not only that, but there were several other faces peering through nearby windows and doors, trying to see what had blown up. We might have woken a few people up with our diversion, which meant more witnesses. But it had had the desired effect of drawing attention away from the strike team, at least for the moment. We'd hopefully sowed enough chaos that we could get in and out without too much interference. Nobody was going to know what the hell was going on for a few minutes, anyway.

Nick braked smoothly just short of the house. I didn't even have to say anything. Larry threw the rear doors open, and he, Eric, and Jack were gone.

Ben had rigged a strap so that he could release the latch on the sliding door and pull it open without having to get up out of his shooting position. I heard the door roll back as we came parallel with the front of the target house.

I'd already had my window down; I didn't feel like eating a bunch of broken glass if we took any return fire, and it made this part that much easier. I lifted my rifle and pointed it out the open window, even as Ben cut loose.

Even with the door open and the windows down, that 60 in the confines of the van was *loud*. It wasn't just the stuttering roar of the gun, either; the muzzle blast was still inside the van. The brake was right behind my seat, so I was getting the brunt of it around the seat back.

I got just enough of a glimpse of the two guys on the porch in the light of the flickering orange streetlamp to recognize at least one of them as one of Fat Boy's security detachment. Then they went down in a welter of blood as Ben hosed the house down at over five hundred rounds per minute.

I added pairs of shots to the quickly-shattered windows, but there really wasn't much my rifle could do that the pig wasn't already doing. The M60E4 had been made famous a few years back by an internet video in which eight hundred rounds were linked together and fired off on a single trigger pull. That's a lot of lead. We didn't have that long a belt, but I knew that Ben had linked quite a few boxes together; he didn't want to waste time reloading. The E4's barrel could take it.

If Larry, Eric, and Jack were engaging anyone on the far side of the house, I couldn't hear it. I couldn't hear anything but the ravening, thumping roar of that machine gun behind me. Then, after just over a minute, the pig fell silent.

"I'm out!" Ben yelled, tossing the 60 to one side. I threw my door open and followed my SOCOM 16 out, with Ben following, grabbing his own FAL off the floor.

Even as we vaulted onto the porch, passing the bullet-splintered porch posts and facing the smashed, bullet-riddled door that was now hanging off its hinges, I heard shooting from around back. Most of it was still muted in my rattled hearing, which wasn't what it used to be anyway, but I could still pick out the heavier *booms* of our 7.62 rifles opposed by the lighter *pops* and *cracks* of smaller caliber carbines and pistols.

I was about to kick the wrecked door in when Eric came around the corner, posted up on the porch, facing back the way he'd come, and bellowed, "*SET!*"

I hesitated. If the flankers had run into stiff enough resistance that they had to fall back, we didn't have time to sweep the house. We had precisely enough time to fall back to the van and make ourselves scarce. If this went Blackhawk Down, we were fucked. We couldn't count on any friendlies in the East Side of Pueblo, and we'd deliberately made sure that law enforcement was a long way away—not that we were going to be seen as law-abiding citizens ourselves at that point.

Jack and Larry came pounding down the side of the house, even as Eric opened fire with a staccato series of controlled pairs. Yep, it was time to go. I rolled away from the door, yanked a frag off my chest rig, donkey-kicked the door in as I pulled the pin, and tossed the frag inside for good measure before slapping Ben on the shoulder and pointing to the van. "Get in!" I roared. "Go!"

Fortunately, I'd chucked that frag in pretty hard. The building wasn't exactly all that solid to begin with; otherwise hosing it down with machine gun fire would have been pointless. As the explosion blew out the remains of the

43

windows and doors, frag whistled through several of the bullet holes and punched some new ones of its own. I felt a hot sting on the side of my neck, as a bit of notched wire came through the wall and scored me. If I'd had the mental energy or time to think about how close I'd just come to blowing us all to bits, I might have gotten the shakes. That probably hadn't been a terribly good idea. It had been born of haste, hate, and frustration.

Ben was already flying off the porch toward the open side door of the van, on Jack's and Larry's heels. I followed, hoping that I wasn't bleeding anywhere else, and that I hadn't fragged Eric with that damned grenade. He seemed to be doing all right. I angled out onto the street behind the van, dropped to a knee where I could shoot past Eric while giving him a clear lane to the van, and lifted my rifle.

There were a few gangbangers back there, mostly spraying and praying around corners, none of them apparently willing to expose themselves more than absolutely necessary. I thought I could see a few dark lumps on the ground that might have explained their reticence. I cranked off three shots at the nearest muzzle flash I could see, then yelled at Eric, "Turn and go!"

He didn't move right away, and I was drawing a breath to repeat myself when he glanced back, saw me in place, then turned and sprinted for the van. I saw another head and what looked like a weapon appear down the alley, and shot at it. The head vanished.

The van rocked as Eric got in, and then Larry was leaning out of the open rear door and yelling at me. "Get in, get in, get in!"

There wasn't any more fire coming from behind the house by then, so I got up off the asphalt and sprinted for the front. My rifle banged off the door frame as I piled into the passenger seat, and I had to wrestle with it a second to make sure I could close the door, but Nick was already rolling before I even got the door slammed shut.

"That was interesting," Jack said as we careened away from the target, rapidly leaving the neighborhood behind. "Did one of us toss that frag, or did they have grenades, too?"

"I did," I replied ruefully. "I wanted to make sure of anybody left in the house, since we weren't going to be able to sweep it. Should have thought that one through a little more."

"No, it was good," he said. "We were taking a lot more fire before that went off. I think you scared 'em."

"Hell, it scared the shit out of me," Eric said. He didn't sound nearly as ambivalent about it as Jack had. "Dude, it was a stick house!"

"I know, it was stupid," I replied. "It won't happen again."

"It might have to," Nick said suddenly as he checked the rear-view mirrors again. "Let's face it, if we're going to make this work, we're going to have to be crazier and more dangerous than the sons of bitches that we're killing. If we want to be safe, we need to head back to Wyoming and dig in.

44

And even then, I don't think anybody in this van thinks that's going to work for long."

His words kind of hung in the air as we rounded another corner and kept going into the dark.

***

We picked Derek up about half a mile away; he'd made good time once he'd done his bit. Nick pulled over just as Derek shuffled out of the shadows of some trees in an overgrown yard, and Ben hauled him in through the side door. I don't think Nick had actually brought the van to a complete stop before the door was sliding shut and we were rolling again.

"Head to Bryan's RV," I said quietly. Nick didn't ask questions, but just nodded. It was still quite possible that we were wasting our time; Bryan's part obviously had not gone according to plan. It was entirely possible that the gangbangers had shot him, then accidentally set off the backpack while searching his corpse. On the other hand, he might have been shot, crawled away, then detonated the pack. If he was alive, he might not have been able to make it to the RV. But we weren't going to bail on him. If there was a chance that he was still alive and at large, we were going to be there to pick him up.

It was a winding, roundabout route to get to the next RV. We were steering well clear of the target area; that place was almost guaranteed to be crawling with bad guys by then, and quite possibly cops. There was no way the local PD could ignore the explosions. Or at least, that was what I thought.

Nobody said much. There didn't seem to be much to talk about. I'd owned up to my own fuckup with the frag, and the rest of the team seemed satisfied. After all, we knew each other, and had trusted each other with our lives in some pretty hairy places for a long time now. "I fucked up, won't happen again," was generally accepted, so long as it really didn't happen again.

The silence was also fueled by uncertainty. We'd already lost Jim. Little Bob was in the hospital and in a bad way. None of us wanted to have to either bury Bryan or leave him to be buried by somebody else.

It wasn't as if we hadn't lost people before. The list was not short. Of the original team that had gone into Djibouti, what felt like forever ago, Alek, Larry, Nick, and I were just about the only ones left. Several had gone in the ground in East Africa, more in Iraq.

And the butcher's bill just kept getting longer.

***

The rendezvous was at a park; it was a good place to loiter if you were trying to look like a bum. There were quite a few huddled lumps of rags and dirty coats at the bases of trees and lying on park benches in the light of the van's headlights, which, by some miracle, hadn't been broken by gunfire.

One of those lumps moved as Nick turned the turn signal on for exactly three blinks. The lump stood up and strode toward the van. Even

45

before seeing his face, I recognized Bryan with a surge of relief. He was alive, and, judging by the way he was moving, he wasn't hurt.

Ben hauled the side door open again, and Bryan piled in, his lanky frame only adding to the crowding in the back.

"Well, that sure was fun," he said sarcastically as the door slid shut and Nick started to roll out of the parking lot. "Holy shit."

"What the hell happened?" I asked. "The boom was late, then we heard shooting and figured you'd gotten smoked."

"I almost did," he answered, reaching out to brace himself against the sides of the van as Nick turned us out of the parking lot. Bryan's callsign wasn't "Albatross" for nothing. "Those motherfuckers really didn't want to play according to the script. They were acting more like guys on security than gangbangers just loitering around the street looking for trouble.

"The first time I went past, they watched me but didn't say anything. Didn't yell, didn't try to stop me, didn't even act curious. Which, of course, kinda fucked the entire plan. So, I went around the block and tried again, this time getting farther out into the street so I'd pass closer. I figured if worst came to worst, I'd toss the pack at their feet and run. Maybe I could get far enough away and set it off before they came after me." When I turned around in my seat to raise a skeptical eyebrow, he just shrugged. "Hey, it was a thought. I'm not saying it was a *good* thought, but it was a thought."

"Tonight seems to be the night for that," Eric commented. Bryan shot him a quizzical glance, but then shrugged again and continued his story.

"Anyway, the second time around they must have gotten suspicious, because one of them yelled at me. They all pulled guns and started toward me. I thought this was a good sign, at first; I figured they might rough me up a little, take the pack, then shove me away and tell me to get lost. Instead, they start pointing their guns at me, and telling me to get on my knees.

"Needless to say, I thought that this wasn't good, but since they were all watching me, I just cowered and did what I was told.

"Fortunately, one of them got kinda impatient. He yelled at me to toss my pack, so I did. I gave it a pretty good swing, too. By then I kind of figured that they were going to search me a little more thoroughly, and since I didn't want them to find my gun or the detonator, while the pack was in the air, I drew down and started shooting."

"You mean the shots we heard were yours?" Nick asked.

"Best damned shooting I've ever done," Bryan said. "I'm still not sure how I pulled it off. Four shots, four kills—or at least all four of them were down in the street and not shooting me in the face. I booked it out of there and hit the detonator once I was far enough away. Then I E&E'd for the rendezvous point and hunkered down until you guys showed up."

There were some muttered comments, but nothing of real operational significance. I think at that point, it was really starting to sink in to all of us

46

that we were flying by the seat of our pants more than normal on this op. It was somewhat sobering, offering to put a chill dash of reality on the flames of rage and vengeance. We'd dodged a bullet twice that night, and the night wasn't over. We were going to have to calm down and start stepping more carefully if we wanted to get through this alive.

"All right," I said, loudly enough to be heard in the back. "I know I don't really have to go over this, but we're not going to have a lot of time once we get clear, so I'll hit it anyway, to make sure we don't skip anything. Once we stop, the van gets sanitized, weapons and gear gets put out of sight, everybody gets changed over, and we split back into buddy pairs and get out to our surveillance points as quickly as possible. We just kicked the hornet's nest, and we need to see as much of the reaction as we can before we can properly plan our next moves. Nick and I will handle ditching the van, then we'll get out to our spot. Any questions?"

There were none. We'd already gone over the details in the initial planning, even before meeting up for the brief earlier that night. Nick pulled up to the old, ramshackle abandoned house that we'd picked out as the refit area, and we piled out and got to work.

***

Only a few, hectic minutes later, Nick was back behind the wheel of the van, heading southwest on the 78. I was following in the beater Jeep Cherokee that we'd be using for the rest of the night. He kept driving until we were far enough out into the desert that ours were the only two pairs of headlights in sight, then he pulled over to the side of the road, parked, and shut off the engine. I pulled up behind him, dousing my headlights as I did, just as he got out of the driver's seat, chucked the keys off into the desert, and jogged back to the Jeep. He climbed in, shucking the black nitrile gloves off his hands as he did so and tossing them in the back seat.

"We'll have to dispose of those, too, you know," I said as I pulled a U-turn and headed back into town.

"I'd be more concerned with the duffel bags full of guns, ammo, and explosives in the back," Nick pointed out, "than with a pair of black rubber gloves lying on a black carpet."

"I guess you've got a point," I replied. "Especially in Colorado." Most of our long guns and all of our mags were illegal in that state, which was part of why we had our base of operations in Wyoming, not Colorado. That alone was a good reason to avoid getting pulled over, though we had a short window of time to get to our position across town.

We'd just offed a cartel rep in the middle of what should have been relatively safe territory. There were two possibilities as to what would happen next. Either they would tighten security and start to watch each other more closely, in which case we would watch and take notes, tailoring our plans to deal with the rest of them accordingly, or they would run like rabbits, in which

47

case we were going to have to move fast to make sure we got a few more of them before they disappeared.

Either way, one thing was certain. One dead Fat Boy was not enough of a message.

You kill Praetorians, you pay the bill, and that price tag is pretty fucking high.

CHAPTER 6

Twelve hours later, aching with fatigue and sleep-deprivation, we pulled off and headed to another one of the myriad abandoned houses that we'd picked out as safe havens elsewhere in the city.

***

"Well, that's interesting," I said, looking around at the weary, grimy faces gathered in the shadowed living room. At least, I thought it was supposed to have been a living room. It was just an empty space covered in dust and debris at that point. We were keeping well back from the broken front windows to avoid being easily spotted from the street. "Nobody saw any police response at all?" I looked at Derek. "I know you were monitoring their comm freqs. Even the IED wasn't enough to stir 'em?"

He shook his head. "They were aware of it. Several calls came in, from locals and police units. But there was no response from dispatch except to say, 'Yeah, we know.'" He shrugged. "They knew that the wild goose chases I had them on were probably connected to it, too, judging by a couple of the responses to the bots' 911 calls. But they still didn't lift a finger to go into the East Side."

"That is *very* interesting," I mused, scratching my beard as I stared at the map.

"I guess the East Side is more of a 'no-go' zone than we thought," Eric said. "Just like down by the border."

"It's more than that," Jack said. "It's parallel governance, just judging by what we saw last night."

I had to nod. Parallel governance was an old concept, though it had really only started getting called that, occasionally substituted with "shadow governance," in the aftermath of the COIN wars in Afghanistan and Iraq. It was essentially a situation where an irregular force established its own, parallel set of laws and public services, in direct opposition to the local, legitimate government's institutions. We'd seen a lot of it in the Middle East. Hell, we'd been *part* of it in Basra, before the alliance of militias that we'd helped to push out the Iranian-backed Provincial Police Force had turned on us.

Jack was right. What we'd seen the night before, in the aftermath of the hit, had been textbook parallel governance. Groups of gangbangers had descended on the target shortly after we'd gotten clear, and immediately taken control of the scene before starting to patrol the neighborhoods and search

49

nearby houses and people, looking for us. It had been characteristically brutal and sloppy, as one might expect from MS-13, but it had been crudely professional all the same.

"It might explain why the cartel reps came here," Larry suggested. "If MS-13 has firm enough control of the East Side, the underground had to know that it was a good place to go if you wanted to contract them in the States, especially with the target sitting only a couple hundred miles due north."

"Makes me wonder how long they've been in control here," Nick muttered. "If they've got the cops scared enough not to risk crossing them at all."

"Doesn't need to have been that long," I mused. "Look at what happened down south after Gila Bend." A very well-known—one might almost say "infamous" in certain circles—sheriff had been gruesomely murdered in the town of Gila Bend, after which local law enforcement in Arizona generally stayed out of the cartels' way south of Phoenix. "First, they start pushing other gangs, then they start offering protection to locals against them. Then they start enforcing their own taxes and tariffs on the locals. Kill a couple cops who get nosy, along with a few locals who might stand up to them. For all we know, they deliberately staged it so that the locals called the cops, then had to watch the cops get murdered, before they killed the locals who called. I'd be willing to bet that with as much anti-cop sentiment as there is floating around, the local PD decided it was better not to risk new riots over dead gangbangers and stay out. The locals might not like having MS-13 run the show, but they'd prefer that to getting gruesomely murdered for talking to the cops."

"That would explain why we got fuck-all for intel when we first got here," Jack said. "They're de facto loyal to the gangs because they don't want to rock the boat, so they're not going to talk to a bunch of outsiders asking questions."

"Well, that means one thing," Bryan said. "We shouldn't have to worry about the local cops getting in the way. Open season, motherfuckers."

"Not for a while, anyway," I said. "But I'd be hesitant to put too much faith in that. Bombs going off or no, last night could be put down as an isolated incident. Once we start really stacking bodies, that could very well change. Remember, we found out the hard way that there are never only one or two factions at work once this shit starts hitting the fan. We leave enough corpses in the streets, the Feds might get involved. Then it's going to be a different ballgame."

"Getting back to the more immediate stuff," Ben said. "It does look like the targets just hunkered down and didn't try to run. They must be relying on MS-13 pretty heavily for their security. We saw some extra firepower out on the porch where White Jacket's staying, but he didn't go anywhere."

"Same here," Bryan said. "Slick stayed put. There were armed men in the windows, but nobody outside."

"Again, good news for now, but subject to change once things get hot enough," I said. "For the moment, I think we can essentially consider the East Side to be Indian Country, and the rest of the town to be a—relatively—safe zone. That's going to make it easier. Let's not get too comfortable and fuck it up, though. *Mara Salvatrucha* might not control the rest of Pueblo, but I guaran-fucking-tee that they've got eyes everywhere." I checked my watch. It was getting toward noon. "Let's bed down and get some rest. At least five hours each. Larry, since Jim's gone, you're ATL. Set the watch up." I didn't even choke when I said that, though I did feel my throat get momentarily thick.

"We're taking White Jacket tonight," I said, letting the hate burn out the grief. "We'll approach it a little differently. I've got some ideas, but we'll get to that at the brief. For now, everybody get some shut-eye."

I stayed up just long enough to work out the watch rotation with Larry. I could tell it was bothering the big guy to be taking Jim's job. It bothered all of us. It wasn't like replacements were new, but something about this time just felt different.

After making sure I got the middle watch, giving the rest of the guys as much uninterrupted sleep as possible, I promptly crashed in the corner.

***

It was stuffy as hell lying under that dusty, probably moldy, tarp in the bed of the old, rusty Duramax. I thought back to Basra, where we'd ambushed a bunch of Ansar al-Khilafah fighters in the cemetery. That time, we'd buried ourselves under a tarp in a shallow ditch and waited. This wasn't that much different.

I was behind my SOCOM 16, with the tarp carefully arranged to conceal me and the rifle, while still allowing enough of a peephole that I could see through the scope and shoot without *too* much blast giving away my position. The tarp was still going to move when I fired, but then, this wasn't a schoolhouse stalk, either.

For the moment, I was staring down about three hundred meters of empty street, my scope dialed back to widen my field of view as I watched the house where Jack and I had observed White Jacket and his cronies. Or tried to, at least. There were trees and other houses in the way, but I could still make out the cars in the front and the street was clear. That was all I needed for this part of the hit.

"Anything moving?" Jack asked from the driver's seat. We had a hole drilled between the cab and the bed, so we could chat without having to raise our voices.

"Nope," I replied. "Looks like two guys in a car parked out front, but nobody seems to be moving around. I think they're still hunkered down."

"Guess it's time to get them moving, then," Jack muttered.

Almost right on cue, the radio came to life. "I'm in position whenever you guys are," Eric announced.

I reached up carefully to dial up the scope's magnification before tucking my off hand against the stock. The rifle's forearm was resting on a sandbag in front of me, and I'd taken the time earlier to get it well-seated. Recoil would move it a little bit, but it was about as stable a shooting platform as I was going to get in the bed of a pickup truck.

I had to shift my position slightly to make sure as much of my body was behind the rifle as possible as I set the reticle on the first guy, the dude in the dark collared shirt buttoned all the way up sitting in the passenger's seat. It wasn't a long shot, not by any means. Hell, I'd killed a Somali militia leader at almost four times the distance a few years before, lying on the roof of a van. But fundamentals are fundamentals.

Letting out my breath, my finger tightened on the trigger. It broke as cleanly as ever, and the rifle *boom*ed, painfully loud inside the truck bed, despite the folds of tarp trapping some of the blast. The flapping plastic cut off my view through the scope momentarily, but I knew right where the reticle had been when the shot had broken, so I wasn't too worried. I just had to get my loophole back so that I could deal with the second guy.

Fortunately, it didn't take long to get the tarp out of my way, and I focused in on the target car again. As I'd figured, the guy I'd shot was sitting slumped in the passenger seat, behind the neat, spiderwebbed hole in the windshield. He wasn't moving. If my shot call was right, I'd put the bullet right through the top of his heart.

There was no sign of the second gangbanger. The driver's seat was empty. They must have been jumpy after the night before; old boy had bailed out as soon as his buddy got schwacked.

For a long moment, nothing else happened. There was no immediate response to the killing, though I had no doubt that the surviving sentry had low-crawled his ass inside and was at that moment screaming at the rest of his *ese*s that they were under attack. They were probably arming up and getting ready to shoot back as soon as the anticipated drive-by started.

But we weren't playing the same game we had been the night before.

My shot had been the signal to Eric, who had been crouched in an alley not far from the target house. As soon as I'd fired, he would have started moving.

A flash was followed by a heavy, window-rattling *thud* and a boiling cloud of smoke rising into the evening air. Eric had just tossed a grenade into the target's back yard, and, if he was following the plan, was even then booking his ass away from the scene, hopefully in a different direction than he'd used on approach.

At first, there was still no response. They had to be hunkered down, ears ringing from the blast, wondering just what direction the attack was really coming from.

I heard the rear window slide open, as Jack got himself positioned. I'd initially wanted him to stay behind the wheel. The driver drives. If we needed to get clear in a hurry, the seconds it could take him to get turned back around could be the difference between life and death. But he'd pointed out that I might be a good shot, but one rifle against however many *chollos* came pouring out of that house was probably not a good set of odds.

The quiet, broken only by barking dogs and surprisingly few people shouting, stretched out. MS-13 must have really had that part of the city cowed, if that kind of violence went relatively unremarked and unresisted. Of course, the other possibility was that we'd misread the situation, and these people were just too shocked by explosives going off in their neighborhoods to have the presence of mind to do much more than keep their heads down.

From what I'd seen, my money was on the first option. I'd seen *Mara Salvatrucha* in action, more than once, and if they were operating this openly, without police interference, then they had to have spilled quite a bit of blood to make sure nobody got in their way.

The stillness dragged on, as the cloud of smoke and dust from the grenade detonation drifted down the street. The local dogs were still barking furiously, but the neighborhood had otherwise gone silent, as the more vocal inquirers were hushed by the more cautious of their families, friends, or neighbors. Whatever was going on out on the street, it wasn't their concern. Let the gangsters and narcos fight it out.

Finally, there was movement. Half a dozen figures ran out into the street, scrambling into cars. We were close enough that even in the low light, I could make out White Jacket, though he wasn't dressed as fancily as he had been before.

Jack and I opened fire at almost the same instant, without saying a word of coordination. The targets were there, it wasn't a hard shot, and we went to town.

I started on the right side of the street, killing White Jacket's driver with the first shot. The tarp flapped with the muzzle blast again, covering the scope, and I hastily ripped it back so that I could see. I could worry about concealment later. Right at the moment, I wanted to make sure that we didn't let any of these bastards get away.

White Jacket had ducked down below the seat backs, though he hadn't gone down far enough. I could just make out movement through the shattered windshield. I pumped three more rounds through the seats before moving on.

Jack had already dropped the three who had crossed the street to the lowrider pickup parked there, so that just left one, and I couldn't see him.

"Where's the last one?" I asked.

53

"I think he's hiding behind White Jacket's car," Jack answered. He hadn't had his visibility cut off by the tarp. "I can't hit him from here." He paused. "You want to close and finish him off?"

I thought about it for a second. After the night before, MS-13 was going to be descending on this neighborhood pretty quick. And letting one guy survive to tell the tale might not be a bad thing. "Nah, let's get gone."

"Roger." I heard him slide the back window shut. A moment later, as I rearranged the tarp to conceal myself, he fired up the truck and started to pull away from the curb.

Another one down. One more to go before morning. There was still plenty of darkness to work with.

***

I hadn't been wrong about MS-13 responding more quickly. We'd hardly gone a block before I heard engines roaring and tires squealing. I couldn't see shit until they were past, but I tensed up. If we were spotted, they were going to come after us, and we were going to have to fight our way out. We could expect none of the niceties of even Middle Eastern cops, not here. These were bad guys, and we would either go undetected, or we were going to have to kill them all.

I remembered Jim talking about the necessity of avoiding engagements that could be avoided, when the mission wasn't just killing everybody. They presented more points of failure, increasing the odds that the whole mission would go pear-shaped without being accomplished.

That thought just made me want to bang on the cab and tell Jack to stop. I wanted to slaughter all those sons of bitches. But Jim, or Jim's ghost, was right. That wasn't the mission. Not this time. Kill the ones who gave the orders. That was the mission, and killing a bunch of cannon fodder wasn't going to get that done. It would only tie us up and give the real assholes time to run for it.

It would probably get us all killed in the process, too, but my fixation on killing the animals who had killed Jim in our own backyard had shoved that to a secondary consideration.

If I'd had more time and inclination for self-reflection, I might have wondered why losing Jim had driven me to this point more than losing Colton, Hank, Rodrigo, Bob, Paul, Mike, or any of the others who had gone down in the years we'd been running around Third World hellholes killing people and breaking their shit. Looking back, I could only figure that having it happen Stateside, on our own turf, had been the breaking point.

None of that was going through my head as Jack slow-rolled the Duramax around the corner, the lights out, then slowly accelerated away. I just gritted my teeth, braced myself against the wheel wells, and started getting my mind on the next target.

***

54

White Jacket had been easy. He'd had a relatively small entourage, and his safe house had been equally small and in a relatively quiet, dark neighborhood.

Slick was going to be another matter.

While he was by no means the toughest nut we had to crack in Pueblo, he had taken over a garage on the south side of Highway 96 as his safe house, and had a lot of *sicarios* with him, close to a platoon. Deeper into the East Side, there were lots of shadows to hide in, alleys to slip through, and vehicles to cover our approach. Slick's garage, out on the fringes as it was, had some long sightlines and a lot of open ground around it. Getting close was not going to be easy.

Eric had nicknamed this guy "Slick" both because of his hair, which he wore longish and slicked back, and because he looked like he was more than a little wet behind the ears. None of us actually thought he was. He wouldn't be representing a cartel this far north if he hadn't done his bit. Baby-faced he might be, but he was a made man, and probably had a *lot* of blood on his hands.

If we'd had more firepower along, I'd have been more than happy to launch one of those thermobaric RPG-27 rounds we'd had in Iraq into the garage and call it good. We'd nailed an Iranian target in Basra that way. As long as we hit the garage, nobody inside would be getting out. They'd be cooked as the round mixed its fuel with the inside air and ignited it.

But we didn't have RPGs or thermobarics, so we were going to have to approach this a little differently.

There was an open field to the south of the target building, and Eric had spotted what looked very much like sentries on the perimeter. East and west were residential houses, and there was a gas station across the highway to the north. Our approaches were limited, and Slick's security was going to be on the alert.

My first thought had been to do something not unlike our approach to taking White Jacket out. Considering what we'd seen of Slick's PSD, they were a little more arrogant and aggressive than some of the other gangs in the area. My idea had been to stage a drive-by shooting, then ambush them when they came out and pursued.

Larry had pointed out the flaw in my scheme. Given the events of the previous night, and the attack on White Jacket, word of which was probably going to spread quickly as MS-13 tried to lock down the East Side, it was entirely possible that the bad guys would refuse to be cocky, and would hunker down and wait for us to either come in after them, or for reinforcements to get there. That would throw our entire plan sideways. It's never a good idea to make your plan hinge on the enemy being stupid. He could surprise you.

So, we came up with Plan B, which sort of wound up becoming Plan A. Prep had taken a bit of doing; after all, we had come south with enough firepower and explosives to fight, not to get fancy.

Which was why I looked up at the ramshackle contraption that we'd thrown together in a couple of hours that afternoon with a certain amount of skepticism.

"I am still in no way convinced that this is going to work," I said.

"Well," Derek said, "it either works or it doesn't. There wasn't exactly a good way to test it beforehand."

"Oh, I know," I replied. Derek, Larry, Jack, and I were presently crouched in a darkened alley just about straight across the highway from the target garage. Derek was putting the finishing touches on his latest monstrosity, while the rest of us held security and tried not to think of all the ways this plan could go very, very badly.

Plan A, or Plan B, or whatever it was called—Derek had started calling it Plan F U—was a flatbed with half a dozen 55-gallon drums of gasoline strapped down in the back, along with a few of the carefully rationed explosives that we'd brought south with us. It wasn't pretty, and it was going to be anything but precise, but it was the best we could come up with on short notice. Call it a suicide truck bomb, hopefully without the "suicide" part.

"If this was a manual," Derek continued, his voice muffled from where he was buried in the truck's cab, "I don't think this would even work at all." He grunted as he fixed the anti-theft rod to the steering wheel. It should keep the truck from veering too significantly off course, though any kind of significant obstacle could still knock it aside. "I'm still not sure we're going to get enough speed going quick enough."

"It just has to get through a roller door," I pointed out. "With as much weight as this thing is carrying, it doesn't have to be going full speed."

He reached up next to the steering column and turned the key. The engine coughed to life with a roar. "I hope those boys are ready," he said, just audible over the noise. "Thumbs up, let's do this."

Holding down the brake with all the weight he could put on it, he proceeded to wedge a brick against the gas pedal. The engine roared even louder, and the truck started to inch forward, despite his pressure on the brake.

I reached up and grabbed him by the back of his chest rig, yanking him out of the cab as hard as I could. I did *not* want Derek getting dragged along with that thing. He still got a little banged up as the truck surged forward, catching his side with the door column as it rolled out onto the highway.

I barely caught him as he was knocked sideways by the impact, both of us staggering against the wall of the bicycle shop that flanked the alley. "Ow," he muttered.

The truck was trundling across the highway by then. As Derek had expected, it was not picking up a great deal of speed, but at least it was still moving in a more or less straight line. It drifted to the left just enough to hit the curb at the entrance to the alley that Derek had aimed it at, but bumped over it and kept going. If anything, instead of getting hung up, it had bounced off the curb and gotten back on course, the impact correcting the drift.

It continued to accelerate, smashing through a signboard before hitting the garage. It wasn't quite centered on the rollup door, but by that time it was moving fast enough that it didn't really matter. It pulverized the wall and the doorframe as it plunged inside the garage.

I hoped that it would run up against something solid enough in there to stop it, but I was careful with my timing, just in case. Jack was still watching our six, down the alley, but Derek, Larry and I had spread out to cover the open parking lot between us and the garage, though only Derek and Larry had their guns up. I had a small burner cell phone in my hand.

As the truck smashed its way inside the garage, I mashed the "call" button.

A lot of the pyrotechnics at air shows and in Hollywood movies are created by putting a small amount of explosive, usually TNT, in a barrel of gasoline and setting it off. It produces a nice, big, impressive fireball, without a lot of frag or blast. Given the nearness of residential houses, and our own relative lack of explosives, we made it work.

With a rolling *boom*, a roiling orange fireball blasted through the inside of the garage, licking out of every opening. In seconds, the entire building was fully involved, a thick cloud of black smoke rising into the night sky.

Dropping the cell phone into a side pocket of my trousers, I brought my rifle up and watched for squirters. A few shots *crack*ed off in the distance; Ben, Eric, Nick, and Bryan were set up in pairs along a couple more avenues to pick off anyone who got out, or any sentries who were outside the building when the VBIED hit. They were doing their work, but it didn't sound like they had many targets. I doubted anybody had gotten out of there, at least not in any condition to need a bullet.

It was a hell of a way to go, but war is hell. They shouldn't have come north.

In the distance, for the first time that night, I heard sirens. I looked west, but couldn't see anything. Still, it sounded like they might be coming closer. Maybe we'd crossed the line where law enforcement couldn't look the other way anymore.

That was not a good sign. I keyed the radio. "Everybody pull off, regroup at One Two Seven." As always, we'd gridded out the city and set numerical reference and rally points to use over the radio. We were encrypted, but there were a *lot* of EM sniffers out there.

57

The four of us turned and hustled down the alley. We'd hit our targets for the night, but I didn't think we were done.

I had a nasty suspicion that we were about to have to pull some cops' asses out of the fire.

CHAPTER 7

By the time we hit the rally point, it was pretty obvious that things were threatening to spiral out of control.

Gunfire was echoing through the night, more intense than anything we'd unleashed yet, except for maybe the mad minute into Fat Boy's safe house. Red and blue flashing lights were clearly visible, as were the flames from something having been set on fire not far from them. The local PD was in the middle of one hell of a firefight. Given what I'd seen, I didn't imagine it was a fight that they were remotely prepared for.

Even though it had been a fairly successful night, we were all pretty subdued as we gathered around the vehicles in a field south of town. Granted, some of our silence was simply professional habit; once you've spent as long as we have running around hostile environments, outnumbered and generally outgunned, you don't get loud and chatty very easily. Some of it was because of fatigue. There hadn't been a lot of sleep since Jim's death.

But some of it was because of the glances we kept shooting toward the clusterfuck on the edge of the East Side. Those cops were in deep shit, if I was reading the noise right, and it was at least partially our fault. Now, I would be the first to say that they had also brought some of it on themselves by going along to get along until it was too late. But since they'd been responding to our bombing, I couldn't help but feel just a *little* responsible for their predicament.

"Decision time, gents," I said quietly. "We can use that fight as cover to go after El Presidente, or we can hit the assholes who have those cops pinned down right now. Either way, I expect that come tomorrow, the East Side is going to be far more non-permissive than it has been."

"I'm pretty sure those are automatic weapons I hear," Bryan said sarcastically. "Aren't those supposed to be illegal in Colorado?" He spat. "Fuck 'em. We came here to kill the shitstains who ordered the hit on The Ranch. Let's do what we came here to do and get the fuck out."

"Colorado's fucked up laws aren't the cops' fault," Larry said. "If it was Brett down there, wouldn't we feel at least a little obligated to go lend a hand?" Especially with Jim gone, Larry was generally the team's voice of reason and compassion, such as he was.

59

"But that ain't Brett down there," Jack said. "Jeff's right. We've got a choice between killing El Pres and finishing the mission, or helping the cops. We won't get a chance at both."

I was torn. And looking around at several of the faces, those I could see in the dark, I wasn't the only one.

"If we hit El Pres hard enough and loud enough," I said after a moment, "it will probably take more of the pressure off the PD than if we went in and tried to intervene directly. There will also be less chance of a blue on blue." That was a real concern, and there were several nods in the darkness. Let the already beleaguered cops see yet another bunch of armed guys come in and start shooting, and they might think we were just another group of bad guys. Getting shot or thrown in jail by the Pueblo PD was going to be just as bad as accidentally shooting any of them.

I looked at my watch. "Presuming he's hunkered down like the rest of them, we should be able to get in position to hit El Pres in thirty minutes."

"What's the plan?" Eric asked with a bit of a dubious note in his voice.

I grimaced, though he probably couldn't see it. "No time to get fancy, but we haven't got the numbers or the firepower for 'hey-diddle-diddle-straight-up-the-middle, either. Fuck."

"It will take some more time, but maybe we need to just go a little more old-school," Larry suggested. "Like we did on some of the hits in Basra."

That jogged a memory, and though I couldn't really see his expression in the dark, I nodded, as the gears started turning. It was simple enough, though Larry, Nick, and I were the only ones left of the Basra team, so there would be a little bit of explanation involved. "We don't have a lot of time to plan, but here's the gist…"

***

"El Presidente's" house was one of the larger residential houses on the East Side, a two-story white-painted bit of Americana with a covered porch and a bay window. The picket fence around the back yard only added to the incongruity of it being used as a safe house for a cartel rep, particularly one that we had tentatively identified as belonging to the CJNG, the *Cartel Jalisco Nueva Generacion.*

We'd started calling the guy "El Presidente" because of the professionalism of his Personal Security Detachment, which was packing better weapons and gear than anyone else in Pueblo, including us, and most definitely including the Pueblo PD, along with the target's polished appearance and general air of "better than you." He usually wore slacks and a nice shirt, with his hair immaculately coiffed. He was definitely more of the "businessman" sort of narco, as opposed to the flashier Sinaloans or the really gleefully savage types, such as the cartel we'd systematically dismantled in Mexico, *Los Hijos de la Muerte.*

His outer security was still rather low-key, usually consisting of a couple guys in a car out front, and another two on the porch, during the day. They might be there in the wee hours of the morning, too, given everything else that was presently going on.

As I strolled down the street, keeping to the shadows of the trees planted along the narrow, cracked sidewalks, I could still hear the shooting off to the southwest. The cops weren't giving up, though it did sound like it was getting more distant. I found myself hoping that they hadn't gotten themselves surrounded, and would just fall back to safer parts of the city. It would keep them out of our hair.

The truck was parked three blocks away, locked up, with my rifle and chest rig hidden in a duffel bag beneath a bunch of junk and detritus in the cab. I had one of Logan's little party favors slung under my jacket, with spare mags shoved into pockets inside the jacket and in my pants. Being seen on the streets at three in the morning was one thing; most people in the East Side were more concerned with keeping their heads down, and wouldn't ask many questions, even if they thought it was weird. Being seen packing a long gun might alert the wrong people.

I had eyes on the target house, and the low, dark sedan parked out front. I could just make out the shapes of two figures inside the car, though they helped a little when one of them lit up a cigarette. I was pretty sure it was a cigarette; every indicator we'd gotten so far suggested that El Pres wasn't the type to condone drug use in his PSD. So, it probably wasn't a joint. The loss of night vision due to the flame would be slightly offset by increased alertness thanks to the nicotine.

Keeping to the shadow of the tree, I scanned the streets. I could just make out the shapes of the rest of the team, spread out in a rough L-shape to the east and north. The rest were sticking either to tree trunks or parked vehicles. A quick count confirmed that everybody was in position. Time to do this.

I had taken the role of initiator, so, adopting as shuffling and drunken a gait as I could, I started across the street. There hadn't been time to change, so I wasn't in full derelict mufti, like Derek and Bryan had been the night before, but I didn't have to be. There was certainly enough substance abuse going on in Pueblo for anyone acting drunk or high to be a relatively normal sight.

I shuffled and staggered across the street, tripped over the cracked, weed-grown curb, and almost fell. In fact, I had miscalculated the act, and damn near face-planted for real, though I caught myself before the subgun could swing out of my open jacket. That could have been bad. I knew that if they were on the ball, those two *sicarios* in the car were watching me carefully. Too much had happened in the last forty-eight hours for them to be too relaxed about anybody moving toward them in the dead of night.

I kept going, veering off the sidewalk onto the gravel and weeds to either side. The target house had a really shitty front lawn, more dirt, rocks, and weeds than grass. It kind of detracted from the "Leave it to Beaver" look of the house itself.

Swaying, I pretended to almost fall over again, before overcorrecting and staggering toward the car. As I stumbled once more, I let my hand go into my jacket and wrap around the submachine gun's grip. I heard a sneering comment in Spanish and a laugh.

Game time.

As I heaved myself upright again, I checked to make sure that I had penetrated far enough that my background was clear, and I wasn't about to accidentally put a bullet into one of my teammates. There was the chance that something would over-penetrate and hit the house across the street, but there really are only so many angles that can be called "safe" when you're opening fire in a residential neighborhood.

The subgun came out of my jacket, hitting the end of the sling, the fiber-optic sights gleaming even in the dark. I was only a step away from the car, and while they had been watching me and laughing, neither of the *sicarios* had gotten out, though their windows were rolled down to let the smoke out. I could see just enough to see the surprise on the closest *sicario*'s face, just before I obliterated it with a four-round burst of 9mm hollow points.

His companion didn't even have time to register shock as the contents of the first guy's skull splattered all over him. The other advantage of my position was that, instead of having to traverse the width of the car, as I would have if I'd opened fire through the windshield, I only had to move the muzzle a little over an inch to give Number Two the same treatment. Dark, glistening liquid splashed out the open window and his cigarette fell to the street as his lifeless corpse sagged against the door column.

The entire assassination had taken about three seconds, and the only sound had been the clicking of the action and the faint tinkle of the brass hitting the rocks.

As soon as I was sure that both were dead, I spun around toward the house. I did *not* want to get shot in the back because I was facing the wrong way after I'd just presumably alerted anyone looking out the window that they were under attack.

The rest of the team was closing in at the same time, sprinting across the street, even as I ran for the porch. The usual daytime sentries weren't there, but I wasn't laying any bets that the two in the car had been the only ones up and about, even that early in the morning.

Ben beat me to the porch by a half a step, vaulted the stairs in a single bound, and hit the door without breaking stride. His boot crashed into the door itself right below the knob, the impact shattering the glass and smashing the latch through the doorjamb. The door slammed open with a crash, and I pushed Ben through the opening, my subgun up over his shoulder to cover him.

The lights were off, and we didn't have flashlights attached to the subguns, for the simple reason that Logan hadn't bothered to put rails on them. They were throwaways, after all. But we all had smaller handheld jobs in our pockets, and I'd been fishing mine out on the way up the porch steps.

Brilliant white light blazed in the darkened living room, blinding the two figures that were stumbling through the door to the stairs and the back hall. They didn't have a chance. One of them tried to lift a pistol to shoot at us, blind or not, and Ben cut him down. I was a fraction of a second behind Ben, having hastily swept my eyes and muzzle to clear the rest of the living room, and put a five-round burst into the next guy, who was in the middle of tripping over his buddy's corpse. Between Ben and me, he took ten or twelve rounds to the chest and head. He hit the floor hard, his ruined skull bouncing off the floorboards with an audible *clunk*, spilling blood and brain matter across the doorway.

There must have been somebody at the top of the steps, because there was a sudden loud, profane shout in Spanish. I had cleared the doorway by then, and had stepped out into the room, closing out the angles on the single door that was now partially blocked by two bodies as the rest of the team poured in behind me. On a hunch, I aimed high and dumped the rest of the mag through the wall and ceiling where I guessed the top of the stairs was.

There was a high-pitched scream of agony and the sound of a body falling down the stairs, even as I ripped the mag out and dropped it to the floor, reaching for another one. Old boy was hurt, but still alive, as he was still making a lot of noise as he got to the bottom of the stairs. Larry silenced him with a short burst.

A rapid series of shots roared down the stairwell, followed by a shotgun blast that did little but turn the already dead bodies further into bloody hamburger. Apparently, whoever was up there hadn't taken the lesson from the guy I'd shot through the wall, and was trying to dissuade us from coming up by shooting down the stairs.

Jack, Eric, and I lined up, lifted our weapons, and hammered a good twenty rounds apiece through the walls and ceiling. Drywall was blasted to powder and splinters flew, but none of it was slowing the bullets down appreciably. Another *sicario* came tumbling down the stairs, preceded by his shotgun, which made one hell of a racket bouncing off the walls and the banister.

We still had the advantage of surprise; they were still waking up and wondering just what the fuck was happening, judging by the responses we'd seen so far. But gunfire has a way of focusing the mind if the enemy has any breathing space. The longer we stayed downstairs, the sooner they were going to come to their senses and start doing the same thing to us we were doing to them—shooting us through walls that provided concealment but no cover.

With visions of Bob Fagin's death in a similar situation in Iraq dancing in my head, I dashed for the stairs. Without plates, I was running one hell of a risk, but it was either possibly die on the stairs, or almost certainly die on the first floor. Speed was our security.

Jack and Eric, seeing what I was doing, poured another pair of long bursts up at the head of the stairs, providing me a little bit of covering fire as I bounded up the steps, two at a time. Bryan was behind me; Larry and Ben had pushed into the kitchen, while Nick and Derek were posted up on the doorway, covering what might have been a bedroom.

Looking up, I could see that there was somebody at the top of the stairs, though they had ducked back from the hail of bullets tearing up through the floor and the wall, so they couldn't see me, though I could just see their shadow. It wasn't going to be all that accurate, and in the old days I would have cringed at this sort of shooting, but I punched out the subgun and ripped a burst through the corner. Drywall was pulverized and somebody hit the floor with a scream.

Jack and Eric's fire ceased at the same time. I went around that corner as I hit the top of the steps. I was breathing hard and my legs were burning, but I had never gotten through a CQB fight *without* feeling like I'd just run a marathon, so that was nothing out of the ordinary.

The stairs opened up on a hallway going back the other direction. There was a door to the right and another across the landing to the left. I faded right for a heartbeat, covering down on the door across the hall to the left just long enough to make sure I wasn't about to get shot in the back, then stormed into the right-hand door as soon as I was sure Bryan was going to be on my ass. I could feel the shudder of boots on the stairs as two more started up behind us.

Bryan and I burst into the small room, where a cheap, Walmart floor lamp had been switched on, probably about the same time that Ben kicked the front door in. It looked like the room had been a kid's bedroom once upon a time; there was colorful wallpaper still up on the walls. Whoever was presently renting the house, however, hadn't cared, and had just thrown a mattress, a couple of folding chairs, and a lamp into the room.

The room was otherwise empty; I guessed that whoever had been sleeping in there was either lying on the floor across the hall or dead at the base of the stairs. I still crossed to yank open the closet, making sure there weren't any little *vatos* waiting in there for us to turn our backs. It was empty.

More gunshots roared across the hall, with softer, almost inaudible *clicks* sounding in reply. The unsuppressed gunfire was painfully loud inside the house, even through three walls.

Bryan led the way out the door and across the hall, just as Jack and Eric appeared in the doorway we'd bypassed. There was a tense fraction of a second as all four of us quickly IDed the men with guns across the hall, but nobody shot a friendly.

A glance down the stairs as we passed only showed the dead bodies at the bottom. Larry, Ben, Nick, and Derek were otherwise engaged, but as long as there weren't calls for help or more bullets ripping through walls or floor at us, I figured we were okay. Our focus needed to be on the top floor for the time being.

Bryan led the way to the third room. The door was shut. Bryan rolled past it, turned his back to the wall, and donkey-kicked it just below the doorknob.

The doorjamb splintered. The door cracked and swung open a whopping three inches before whatever had been stacked against it provided enough friction to grind to a halt.

At the same time, there was a roar of automatic gunfire from inside, and bullets smashed out through the wall and the door, filling the hallway with splinters and dust.

Bryan dropped flat on the floor; I didn't know if he'd been hit or if he had just sensed the gunfire coming and hit the deck as soon as the door didn't open all the way. I lifted my subgun and ripped an answering burst through the wall, dumping the magazine as Jack and Eric came up behind me.

There wasn't time to think, plan, or even to see if Bryan was all right. If we didn't get in there and kill that son of a bitch, we were all going to die in the hallway. Hesitation was going to be fatal. So, I moved.

I took one step over Bryan's prone form, reloading as I went, and aimed a kick as high up the door as I could get, hoping to smash the hinges off the doorjamb and lever the door over whatever obstacle was inside. It was not the first time I'd encountered a barricaded door on a raid.

Naturally, it didn't work. The jamb cracked a little, but my boot rebounded from the door as the painful shock of the impact traveled up my leg. Eric had shouldered past behind me and was putting another burst through the wall just to give whoever was inside something to think about besides turning me to hamburger.

I could stand there and try to kick that door all day, and only buy the asshole inside more time. So, I changed tactics. I stepped back against the wall over the stairs and bull-rushed the door.

I hit it low enough and hard enough that the barricade slid on the carpet. It was still heavy enough that it stopped me and the door a good two feet inside, but that was enough.

I was low, almost lying on the floor, my submachine gun aimed in the opening to the darkened room, somewhat lightened now by all the bullet holes in the walls. I heard the *ping* of a spoon flying free as Jack tossed one of our few flashbangs in over my head, and closed my eyes. This was gonna hurt.

A fraction of a second later, the bang went off with a deafening blast of noise, painting an actinic flash on my retinas even through my eyelids. Smoke filled the room, and I was pretty sure that something was on fire. Meanwhile, Jack jumped over me, knocking the door a few inches further open as he went.

I had to stay down for a few more seconds, because Eric was already heading in after Jack, and if I stood up, I was going to trip Eric up. As soon as he was clear, I scrambled to my feet and shoved the door the rest of the way open, even as suppressed gunfire tore through the room.

Something was burning. The flashbang had somehow landed on the bed and set the covers on fire. The rest of the lights were off, and Jack's and Eric's flashlights stabbed brilliant white beams through the drifting smoke, making the blood splashes against the drywall look particularly bright.

There had been three men in the room; two *sicarios* and El Presidente. All three were now rapidly cooling piles of meat and bone. The *sicarios* had gone down fighting; one had a pistol clenched in his hand, while the other had an AK.

El Presidente had not died well. He was still in his underwear, huddled on the floor on the far side of the smoldering bed, unarmed. If he'd been smart enough to stay down, he might have lived a few moments longer. But he apparently had peeked over the top of the mattress just as Jack and Eric were doing for his bodyguards, and had taken a round right in the T-box. One eye was slightly bulged out from overpressure, just below a gently smoking hole right over his eyebrow. A sizeable chunk of the back of his skull was gone.

"Clear," Jack said, his voice only slightly louder than normal, probably because of the ringing in the ears we were all experiencing thanks to the opposition's unsuppressed gunfire. His face was blank as he looked at the corpses crumpled on the far side of the room. For all his sarcastic belligerence, which had earned him the callsign "Anarchy," most of the time Jack did his damnedest to affect a demeanor of bored cynicism. That extended to combat, as well. The guy never got visibly excited.

Of course, few of us did, anymore. We were all too old, too jaded, and too combat hardened.

I didn't say anything but, satisfied that I wasn't going to get burned down as soon as I turned my back, I went back to the door to check on Bryan, hoping and praying that we hadn't lost him, too.

But he was already levering himself painfully off the floor. He was alive, but I put out a hand to stop him before he moved too much. "You're bleeding," I told him.

"I know," he said with a wince. "I got burned on my right trap as I went down. It hurts like a motherfucker, but I'm all right."

66

I ran my hands over him anyway, checking for bleeds or holes that he might not have noticed. Aside from his shoulder, he came up clean.

"I love you, too, Jeff," he said as I worked.

"Fuck you, Bryan," I said. I finished, got to my feet, and held out my hand to heave him up. "Let's get out of here before the hordes show up."

Fortunately, there was no sign of any response mustering as we cleared out of the bullet-riddled house of corpses. Yet. The shooting off to the west had died down; whatever had been going down between MS-13 and the cops appeared to be mostly over. But it also appeared to mean that the *Mara* hadn't had a chance to re-orient themselves to the hit going on deeper in the East Side. We scattered to the winds, jogging away singly or in pairs, bombshelling into the fading night even as the first pale light started to grow in the east.

***

We didn't link up again in Pueblo itself. As soon as I got back to the truck, I sent a mass text to the whole team giving an RV point way out by the Pueblo Reservoir. Our target deck was clear, at least for the moment. I was reasonably certain that we'd eliminated the major players who had ordered the hit. It should give our enemies pause while we got to work on a more strategic plan.

I knew on some level, even as we drove west, that what I had in mind wasn't going to work. There was no way to kill *everybody* who wanted us dead, not least when so many of them were powerful and violent men south of the border. I hoped that we'd sent a message not to fuck with us on our home ground; we'd lost Jim and almost lost Little Bob, but we'd reaped a lot of souls in recompense. But it wouldn't stop the cartels, or the other assholes who had it out for us.

I didn't have any answers, not then, other than continuing to build the target deck and taking down enough big boys that they got the message to never fuck with us *ever* again.

I wasn't going to have time to complete the plan, never mind put it into action.

CHAPTER 8

We had just passed Franktown, north of Colorado Springs, when my phone buzzed. I cursed, since the phone was in my pocket and I was driving. Risking a little bit of swerving, I dug the phone out of my pocket and passed it to Jack.

"Fuck," he said flatly. "Tom just sent us 'Extremis.'"

"Motherfuck," I said. "Details?"

"Hold on." He squinted at the phone.

"I keep telling you, you need glasses, dude."

"The fuck I do," he replied. "Let me read."

I kept driving, though I was checking my mirrors a little more often. Intellectually, I knew we were clean, and there was no way in hell the bad guys could have picked us up once we got clear of the Springs. Too many miles and too many other vehicles on the road. But "Extremis" meant that The Ranch was under attack, and that meant we were all under threat.

"Holy shit," Jack said, still focused on the phone's screen. "It's like Waco all over again."

I risked a glance over at him. "The Feds?" That a Federal raid was only about midway down our list of nightmare scenarios said something about some of the enemies we'd made over the years. Nothing good, but something.

He shook his head, frowning, his lips tight behind his sandy beard. "He says that they look like it, but there are no markings on any of the gear or vehicles—no 'FBI,' 'BATFE,' or anything like that. Just blank black." He tapped the screen and turned the phone to squint at something. "Sure looks like a lot of 'em, though. A couple of infantry companies worth, at least, with MATVs and a couple other armored vehicles I don't recognize right off."

He read on. "Tom says that they're secure; they've taken a couple of casualties." He shook his head. "A couple of the new guys, out by the gate, it looks like. They're dug in, but they can't get out, and he doesn't recommend trying to get in without a lot of firepower and backup." Which were things that we did not have at the moment.

"That's about all he's got," Jack finished, looking up from the phone. "Or at least, it's all he was willing to put in a text message."

"Send an All Call," I said. "We need to link up once we get back into Wyoming." I started racking my brain for a good spot.

"I'll call it just south of Tie Siding," Jack said after a moment of squinting at the map. "It's 'middle of nowhere' enough."

I just nodded and tried to concentrate on driving. There were a lot of miles to go before the rendezvous. A lot of miles to try not to think of how bad things could be getting back at the only home we had left.

***

It was almost dark when we pulled off the side of the 287 and joined the other two vehicles that had beaten us to the RV point. Larry and Ben were waiting next to the old, beat-up Pathfinder, no weapons in sight but eyes out and alert. The Bronco parked ahead of it was dark, but I could see Nick's silhouette in the driver's seat.

I parked and got out. There was nothing to see around us but sagebrush and bunchgrass. This was cattle country; miles and miles of rolling plains and dry washes. We had plenty of long lines of sight and open fields of fire.

It didn't mitigate the feeling of being a hunted, cornered animal. We were still free and at large, but our home base was surrounded, and I was only too aware of how many people wanted us dead, or at the very least, buried in a deep, dark hole where no one would ever find us and we'd never cause trouble for anybody ever again. We'd been making political enemies since we'd shot our way out of Kismayo in Somalia, rustling the jimmies of a lot of people who'd never heard a shot fired in anger, but presumed to dictate the use of firepower by those they'd sent into an untenable situation with inadequate support and top cover. Since then, it had only gotten worse. We'd uncovered rogue operations, discovered links between American companies and Mexican cartels, embarrassed our own employers by killing a lot of people who'd had it coming but hadn't been on their target deck, and done a lot of very bad things to very bad people, setting some carefully laid plans back years.

And when it all came to a head, here we were, alone, low on ammo, cut off from the only safe place we knew of, and pretty sure that we had nowhere to turn. We'd fought, bled, killed heaps of people, and buried friends, all in the hopes that we were doing the right thing in the end, and this was where it had led us.

Anyone who says that he can have peace just by killing all his enemies is a damned liar. Kill one, and two more will pop up in his place.

Alone as we were, there still wasn't really any conversation. I think we were all thinking that we were going to be talking over the same things over and over again, anyway. And with our paranoia at a peak, we were just watching the plains and the sky, staying quiet lest some unseen enemy hear us.

Even so, it wasn't a long wait. Derek and Bryan pulled up in their battered old Ford and shut off their headlights. The sun was right on the western horizon. It was going to be full dark in a matter of minutes. Which didn't mean anything if there *was* an eye in the sky watching us. Any drones

70

our enemies in high places might be using were guaranteed to have IR and thermal capability. But there weren't a lot of other places to hide at the moment, and time was a-wasting.

Doors slammed loudly in the empty quiet of the open country, and we gathered down the slope from the highway. I stuck my hands in my pockets and looked around at the team. Bleary eyes met mine. We all looked a little ragged. We were all tired as shit, feeling the last week of driving, snooping, prepping, fighting, and more driving.

"I take it everybody's up to speed on what's going on?" I asked. "At least as much as Tom sent?" There were nods all around.

"How the hell are we going to get through that cordon with eight dudes?" Ben asked. "Especially eight dudes who are guaranteed to be on their 'Most Wanted' list?"

"The same way we've gotten through just about every other cordon," I said grimly. "We smash through it."

"With what?" Ben looked around at the rest. He seemed to be getting annoyed that he was the only one voicing doubts. Nobody else looked at him, but stayed silent, either looking outboard, toward the highway, or down at the ground, thinking. "We're kind of low on ammo after the last few days, and we weren't exactly rolling heavy enough before to be in any position to take on what looks a hell of a lot like a Federal task force."

"Well, Tom's pretty sure they're not really Feds," Bryan pointed out. "No identification as such. They might not be as well-equipped."

"They'll be just as well equipped as we would be, taking on a hard target like The Ranch," Larry replied. "And I doubt those are fake MATVs, or whatever those other things are."

"They won't be," I said. "Whoever these guys are, they are going to be as well-funded and well-equipped as their sponsors can make them, and if they came after us this quick, you can bet that there's a lot of money and influence behind those sponsors. Our list of enemies isn't exactly a short one, I'll remind you."

"We need to stay well away from The Ranch until we've had a chance to refit and resupply," Eric said. "The Pat O'Hara Mountain cache should have everything we need, it's on the way, and it's far enough away from The Ranch that nobody else should know about it, presuming that they haven't compromised *everything*."

"That's a pretty fucking big presumption," Jack said, his arms folded across his chest. "They moved fast enough after the MS-13 hit that I suspect they had all this ready to go weeks ago, maybe even months. In that case, they will have done their homework." He spat. "We might not have *any* bolt-holes they don't know about."

"That's paranoid as shit," Nick said.

Jack shrugged. "Times we live in," he said.

71

"Not saying you're wrong," Nick said. "I'm actually kinda impressed."

Jack gave a sardonic little bow.

"If we start thinking that they're always five steps ahead of us, we're just going to paralyze ourselves," Larry said, getting the discussion back on track. "I say we shoot for the Pat O'Hara cache, and make sure we recon it thoroughly before we move in on it. As we know all too well, there's no such thing as really undetectable surveillance. If they're watching it, we should be able to spot them."

"Larry's right," I said. "We know the ground better than they do, and I guaran-fucking-tee these assholes haven't done as much field work as we have. That said, if we get cocky, we're dead, and so is everybody back at The Ranch. Careful and methodical, and don't drop tradecraft for a second. I know we all do this already, but it's cash only from here on out. No plastic, burner phones only. We'll split up again as soon as we start rolling, and ditch the vehicles not less than ten miles from the cache." I turned to look at Derek. "How confident are you that we weren't tagged on the way out of Pueblo?"

He grimaced in thought, then shrugged. "Eighty percent, maybe? We were pretty careful; we didn't have any tails on the way through Colorado Springs or Denver, and unless tech has advanced farther than even I know—and trust me, it hasn't—we should have seen or heard some sign of a drone following us if they had an eye in the sky on us. No, I think we're clean."

I nodded. "Even so, be ready to ditch the vehicles and E&E as soon as it looks like we might have picked something up. It'll fuck our timetable, but better late than rolled up or dead." The nods I got were of the, *yeah, we know, teach your grandpa to suck eggs* variety.

"Do we have any theories about who's behind this?" Eric asked after a moment, just before I was about to break the meeting and hit the road again.

"The list is a pretty long one," Nick said. "Take your pick."

"There isn't enough information to say, yet," I said. "But trust me, once we get this sorted, we're going to find out." My tone promised that there was going to be retribution for this. It might not have been the "civilized" way to deal with such problems, but if anyone Stateside knew just how uncivilized our times were, it was the eight men gathered on the side of that highway in the deepening twilight. We'd been an instrument of policy, several times, though a deniable instrument, employed through multiple layers of shady organizations and contacts, but useful or not, when it all came down to the wire, we were expendable, which meant we were outlaws. We could count on no support but each other.

"All right," I said, after a brief pause, "we'll RV at the Pat O'Hara cache, no later than EENT tomorrow." End of Evening Nautical Twilight was when the last light of the sunset disappeared in the west. In northern Wyoming, at that time of year, it would be around eight thirty at night. "We'll depart here at staggered intervals; I want us spread out no less than five miles between vehicles. In the event that there is an eye in the sky, I don't want a convoy showing up. Find someplace to hole up and grab some shut-eye tonight or in the morning, but be at that cache by the time it's dark tomorrow night. Questions?"

A few guys shook their heads. No one asked a question. "Let's go, then," I said. "We're wasting darkness."

***

Jack was driving and I was dozing as we went up Wind River Canyon in the early morning. The road was still in shadow; the sun hadn't risen over the bluffs to the east yet.

I was yanked out of my fitful slumber by a phone buzzing. We'd stopped for a few hours to sleep in Boysen State Park, but we'd gotten moving early, knowing that once we got to the foot of Pat O'Hara Mountain, we were going to have some slogging to do to get to the cache. I wanted to get to the foothills by mid-afternoon at the latest.

A moment's bleary rummaging produced my main phone, but it wasn't the one ringing. "What the hell?" I muttered, and started digging in my go bag some more.

"Oh, fuck," I grumbled, as I pulled out the offending phone. It was another burner, the simplest, cheapest pre-paid job you could find in a local truck stop. There was no contract attached to it, no name associated with the number, especially as the phone and the card had been purchased with cash. There was only one other person who had that number. And I was in no way, shape, or form convinced that I could trust him, not with what he knew in light of everything that had happened over the last two weeks.

I stared at the phone in my hand for a long moment, while it kept ringing. I felt more like a hunted animal than ever. The man on the other end of the line could help pull our asses out of the fire, or he could be drawing us out for the hammer to fall.

"Is that who I think it is?" Jack asked.

"Yeah, it is," I rasped. The phone kept ringing. He wasn't giving up. He probably knew me well enough to know that I wasn't going to answer right away, so he was being patient.

"Fuck," I finally muttered, and hit the green "Accept" button. Lifting the phone to my ear, I said, "Give me a reason not to chuck this phone out the window right now."

"Relax, Mr. Stone." I could hear the smooth, reassuring smile in the other man's voice. "I didn't sell you out, and no one else has either of these numbers. We are still secure, for the moment." His tone changed suddenly. "That can, however, change, depending on what you do in the next twenty-four hours. Take my advice and do what I tell you, and we can ensure that all of us remain relatively free and at large to deal with this situation. Ignore me, and you are on your own. I cannot guarantee that it will work out well for you or your compatriots."

The Broker, or Mr. Gray, as we had come to know him, was, at least by implication, a former US intelligence officer of some stripe, who had gone renegade shortly after the fall of the Soviet Union. He had since become something of a powerhouse in the international underground, what the big brains called a "shadow facilitator." If you needed information or logistics for all manner of skullduggery, he was the one to find, provided you could meet his prices.

He had involved himself in our hunt for the elusive—and illusory—underworld kingpin known only as "El Duque." He had been the one to inform us that we were chasing a phantom, who had been invented precisely for that purpose, and put us on the trail of one of the more dangerous conspiracies brewing south of the US/Mexican border. We had proceeded to dismantle a Mexican cartel and several of their international sponsors, including a Chinese front company, in a series of bloody strikes across several Mexican cities.

Exactly what The Broker's game was, I still wasn't sure. That his hands were as dirty as anyone else's in the shadowy world where organized crime and fourth generation warfare overlap was without question. Yet he'd gone out of his way to convince us that he had ulterior motives that did not jibe with being an evil mastermind only out to build his own underworld empire. He had some other play in mind, and I still didn't know what it was. He'd definitely helped us out; we probably wouldn't have made it out of Latin America alive if he hadn't interfered. But I was under no illusions that he had taken us under his wing purely out of the goodness of his heart. He'd done us favors, and I was sure that those favors were eventually going to have to be paid for.

But we were not presently in a position to refuse his help. "I'm listening," I told him.

"I expect that you are en route to one of your supply caches as we speak," he said. The man's resources were definitely extensive, as was his knowledge of human nature. It was still a little eerie to hear it from him. He was a step ahead of me, and it pissed me off.

"Stay away from them," he continued. "I cannot say for certain that whichever one you are making for is on the list, but at least a majority of them are compromised, and under surveillance. If you show up at one of them, you *will* be targeted and run down within hours."

"Who the hell are these people?" I demanded. "And how the hell do you know so much about their operation?" My paranoia was running pretty high. I still couldn't shake the nagging thought that we were being set up, and that this entire conversation was just bait.

"Not a conversation to be having over the phone," he said. "Go to the junction of Highway 72 and Robertson Draw Road. It's north of the border, in Montana. Call me when you get there, and I'll give you the next set of directions." Without further ado, he hung up.

"Motherfucker," I snarled. I tossed the burner back in the go bag and started digging out the road atlas. Where the hell was Robertson Draw Road?

***

Long hours and longer miles later, we were driving north on Highway 72. Squinting at the sign up ahead, I saw "Robertson Draw Road." It was time. Jack was back behind the wheel, so I dug in the go back, turned the burner on, and called The Broker.

"We're here," I said flatly, as soon as he answered.

"Good," he said. "Take Robertson Draw Road across the river to Meteetsee Trail, and follow it to Stagecoach Trail. Go down to the wash when you hit the end of Stagecoach."

"Got it," I replied. He hung up again. I powered down the burner and pulled out my team phone. A mass text to the other vehicles said only, "Meet at the bridge."

Technically, we didn't stop on the bridge itself, but crossed over the Clark's Fork of the Yellowstone River and turned off on the fishing access. Jack parked, as I dragged my chest rig out and shrugged into it, pulling my rifle onto my lap and slinging it.

By the time the other three vehicles arrived, both Jack and I were kitted up and scanning the surrounding fields and hills. It wasn't that we were necessarily *expecting* an ambush, per se, at least no more than we usually did. But under the circumstances, this could just as easily be an elaborate trap as a chance for help and support.

We weren't just looking for people watching us. We were watching for drones. They were getting pretty small, but if you can see a bird, you can see a quadrotor, and nobody who's really looking is going to mistake a quadrotor for a bird. The tech to realistically disguise a drone as something natural just wasn't there, yet.

When the rest of the team piled out and joined us around the Duramax's hood, everybody was kitted up and armed. We were far enough out in the boonies, despite the farms right across the river, that we were more concerned with being ready to fight than we were with staying covert. By the time the locals called anybody—if they bothered; this was rural Montana, after all—we'd be long gone.

I had a tablet on the hood, with overhead imagery of the area. As much as I was trying to go low-tech as much as possible, in the interests of leaving any sort of electronic surveillance blind, I wanted something a bit more detailed than I could get in the road atlas, so I'd pulled out the tablet and plugged it into the satellite puck. I'd stayed connected just long enough to download the imagery I wanted, then pulled the puck and stowed it.

"This looks like our meeting spot, right here," I said, pointing to the wash, lined with brush and trees, that during the spring and late fall must be a tributary of the Clarks Fork. "There's not a lot of high ground, so we're going to have to do an L-shape, and get closer than we might otherwise like. It does mean that any security that The Broker has out will be likewise constrained, and should, hopefully, be easier to spot and neutralize, if necessary. I don't want anyone but me and Jack getting closer than three hundred, though, not until we're sure that it's not an ambush. I'll signal the all clear when I'm satisfied, then you guys collapse in."

"Comms?" Larry asked.

"Stay on the radios, but no talking unless it's necessary," I said. "If you happen to stumble across any flankers he has out, neutralize them if possible, but don't shoot unless you absolutely have to." I took a deep breath, letting out a bit of a frustrated sigh. "We don't know for sure if he's friend or foe yet, and it's probably not going to be a good idea to alienate an ally like The Broker without knowing for sure that he's out to fuck us."

There were a few short coordinating instructions that we had to work out, then we were saddling up again and trundling down the dirt road toward the meeting.

***

Stagecoach Trail was aptly named; it was more a trail than a road. The Duramax handled it okay, though I rather missed my old Ram, which felt more solid on unimproved roads. The GMC was bouncing and rattling more than I liked, but I had to remind myself how little we'd paid for the thing, and the fact that we were driving it precisely *because* it was expendable.

We'd been expecting to go all the way down into the wash, but The Broker was waiting for us next to a line of trailers parked in what looked like a staging area for the local ranchers. The place was otherwise deserted, but The Broker was standing in front of a good-sized panel truck, his hands in his pockets, giving every impression that he was just waiting patiently.

Jack brought the truck to a halt some two hundred meters from The Broker. We sat there for a long couple of minutes, letting the others get into position. The Broker just stood there and watched us calmly, the sunlight glinting from his sunglasses.

Finally, figuring that we couldn't hold this off any longer, I opened the door and got out, my rifle slung around my shoulders and my chest rig showing under my open jacket. I didn't give a fuck at that point if The Broker thought we were being hostile. We'd been attacked twice on our own turf. Damned straight we were hostile.

The Broker still didn't move or visibly react as we walked toward him, our rifles at the low ready. He just watched us, his head slightly tilted to one side in an attitude of amused curiosity that I'd come to expect from him.

He was a small man, going bald, with a round head and a generally soft, genial way about him that disguised the fact that this was a very, very dangerous man, indeed. I'd first met him in a very expensive restaurant in Panama City, where he had been dressed in a suit and tie, which had suited him perfectly well. He was presently dressed in jeans and a Carhartt jacket, and seemed just as comfortable dressed that way. He was a chameleon, able to move through numerous environments easily and unobtrusively. It was how he had become as powerful, and as dangerous, as he was.

He smiled as we approached him, though with his sunglasses on it was impossible to see if the smile reached his eyes. It probably did; he was too good at tradecraft to have so obvious a tell.

"Good to see you, gentlemen," he said jovially. "I'd tell you that the rest of the team can come in; there is no ambush waiting for you in the weeds, and I am certain that the area is clean. But I don't imagine you'll take me up on the invitation."

"You have a problem with that?" I asked. Jack just watched him, his eyes flicking back and forth between The Broker and the truck, where there was at least one guy behind the wheel, more than likely just as heavily armed as we were.

"Not at all," The Broker replied, his voice growing more serious. "Under the circumstances, paranoia is not only natural, it's commendable. I'd be worried if you weren't suspicious."

That actually made me relax, fractionally, though the little voice in the back of my head that told me not to trust *anybody* who wasn't a Praetorian kept suggesting that he'd known his words would have that effect. "What have you got?" I asked him.

He jerked his thumb at the truck behind him. "Refit and resupply, to start," he said. "I imagine that you're running a little low after your adventures down in Colorado." He nodded. "Oh, yes, I know that was you. I knew as soon as it started hitting some of the information streams. You have your own patterns, for those who know how to look. Everyone does."

"You didn't want to talk over the phone, but now we're not on the phone. Who sent these assholes after us?" I asked.

"I'm working on that," he replied. "Suffice it to say, for the moment, that there's a major power play at work, and you gentlemen are in the middle of it, if only a part of it. What you need to concentrate on for now is getting in there, getting as many of your people out as possible, and getting someplace more secure. I know a few fallback positions where you can hole up for a while, positions that are *not* compromised." He tossed an envelope to me. I let it fall at my feet. He might be on the level, but I was not falling for the "catch" trick if there was some skullduggery afoot. "That's all the reconnaissance reports from a few of my people on the task force's numbers and dispositions. Yes, I've had them in the vicinity since Mexico. I like to keep an eye on my friends as well as my enemies."

I didn't look down at the envelope. "We'll take it under advisement," I said. I was already starting to think ahead, think of staging areas and hiding places in the hills above The Ranch. The last time The Broker had given us intel, it had been extensive, thorough, and spot-on. It still didn't mean he wasn't double-crossing us this time, but that was why we always ran our own reconnaissance and moved carefully.

Well, mostly carefully. If I was being honest, Pueblo had not been a good example of us at our most professionally cautious.

"If you want to get the rest of your stuff out of that Duramax," The Broker went on, "we'll trade vehicles. John and I will take your truck, and you take this one. There's a new set of burner phones in the glove compartment, programmed with a new contact number, so that we can keep in touch. With that, I will get out of your way, at least until it is time to proceed."

"One more question, Gray," I said. "Why the favors? What does this get you?"

His smile thinned slightly. "Your company is a hell of a wrecking ball, Mr. Stone. And the time is rapidly approaching when some edifices will need smashing. I'd like to have you around for that. Now, I'd suggest that you concentrate on getting your people out. We can discuss the strategic situation when time is slightly less pressing."

CHAPTER 9

The Ranch was too big to be properly surrounded by anything less than a battalion. Not only that, but it was backed up against the Beartooth Mountains, and no mechanized force was getting up there without considerable difficulty. Add in our own not inconsiderable defensive measures, and, for the moment at least, the unknown task force was stalled at our two entry gates.

Nick and I were watching one of those task force encampments. They had set up just outside the North Gate, where the MS-13 attackers had been turned into hamburger. There were few traces of the fight out there anymore, just some shattered glass in the ditch alongside the road. Anyone who didn't know what had happened would probably think somebody had wrecked their car and nothing else.

The two of us were lying on our bellies, peering over the crest of a finger that ran roughly southwest-to-northeast, draped in tan and brown camouflage ponchos, watching the gate and our mysterious adversaries through binos.

The task force had fallen back down the slope from the gate, and was circled up just above the dry streambed to the north and the Harricks' hay fields beyond it. They were within rifle shot of the gate and the concealed bunkers flanking it, but it didn't look like they'd exchanged much in the way of fire. Our guys weren't visible, but the task force personnel we could see weren't showing too much concern; they weren't going out of their way to stay behind cover.

They were *very* well equipped. I counted four black-painted MATVs, the towering armored replacements for the up-armored HMMWV, along with another six vehicles I didn't recognize. They were long, sleek, and angular, with eight wheels on what looked like independent suspensions. If there had been any doubt that our enemies had a lot of money and influence—and there really wasn't—then the presence of what looked like advanced armored vehicle prototypes did a good job of dispelling it.

While the vehicles were painted black, they displayed none of the block-letter alphabet soup that might be expected of Federal agencies, whether the FBI, BATFE, or DHS. The personnel's pseudo-uniforms and equipment were similarly blank, though if they had any badges or patches, I couldn't tell, not from seven hundred meters away, through binoculars. They were kitted up, but not to the extreme level of most SWAT teams, who tend to look like they can barely move, so covered are they in armor, drop leg panels, knee pads, elbow pads, helmets, etc. No, these guys were mostly wearing 5.11 tuxedos in tan and green, with plate carriers and battle belts. Ball caps predominated, instead of the ubiquitous SWAT/Hostage Rescue OpsCore helmets. My grudging respect for their choice of kit was offset by the fact that these assholes were besieging my home, and that a few of them were wearing shemaghs wrapped around their necks, though there was no desert sand to keep off and it wasn't cold enough yet to need to keep body heat in during the day. Tacticool jackoffs.

We had been in position since before dawn, and it had quickly become evident that we were going to have to stay put and move as little as possible until after dark. We'd been clean on the way up, but these guys definitely had UAVs out; we'd heard one quadrotor already. I was watching a couple of them, in the shelter of one of the eight-wheelers, setting up another one. They leaned back and it started to wobble up into the sky.

It didn't make it far, though. I guessed it had just passed a hundred feet when it suddenly jerked, tilted hard to one side, and fell out of the sky. The two who had launched it had to scramble to avoid getting hit. A moment later, the *crack* of a shot echoed up the hill.

"The boys are getting a bit of skeet shooting in, I see," Nick whispered.

It was a good sign; it meant not only that our guys weren't lying down for this little invasion, but that the opposition had limits on their overhead reconnaissance capability. I briefly wondered how many drones they'd already lost.

Carefully, achingly slowly, so as to avoid showing enough movement to catch a drone operator's eye, I put down the binos and picked up the camera. A few shots framed the general disposition of the task force personnel and vehicles. As I was just about to put it down, though, Nick whispered, "Don't put it away, yet."

I wasn't sure why not, but then I heard the distant growl of helo rotors. That was certainly a familiar enough sound, and given the fact that all our helos, to the best of my knowledge, were currently either still in Kurdistan, where Alek was running the bulk of the company's overseas operations, or out at sea aboard the *Frontier Rose*, the freighter that we'd liberated from Somali pirates and turned into a maritime operations platform, it probably didn't mean anything good. I kept the camera up, scanning for any sign of the bird.

In a moment I had it, a dark dot moving low over the flats. I didn't get too fixated on it, but kept scanning, looking for a follow aircraft. There wasn't one within my line of sight; it appeared to be alone. A glance down at the TF showed that they were expecting the helo; two of them were laying out an LZ, as far from the gate as they could get, in the middle of Dave Harrick's hay field. Old Man Harrick was gonna be *pissed*, but I expected they'd already threatened him with all sorts of imaginary charges and a long stay in a black site if he didn't keep his mouth shut. They probably wouldn't have threatened his life directly; that might not have maintained the cover that this was some kind of legit Federal operation.

We watched and waited as the helo came closer, flying low and fast before flaring just above the LZ. It was a Bell JetRanger, not unlike a couple of our helicopters, only painted black. Just like the armored vehicles on the ground, there were no other markings except for a white tail number, which I suspected was a decal that could easily be replaced.

The bird settled in a cloud of dust and hay clippings. No shots were aimed at it from the gate; Tom must have instructed the boys to be a little circumspect in their shooting. I didn't know how they'd convinced the TF to back off when they'd first approached; what little contact we'd had with Tom since the "Extremis" signal had been necessarily terse and of a strictly operational manner, with only absolutely necessary information being passed, and that as coded as possible. We were kind of stuck using a commercial satellite uplink for all our comms, and if these assholes were as well-connected as they appeared to be, we had to assume that they were tapping into every data stream they could find, including commercial sat-comm. Our encryption was top of the line, largely thanks to Derek, but we still had to be careful. It was entirely possible that we were being overly paranoid, and Derek insisted that we were, but under the circumstances, few of us were willing to chance it.

At any rate, there wasn't any attempt made to shoot the helo down, though I could see a lot of rifles pointed toward the gate as the bird got closer. They were nervous, and they weren't taking chances.

I kept snapping pictures as a figure got out of the helo and ran, hunched over below the still-turning rotors, toward one of the unidentified armored vehicles. It took a second to make out, since the figure was kitted out just like the rest, but after a moment I saw that it was a woman, her long blond hair tied up in a ponytail that stuck out from the back of her olive-green ball cap.

"Who the hell is this?" Nick asked, his eyes still pressed to his binos.

"I think this is somebody working for a higher echelon," I replied, still snapping photos. We'd have more pictures than we knew what to do with, but the more information, the better. We could sift through it later. Somewhere in the ocean of imagery, we might find a vital clue to what the fuck was going on.

A barrel-chested man in kit, with a bald head and a beard down to his mag pouches, got out of the armored vehicle and shook the blond chick's hand before ushering her into the undoubtedly cramped compartment inside the vehicle.

The TF's security was still on alert, watching the gate from behind rifles and machine guns. To their credit, the boys at the gate didn't do anything, but were presumably watching and recording as much as we were.

81

After about a half an hour, the blond came out of the vehicle and ran back to the helo, which quickly spun up again and rose into the sky, banking hard and staying low and fast as it flew back down the valley. I spared only a couple of shots for the bird, as I turned my attention back to Big Beard.

Old boy was yelling, though he was far enough away that we couldn't hear what he was saying. He was getting responses, though, as several individuals came running to his vehicle. I counted one per MATV or eight-wheeler, suggesting he was calling in team leaders.

"I don't think we've got a hell of a lot of time," Nick whispered. "That looks like something's getting ready to kick off."

"I think you're right," I muttered, as I slowly and carefully put the camera down and pulled out the tablet and the satellite puck we were using for comms. The boys might be skeet shooting drones every chance they got, but I knew I'd heard at least one up there, and still wasn't going to take chances on being detected by moving carelessly.

I hastily laid out the situation in as brief a message as possible, and squirted it up through the satellite before shutting off the puck and stowing it and the tablet in my pack again and focusing back on the TF. We couldn't move until dark, and even then, we were going to have to move with extreme care.

I just hoped that the TF didn't decide it was go time before then.

***

By the time the sun went down, it was pretty damned obvious that go time was fast approaching. I've been on enough teams getting ready for an assault to know what it looks like. As it got dark, they were donning helmets and NVGs and sitting in their vehicles, even if they were keeping the doors and hatches open, the up-gunners focused on the gate.

And we were still stuck in our OP, watching, afraid to move lest we give our position away.

"We could get Big Beard from here," I muttered. "It's only about six hundred yards. Easy shot with a 7.62."

"I don't know," Nick replied. "Can we get back under cover before they light up the whole fucking hillside? And would it slow 'em down, or just make 'em step up the timetable?"

"It would at least give them something to think about," I pointed out. "You and I would probably try to assault through, but can you think of anyone trained up in the last decade who'd do the same? They're trying really hard to mimic some kind of Federal law enforcement task force, whoever they are, and I haven't heard of Federal LE taking fire and counterattacking with overwhelming force in the last few years."

"These guys might be trying to mimic Federal LE," Nick answered, "but we're pretty sure they're not. Which means, when push comes to shove, we can't count on them to react the same way."

Which was a good point. As much as I was itching to do something, *anything*, to put the hurt on these fuckheads and drive them off, there were no guarantees that taking a shot wasn't going to have disastrous consequences.

But then, there are never any guarantees that violence isn't going to have disastrous consequences. The nature of violence is that it's violent, which means it's unpredictable. You can only be certain of so much. After that, you've got to make a decision.

We had a rough plan already worked out, that had taken shape throughout the day, through brief messages sent during carefully planned comm windows. It involved a series of strikes at the two staging areas, mainly focused on sowing as much confusion as possible, followed by getting the rest of the Praetorian personnel out and into the mountains. We'd ID'ed the two overwatch positions that had been set up watching The Ranch, which had prevented an earlier breakout—Tom hadn't been sure they could get clear before the overwatch had the TF coming down around their ears.

The siege had been a delicate balance of power for the last couple of days. Our guys had demonstrated that they had enough firepower to put some serious hurt on any attacker, which had led the TF to fall back and reconsider its position. But those overwatch positions had to be feeding the staging areas enough information, coupled with however many drones that they could get in the air, to let them know by now just how narrow the margin was. We were heavily armed, sure, but even we didn't have the kind of clout to stop a coordinated assault, with air and armor assets, cold.

Tom hadn't moved for the same reason you don't turn your back on a pissed-off dog. As long as he had a gun pointed at the TF's face, that delicate equilibrium stayed in place. As soon as he pulled back, they were going to be coming in, and then things were going to get ugly.

Of course, now he had us on the outside, so the dynamic was going to change a bit, especially given some of the toys that had been in the back of that panel truck. The problem was, the plan required time, time that I was no longer sure we had.

I decided to take a chance. It sure looked like they were saddling up to move down there, and they weren't going to just drive away. If that had been the plan, they would have done it as soon as Blondie left on that helo.

I pulled out my tac radio and turned it on. After giving it a moment to boot up, I keyed the mic. "North Gate, this is Hillbilly," I sent.

"Hillbilly, Geek," Eddie replied a moment later. Eddie had been Mike's assistant team lead until Mike had caught a round outside of Veracruz. Since then, Eddie had been my counterpart, taking over Mike's team and trying to rebuild it after losing Mike and Chad.

I hadn't known that Eddie was out on the North Gate, but it wasn't worth commenting on, especially since he'd treat any question about it as a waste of time. Eddie was one of the most dispassionate killers in the company. He'd once told me that he got mistaken for a borderline sociopath a lot.

"It looks like our visitors are getting ready to introduce themselves again," I said. "Are you guys set, if they do?"

"Ready and, well, not quite eager, but at least ready," he replied. "We have eyes on."

"Roger," I replied. "I'm going to try to throw them off a little. Send to the rest that go time just got moved up; I don't think these guys are going to give us much more breathing space. Hopefully we can disrupt them before they move. The main effort's going to have to go as soon as the shooting starts. Just be ready to repel if they decide to counterattack, and cover our retreat, if need be."

"Roger," he replied calmly. "We've got a few party favors waiting for them down here, too. Standing by." Eddie and I knew each other well enough by then that there weren't a lot of questions. Just rolling with the punches.

Stowing the radio, I looped one arm through my pack strap and pulled my rifle forward. It had been lying close to my hand all day, just in case, but now I got behind it properly, carefully moving the pack forward to act as a rest. Then I got behind the gun, turned on the lighted reticle, and looked for Big Beard.

He was right where I expected him to be, standing behind his vehicle, holding a phone to his ear, either getting last minute instructions, or running last minute coordination. He and his boys had made the mistake of focusing all their security on the gate; they hadn't taken shooters in the hills into consideration. He wasn't even trying to stay behind cover from anywhere but the gate.

Gauging wind is always difficult after dark, and we hadn't brought a Kestrel with us to measure it precisely. But I could feel a faint breeze, enough to at least make a decent guess for a six-hundred-yard shot. Of course, since it was downhill, I had to adjust my hold ever so little, aiming slightly below where I wanted to hit him. Making sure I was squared up behind the gun, I let out a breath and squeezed the trigger.

Suppressed or not, the shot *cracked* loudly across the empty slopes of the mountainside. The suppressor contained the muzzle blast, but didn't quiet the supersonic shockwave of the bullet breaking the sound barrier as it flew toward its target. It was an unmistakable sound, especially in the quiet of rural Wyoming in the evening.

Big Beard was kitted up and armed, wearing a plate carrier and carrying a SCAR slung across his chest. But plates only work if you're standing head-on with the shooter, and he'd been facing the gate. The bullet went into his side, a couple inches behind his front plate. If I had my angles right, based on where the reticle had been when the trigger broke, it had just blown right through both lungs and the top of his heart.

He dropped like a rock.

Now, I'd been hoping to sow confusion and chaos. But there was no reaction, aside from the tiny glints of NVGs searching the hills for where the shot had come from.

I realized that, with everybody mounted up and ready to go, no one actually had eyes on their boss. I'd just decapitated this part of the TF, and none of them even knew it yet.

Under different circumstances, that would have been a feat to be proud of. At the time, however, it was just an annoyance. I'd lopped off one of the Hydra's heads, but its heart was still beating, and it was still about to come after us with the other eight.

"Holy shit," Nick whispered. He'd noticed the same thing.

I didn't say anything. I just did the only thing that I could do that made sense. I shifted targets.

The eight-wheelers had their hatches in the rear, and they were all facing the gate, presenting their armored flanks to me, so I didn't really have a shot there. But the MATVs had doors like ordinary trucks, and most of them were open. One smart guy had closed his door when the first shot echoed across the hillside, but the others hadn't *quite* caught on yet.

I put a second bullet into the vague outline of a man in kit and helmet, who still had one leg hanging out of his door. His scream sounded faintly and he slumped, though he was trying to close the door. I put another bullet through the opening before he could get it closed, and the door swung all the way open again.

By the time I'd shifted to the next truck, its occupants had wised up and closed their doors. A MATV is impenetrable to most bullets, so I shifted higher. The gunners in the turrets were hunkered down and swinging their heavy guns toward the hillside, but I had a good enough angle that they couldn't *quite* get low enough. I knocked one down into the cab, then shifted to the next. By the time I steadied the reticle on the turret, he'd already ducked inside.

"This might be a good time to make ourselves scarce," Nick said. The eight-wheelers were swinging their turrets around. "If they've got CROWS on those things, they'll have thermals."

Whatever those eight-wheelers were, even if the turrets were manned, I suspected they'd still have thermals. Nick was right. It was time to get the fuck out of Dodge.

We didn't need to go far; we were right at the crest of the finger, and we just had to clamber a few feet backward and down to get a good chunk of dirt and rock between us and anybody trying to shoot us. Still, haste was called for, so I dragged my pack to me, threw off the poncho, which Nick swept up under one arm, and we skedaddled down the slope, even as one of the gunners down below opened up on the hillside. A few shots *snapped* by overhead as we dropped below the crest, but for the most part, they didn't seem to have zeroed in on us before we disappeared.

There was a louder, heavier *boom* from down below. I knew what that noise was, even without being able to see the shot.

Logan Try, in addition to being a sour, anti-social son of a bitch, was something of an evil genius. He'd managed to build four reasonable facsimiles of a Lahti L-39 20mm anti-tank rifle. He'd been something of a ballistics nerd for a long time, always fiddling with various wildcat cartridges, and had started fabricating his own rounds for the 20mms. I didn't know where he'd gotten the sheer amount of tungsten needed for the penetrators, and I didn't ask. I suspected that I didn't want to know. With Logan, hijacking and/or murder was not entirely outside the realm of possibility.

We'd been careful to keep the capability that the 20mm rifles provided under wraps. Even Brett didn't know we had those, and we'd run him through his paces with some pretty cool toys. I hoped that meant that the Task Force down there was shitting its collective pants as soon as the first round punched into one of those MATVs.

As soon as we were behind cover, Nick and I took a brief second to properly get our gear set to move, then we stepped off. We were going to have to pick our way carefully to make sure we kept some terrain between us and those armored vehicles down there; I didn't want to catch a round from somebody who decided to keep an eye on the hillside while his buddies confronted the 20mm blasting at them from deep inside a pillbox.

We didn't have any time to waste moving slowly, though. Opening fire had, hopefully, forestalled the assault, but we had to move fast. They were going to recover and come after us sooner or later. Leading out, I started dog-trotting up the draw.

* * *

We actually got to the ranch house itself just ahead of Eddie and the boys at the gate. They were coming at a trot, rifles in their hands, looking almost as smoked as I felt at that point. Training aside, climbing a fucking mountain at speed while trying to keep cover between you and an enemy down in the valley is a bitch.

"They fell back after we disabled two of the MATVs," Eddie said between breaths. "I think you threw 'em for a loop with that sniper fire, Jeff."

Tom stepped out onto the porch, dressed in woodlands, with a chest rig on, pack on his back, and his rifle in his hands. A cigarette was dangling from the corner of his mouth. "It slowed 'em down, but it didn't stop 'em," he said. "They hit the East Gate hard, and broke through. Miguel and those boys took the secondary exits from their positions and are E&Eing as we speak. We need to do the same."

A deep, earth-rumbling *boom* sounded from the north. "That would be the demo charges on the bunkers detonating," Eddie said. "Did Miguel get the east bunkers wired?"

A similar rumble a second later answered his question. "There's nothing left here that can't be replaced," Tom said. "All the drives are wiped and we've been hiding most of the sensitive stuff for the last few days anyway. Let's go."

"Lead out," I told him, pointing up into the Beartooth mountains. I specifically pointed to the left of the big pyramidal peak that loomed behind The Ranch. That was where Larry and the rest of the team except for Jack and Ben, who were out on the southern flank to provide some more harassing fire, were waiting to cover our exfil.

We could hear the rumble of engines as the armored vehicles trundled up the dirt road from the East Gate. I had little doubt that the other element would be along soon, since Eddie had blown the bunkers at the North Gate. They were a bit discombobulated, thanks to losing their TL, but they'd rally if they were any kind of professionals, which they appeared to be.

Tom led the way, jogging around behind the house and past the barns. Fortunately, we didn't have far to go to get to the woods, where those armored vehicles couldn't follow. They'd have to dismount and follow on foot, and we knew the hills better than they did.

With one last glance back from the treeline, I caught a glimpse of a dark hulk rumbling up to the front of the ranch house, before I turned and plunged into the shadows under the trees.

We'd be back. We'd wreaked our vengeance on the *narco* assholes who had ordered Jim murdered. We'd catch our breath and deal with these fucksticks, too.

CHAPTER 10

It was a tough slog. We had a nine-thousand-foot tall mountain to climb, and we weren't going to be able to stop once we reached the top. And we had to expect to be pursued the entire way.

It was getting dark, and the trees and the terrain would deny our adversaries the use of their vehicles, along with the heavy weapons and high-powered night and thermal optics that went with them. But as I hiked up the rocky slope of the mountain, sometimes half supporting myself on the trees growing just down-slope, I could hear the faint buzz that announced the fact that our pursuers still had drones up. They'd probably launched a couple new ones since the gates had been evacuated. Those little quadrotors weren't *that* expensive, especially for somebody who had managed to assemble and equip a mechanized paramilitary force like that.

The people and the equipment weren't the only factor I was thinking of, either; they would need the sort of money and influence that gets Federal law enforcement to look the other way. There was no way this was legal. Which was why my conscience wasn't bothering me that much about smoking any of them without warning. It wasn't like they'd come to the gate and presented a warrant.

The terrain necessitated a single file. It was too damned steep for much else. Tom was up front, leading the support people with a couple of the newer teams. I'd seen Mia with them, briefly, so she'd made it, at least. Eddie and I were in the rear, with our shrunken teams, looking over our shoulders for pursuit, wondering if we weren't at least half hoping that they'd come after us. They might be well-equipped to beat down doors, but coming after us with LAVs and MATVs didn't speak well to their preparedness for the mountains. We trained up in the Beartooths for *fun*. We knew those hills like the backs of our hands.

I was actually really looking forward to one of their forward scouts running into a grizzly. They'd been seen more frequently in the area lately, and more than one training patrol had had a close encounter with one, fortunately without anybody getting mauled. Somehow, I doubted that our friends down there had considered that factor. The only problem with my rather uncharitable hopes was that they were probably making too much noise for a bear to let them get that close.

Eddie and I were letting the others get ahead, while we paused more often for short security halts, essentially leaning against the side of the mountain, or wedging ourselves against trees and watching and listening for our enemies.

Some of the halts were more impromptu than others. As a drone buzzed by overhead, we flattened ourselves against trees, hoping the evergreen boughs would be enough to shield us from thermals, if the drones were carrying them and not glorified GoPros. For all the mythologizing that Hollywood has done, thermals can't see through foliage. Not well, anyway.

I took a knee next to a tall, wind-twisted spruce and aimed my rifle back the way we had come, using the tree as something of a rest. I kept moving my attention from our back trail to the sky, though I couldn't see shit through the tree branches, especially in the dark. That quadrotor was up there; I could hear it plainly enough that it had to be only a hundred yards away at most. But it wasn't going to be showing lights, and it was just too dark to see.

I don't know how long that thing loitered up there, weaving back and forth over the mountainside, but it felt like an eternity. I had my skullcap mount on, and was peering through the trees with NVGs, waiting for the bad guys to come through the trees. If they had thought it through, they could just keep the drones running back and forth across the mountain all night, and keep us in place until they caught up.

That thought almost got me up and moving before the faint buzz of the quadrotor faded away down the draw. But I stayed put. The last thing that any of us needed to do was panic; they'd catch us and cut us down like grass if we did.

As the sound of the drone faded, I strained my ears for sounds of pursuit. My hearing wasn't what it used to be; too many explosions and too much gunfire. But unless they were real woodsmen, I should still be able to hear *something* if they were getting close.

The only sounds were the faint, receding noise of the drone and the wind in the treetops. If they were on our trail, they were still a good distance behind us.

My knees had stiffened as I'd crouched there, waiting, and the left clicked a little as I levered myself to my feet, hoping that nobody else saw me using the tree to help myself up. I needn't have worried, though; as I turned around I saw Eddie doing the same thing. He looked up as I turned around, and while the NVGs masked both our faces, I got the fleeting impression that both of us were about to bust out laughing at having caught the other moving like an old man.

The moment of levity didn't last. Our situation was still too dire. I pointed uphill and Eddie nodded. Tom and the rest should have been a good distance ahead by then. With the drone gone and pursuit still not having caught up, we needed to open up that time-distance gap. It was going to suck; the mountain only got steeper as we got higher. But that was where the rendezvous was.

Legs burning, we kept going.

***

First light was less than an hour away by the time we reached the RV point. Most of the new guys were holding up well, better than some of us older guys, truth be told. Several of the support people, including Mia, were visibly exhausted. It had been a punishing climb; if it had been a patrol rather than an escape, I probably would have split that movement into two nights, hunkering down in a hide site somewhere on the side of the mountain for a day. Instead, we'd pushed all the way up to the grassy top of Tibb's Butte in about eight hours.

The Broker was waiting with transportation just as he'd promised, though it probably wasn't what most of the support guys, or even some of the shooters, had had in mind. But we were in the backwoods, so trucks or even four-wheelers weren't ideal. This way was slower, but fairly reliable over rough terrain and a good deal quieter.

We also weren't going to be able to rest much until we got where we were going. Horse-riding and mule packing are still work.

The Broker's guys already had the horses saddled and the mules had pack frames set up so that we could drop our kit in the pouches and go. It took a few minutes, and a little bit of whining and grumbling from all hands, including some of the self-proclaimed hardasses, but we got everyone saddled up and ready to go. Or, at least, as ready as they were going to be. We had done a little bit of horse work in the backcountry just because, but few of us were what you'd call accomplished horsemen.

Fortunately, the gelding that I'd gotten was a good-tempered and docile animal, and responded readily to my clumsy and hesitant direction. I brought the horse up next to The Broker, who, in the faint gray light of pre-dawn twilight, looked as perfectly at ease on horseback, dressed in jeans and a Carhartt jacket with a broad-brimmed felt hat on his head, as he had in a suit, sitting in a posh, five-star restaurant in Panama City.

"We've only got about four miles to go," he said quietly. "I've got a camp set up, well-concealed, on the other side of the Butte. We should be under the trees and out of sight by the time the sun's all the way up."

"They've got drones up," I pointed out. "We're going to stand out crossing four miles of open country."

"They are probably looking for a group on foot," he pointed out, turning his horse toward the long, low slope to the west, "not a group on a horse packing trip. To make matters more interesting, I have several similar groups moving around the nearby hills for the rest of the morning. That should give them more than enough to look at."

91

I just nodded. I was exhausted. The night air in the mountains had chilled down, but the hike had been murderous enough that I was soaked in my own sweat. I wanted nothing more than to lie down on the rocky ground and pass the fuck out. But my own still-simmering anger and determination to live through this and wreak bloody vengeance on the motherfuckers who'd come trying to knock down our door kept me upright in the saddle and my aching eyes searching the horizon and the sky for enemies.

We rode with the rising sun at our backs, making decent time but keeping the pace slow enough that we didn't have too many accidents. A few of the less-capable riders fell off their horses, anyway. Eric seemed to have drawn a mare who liked to blow up her stomach when she was being saddled, then relax once the cinch was tightened. His saddle kept sliding to one side or another, and we had to stop to tighten it twice.

Finally, we descended into another draw on the far side of Tibb's Butte, getting off the open ground and back into the trees. I'd felt like there were eyes on us the entire ride, especially as we'd heard drones a couple of times, though they never got quite close enough to spot. That didn't mean anything; they would be equipped with top-of-the-line cameras that could have picked us out from miles away. I just hoped that The Broker's plan to camouflage our movement worked.

The Broker led us about three hundred meters down the slope and through the trees, to a small bowl in the mountainside, lined with pine and spruce. There was a camp there, though it was all but invisible until you were right on top of it; the shelters were covered in brush and pine boughs, and there was very little in the way of equipment out. Several of The Broker's shooters were on security. I wondered where exactly he was getting his personnel, but a man of his obvious resources would have his pick of operators with the price tag he could probably offer.

Reining in beneath the trees, we slowly, painfully dismounted. A couple of the new guys were rather less than graceful, and Herman, one of Eddie's guys, managed more of a fall off his horse than a dismount. He lay under the horse and groaned for a long moment before Eddie hauled him away from the animal's hooves.

I swung down, feeling every muscle in my body, including a few that I could have sworn hadn't existed before. It took a few minutes to get everybody situated, while maintaining our own discreet security. So far, The Broker had played straight, but I was not in a particularly trusting mood, and neither were Eddie or Tom.

Mia looked like she wanted to talk to me, but as soon as she leaned back against her pack, she was asleep.

The sun was filtering down through the trees, having risen above the bulk of the butte behind us. Eddie, Tom, and I joined The Broker inside one of the shelters.

"Have you contacted Renton since this started?" The Broker asked.

I shook my head. "Renton's organization is as leaky as a sieve," I said. "Considering that it was because of his people that our identities got spread all over the hell-and-gone in the first place, I can't trust them."

"Certain members of his organization are certainly compromised, at least morally," The Broker said mildly. I didn't comment on the incongruity of an international underworld shadow facilitator talking about moral compromise. "But Renton is still clean. You can trust me on that."

"I hate to say it," I replied, before Tom could say anything, though I caught his wintry warning glance, "but trust is in *very* short supply right now. I know, you pulled our asses out of the fire back there, but just based on your own statement, I can't trust that your agenda is anything more than saving us as sacrificial lambs for later, when it suits you better."

Even Eddie gave me a look at that, but The Broker maintained his bland smile. The son of a bitch was *impossible* to ruffle. "Your paranoia is impressive, Mr. Stone," he replied, "if slightly misplaced. Yes, your continued life and freedom does play a part in my plans for the future. I would not have expended the resources and risked the exposure of operating on American soil otherwise. But you need to think; have I ever, to your knowledge, demonstrated such depth of caprice, such *stupidity*, as to go to this kind of effort on a lark? You gentlemen are a valuable asset; far too valuable to throw away." He sighed, the first sign of frustration I'd ever seen him indulge in. "If I wanted you disposed of, do you really think that I couldn't do it in a more straightforward fashion? I would have done exactly what the people who sent that task force out there did, except that I would have done it more competently, and you would not have seen it coming until it was far, far too late."

He tilted his head slightly to one side, in that odd sort of way he had, and continued, in a slightly warmer tone. "You do have friends, Mr. Stone. Few and far between, perhaps, but you do have them. Though it is ultimately up to you to decide whether or not to trust me, and therefore trust my word that Renton is also trustworthy, I would suggest that the weight of evidence is on my side."

He had a point, and even through the fog of fatigue, I could see it. I still didn't especially like it. I knew what this man was, and the fact that he was one of our only real friends bothered me, almost as much as my near-murder of that gangbanger in the barn had. My defensive wall of killing fury weakened by weariness, the thought snuck through, *What the hell is happening to us? How did we end up here, where our only friends are shadowy networks of spooks and international underworld kingpins? We're supposed to be the good guys, dammit!*

93

I quashed the thought as quickly as it came. There would be time for self-examination and recrimination later, if we survived. For the moment, the world was the way it was, and we were going to have to roll with the punches.

But even as I thought it, I felt a tiredness that went deeper than my physical exhaustion. I hadn't taken up the gun thinking I'd end up here, hunted in my own country, buddying up with shadowy conspiracies and criminal kingpins.

I suddenly remembered a brief conversation with Jim, back in Nicaragua, while we'd been hunting down Reyes, the drug kingpin who had been the lead that drew us into the hunt for the shadowy, and illusory, El Duque. Jim had been the oldest of us out in the field, and he'd wondered if it wasn't getting past time to get out.

He hadn't. He'd been brutally murdered before he could.

I needed to focus on the task at hand. Fortunately, everybody else was just as smoked as I was, so I didn't think anyone else had noticed my little reverie, though when I looked The Broker in the eyes, I suddenly thought that he at least suspected what I had been thinking. The guy was scary smart, and you didn't dare do or say anything around him that you didn't want getting added to the dossier in his head.

"Fine," I said. "You've got a point." I rubbed my aching eyes. "We'll contact Renton, but not until we've had some time to rest. It's been a long forty-eight hours."

"We should be secure here," The Broker said mildly, as if there had been no clash of wills at all. "Get some chow and some sleep, but don't take too long. Things are moving quickly, and we don't have a lot of time to spare."

***

We might have simply called on a sat-phone, of which The Broker had several, from the campsite, but at the same time, I wanted to both avoid the possibility of being back-tracked electronically and get a bit better view of the lay of the land. We'd concentrated on the task force's local dispositions around The Ranch, for the obvious reason that the immediate threat needed to be dealt with or otherwise counteracted first. But there was no way that any kind of paramilitary force, particularly one that size, was going to be operating without a support base somewhere, and I wanted to know where it was.

I was pretty sure I knew just where to start looking, too, and my suspicions just made me angrier.

So, just before dawn, after far too little sleep, Larry and I saddled up and headed down the mountain. Both of us were dressed to appear more like regular old mountain trekkers, rather than mountain fighters; we'd ditched our chest rigs and were riding with pistols only. They'd be less than ideal if we got in a firefight, but if the drones that were still up were looking for dudes decked out in the latest in Tacticool Fashion, they might overlook two guys in Carhartts and broad-brimmed hats on horseback, not visibly armed.

It was a long ride, over some not insignificant terrain. While the Beartooths got a lot steeper and rougher to the north and west, the draws and slopes we were covering were still plenty steep enough to make riding difficult, especially for two not-so-practiced riders as Larry and me. We were both staying in the saddle, but between the steepness of the slopes, the rocky ground, and the piles of fallen trees we often had to work our way around, we weren't comfortable. I doubted Larry's horse was all that comfortable, either. He was a *big* dude, and it had to be rough going hauling his enormous frame up those mountains.

We worked our way west, first, crossing the steep-walled canyon that led down toward Deep Lake, and swinging north around Sawtooth Mountain. By the time we hit the Morrison Jeep Trail and headed southeast, it was already late morning. The sky was clear, and I was keeping an eye turned upward, though I was careful to keep my hat brim at such an angle as to obscure my face from any great distance.

I had good reason to. Even as we cleared the treeline and rode out onto the grassy meadow, the faint buzz of a drone overhead got louder. They knew we'd disappeared into the mountains, and they were searching for us.

Keeping my head down, I scanned the sky. At first, I couldn't see anything aside from the eagle or hawk that was gliding in great, looping circles above Sawtooth Lake to our west. I knew guys who would insist that it wasn't a hawk or an eagle, but a disguised drone, but I kept my ear enough to the ground, especially through Derek's unending tech talk, to know that there weren't any devices out there, yet, that could reliably disguise a drone as a bird. There are ways an animal moves that a machine just can't reliably mimic.

As I let my eye rove, however, I eventually saw it. A glint of sunlight on metal, high above. I squinted at it, just barely able to make out the tiny outline.

Larry had ridden up next to me, visibly uncomfortable and more than a little stiff, intent on staying in the saddle, but watching the sky instead of concentrating too hard on the horse. Larry might not have been much of a rider, but he was a pro.

"Scan Eagle?" he muttered, squinting at the drone. It was a lot higher up than I'd thought, and quite a bit farther away, but still noisy enough to be picked out from several miles away.

"It sure sounds like the flying lawn mower," I replied. I couldn't make out enough detail from that distance to definitively identify the machine. "But why would they be using a bird that old? It's not like they can't afford next-gen systems, just going off of what we've seen."

"Maybe they're trying to look respectable?" Larry suggested. "As far as I know, the Scan Eagle's the only drone in its class that the FAA's okayed to operate in US airspace. Maybe they don't want to press their luck too far from their main body."

95

"Or," I countered, as an ominous thought occurred to me, "that thing is the one we're supposed to be watching, and the real deal is staying quiet and out of sight."

"Devious, if that's what they're doing," Larry replied. "You know the best way to handle either case, though."

"Yep," I replied, kicking my horse into an easy walk down the jeep trail. "Make like we don't notice anything. We're just a couple of yokels out for a ride."

"I just hope there aren't any horse people watching," Larry said. "If they see the way we ride, they'll see through us in a minute."

I glanced over at him. "You really think there are going to be horse people sitting in a control trailer, working for the poster children for the worst fears of the black helicopter set?"

He shrugged. "It was a joke, but I've seen stranger things. I knew a bleeding-heart liberal Ranger once."

I had to nod. I'd known a few of those, too. They were few and far between, but they did exist.

We rode on, trying to act like we hadn't noticed anything out of the ordinary, while still keeping our eyes peeled for enemies, aircraft, and the perhaps more mundane, if no less dangerous, four-legged predators. I had my TRP on my hip, loaded with Buffalo Bore +P rounds, but getting surprised by a bear, a cat, or a wolf pack would still be a bad day.

***

We rode through breathtaking country, with jagged, stony mountains rising above their fir-clad shoulders to our north and west. The crest we followed was open and grassy, but with scattered low pines and solid pine and fir forests rising on the lower slopes. Fleecy white clouds scudded across the bright blue sky.

It would have been an idyllic ride, if not for the fact that we were being hunted. This wasn't like running and gunning in some Middle Eastern shithole, or even the much more attractive terrain of Latin America. These high alpine spaces were *home*. And yet here we were, doing precisely what we'd hired out to kill people and break their shit in distant lands for years to avoid. We were fighting the war on our own turf.

It was a depressing thought, casting a pall over the awesome scenery. I should have been up there hunting, or fishing in Deep Lake, not riding back down toward Cody with killing on my mind.

Cody itself was too far to make it in any sort of timely manner on horseback, and The Broker had been insistent that time was of the essence, so we weren't going to go all the way mounted. Instead, we worked our way down into the Clarks Fork canyon, and followed the river until we reached the gravel parking area where Morrison Road met the paved Canyon Road.

We had still heard the drone overhead intermittently for hours. I didn't think the hackles on the back of my neck were ever going to go all the way down; it had felt like we were being watched every step of the way. That uneasy, hunted feeling didn't go away as we approached the horse trailer and the old, beat-up Honda Civic parked on the dirt.

I thought I recognized the grizzled character who got out of the truck and lowered the gate of the horse trailer, but I couldn't quite place him. He might have been a local, though I suspected he was far more likely to be one of The Broker's network. This didn't seem like a time that The Broker would be contracting out to random locals. The balding old gent with the thick, white handlebar mustache didn't betray any recognition as he held our bridles for us while we got painfully down from the weary horses, though, so the sense of familiarity might have been nothing.

The old gent led the horses up into the trailer, then came down the ramp and tossed me a set of car keys. "The Broker told me to tell you to contact him for the next RV point," he said, his voice just as gravelly as his appearance suggested. "He said you'd know how."

I just nodded tiredly and made my way to the car, noticing that I was moving a little more stiffly than I would have liked. That had been a *long* ride, and on very little sleep. I was going to have to be careful not to nod off behind the wheel.

Larry and I got in, the car sagging visibly on its suspension as he wedged himself into the passenger seat, and headed for Cody.

***

We stayed outside of town until a little after midnight. We weren't well known in Cody itself, aside from some of the sheriff's department, but there was no sense in taking chances. After all, it wasn't like we had been exactly anonymous for a while, in large part thanks to our occasional employers.

When we finally headed into town, I didn't drive to the Sheriff's Office. If my suspicions were correct, that would be suicidal, and even if they weren't, it still wouldn't be a good idea. Instead, I made for a small house on the other side of town.

I took a pass by the front of Brett's house, and saw two SUVs sitting out front that didn't belong there. Brett's truck was in the driveway, but those dark Ford Expeditions meant he had security. Which meant somebody was expecting us.

Without a word, I circled the block, then turned into the narrow gravel alley that led behind Brett's house. If they were on the ball, there would be security there, too, but we had better odds of success coming in the back.

I parked three houses down, and we got out, careful not to slam the doors. I drew my TRP and held it down by my leg, even as Larry slid his STI

97

into his gigantic mitt. That 2011 was not a small pistol, but it sure looked like it in Larry's grip.

Silently, we slipped through the shadows of the trees toward Brett's back fence. There wasn't a lot of light back there; Cody was nearly as low-crime as Powell had been. The odds were actually pretty good that most of the back doors we passed were unlocked. Even as rough as times had gotten, Wyoming, as sparsely populated as it was, had stayed pretty much the same.

We got to Brett's back yard without even eliciting a bark from a local dog. Both of us were a lot better at moving on foot than we were at horseback riding. As big as he was, Larry could move like a cat.

Larry put his back to the plank fence around Brett's yard and cupped his hands for my boot. I put my foot in his impromptu stirrup and lifted myself up just high enough to peer over the top of the fence, checking for more goons watching the back.

If they were there, they were inside. The yard was empty and still. I clambered up and over the fence, making as little noise as possible.

Larry had a bit of a harder time getting over; the fence swayed and creaked under his weight. He got over, though, as I crouched in the corner by the garden, my pistol out and trained on the back porch.

There was still no sign that we'd been seen or heard as we padded across the lawn toward the back. I started to hope that we could stay soft the whole way through this.

We got onto the back porch, stepping carefully to avoid letting our boots drum on the planks. There wasn't much we could do about the occasional creak, but fortunately, they were few and far between.

The screen door creaked threateningly as I eased it open. I just *knew* that the hinges were waiting to unleash the screaming of the damned any moment. I was pretty sure if they did, I'd be staring down the barrel of a gun in seconds.

But I got it open with a minimum of noise, and tested the back door. The knob turned and swung open, leading into the darkened kitchen.

The kitchen was reassuringly abandoned, and since we had both been to Brett's house before, we knew where we were going. Carefully and quietly, we stalked toward the bedroom.

If the goons weren't in the house, I was relatively sure we could do this quietly. Brett was divorced and his kids long since grown. If there weren't task force security personnel watching the doors, then Brett was alone inside.

My eyes were well enough adjusted to the dark by the time we got to the bedroom to see Brett's form under the covers of the bed. He still slept on one side of the queen, leaving an empty space where his wife had slept.

I froze suddenly, listening. I didn't think Brett had picked up a girlfriend lately, but if he had, and she was in the bathroom at the moment, this could get real complicated, real quick. But the silence continued, and, confident that we were still alone, I stepped into the room and moved to the side of the bed. Larry loomed at the foot.

I clapped a hand over Brett's snoring mouth. He started awake and began to try to rise, stopping as I placed the cold steel of my .45's muzzle to his forehead. "Yell for those assholes outside and you're a dead man," I hissed.

I felt him relax and cautiously took my hand away. "Holy shit, Jeff," he whispered hoarsely. "Where the hell have you been and what the hell did you do?"

I'll admit, that threw me a little; it was not what I expected to hear from a man with a pistol held to his head, while his security waited outside. "What," I asked, "your new buddies didn't clue you in?"

"Buddies!" He almost came off the bed at that, but subsided at the pressure of the 1911 barrel. "Those cocksuckers outside? They haven't told me shit, except where to keep my people and to keep my mouth shut."

I glanced at Larry, then took a long step back, letting Brett sit up while still keeping my .45 trained on him. "Keep talking," I told him.

He sat up, swinging his legs out of bed, though he didn't move to stand up. "You think I'm working with these clowns?" he asked.

"There do appear to be two carloads of them out front of your house," I pointed out.

"Yeah," he said bitterly. "To make sure I stay put. I don't know who they are, but they seem to know a lot about me, including the fact that I've trained on your facility. They don't seem to think they can trust me."

"Who are they?" I asked. There was still the off chance that he was bluffing, but I'd known Brett long enough that I was pretty sure he wasn't. He was pissed, clear down to his bones, mad enough not to bitch me out for putting a gun to his head.

"Shit," he said, "I was hoping you could tell me. Three days ago, these assholes come roaring into my office with some official-looking guy in a suit, making noises about national security and telling me to turn over every bit of info I've got on The Ranch. When I asked who they were, they waved some papers in my face and told me they had authority and I was required to comply with anything they said. When I pressed the issue, the guy in the suit just laughed at me and pointed out the two armored vehicles he had parked out front. The implication was pretty damned clear."

"Have they solicited any other support?" I asked.

"Nope," he replied. "They just wanted anything we knew about The Ranch, and then we were told to stay out of the way. The guy in the suit never said it outright, but if any of my people got in their way, they were going to either disappear or get killed in a tragic accident."

"Did you try to contact anyone else?" I asked.

He shook his head, barely visible in the dark. "I tried once. I called the State Attorney General. That son of a bitch in the suit broke into the call before anyone could answer and warned me to 'stay in my lane.' After that, I didn't dare."

This was bad, all right. At least I could now be reasonably confident that our friends in the sheriff's department, at least, hadn't willingly betrayed us.

"What the hell is going on, Jeff?" Brett asked.

Before I could answer, Larry posed another question. "Is Little Bob still all right?"

That startled Brett. "You mean...? Oh, shit."

"What?"

"Bob disappeared out of the hospital just before these guys showed up," he said. "I thought you guys had gotten him out. He sure as hell wasn't in good enough shape to get himself out."

"Fuck," I muttered. I hoped like hell Little Bob was still alive. Those cocksuckers in the task force had better hope he stayed that way, too.

"Look," I told Brett, thinking fast, "we can't stick around. I just wanted to make damned good and sure you hadn't sold us down the river. Whatever's going on, there's a pretty long list of people who want us dead after the last few years. I don't know which set this is. But you're in a good position to be our eyes and ears down here. We're still at large, and intend to stay that way." I dug in my pocket and pulled out the burner phone I'd brought for comms. I had two more in the car. "Take this. If things start getting squirrely, or you notice something that we need to know about, call. Any of the numbers programmed in will get to one or another of us, and the word will get back to me."

"What are you guys going to do?" Brett asked as we started to leave the bedroom.

"We're going to get Little Bob back, and then we're going to raise some hell," I told him.

100

CHAPTER 11

The phone call with Renton was vanishingly brief, just long enough to establish a rendezvous point and meet time. Whoever we were up against, if they could mobilize a task force of that size, with those armored vehicles, then they had the scratch to be able to, at least potentially, listen in on any electronic communications. Out there, even if they couldn't crack the encryption, they could probably DF the transmissions. Security meant going low-tech, and I really didn't have a problem with that.

There was a noticeable tension in the air during the brief exchange of words and information, suggesting that Renton was none too happy with me. That was fine; I wasn't feeling all that friendly toward him or his organization at the moment, regardless of The Broker's assurances that he was still one of the good guys.

Leaving aside the anger at having to fight this fight at home, there were definite advantages to operating in rural Wyoming. For all intents and purposes, particularly as far as most of our adversaries were concerned, we were in the back of beyond, outside of their comfort zone. Meanwhile, we were on our home turf, and knew the country and the people intimately, far better than we ever had overseas or south of the border.

There were also plenty of spots out in the wilderness with long sight-lines where you could be reasonably certain not to be observed, at least not without any observers giving themselves away in the process of either getting into position or following you there.

Our chosen RV point was one of those places. It wasn't quite in the middle of nowhere, since we wanted to be able to drive to it in a reasonable amount of time. But there weren't a lot of tourists at the Heart Mountain trailhead in the fall, and when we pulled into the gravel parking lot, it was nearly empty.

There was one other vehicle there, a four-wheeler parked next to the cinderblock outhouse. Since Larry and I were half an hour early, I didn't think it was Renton. I knew he was in the vicinity, but somehow it didn't look right.

It wasn't Renton. When the outhouse door opened, Mia stepped out, dressed for the woods and packing a Glock on her hip.

While I had glimpsed her during the evacuation, I hadn't really looked at Mia since we'd last met at the hole-in-the-wall bar where I'd had my little confrontation with Janson, another one of Renton's organization, who had had something to do with leaking our identities to the cartels while we'd been in Mexico.

She was a reasonably tall, fit woman, with dark hair and just enough tan to her skin to let her blend into the background in most parts of the world, particularly in Mexico, where I'd first met her.

She had a way of keeping you from noticing unless it suited her purposes, largely through her dress and cool, professional demeanor, but she was a *very* attractive woman. Unbidden, my mind turned back to that week in Veracruz, and just how pretty she was when she cleaned up, not to mention how she had felt under my arm. I forced the memory aside.

I was rather surprised how glad I was to see her, considering how little I really trusted her. We knew she'd been put with us as a bird-dog, with the added fact of her sex being a way to get under our skin. She had tried to flirt her way into my confidence early on, though she'd backed off and acknowledged that it had been a bad idea. Later, she'd worked her ass off to make the mission succeed, and as she had pointed out several times, she'd been burned and put on the bounty list of every cartel and underworld hitter with access to the Dark Net along with the rest of us.

Being hunted together tends to form a bond between people, and Mia wasn't an exception. Even so, I had to remind myself that she had been an Agency Case Officer once upon a time, and was therefore a manipulator by trade. I still didn't know which side she was really on; hell, I didn't know what the sides *were*. So, I kept my face as neutral as possible when she looked up and saw me, and kept reminding myself to trust no one who wasn't a Praetorian.

Maybe it was my imagination, but her eyes seemed to soften a little when she saw me. Or maybe she just wanted me to see it. "Hi, Jeff," she said.

"Mia," I replied. "What, exactly, are you doing here?"

A look that might have been a combination of amusement and irritation crossed her face. "Renton isn't entirely comfortable meeting you in the middle of nowhere alone," she said. "He thought that I'd be a familiar enough face to provide him a little backup without exacerbating your paranoia further."

He really doesn't know me as well as he thinks he does, I didn't say. Mia might be a friend of sorts, but her presence wasn't going to ease my paranoia any.

"Heads up," Larry called. "Company's coming." I followed his gaze to see the dust cloud of an approaching vehicle on the road.

I drew my .45 and leaned against the trunk of the car, making no effort to conceal it. Let the tone get set right away.

I couldn't help but think that the little Toyota RAV4 looked like a plastic toy as it pulled up, its fancy green paint job covered in trail dust. The little SUV came to a stop about twenty yards away, and Renton got out.

He was a thoroughly unimpressive-looking man. Neither conspicuously fit, nor fat, he had sandy brown hair, a tan slightly lighter than Mia's, and a touch of five-o'clock shadow. The first time I'd met him, he'd successfully disguised himself as a Basra Provincial Police Force officer, despite having no Arab blood, that I knew of, in his ancestry. He was what a spy was supposed to be—a gray man, moving quietly, unnoticed, through the shadows. And he was good at it; he'd effectively disappeared out of the Intelligence Community a number of years before to work for the shadowy Cicero Group, the same people who had employed us several times now, and the same group that I no longer trusted farther than I could throw his car.

His gray eyes flicked down to the 1911 in my hand. He was composed, but his eyes were wary, and I was pretty sure he was packing heat, himself. This wasn't shaping up to be the friendliest meeting, and I didn't mean for it to be.

"Is that how this is going to go?" he asked, standing a few yards away.

"Depends on you," I replied shortly. "You came alone, which is a point in your favor. You understand that I'm not in a particularly trusting or complacent frame of mind at the moment, given that Jim's dead, Little Bob's missing, and what looks suspiciously like a larger version of Janson's wannabe SWAT team just drove us out of The Ranch and into the hills."

He shook his head angrily. "The Group didn't send that task force, though it was certainly raised as a possibility, after that loose-cannon stunt you pulled in Pueblo. Between the bloodbath you started down there, and its aftermath, there are some powerful people in the Group who are beginning to think that you're too much of a liability."

I confess I sneered. "Really? We're a liability? Last I checked, we weren't the ones leaking assets' targeting information to cartels. We were the ones getting set up to have our own people murdered in our own *fucking* backyard!"

"And if you'd contacted me instead of flying off the damned handle, we might have handled it without throwing the door wide open to the kind of people who get off exploiting dead bodies in residential neighborhoods!" he snapped. "Do you have any idea what your little set of raids has led to?"

"I was supposed to trust you and your people, after what happened last time?" I replied. "*Your* organization is leaky as fuck, and I still can't be sure that Janson or Sherman or one of those assholes didn't put the narcos or these black-helicopter fucks on us, to remove the 'liability.'" I stabbed a finger at him with my non-firing hand. "Your people made damned good and sure that this was the only option open to us after the way they fucked us in Mexico, Renton."

"He's right, Renton," Mia said suddenly, "and you know it. Face it, we knew this was coming, and we didn't move fast enough."

His shoulders sagged a little. I saw an echo of the dead, defeated look in his eyes that he'd worn after I'd called Janson's bluff and forced him to back down, the day that our relationship with the Cicero Group had become a few degrees colder. It was the look of a man treading water and starting to feel a cramp.

"Janson's on the outs with the Group as it is," he said quietly, "and Sherman didn't order the raid. I'm ninety-nine percent sure that nobody in the Group had anything to do with giving the cartels the target package that kicked this off, either."

"Then who did?" I asked coldly.

"And if I tell you?" he asked sharply, looking me in the eye. "Then what? Another bloodbath? A few more steps toward the edge? Do you have any idea how fragile the situation here Stateside is right now?"

"That's the second time you've said that," Larry pointed out. "Maybe you'd better elaborate a little for those of us who have been running and fighting for our lives for the last couple of weeks."

Renton reached into his pocket. I tapped my trigger finger against the slide of my 1911, just to make it clear that pulling anything lethal out would be a very, very bad idea. He noticed it, but studiously ignored it.

He came out with a smartphone. When I raised an eyebrow, he snorted. "This thing isn't what it looks like. It's encrypted six ways from Sunday, and if anyone was actually, by some magical tech wizardry, able to tap its IP, it would show up as being somewhere in the middle of Lake Superior. *And* anything they could get off it would still be gibberish. Give me a *little* credit."

He tapped at the screen, then stepped closer and held it out. To his credit, he came to me, instead of trying to make me cross the distance to him. Maybe I'd gotten a bit too sensitive to little power and manipulation tricks, but when you're a trigger puller in a world of spooks and manipulators, you get that way.

Taking the phone, I looked down at the screen. It was set to a social media page, entitled "The People of Color Revolutionary Front." The cover photos were about what you might expect from a group with that name; lots of pictures of masked young people waving their fists in the air, banners calling for "Revolution Now!" "Fuck the Police!" and "End the White Race!" along with several stylized portraits of the likes of Che Guevara and Malcom X.

Below the banner of images, the top posts were a series of gruesome photos, including several of the cartel assholes we'd waxed in Pueblo. Several of the others were obviously nowhere near Pueblo; I thought I recognized one from Mexico about three years before.

Accompanying the photos were lurid descriptions of a cold-blooded, house-to-house massacre of Hispanics in Colorado. It had very little to do with what had actually happened, but to someone who had no idea, it certainly

104

would sound like some kind of white supremacists had decided to start purging the Latinos from the US, beginning in Pueblo of all places. It really didn't make a lot of sense, but in my experience, propaganda rarely does. It relies on emotion and outrage to override the reader's or hearer's reason, and to the unprepared reading this, it would sure do the trick.

"That's only one example," Renton said grimly. "There's been a full-court push in the last ninety-six hours, ever since you finished your hits in Pueblo. And it's getting traction; there are enough people out there who already believe this kind of thing that they're primed for it."

"What kind of traction?" I asked, handing the phone to Larry.

"What kind do you think?" was the answer. "Demonstrations in a dozen major cities, several of which have already turned into riots. Entire city blocks are being burned down. Several cops and other public figures have been assassinated already, and at least twenty random people who happened to be the wrong color in the wrong place at the wrong time have been dragged out into the street and beaten to death. At least one was doused in gasoline and set on fire."

I frowned, studying the images and thinking about what he'd said. "That's awfully fast," I pointed out.

"No faster than the Ferguson shit-show and the rest that followed it," he replied, "if slightly more intensely violent." He ran a hand over his face. He seemed a little calmer. "Granted, this isn't unprecedented. Social media has been known to be a major tool for propaganda and coordinating street action for a long time. And like I said, the pump was primed a long time ago. The people behind this were just waiting for an opportunity, an opportunity that you handed them on a silver platter."

"Don't give me that bullshit," I snapped, getting angry again. "If we had to walk on eggshells because of the possibility that bad guys would use what we did for propaganda purposes, we'd have been even more paralyzed than we have been for the last twenty fucking years. They'll *always* lie, always twist things to make us out to be monsters, no matter how justified we might be. Hell," I added, pointing to the phone in Larry's enormous hands, "half of these pictures aren't even from Pueblo. I recognize a few of them from the intel reports on Mexico a year ago, and *that* one's from Gila Bend; it's not even a cartel shithead. It's one of that sheriff's family."

"My point is, that regardless of your intentions, you've provided some very unscrupulous people with a made-to-order atrocity, whether it really was one or not," he said heavily. "I told you a while back that there were people dead-set on sowing chaos at home and abroad, mainly to forward their own agendas, mostly by consolidating power and influence behind the scenes. Well, it looks like this is their golden opportunity."

"You said it yourself, Renton," Mia said. "This was an opportunity. If it wasn't this, it would have been something else. And I'm not going to get my panties in a knot over some dead cartel reps in Pueblo, not when they sent *Mara Salvatrucha* gangsters after me, too."

Renton shot her a glance. She wasn't really providing the backup he'd been expecting her to, though she made a good point.

The fact was, I realized that part of why I was getting my back up was that in a way, Renton was right. We'd gone south half-cocked, pissed off, and hungry for blood. We'd lucked out and accomplished the mission without losing anyone, but we'd made life a lot harder for the Pueblo PD in the process, and I was still trying not to think too hard about all the ways that op could have gone horribly, horribly wrong. Vengeance is rarely a good motive for operations; it's an emotional response and leads to poor planning and occasionally poorer decisions.

Renton's anger at our killings was only highlighting some of my own growing misgivings about my own motives and actions. I hadn't *quite* done anything I regretted, yet. But I was starting to realize how close I was getting to that line, and Renton was reminding me of it.

"It looks like we're not the only ones providing fodder for the Outragey Outrage Patrol," Larry said suddenly. He was studying the phone, and had apparently gone digging further. He held it up. "It seems the Three Percenter types are getting stirred up over that task force in our backyard."

"Let me see that," Renton said, holding out his hand. Larry handed him the phone. He studied it, then tapped the screen a few times, presumably doing some further checking of his own. "Hell," he muttered. "This might be it."

"Maybe you should share with the rest of the group," I said sarcastically.

"Yes," Mia said sternly. "Maybe you should lay out what we know *before* going on a tear, Renton."

I shot her a look, even as I noticed Renton look a little shamefaced. "What *do* we know, Renton?" I asked, my voice low and dangerous. I still hadn't holstered my pistol, and the look in Renton's eyes when he met my gaze told me he'd noticed.

"We didn't get any indicators in time to warn you," he said wearily. "Trust me, if we had, I'd have been blowing your phone up every thirty seconds until I got in touch with you. This caught me as flat-footed as it caught you.

"I told you about the back-room power struggle that's been going on. The Project in Iraq and Syria was part of it. Other parts of it were wrapped up in the El Duque fiasco; you helped uncover some of them. The whole thing is a lot more complicated and murky than anything you've ever imagined; there are no set battle lines, and different groups and personalities can be deadly enemies one day, then bosom buddies the next, before going back to hating each other. It's all a matter of momentary advantages. But we've generally

106

identified two fairly nebulous factions. They're related by social and money networks, not ideologies. There are hard-core right-wingers and frothing leftists on both sides, and some that skip back and forth depending on the situation at the moment. There are also a *lot* of foreign influences, sometimes asserted through donations to non-profits and NGOs, sometimes through connections with trans-national corporations and trade agreements.

"A few of us have started calling these two factions 'Marius' and 'Sulla.' 'Marius' seems to be the more hawkish group, relatively speaking, while 'Sulla' has more connections with 'revolutionaries' and organized crime. Again, none of these are hard and fast categories; the connections and rivalries vary depending on the situation and the people involved.

"We've been able to determine that it was mostly 'Marius' behind The Project. Both factions had their fingers in the El Duque mess. Both factions have reason to want to see you gentlemen out of the picture, and it appears that both decided to move against you within days of each other. I'm pretty sure the task force that just beat down your door was put together by somebody within 'Marius,' somebody with enough money and clout to get the legitimate authorities to look the other way. 'Sulla' beat them by a couple weeks, preferring the more deniable avenue of meeting with a convocation of cartel leaders who were concerned about the precedent set by letting a bunch of gringos dismantle a cartel without retribution, and providing them with a target package."

"Who the hell are these people?" I asked. "If they don't really give a shit about politics, then what are they organizing around?"

"Like I said, carving out their own little virtual fiefdoms," he replied. "Politics is only an end for the people they use. To them, politics and ideological crusades are only means to the end, namely being rich, powerful, and important. Patriots and revolutionaries alike are little more than useful morons to these people. Most of what organization exists consists of personal friendships, patronage, business connections, and blackmail. Who knows who, who gets money from who, and who has dirt on who."

"That sounds an awful lot like a conspiracy theory," Larry pointed out. "Bilderberg, Trilateral Commission sort of stuff."

"It does, doesn't it?" Renton replied. "But just because most of the conspiracy theories floating around the internet are insane doesn't mean there are no conspiracies. They're just generally far less competent, less over-reaching, and less disguised than people expect. Hell, most of this shit happens in plain sight, and gets papered over by partisan so-called 'journalism' on one side or another."

"So, when you said, 'this might be it,'" I ventured, "what exactly did you mean by 'it?'"

He paused. For a moment, the quiet of the wilderness was broken only by the wind in the grass and the distant scream of a hawk.

"There are indicators," he said slowly, "that certain movers and shakers among 'Marius' and 'Sulla' have developed enough of an antipathy for each other that they might begin resorting to violence to remove one another as obstacles. One of our probable COAs has been sowing violent unrest as a cover for other actions, such as raids and assassinations." COA was a military term, standing for Course Of Action. "This is starting to smell like that. It might not have been the initial plan; in fact, I suspect it wasn't. Taking you guys out because you knew about too many skeletons in too many closets was almost guaranteed to be the primary objective, but when that went awry, 'Sulla' saw an opportunity."

"Do they realize how this could spin out of control?" Mia asked.

"Of course not," Renton snorted. "They're the smart ones, remember, so much better than the stupid dupes whose strings they pull. It didn't spin out of control after the Black Lives Matter fiasco, so they're sure they've got it figured out."

"That's what you're really worried about, isn't it?" I asked. "If these 'Marius' and 'Sulla' fucksticks start offing each other, who gives a shit? Good riddance. But if they start a firestorm to cover it…"

He nodded wearily. "It's been a long time coming, but after decades of mob politics, this country is a fucking powder keg. You've got two-thirds of the population hating each other with every bit of intensity as the Shi'a and Sunni in Iraq. These assholes have pushed and pushed and pushed, stirring up the mob at every opportunity, because it's the easy route to votes and money, and besides, once you've got the mob stirred up, you don't dare back down or it'll turn on you. So, here we are. Maybe we can stop it, maybe the US turns into Sierra Leone writ large."

"And how do you propose to do that?" I asked, already having some suspicions of my own. Unfortunately, if he said what I thought he was going to say, it was going to line up with about the only workable plan for our own survival that was forming in my own head.

He sighed. "I don't know for sure. Short term, the hope in the Group is that if we can take down the worst of 'Marius' and 'Sulla,' then the provocations will die down, and we can at least put a lid on the kettle for a while longer, maybe long enough for calmer heads to start to prevail. Long term, I really don't know."

Which was about what I'd expected him to say. Maybe I was getting better at reading the spook's spook. Or maybe he wasn't really the master manipulator that he appeared to be, but just a guy trying to do a job in murky and ever-shifting circumstances.

Rather like us.

Even so, I couldn't afford to think like that. Renton was still a client, not a friend. And when your business is violence, it's just as bad an idea to let your guard down around clients as it is around enemies. Sometimes the line between the two gets pretty damned thin.

"And I take it that you are hoping that we'll take a hand in dealing with these factions." I didn't phrase it as a question.

"More than likely," he said. "It would probably be in your best interest, given the unhealthy interest both factions have taken in you, though I'm sure you've already thought of that." He sighed again. Damn, but that man looked tired. My sympathy was, of course, limited by the fact that he hadn't just spent the last week and a half running and gunning and sneaking through the woods and mountains like a hunted animal. "I don't have anything set in stone yet. The Cicero Group's not even all on the same page as to what's happening. I came out here to make sure you were still alive and to try to get you to stop killing people where their corpses can be used as propaganda footballs."

"We'll take it under advisement," I replied dryly, getting a little angry again, "right after they stop trying to kill us. For the time being, my primary concern is breaking these paramilitary clowns who just drove us out of our home, and finding Little Bob. Come talk to me again when you've got something useful."

The air had gone tense again. We'd been burned trusting Renton's Cicero Group before. It was the reason we were in this fix in the first place.

Somewhat to my surprise, Mia's reaction to my hostility was to step up next to me, facing Renton. I saw his eyes move to her for a moment, then back to me. There was a flicker of surprise, and then he was the dispassionate professional spook again.

"I'm not your enemy, Jeff," he said. "We really are on the same side. And to prove it, I'll send you any intel I get on the task force or where Little Bob might be. In return, I only ask that you be a little more circumspect. This isn't Iraq, or even Mexico. Stacks of bodies attract attention."

As much as I hated to admit it, he had a point. "We'll see," I said. "There are a lot of woods and empty spaces to hide the bodies out here."

He studied me for a moment, as if unsure whether I was joking, or if he had reason to be worried. To tell the truth, I wasn't entirely sure myself at that point.

CHAPTER 12

Even with The Broker's support, the task force was going to be a tough nut to crack. They had some serious money backing them, and that meant some serious numbers and hardware. The armored vehicles alone presented a problem that we weren't all that well equipped to deal with, especially since Logan's hundred-pound 20mms had been left behind, being too heavy and unwieldy to lug through the mountains.

Fortunately for us, we had kind of gotten used to facing off with enemies who had a lot more men and materiel than we did. It was how we'd made our money in dangerous places, usually alone, outnumbered, outgunned, and under-supported.

So, we kept our heads down in the hills, moved camp every couple of days, and ran recon. A lot of recon.

***

"Complacent, trespassing bastards," I muttered.

"You say that as if it's a new observation," Bryan whispered from beside me. He was right; this was the fifth time in the last week that we'd gotten eyes on The Ranch, which was now occupied territory. Our front yard was now filled with armored vehicles, and what grass had been growing there had been churned to dust by the big eight-wheelers.

"I know, but it's just that they're so fucking *lazy* about it," I answered. This was, again, the fifth OP we'd put on The Ranch, and they hadn't come close to catching us yet. They had sentries on the porch, but no patrols out. There were drones still buzzing overhead, but we had gotten *very* good at hiding from them. They made enough noise that we could usually tell where they were, and careful camouflage kept us hidden. Believe it or not, a good blanket not only keeps you warm during a fall night in the mountains, but it also acts as a surprisingly good thermal barrier to hide you from thermal cameras.

We were taking our time, carefully cataloging their personnel and equipment, recording their patterns of life, and looking for weak points in their security for a couple of reasons.

For one, given how outnumbered we were, and how little support we could really count on, either from The Broker or Renton, we wouldn't have a second chance if things went pear-shaped because we got caught with our britches down. We had, hopefully, learned our lesson from Pueblo, and were approaching this new threat in a more coldly pragmatic and careful way.

The other reason was to encourage the kind of complacency that Bryan and I were observing right at that moment. They had security in place, but it was lazy. I was reasonably certain that there were no eyes on the mountain where Bryan and I were perched. As I had noted before, there were no patrols out looking for us. They were relying almost exclusively on their drones. And drones have drawbacks that men on the ground don't. They can only look where the operator tells them to look, and staring at a video feed for hours not only gets tedious, it also denies the drone operator a lot of other environmental cues that a man on foot or on horseback—or even in a vehicle—can pick up.

Granted, they weren't necessarily just sitting there. They had tried to push up into the hills after us, the day after they'd taken The Ranch. They hadn't made it far; they were in no way prepared for extended ground operations in mountainous terrain. We hadn't even needed to ambush them. One of their "operators" had fallen down a draw and broken his leg. It had taken them the rest of the day to get the casualty out. They hadn't tried since. I'd be willing to bet that they'd expected to steamroll over us and be done, taking us down quickly with a fast "shock and awe" raid. It hadn't worked out that way, and they didn't seem to quite know what to do about it.

Derek was, somehow, still doing his voodoo, using a laptop he'd gotten from The Broker before carefully scouring just about every line of code to make sure that our "benefactor" wasn't snooping—which I was sure he still was, anyway—and a satcom puck. He told me that, even though he couldn't necessarily read it, he could see a lot of comm traffic going between The Ranch, the other TF headquarters that we'd pinpointed near Cody, and a third location, which he still couldn't quite nail down. My guess was that they were asking for mountain gear and more backup.

The other reason we were taking our time was because of that second HQ. We still hadn't gotten eyes on Little Bob, and Derek hadn't cracked deeply enough into their comms to be able to find any mention of him. They had some decent encryption on everything, he told me; not completely unbreakable, but it was going to take time, time we probably didn't have. They were running advanced enough setups that the usual hacking tricks—tricks that had worked even on official government agencies—weren't necessarily going to work. But until we knew where Little Bob was, we would be risking his life if we hit the wrong place and he wasn't there. Better to hit both simultaneously, but to do that, we were going to have to have everything carefully plotted out ahead of time.

I was thinking about all of that while I peered through the spotting scope at The Ranch below me. There was some security around the barns, but the vast majority was around the main house. They didn't appear to be using any of the outbuildings. Just the house. That would make matters a little simpler.

I was mostly only confirming stuff that we'd already observed and recorded. The armored vehicles were sitting shut down and unmanned, the turrets still. It was still conceivably possible that they were keeping gunners in the vehicles, but the turrets weren't oriented outboard, like they should have been if they were using the vehicles to hold security. The dismounts were the only visible sentries.

There were two or three roving around the back of the house and the outbuildings at any one time, all wearing body armor and carrying SCAR 16s. They were roving in what might have initially appeared to be random patterns, but after a while we'd determined that they went out about every half hour to forty-five minutes. They varied the timing, but only by about the same five to fifteen minutes.

Not good enough, cockbags.

"Heads up," Bryan whispered.

I didn't need him to point out what he'd seen. We had a good line of sight on the main road leading up to the house, and there was a trio of pickups trundling up the road in a cloud of dust. Whoever it was, they were making good time, and were obviously in good with either the task force or its masters. We knew they had security on both gates, and besides, the half-dozen shooters on the porch were still relaxed as the vehicles approached. These guys were expected.

They pulled up in front of the house, and the figure that we'd tentatively ID'ed as the task force's field commander stepped out. Even with the quality of the spotting scope, I couldn't make out a lot of detail, so while I could ID him from his build and coloring, I couldn't make out his face. But he seemed slightly nervous. That was interesting.

The doors of all three trucks opened almost simultaneously, and I counted ten men getting out. Most of them started pulling packs and gun cases out of the beds, but one strode up to the porch to greet the field commander.

There was something familiar about him, though I couldn't make out enough to say why. Something about the way he carried himself struck a memory, somewhere in the back of my mind.

I wasn't alone, either. "Who the hell is that?" Bryan muttered.

"He looks familiar to you, too?" I asked, my eye still glued to the scope.

"Yeah," he answered slowly. "I'm not sure from where, but there's something about him that's ringing a bell."

That had me racking my brain, wondering who it might be, that both Bryan and I thought we recognized him, even from a distance. We'd both kicked around the Marine Recon and Special Operations communities for a while before our contractor days, but we'd seen a lot more since getting out and going private sector.

I suddenly thought of Cyrus. He had been one of Mike's guys, who had been seconded to my team in Iraq after the battle for Basra. I'd lost Bob Fagin, Paul, and Juan during that shit-show, and had gotten Marcus and Cyrus from Mike to balance out our teams for follow-on operations. Cyrus and I had never really gotten along, though he'd been competent enough, up until the point where he'd objected to taking the contract with the Cicero Group to take down The Project, a rogue special operation that was training and supporting some of the worst jihadis in Iraq as a proxy weapon against the Iranians. He'd quit angrily and flown home from Baghdad. None of us had heard from him since, but our adversaries had to know that he'd been one of us, and that we hadn't parted on the most amicable of terms.

The guy below us wasn't Cyrus, though. Cyrus was a short, skinny guy. This dude was tall and, while not enormous like Larry or Little Bob, he was still considerably burlier than Cyrus. He was also gray-haired, if I was seeing him right.

Who the hell did both of us know who fit that description? I couldn't place anyone off the top of my head, but I had a nagging suspicion that when I did figure it out, it wasn't going to be good news.

The mystery man was talking to the field commander, and just from watching their body language, I could tell that there was a new sheriff in town. The gray-haired guy was now rather obviously in charge, whether the guys already on the ground liked it or not.

"I can't tell for sure, but you want to lay bets that those packs are mountain rucks and these guys are the backcountry manhunters?" Bryan murmured.

"No bet," I replied. I grimaced, though Bryan couldn't see it, since we were side by side in our tiny hide, under the same camouflage blanket, peering through carefully selected loopholes in the rocks. "That tears it. We're going to have to move soon, before these assholes put us on our back foot and we can't."

I was worried that the hunters were going to step off right away. If that happened, it could throw everything into a cocked hat; we'd have to break out the comms and risk a transmission, telling Tom that he needed to move the camp and push farther back into the mountains. We'd lose our staging area for both raids, necessitating longer approach marches and stretching the timeline farther than I was afraid it could stand. Coordinating near-simultaneous hits without comms got more difficult the longer the approach was, not to mention the added risk of something going wrong, such as compromise or injury.

But the hunters took their packs inside, while Gray Man and the field commander stayed on the porch talking for a while before following them in.

We couldn't really move until nightfall, anyway. Well, we *could*, especially as long as we were careful to keep under cover from the sporadic drone coverage, but the risk of compromise was still higher than if we crept away under cover of darkness. Technology alters things a lot, but never entirely eliminates certain advantages and disadvantages.

So, we waited and watched, poised to send the warning that would throw all our plans back to square one, and quite possibly kill any chance we had to retrieve Little Bob. I was already revising the strike plan for The Ranch as I watched; ten more shooters could complicate things, and just from what I could see, these guys were competent. They'd present a challenge.

The anticipated formation of shooters heading into the hills didn't come, though. More than likely, Gray Man wanted to get as complete a picture of the situation first-hand as he could before going into the planning phase. Ops generally don't get started on terribly short time-schedules, particularly one as extensive as a manhunt through the entire Beartooth Mountains. Hell, we'd been watching and planning for days now, ourselves, and we had a hell of a lot smaller target area to focus on.

When night finally fell, we stayed in place for just long enough to be reasonably certain that they weren't heading out right away. It was certainly possible that they'd wait until the wee hours of the morning, say around 0300, to step off. But even if they did, we could be reasonably certain that we had a little bit of breathing room. Hopefully enough to launch our own strikes. Hell, the more I thought about it, if they did step off at 0300, it would work out better for us. They wouldn't be on-site when we hit The Ranch.

Straining our ears and our eyes for drones, we carefully packed up and sanitized the OP, even though the task force had shown no sign of being inclined to climb up there and look for us, and started over the mountain toward camp.

***

That was one hell of a tough slog. We were already running on short sleep, and had been for weeks. Furthermore, it had been a forced march from hell over some really nasty terrain just to get *into* that OP the previous night. A day lying on rocks, mostly glued to the glass, hadn't been particularly restful.

By the time we got back to camp, Tom nixed any further movement that night. It was already damned near 0400, and we were falling down from fatigue, muscles shaking and with that curiously empty feeling that is the warning sign that you've used up all the gas in the tank. We were in no shape to mount a raid.

Tom listened to our report, then said he'd strengthen our exterior security, but we were staying in place for the moment. We had enough guns that unless they bird-dogged us for a larger force, which would have the same difficulties getting up into the mountains and the woods after us that the Task

115

Force had already run into, they'd find us a pretty tough nut to crack, especially given the harsh, extremely defensible terrain we'd set up in. We were hard to find, and we'd be harder to attack.

So, with security set and sunrise only a couple hours away, we rolled up in our blankets and passed the hell out.

***

The sun was well up by the time I woke up. I still felt groggy and sore, though I hadn't noticed the rocks and tree roots under my back until just then; I'd been that wiped out.

My rifle was by my side; I'd run my arm through the sling before I'd passed out, though I didn't remember doing it. It had become one of those things done completely by instinct, after years of living and working in conflict zones, where having a weapon within arm's reach was a matter of day-to-day survival.

As I sat up, pulling the weapon onto my lap, my hand brushed a warm, blanket-wrapped body next to me. I looked over to see Mia, leaning against the same tree I'd bedded down under, watching me.

"I'd say good morning," she said, "except that it's almost noon."

I grunted as I reached for a canteen. I still felt wrung out, and every move made me want to groan. My head was pounding, every muscle in my neck and upper back tied in iron-hard knots.

"How long have you been sitting there?" I asked, temporizing. I hadn't been this close to her since Veracruz, and, my battered and aching body notwithstanding, I was uncomfortably conscious of her nearness.

"Not long," she said with a yawn. "I only got off security just after stand-to, about five hours ago. You were already dead to the world." A smile quirked the corner of her mouth. "I almost got under your blanket, but I didn't want to wake you. You needed the sleep."

My brain and mouth went into lock. It might not have been *early*, per se, but I was way too sore and groggy to deal with her flirtation. I growled inarticulately, while I reminded myself that the last time she'd tried the flirtation bit, it had been an admitted shortcut to ingratiating herself with me.

My growl only made her smile wider. "You know, Jeff, sooner or later we're going to have to do something about all this sexual tension between us."

I glared at her, trying to ignore the jolt that her words sent through me. In response, her little smile turned into a dazzling grin. "You know, you really are cute when you're flabbergasted and annoyed," she said.

"Haven't we already been through this?" I grumbled, as I got up slowly and painfully, and started rolling my blanket up to stuff it in my pack.

She ignored my question, but her expression got serious, and tinged with concern. "Seriously, though, Jeff, you're running yourself ragged. The

116

world could have ended an hour ago, and you would have slept through it. And here you are, awake but barely able to move."

"And what alternative do you have in mind?" I asked, back on somewhat more solid ground. "It's not like we've got a lot of breathing room right at the moment. The Ranch is occupied and we've got more hunters on our trail, more competent ones by the looks of it. Our list of friends is damned short, almost nonexistent. And Little Bob's life could very well depend on our moving quickly. So, when do you suggest I relax?"

"You've barely slept and barely eaten more than a few bites at a time in the last week," she replied. "I've noticed. Some of the others have, too. You know better than that. You're not eighteen anymore. Food and rest are as important as recon and ammo. But you're trying to have a hand in everything, going out on the longest patrols and then staying up and trying to put together the reports and plan afterward, even when you're utterly exhausted." She sat up and put a hand on my arm. "You're going to kill yourself if you keep this up." Her voice got quieter. "Personally, I'd rather you didn't do that. I'm sure the rest of your team would agree."

"She's right, you know," Larry said, looming suddenly beside the tree to my other side. I squinted up at him against the sunlight filtering down through the needles.

"You too?" I asked, mock-indignantly. "I'm getting ganged up on here."

Larry's presence seemed to ease a bit of the tension under the tree, though Mia still didn't move away. "Bitching and moaning about common sense really isn't your style, Jeff," Larry replied. "Listen to the lady."

"All right, I'll try to slow down and spread the weight around when I can," I said. "Is there any word on the newcomers?"

"Eric and Jack went out early this morning, and saw a couple of them starting to probe the woods," he replied. "They didn't get far before they headed back in; Eric thinks they were looking for spoor that hadn't been contaminated by the lead-footed morons that tried the first time."

"We've still got a little bit of time, then," I said.

"I'd say at least until nightfall," Tom put in, coming over to join us. "But we do need to move tonight. The newcomers aside, if we wait much longer, we might never be able to get Robert back."

I nodded. Mia and Larry mother-henning me about overreaching myself aside, we really were short on time. "Did Eddie have anything new about the Cody site?" I asked.

Tom shook his head. I noticed he wasn't smoking, and realized he must have run out a day or two before, since none of the rest of us smoked. His head had to be pounding. "No," he said. "Our best guess is that the target is still that trailer near the center of the site," he said.

"Is everybody back in?"

"Aside from the new guys out on the LP/OPs, yes," Tom replied. We had Listening Post/Observation Posts on several of the nearby peaks, with commanding views of the most likely approaches to our rocky aerie.

I looked at my watch. "We've got at least ten hours before we need to step off," I said. "Should be plenty of time for final target studies and mission prep."

"Not before you eat," Mia insisted. Tom nodded, fixing me with those pale eyes of his, raising one gray eyebrow.

"Everybody's a mother hen all of a sudden," I grumbled, as I stuffed my blanket back in my ruck. "Fine, I'll eat. Then can we get to the job?"

CHAPTER 13

I couldn't quite believe that we'd gotten this far.

It was 0300, and I was crouched not ten yards from the outermost barn on The Ranch, watching the obviously bored and sleepy night patrol checking the barns and the treeline through my hybrid NVGs. We had used PVS-14s with small thermal attachments for years, but Logan had found an outlet recently for the purpose-designed PSQ-20s, which had thermals built-in. They were clearer and crisper than the 14s, casting the world in grayscale instead of the shades of green we'd always been used to.

Jack and Nick were behind me, similarly kitted out, cammied up, and armed. Larry, Eric, and Bryan were higher up the mountain with long guns, ready to provide some support by fire.

At least we didn't have to worry about Gray Man and his manhunters. We'd gotten the signal from the LP/OPs that they'd pushed into the mountains only a couple of hours before, fortunately along a different route than we had taken for the approach; they'd headed west on the north side of the ridge, while we were pushing east on the south side. So, we just had to deal with the original task force clowns.

I could hear them bullshitting as two of them walked around the corner of the barn.

"Only a matter of time now," one of them was saying. "Once Baumgartner catches them, we can burn this place down and get out of here."

Baumgartner? That name sounded damned familiar. But it couldn't be the same guy, could it? I hoped not, because if it was, it was *really* fucking bad news.

"It ain't that bad," the other said. "Scenery's nice."

"Maybe," was the reply. "Fucking Gage won't let us drink, and there's no pussy around here."

"Sure there is," the younger-sounding guy said, a joking note in his voice. "I'm sure some of the ladies at that strip club outside the truck stop down the mountain would be happy to go across the street with you, for the right price."

"I just threw up in my mouth a little," the first one said. "I like my hookers with all their teeth. And preferably not-pregnant."

"I've never had a toothless blowjob. At least you wouldn't have to worry about the chick *using* her teeth." They were moving away, down the

119

barn wall. "Besides, it's not like we've been in there; you don't *know* that they're all toothless and pregnant."

"We're in the middle of fucking nowhere," was the growled reply. "You know it's all meth queens and trailer trash in there."

"Pussy's pussy, man." The voices were fading as they headed back to the house.

While I was rather disgusted at their lack of professionalism, as they had obviously been too focused on their conversation and their blue balls to pay too much attention to the perimeter, at the same time, it was something of a relief. Though it was merely a confirmation of what we'd observed from afar, it made it clear that, while they were at least going through the motions of security—which was more than we'd seen a lot of the jihadis we'd waxed do—they were complacent as all hell. They figured that we were on the run, soon to be brought to ground by Baumgartner—holy shit, I hoped that wasn't who I thought it was—and they had the local law buffaloed. They were on guard out of force of habit and a certain ingrained professionalism, but that was it. They didn't figure we'd come out of the dark and hit them.

That was, of course, assuming that we hadn't been spotted by one of the drones that they still had up, that we'd heard on the way down. I was pretty sure we hadn't, though. We'd have been met by a watchful perimeter if that had been the case. If it was me, at my most sadistic, I might have let us get deep inside before cutting us off and gunning us down. But I was not getting a "subtle trap" vibe from these assholes. They were, after all, the same tards who had tried to storm a mountain compound full of proven hardasses who were known to be armed to the teeth using urban assault vehicles.

Once they were out of sight, heading back to the house, I knew that we had anywhere from thirty to forty-five minutes to work with. Considering that forty-five minutes was a *long* damned time to spend on a target site, we had plenty of time. We just had to do this carefully and stealthily. The advantage of surprise notwithstanding, we were still wildly outnumbered. If Little Bob was in there, and if we were going to get his incapacitated ass out, we were going to have to do it really sneaky-like.

A glance back confirmed that Jack and Nick were with me, Jack trailing a little behind. Jack was smaller than either of us, and while plenty competent, he was a bit of a city boy. Nick and I were country boys and backwoods hunters, and had been quietly woods-running for a lot longer than Jack had. We could move quicker and quieter, with ingrained habits that he'd had to learn on the fly.

Silently, weapons up and ready, the lighted reticles set to their lowest settings so that we could see them through our NVGs, we padded forward. Unlike the guard force, that had kept close to the barn, we stayed farther out. We were in the open, but the ground wasn't entirely flat; there were plenty of hummocks and folds in the ground to use as cover if we needed to drop flat.

We also weren't going to silhouette ourselves against the lighter corrugated aluminum of the barn wall. Our camouflage blended into the grass and the ground and the brush a lot better than the buildings.

The lights were out in the house, though we saw the faint flicker of a flashlight beam through the back windows as the night patrol made their way to whatever they were using as a ready room. More than likely, they'd just moved into our own team rooms, which rankled. Even as we crossed the back forty, closing quickly but quietly on the back porch, the light went out.

In minutes, we reached the back porch. There had been no sound beyond the wind in the trees, the usual nocturnal sounds of the woods, and the faint buzz of a distant drone. *Somebody* had to still be up, watching the drone feed. Hell, I was kind of surprised to see the whole place dark, given that the manhunters were out. Unless this Baumgartner didn't want the pseudo-SWAT guys looking over his shoulder for some reason.

I didn't step onto the porch itself until I absolutely had to; I knew the old planks creaked. When I did have to mount the porch, I was careful to glide between planks and roll my feet as much as possible, trying to spread my weight out and put most of it on the supports underneath.

I kept my SOCOM-16 trained on the door while Jack reached past me to open it. We might have been trying to keep this hit soft for as long as we could, but that never means not being prepared to start shooting motherfuckers in the face at the drop of a hat.

The door swung open soundlessly, and I stepped inside, scanning the back hallway quickly, my NVGs just over my rifle's sights. At those ranges, I really could have just point-shot anyone I needed to, without even using the sights, but old habits die hard.

The hall was clear. I moved forward, while Nick and Jack followed, quietly closing the door behind us. If, by some chance, another patrol went out, randomly out of order, we didn't want them to suspect we were on-site.

Since we had been pretty sure that Little Bob was not being kept in one of the barns, or the various other houses out on The Ranch, we'd thought out how to narrow down which room he was probably being held in. The central briefing room, at the front of the house, was probably the best bet for a man with six extra holes in him. If they were holding him, they were going to be keeping him alive, and that meant a cot and medical supplies. The briefing room, that had been the living room before we'd taken the house over, was the largest room in the house, and therefore the most likely to work.

Fortunately, it was a fairly straight shot from the back door to the briefing room. Carefully, keeping away from the walls, we paced toward the front of the house.

The briefing room was a jumble of equipment cases and boxes of MREs, with our easels being used for tac maps and imagery. One of our folding tables was covered in comm gear and Toughbooks, one of which was open and casting a pale glow over the rest of the room.

There was no sign of a gurney or a wounded man. There were, however, two men in the room, one sitting at the laptop, the other lying on the couch against the north wall.

We'd been quiet, and the hallway and the room were both dark, except for the glow of the laptop. But something made the guy at the computer turn and look toward us as Jack and I stepped into the room.

"What?" he asked, sounding bored. "Are we about to get overrun by a strike force of racoons?" He thought we were the perimeter patrol.

When neither of us replied, with either a flippant remark or obscenity, he frowned, squinting at us in the dark. We were going to be made in the next couple of seconds. So I moved.

There was an equipment case between him and me. I almost went over it, but adjusted at the last moment to dodge around it, lest vaulting it make more noise than we could afford. Of course, if I didn't get this shithead shut down quick, we were going to have more noise than we knew what to do with, and then we were fucked.

Even as I started to charge him, covering the ten feet between us in a couple of long steps, he realized that something was wrong, and grabbed for the pistol that wasn't quite where he thought it was on the table. He opened his mouth to yell as he turned his head to find the gun, his fingers desperately scrabbling at the plastic tabletop, and then I hit him.

A collapsible polymer buttstock is not the ideal tool for buttstroking an opponent into insensibility, but with the weight of that rifle behind it, I gave it the old college try, anyway. He probably could have ducked it if he'd had his eyes on me, but since he'd turned to try to find his pistol, I caught him at the base of the skull with a good, solid *thud*. His brain sloshed hard against the front of his skull, and he went out like a light.

Holy shit, I thought. *I could not have imagined that actually working so well.*

My astonished triumph was short-lived. In trying to get around me to get at the same guy, Jack had stubbed his toe on an equipment case, and kicked it a good couple of inches. While he bore the pain silently, the impact of his boot on the plastic was almost deafeningly loud in the quiet room. The sleeping man grunted and jerked his head up.

Fucking dammit! I whirled toward him, bringing my rifle around, afraid that I was going to be too late; he was going to see me, kitted up and camouflaged, looking nothing like one of his guys and standing over the slumped form of his fellow watchstander. He was going to yell, and bring the entire fucking task force down around our ears.

But Nick took a chance, vaulted over two of the equipment cases, and came crashing down on the groggy sleeper with all two hundred seventy-five pounds of man, rifle, and ammo. There was a grunt of pain, and the couch rocked back on two feet to hit the wall with a painfully loud *thump*.

There followed a series of grunts and meaty *thuds* as they struggled, a struggle that I ended abruptly with the touch of my suppressor to the guy's forehead.

It took him a second to realize what the circle of hard, cold metal against his skin was, but when it sank in, he froze.

"Make any more noise than a whisper and your head turns into a canoe," I hissed. "Understood?"

He made a tiny movement that was just barely a nod. If there had been more light I might have seen him going cross-eyed as he stared at the rifle muzzle pressed to his skull.

"Where's Bob Sampson?" I demanded. But if he knew, I didn't get an answer.

"What the fuck are you idiots doing in here?" a voice asked sleepily from the doorway.

Oh, fuck. I didn't dare turn away from the guy on the couch, especially since Nick had gotten off of him as soon as he'd stopped fighting. I had to rely on Nick and Jack to deal with this; unfortunately, there was only one way this could end.

"What the fuck?!" the voice suddenly had a lot more alarm in it. Whoever it was had heard the commotion and come to bitch out the watchstanders for horsing around in the CP, only to find one of them slumped unconscious at the desk and the other prone on the couch with a gun to his head, not to mention the three unfamiliar figures in field gear and rifles at the ready standing in the middle of what was supposed to be a secure house.

I heard what sounded like two loud *clap*s, almost like a heavy book being smacked against a solid table, followed by the unmistakable sound of a body hitting the floor. There was an extra *thunk* in there that sounded a lot like a pistol falling to the hardwood floorboards, as well.

Suddenly, we could hear the sound of people moving elsewhere in the house, and I caught the reflected illumination of a light being turned on down the hall. *FUUUUUCK!*

Slinging my rifle out of the way, I grabbed the guy on the couch and dragged him to his feet. "You're coming with us!" I snarled quietly, shoving him toward the front door. It wasn't the ideal escape route; they had more security stationed toward the front than they'd had toward the back, but getting through the house to head out the west side was going to be suicide now that we'd awakened the hornet's nest.

There were more loud *clap*s as Jack fired a few more shots down the hallway to discourage pursuit. Meanwhile, Nick, having apparently read my mind, yanked the front door open and rolled through behind his rifle. Driving our unplanned prisoner ahead of me, I followed him, with Jack only a pace behind, stopping at the doorway to cover back the way we'd come one more time before ducking out the door quickly, trying to clear the front windows before somebody could start shooting through them.

Nick was *moving*, heading for the trees where the ground dipped down to the south. It would provide us some cover as well as the concealment of the darkness under the trees. I had adjusted my hold on my captive, letting go of his t-shirt and twisting his arm up between his shoulder blades. I was driving him ahead of me at a trot, my other hand on my rifle's firing controls. If he got too froggy, I was in a good position to shove him on his face and put a bullet in the back of his head, and he knew it. He didn't resist.

A round *snapped* by overhead, and Jack stopped, dropped to a knee, and fired three more shots in reply before getting up and running after us. We were almost to the dip, where we could drop down and be out of the line of fire. It was dark enough in the patch of woods down there that by the time they caught up, we'd be long gone and out of sight.

We hit the slope just shy of a run, and went skidding and slipping over it. I barely maintained control in the dark, and damned near wrenched my prisoner's arm out of its socket. I heard him gasp as he bounced off the trunk of a spruce, but he left it at that.

He was going to have a miserable night, regardless. It was getting on toward fall, and it got *cold* at altitude. And while he had his trousers on, fortunately for him, he was otherwise dressed in a t-shirt and socks and that was it.

Once we were well inside the trees, Nick banged a hard right and started heading uphill. There was a small stretch of open ground we'd have to cross before we got back into the treeline on the south flank of the mountain, but it was pretty well covered by the terrain.

We had to slow down, in part because of the darkness under the trees. NVGs have to have ambient light to amplify, or they don't work so well. It wasn't a high-illum night as it was; the moon wasn't supposed to rise for another hour. Add in a captive who didn't have NVGs or even boots, and we weren't going to be setting any ground speed records.

Behind us, I could hear shouts; the pursuit was getting up to speed. Those shouts were punctuated by the rolling, echoing reports of high-powered rifle shots, followed by calls of alarm and what sounded a lot like panic fire, before somebody bellowing louder than the gunfire got them to cease fire. The boys up on the mountain were doing work.

As we wove our way through the trees, I tried to construct a picture of what was going on up above. The shouting had died down, and for a while, the shooting did, too. Then more shots rang out from up above, on the mountain, the reports echoing down the valley. I counted five shots; the task force must have tried to make a move, and Larry, Eric, and Bryan were nailing anyone who strayed too far from cover. The shooting wasn't all that fast; that had the sound of carefully aimed shots.

We'd first tried out using snipers on an elevated position in place of machine guns for a support by fire position in Mexico. It had worked there, and it was working here. Instead of spraying bullets—and, coincidentally, potentially revealing your position thanks to muzzle flash—we kept the enemy's heads down by dropping them from distance whenever they tried to move.

It took another hour before we were able to swing around the shoulder of the mountain and start really heading up. By then, the shooting had died down altogether. Jack kept stopping and turning to check our six, and Nick had slowed down to backwoods hunter speed, stepping carefully and silently, almost as if he could see the rocks and the roots and the brush even in the pitch black under the trees. I was trying to watch every direction at once while still keeping tabs on and control of our captive. To his credit, he was keeping quiet and he wasn't trying to fight me. He was slowing, though, as the rocks and needles and fallen tree limbs cut his socks to ribbons.

I stopped, signaling Nick to halt when he looked back. There hadn't been time to get the prisoner to put his boots on in the house, but he was already limping, and if we kept climbing for long, he was going to be barefoot and going over rocks and brambles on the shredded meat of the soles of his feet. I made him sit down and hissed, "One wrong move and I'll end you. Nobody's going to be able to localize the shot up here." Unslinging my rifle, I leaned it against a tree nearby, out of his reach, and drew my knife. He tensed, but I just used it to cut off his pantlegs below the knees, then tied the sections of cloth around his feet. They wouldn't last all that long, and he'd still be hurting, but it was better than trying to climb a mountain barefoot.

Still, it was going to be a long movement.

CHAPTER 14

We didn't make it back to camp until well after sunrise. As the first faint light of dawn started to turn the sky above the treetops gray, I started to worry. Not so much about the drones; if they hadn't found us yet, they probably weren't going to. I suspected that the operators really didn't know where exactly they should look, and it was a big, jumbled, steep, tree-lined bit of country. No, my concerns were with Baumgartner and his manhunters. I really didn't want to accidentally stumble on them with only three shooters and a prisoner.

Granted, they were supposed to be on the other side of the ridge, and the odds were against our routes crossing. We'd planned ahead for that. But if my growing suspicions about just who this Baumgartner was proved to be right, it wouldn't pay to make any assumptions.

But we saw nothing on the way up except a couple of small, distant herds of elk, a red-tailed hawk, and too many squirrels and birds to count.

Nick slowed, then halted and took a knee next to a wind-gnarled tree. The slope below us was steep enough that a slip promised lots and lots of broken bones before stopping, whether against a rock, a tree, or the bottom of the draw. I found myself trying to find a spot on the slope with some little concealment where I could wedge myself and my captive. Jack snugged himself up against a tall spruce and faced back the way we'd come.

Nick let out a series of low whistles. They were supposed to sound like a bird, but none of us were very good nature mimics. If we'd been doing it since childhood, it might have made a difference, but as it was, to anyone nearby it would still sound like a man whistling.

Fortunately, it appeared that the only people up on that rocky mountainside were our guys. We got the right pattern of answering whistles in reply, though they were hoarse and labored, as if whoever was on outer security hadn't grown up learning how to whistle at all. Nick gave the proper acknowledgement, got up slowly, and headed in.

I followed, every bone aching, feeling once again the vague lightheadedness that I had come to associate with extreme fatigue. I might have gotten some decent rest the day before this little fiasco, but I was long past burning up whatever reserves I'd managed to rebuild.

My captive wasn't in any better shape. His feet were bleeding and he was limping and shivering. I almost felt sorry for him. Almost.

We wove our way past the outer guard, a pair of new guys whose names I couldn't remember for the life of me at the moment, and onto the slightly more level ground where the main camp was situated. Larry, Eric, and Bryan were sitting against their rucks, waiting. Other than that, the only ones still there were Tom, Mia, Logan, and a couple of the other support folks who'd stayed in the mountains with us, instead of going with The Broker and his people to another refuge, one slightly less austere.

So, even as slowed as we had been by our prisoner, we'd beaten Eddie back. That might or might not be good news; on reflection, if they'd taken the planned exfil route, we couldn't have expected them to beat us back. Even so, knowing how our own mission had gone down, the longer they were out of contact, the longer the darker side of my imagination could run wild.

I found a reasonably flat rock and propelled my captive to it. I didn't need to make him sit down; he just kind of collapsed. "I'd tell you to keep your mouth shut unless one of us asks you a question," I told him, somewhat surprised at the hoarseness of my own croak of a voice, "except that I think it should be pretty obvious that there's nobody up here besides us who can hear you."

He didn't look at me, but just nodded, before slumping down on the rock and curling into a ball. He was in bad shape. It would probably be several hours before we could get anything out of him, which was fine with me. It was going to take at least that long for us to recover from the night's exertions.

I found my ruck, sat down against it, and promptly passed the fuck out.

***

Eddie's return woke me up, though I was pretty damned groggy. I sat up slowly and tried to rub the sleepy out of my eyes as I stifled a groan. I *hurt*.

The first thing I noticed when my blurry vision cleared was that Eddie and his team did *not* have Little Bob. They didn't appear to be missing anyone, so there was that, but it meant that they'd failed as thoroughly as we had.

"No joy?" I asked.

"I hope you had a better night than we did," was Eddie's reply.

"I'd be willing to bet we didn't," I said, "but you go first."

He leaned his Galil ACE against a tree and dropped against his ruck like a sack of rocks. He leaned his head all the way back and stared at the sky for a moment. He was so still that I started to think he'd fallen asleep from sheer exhaustion, and was about to say, "Fuck it," and lie back down for a few more Z's, before he lifted his head and looked at me blearily.

"We were in the LCC," he said. The Last Covered and Concealed position was the "point of no return" on an op. It was the last spot to take a momentary breather and make any adjustments before going loud. "We had just halted and dropped rucks, getting ready to move. Security was set, and I was about to go forward to take a look at the objective with Lee. Then all hell broke loose.

"Somebody opened fire with an automatic weapon, then a whole lot of others joined in. It sounded like several calibers, and if there were more machine guns, we couldn't tell. The volume of fire was just too fucking high. Whoever was down there was throwing a *lot* of lead.

"I couldn't just sit there and listen," he continued tiredly. "If Little Bob was down there, we had to find *some* way to get him out, if it was at all possible. So, Lee and I moved up to find a vantage point."

He ran a hand over his face. Most of his cammie paint had worn off on the movement. It had been a long one, too; I knew the route he'd been planning to take. They'd gone miles out of the way, to try to loop around where the TF might be watching.

"It took some doing to get eyes on," he continued. "The compound was definitely under attack; there was a line of muzzle flashes to the north." If they'd followed the plan, Eddie and his boys would have approached the camp outside of Cody from the mountains to the west. "We had to move north a bit to get a good line of sight.

"The attackers drove up in a convoy of Jeeps and pickups, got on-line, and opened fire. They did it pretty quick; too quick for the perimeter security to do much to stop them before they started shooting. We couldn't see a lot of detail, but it sure looked like a peckerwood version of some of the Arab militias I've seen. Drive up, unass, and start blasting. They didn't seem to be hitting all that much; it looked like they were just turning a lot of money into noise.

"The TF goons might be assholes," he said, "but they reacted quick. They were already starting to return fire by the time we got into position. In a couple of minutes, we were looking at a full-on firefight.

"I don't think the Peckerwood Patrol was quite ready for the volume of fire they got in return. Whoever these TF bastards are, they know how to get fire superiority. They turned a couple of those trucks to scrap in a hurry, and before too long, the fight was over and the mystery shooters were on the run. I don't think all of them made it off the X, either."

He fell silent. "I'm guessing there was no way to get in to look for Little Bob, after that," I said.

He shook his head grimly. "No way in hell," he confirmed. "They were at full stand-to after that. We could have tried, but we'd have been fucked in a hurry. Especially with only six dudes." He eyed me. "So, he wasn't at The Ranch, either?"

I almost said something about stating the obvious, but bit the words back. I shook my head. "We made it farther than you did, but it turned into a shit-show anyway." I filled him in on our own compromise and subsequent escape. He raised his eyebrows.

"Damn, you got lucky as shit," he said. "They must have been in Complacency City if they let you get out of that."

"They were," I answered. "They won't be next time."

"No, I guess they won't." He jerked a thumb at the prisoner's huddled form. "Who's the guest?"

"Don't know yet," I answered. "We haven't had time to interrogate him. And it was a bit of a rough haul to get him up here."

Eddie squinted up toward the rock where I'd left our captive. "I really want to start raking him over the coals," he said with a yawn, "but I'm about dead."

"Tom's about to show him some hospitality," I said, painfully levering myself to my feet. "We'll fill you in when you wake up."

He nodded, lay back against his ruck, pulled his cap over his eyes, and stopped moving. I was pretty sure he was asleep before I straightened to my full height.

Tom was already stepping up onto the rock as I approached the captive. The guy didn't move at first when the retired Colonel nudged him in the ribs with a boot. When Tom kicked him a little harder, he groaned and turned over.

He was slightly shorter than me, fairly stocky, with dark brown hair, a square jaw, and a thick five-o'clock shadow turning to stubble. He'd fit on a SOF recruiting poster, if he weren't playing jackbooted thug on American soil.

His feet were a mess; his socks were shredded and his soles were bloody. We'd covered some pretty rough terrain getting up there. But his brown eyes were alert and wary as he looked up at Tom.

Tom frowned down at him. "I know you," he said suddenly.

The man winced a little. "Long time no see, Colonel," he said.

Tom crouched down to look him in the face. "Bill Gage?" he asked, a distinct note of incredulity in his voice. That was new. I didn't think I'd ever seen Tom caught off guard like that. "I thought you were dead."

The man chuckled without humor. "I damned near was," he replied. "I spent a *long* time in the body and fender shop after that op."

I looked at Tom quizzically. He straightened, his eyes still locked on Gage. I guessed that seeing a ghost could even rattle Tom Heinrich.

"It was my last tour before retirement, in Afghanistan," he explained, still without looking at me. "Some of my boys got into trouble just outside of Herat. I rolled out with the QRF, and came across some DEVGRU guys along the way, who volunteered to come along." He jerked a chin at my prisoner. "Gage, here, was one of them.

"It was a disaster," he continued. "They'd gotten sucked into one of those little shithole villages and surrounded, and we had to go in after them.

There was enough defense in depth in there to make Kuribayashi proud. It was a maze of two-foot thick mud walls with murder holes on every flank.

"The SEALs took point, and got fucked up. I went in after them with my boys. We were...thorough." Knowing Tom, that meant they had left a metric fuckton of dead bodies behind them. I imagined that "thorough" involved a high volume of fire and grenades in every opening they came to, without worrying about collateral damage. That was Tom's way. Protect his own, crush the enemy, and fuck anyone who got in the way. It worked. "The last I saw of Bill Gage, he was over a brother SEAL's shoulders, covered in his own blood and either unconscious or dead."

"I caught about ten bullets and a lot of frag that day," Gage said hoarsely. "I actually did die, or so they told me. Twice. I had fifteen surgeries before I could start to live normally again, and it was another two years before I was back in any kind of shape. By then, the Teams had essentially moved on without me; I could take a leadership or admin position, but I'd never be the shooter I was anymore.

"That was when a guy I'd known from BUD/S approached me, said he had a line on a new contract, something for guys like us. Not as many rules, none of the Navy's administrative bullshit, no annual training wickets, none of that crap. Just 'getting shit done.'" He looked up at Tom. His expression was unreadable. "How could I resist? A desk job versus getting to run and gun again, without having to put up with the idiocy I was seeing more and more of in the service? Sign me up."

"And then?" Tom asked coldly. Tom had never been the sentimental type, and any sense of brotherhood he might have had with Gage from Afghanistan was pretty well DOA thanks to Gage being among those who had attacked us, and on American soil to boot.

Gage looked at his bloodied feet. "'Once in, never out,'" he quoted. He looked up at Tom, then at me. "Ever hear that one? It can sound good; lots of brotherhood implied in the right context." He shook his head. "Not in this outfit.

"It didn't take long to see that 'getting shit done' meant being strongarm guys for a different set of soft-suited assholes in offices who never had to get their hands dirty. Worse; these sons of bitches were accountable to fucking *nobody*. Oh, sure, they gave us the usual line of bullshit, but the cracks started showing pretty quick. Go support these 'freedom fighters,' who are little more than terrorists. Go grab this 'terrorist,' who it turns out is a financier for an opposing interest, and never had any contact with jihadis or anybody else." He slumped. "I kept my mouth shut and did what I was told. Yeah, maybe that makes me a dupe, but by then I was already in too deep. I saw what happened when somebody tried to get out. They threatened him with prosecution for an illegal op, one that had actually happened. That was when

I decided to keep my head down and my teeth together." He shook his head. "At least I got out of the Syria-Iraq op."

"I think I ran into that one," I said grimly. "Was there a shithead who called himself 'Carnivore' on that op?"

He looked up at me. "Yeah, there was," he said. "Maybe still is; it's not like they give us regular updates on anything we're not directly involved in. Or anything we are, for that matter."

"He's dead," I said flatly. "I gutted him like a fish after he tried to send one of you to stab me in the back while we were trying to fight a bunch of ISIS fucks."

"No shit?" he replied. "Hell, I'd like to shake your hand. Never did like that bastard."

"That's nice and everything," I said, "but the fact remains that I just pried you out of *my* house, which you and your cronies just invaded. Mutual enemies aside, that isn't going to make matters easier for you."

"I get that," he answered. "You've got to understand, though, that I really didn't have much choice, not if I didn't want to wind up in the Federal pen or dead."

"'Just following orders' hasn't been an excuse since Nuremburg," Tom said flatly. Given his scorched-earth style of leadership, I found that vaguely funny, though I kept my face impassive. "But if you cooperate, we might go easy on you. As in, we might not tie you to a tree and leave you for the wolves."

As if sensing just how thin the ice he was on was, Gage took a deep breath. "And I'm willing to cooperate," he said. "Hell, this is the first time in years I've really been beyond my employers' reach. I don't know very much; they keep everything pretty compartmentalized, but what I know, I'll tell you. I was never really comfortable with running operations on American soil, anyway. I thought I'd be going after bad guys in the Middle East, not taking out political and business competition at home."

"First things first, then," I said, before Tom could get started. "Where is Bob Sampson?"

"You asked me that before," he said. "I don't know who that is."

"The wounded guy, the big dude with a bunch of bullet holes and stab wounds in him, who disappeared from the hospital," Tom said, following my lead. "He sure as hell didn't check himself out."

But Gage shook his head. "We didn't take him. Shit, I didn't even know he was there; we thought we had y'all bottled up on the ranch. Shows how good our intel was."

"What was the job?" Tom asked. "Start at the beginning."

"Same as always," Gage replied with a shrug. "We got a target package and a list of assets. They wanted it done quick, with overwhelming force, and they wanted *everything* secured. The orders were very specific

132

about that." He grunted. "Obviously, that didn't go according to plan. Which I'm sure is why they sent Baumgartner."

"That's the second time I've heard that name," I said. "Who is this Baumgartner?"

He looked at me curiously. "Gordon Baumgartner," he said, as if I should have known.

And he was right. "Fuck!" I snarled. "I was afraid of that."

"You know him?" Tom asked.

"Crossed paths with him," I said. "Dammit! I knew I'd seen him before. Bryan did, too." I took a deep breath. "The guy's a fucking legend. Ranger, then Delta, two Distinguished Service Crosses, both for going into utter fucking hornet's nests, killing everybody inside, and getting out alive, once in Afghanistan, and then again in Libya. The guy's a beast and a hell of an operator; a few of the more melodramatic types started calling him 'The Terminator.' He's the kind of single-minded killer who makes a great door-kicker but doesn't seem to be interested in much of anything else."

"Sounds like this Carnivore character you told me about," Tom mused.

Gage snorted. "Carnivore wished he was Baumgartner. He wasn't even in the same league. Baumgartner's the real deal. He just doesn't give a shit about who he's working for or why he does what he does, as long as he gets to do it. The Army wasn't scratching his itch anymore, so he went 'private sector.'"

Tom looked at me, and jerked his head to indicate he wanted a word alone. We left Gage where he was and headed downhill to where he couldn't hear us easily.

"If he's telling the truth," he said quietly, "that leaves us rather hanging when it comes to finding Robert."

"The way I see it," I replied, "*if* he's telling the truth, there are three options. Either these 'Sulla' assholes who sicced *Mara Salvatrucha* on us have him, Renton has him, or The Broker has him. Unless there's *another* player who's close enough to grab him to get at us, those are the options."

"You think Renton or The Broker might be holding him as a way to get us to play their game?" he asked.

"I think it's entirely possible at this point," I said grimly. "Yes, both of them have helped us out, but The Broker straight-up admitted that he was helping us because we're potentially useful to him. Same thing with Renton. We're assets, not friends."

Tom nodded. "So, our missing lad is completely in the wind, and we're on the run in the mountains. Ideas?"

I frowned, looking up at Gage. "Our options are pretty limited. We can say 'fuck it,' and head out, see if we can get a line on who has Little Bob from somewhere else and go after him. But this is our rear area; unless we want to rely entirely on Renton and The Broker, neither of whom we can be one hundred percent sure of, we need to secure our own house. And I'm not going to rest easy until Baumgartner's off our trail. Not only that, but we spent a lot of time and effort building rapport with Brett, and he's in one hell of a tight spot right now, largely thanks to us. We owe him. Hell, we may be the primary targets, but having these jackbooted motherfuckers stomping on our neighbors is pissing me off. If this ain't the right fight, maybe we're in the wrong business."

"Agreed," he said. "First things first. We break the TF, then we reassess."

I started back up toward Gage's rock. He might not or might not be telling the truth about having no real big picture info, but I was going to squeeze him dry about the TF's dispositions, or he was going to have one hell of a hard time.

CHAPTER 15

"Fucking amateur hour," Eric muttered.

I hadn't gone on the recon mission this time; I'd been prevailed upon to let somebody else do it. In fact, both my team and Eddie's had stayed back while Tim had taken out one of the newer teams. While both Eddie and I might have had some reservations about leaving it to the new guys, Tom had upbraided us roundly about it, pointing out that both of us had had a hand in the selection process, that none of these guys were wet behind the ears anymore—they wouldn't even have been considered if they had been—that trying to do all of this with only two teams was stupid, and that Tim's boys were getting restless for a piece of the action anyway.

I wasn't sure what to think about that last part. Sure, I didn't think there was a shooter alive who hadn't, at one point in his life, hoped for *Red Dawn* to become a reality, in some way. There is a cleanness, a clarity to defending one's home against an invader that is appealing to the warrior, especially when he's spent most of his adult life fighting murky shadow wars in distant lands with uncertain results for uncertain causes.

But this wasn't so clean-cut. This wasn't a foreign invasion; this was a shadow civil war. Even the foreign invaders, the Mexican *narcos*, had apparently been invited in by our domestic enemies.

I shook off the reverie. We had reporting and imagery to go over.

Eric had some experience in the intel field, so he was our go-to team intel guy. I was looking over his shoulder at the images on the tablet in front of him.

One of the recon patrols had tracked down a couple of the trucks that Eddie had seen among the attackers hitting the Task Force's Cody headquarters a few nights before. Since the mysterious new players hadn't seen anything wrong with driving a lifted, heavily modded Ford Raptor to a firefight, a truck that would stand out under normal circumstances, they hadn't been all that hard to find.

My suspicions about the new factor's identity had proven to be pretty accurate. There was an impromptu camp set up a few miles on the other side of Cody, mostly tents and trailers, with lots of US flags, Gadsden flags, and Oathkeeper banners in evidence. They had security out, in cammies and kit with rifles, though they looked a little anarchic and slipshod compared to the Task Force. Their choice of terrain also sucked; it might make a good campsite, but if the TF decided to roll through there with those eight-wheelers, the militia weren't going to last long.

"We probably should have expected these guys were going to show up," I said. "Hell, this is a dream come true to some of them."

"I'm amazed any of them can move," Eric said. "All the blood must be going to their massive, throbbing erections. They're probably well past the point of needing to see a doctor."

"The funny part is, this is precisely the sort of situation where they're not entirely in the wrong," I said. "They're not right, either; I don't even want to know what kind of fantastical explanation for what's going on they've got cooked up. But they organized to fight back against tyrants and terrorists, and that's kind of what's going on here."

"Kind of," Eric replied grudgingly. "But not exactly. And if somebody really *is* trying to spread chaos? This will just make it worse."

"I'm pretty sure it already is worse," I told him. "Does that look like all of them came from the local Three Percenter group to you?"

He frowned and shook his head. "Nah, way too many people. And I don't remember seeing that Raptor around before. Although," he continued, rubbing his chin with a thumb, "for all we know, little enough information has gotten out about what's going on that the TF might have inadvertently done some recruiting for them."

"Maybe," I said. "But if the rioters can use social media to get things rolling over some dead *narcos* in Pueblo, who's to say that it can't work the other way, too?" I scratched my beard. "How much would you be willing to bet that this same mysterious 'Sulla' bunch made sure that word got to the Three Percenter sites about the 'jackbooted thugs' in Wyoming?"

"No bet," he answered. "What are we going to do about this?"

I thought about the options available. There were a few, none of them particularly palatable.

I stood up with an annoyed grunt. "If we can avoid it, I don't want these clowns getting underfoot." I sighed. "Guess I've got to make a phone call."

***

With Baumgartner sweeping the Beartooths around The Ranch, we had relocated again, pushing our own camp south, and deeper into the mountains. We'd moved far enough that we only rarely heard the buzz of drones overhead anymore, but we were still cautious about open ground.

We were also being extremely careful about phones, whether we were using the sat phones or the local cell network. Alek and the rest overseas had only the barest knowledge of what was going on; until we had more assurance of comm security, we couldn't send more than the most cursory details.

So, I was several miles and a terrain feature away from the camp when I pulled out one of the sat phones and dialed a number.

Van Williamson answered cautiously after a few rings. "Yeah?"

"Van, it's Jeff Stone," I said. I waited for the inevitable.

"Oh, *now* you want to talk to me," Williamson said after a moment. There was a certain note of triumph in his voice, though I wouldn't call it gloating, strictly speaking.

This was going to be painful.

"When we asked to train with you, like you were letting those militarized cops train with you, you turned us down," he continued. "Now, all of a sudden, the cops can't do shit, and here we are to get your asses out of the fire. Not such a bunch of 'delusional wannabes' now, are we?"

I sighed. "You're not pulling anyone's ass out of any fires, Van, you're making things worse," I said tiredly. "You people already fucked up one of my ops." I'd debated telling him that, but figured that it wouldn't tell him, or anyone listening, anything that hadn't already been implied by our hit on The Ranch the same night. "I'm extending you the courtesy of asking you to get out of my AO and leave this problem to us."

There was a long silence. I'd been afraid that this wasn't going to work, and the longer the pause went on, the more likely I thought it was that I'd been right.

"So, that's it?" he demanded. "We're still not good enough? I tried to warn you before, that this kind of thing was coming, and that you were going to need our help, but you didn't want to listen. Now it's come to your own damned door, and you still want to play high and mighty with me?"

"You don't have any fucking clue as to what's really happening, Van!" I snapped.

"I've seen the signs!" he replied, before I could continue. "I've seen it coming for a long, long time, and so have you, or you would have if you hadn't let the powers that be string you along, shutting your eyes and ears with their money! Now that you're no longer useful to them, they're trying to bury you, but you still can't get their narrative out of your head, can you? You *need* us, Stone!"

"Listen to me," *you little shit*, I didn't say. Van Williamson was in his late twenties and had never enlisted, preferring to "prepare for the collapse," while badmouthing those who did serve as being dupes of the aforementioned "powers that be." He wasn't one hundred percent wrong, necessarily, but he wasn't nearly as right as his self-righteousness told him he was. He had a lot of very strong opinions for his lack of experience. "You want to talk about 'powers that be?' You want to talk about corrupt politicians and Leftists taking over the country? There are assholes trying to sow chaos and disorder right now in order to do just that, and the more you follow through with your fucking John Milius fantasy, the more you play right into their hands! You'll get more of your Second American Civil War than you can stomach!"

That was probably the wrong thing to say, and I realized it as soon as I finished talking. I'd just pushed a button, and there wouldn't be any getting through to him after that.

"Well," he said, with that false calm that you usually heard from a green kid who was simultaneously excited as shit and scared shitless at the prospect of facing his first firefight, "maybe it's time. Maybe this is it."

I hung up. There was no point anymore.

"Fine," I muttered, as I turned back toward camp. "I guess we have to do this the hard way."

***

The flash from the direction of the TF camp lit up the underside of the low clouds, bright enough that it had to draw every eye for miles. A few seconds later, the rolling *boom* of the explosion rumbled across the sky, as a great cloud of smoke and dust roiled upward toward the clouds.

That was my cue. I moved as quickly and silently as I could, through the shadows between several tents and trailers, until I got to my target, a small pop-up trailer near the center of the campsite. There were plenty of people up and about, most of them armed, but all eyes were to the west, toward the explosion. Nobody noticed me, or if they did, they didn't notice that I didn't belong there.

Inside, the trailer was surprisingly neat, with clothing and gear stowed with military precision. A copy of *Resistance to Tyranny* was lying on the table, but that was about the only thing remotely out of place.

I sat down on the couch across from the table, hunkered down with my TRP on my lap, and waited.

After a few minutes, as the furor from the IED blast died down, Van Williamson came back into his trailer.

Van was a fit young man, unlike more than a few of his compatriots, though he lacked some of the hardness of the likes of Gage or Baumgartner. He'd grown an "operator" beard that was thicker than mine, and was dressed in the Tactical Timmy Starter Kit: 5.11 tuxedo, Ranger green ball cap with an upside-down US flag velcroed on the front, Merrell boots, and a Glock riding high on his hip. Apparently, drop leg holsters—which I admittedly hated, myself—were "last year."

He didn't notice me, but was reaching for his gear tree, where his plate carrier and helmet were carefully hung, when I spoke.

"Hello, Van," I said, letting every bit of unfriendliness I could muster into my voice. I sat up straighter as he jumped and spun around, starting to reach for his Glock until he noticed the 1911 in my hand, indexed on his sternum.

"Yell, or move one more millimeter for that gun, and I'll kill you," I told him. He nodded ever so slightly, his face gone pale and sick, slowly and carefully moving his hand away from the pistol on his belt.

"You want to know why I don't have any use for you and your pack of glorified airsofters with live weapons?" I asked, my voice low. "Here's a good one: you idiots are so easily distracted by a fireworks show that I could waltz in here without being noticed or stopped. If I'd wanted, I could have snuffed you as you came through that fucking door. I could still do it, and the guys I've got out in the dark would sow so much chaos and bloodshed in here that I could walk out just as easily as I walked in. You're amateurs. Hell, you're not even amateurs; you're kids playing at being soldier, without any of the real-world experience or discipline that I need.

"Which brings me to the heart of the matter." I didn't know how well he could see my glare in the dim light inside the trailer, but then, his eyes were pretty much glued to the pistol in my hand. "I can't trust any of you. You've got these visions of a Second American Revolution crossed with *Red Dawn* dancing in your heads; you think that you'll be the brave guerrillas who will hit the reset button and bring some kind of new American utopia in the aftermath. But how many of you have actually ever heard a shot fired in anger, much less seen what a country tearing itself apart for two *fucking* decades in a civil war actually looks like?

"I've spent the better part of my adult life in places like that, kid. You know what? There is no fucking 'reset button.' This isn't a fucking movie; everything isn't going to be all neatly wrapped up at the end. If this kicks off, it won't be 1860, with set battles and a final surrender. It's going to be fucking Lebanon, and Libya, and Syria, and Iraq. It's going to be neighbor against neighbor, with the grudges lasting the next hundred years, and whatever comes out the other end isn't going to be recognizable as the United States.

"Maybe it's inevitable," I continued tiredly. "But I'm still going to do what I can to head it off. Because this is *my* fucking country, and I don't want to see it turn into the shitholes I've been fighting in for the last twenty years. And that's why I can't trust you. You actually *want* that shit to happen. And that plays right into our enemies' hands."

I stood up. "You've got six hours to get yourself and your drinking buddies out of my way, or I'm going to come back here and put a bullet through your skull. You got me, Van?"

He nodded again, his eyes wide and his face very pale. He looked scared as hell, which was what I'd been hoping for. Hopefully I'd scared some of the piss and vinegar out of him, and he'd listen. I didn't want to have to kill him. I just needed him out of the way, and preferably not flying off the handle and triggering a conflagration that we'd never recover from.

It was entirely possible that we were already past the point of no return. Renton had made that point earlier, and I had to agree with him. But I'd be damned if I'd just go with the flow and bring a civil war on any faster than could be avoided. As matters stood, this was still essentially a war in the shadows. The longer we could keep it that way, the better.

We might still be able to end it without tearing everything apart in the process.

Keeping my .45 trained on Van, I slid off the couch and out the door. He watched me go, but didn't move a muscle. Just as I quietly closed the door, I caught a glimpse of him slumping bonelessly to the floor.

Yep, he was scared. Good.

I moved quickly away from the trailer, while trying not to look like I was sneaking. That's one of the keys to successful infiltration; look like you belong there. I kept waiting for Williamson to pull his nuts out of his throat and yell; while I hadn't been lying about having my team in the grass on the perimeter, ready to cover my exfil, he could still make getting clear plenty sticky with little more than a shout.

But as I walked between tents and trailers, keeping to the shadows and avoiding the knots of hard-talking tough guys who were still discussing the explosion that Tim's team had set off close enough to the TF camp to keep those assholes focused on perimeter security for a while, there was no call, no shots fired, not even any movement from the direction of Williamson's trailer. By the time I reached the perimeter and started to fade into the darkness, I was reasonably confident that Williamson had been the only one to know I'd been there.

It occurred to me that I might well have been the first person to ever seriously threaten Van's life. That kind of confrontation could have some unexpected effects. I suspected, given his silence, that Van was presently sitting on the floor of his trailer, shaking too hard to move.

So much the better. Sometimes a good, heavy dose of pants-shitting fear is what it takes to knock some common sense into some people's heads. On the other hand, of course, he might go the other direction, and double down to cover up the fact that he'd pissed himself when I'd threatened him. I'd known a few of those types, too, and it was entirely possible that there were plenty of them in that camp, the kind who will go over the top and completely fuck shit up just to compensate for the fact that they're scared.

We'd roll with the punches if that happened, but it would make matters that much harder. I hoped, as I carefully signaled to Larry, who was down in the grass behind his FAL, that I was clear. He didn't return the signal, but he didn't shoot me, either, so I could safely assume he'd gotten it.

I got to him and dropped into the tall grass next to him. He had my chest rig and my SOCOM 16 with him, and I quickly donned the rig and took up the rifle, getting into a decent shooting position a few feet away from him.

I'd given Van six hours, but if they decided to do anything but pack up and go home sooner than that, we were in a position to make that a very, very bad idea.

The truth was, I really didn't want to start shooting these guys. As dumb and dangerous as most of them were, they were genuinely sincere, and if they hadn't been a bunch of tards living in a fantasy world, I might have tended to sympathize with their outlook a little more. As it was, if I could scare them off and get them out of the way, I'd be happy.

***

We waited, watched, and listened. At first, I thought maybe Williamson had fainted, but after about half an hour, I could hear raised voices near the center of camp. I couldn't make out what they were saying, but it sounded like things were getting pretty heated. It didn't sound like there was a great deal of agreement about how to proceed.

I started to get a sinking feeling in my gut. Dammit, they were going to make this hard. Granted, I should have probably expected it; it wasn't like these guys were strategic geniuses. They wanted their blaze of glory, and they were just as likely as any other mob to turn on anyone who opposed them as "one of the bad guys." I could just see some of them starting to think that they had to "secure" the area against the Task Force *and* us.

Larry inched closer so I could hear him. "Are we going to need to go to Plan B?" he whispered.

"Maybe," I replied.

"Jack and Derek are already in position if we do," was all he said, then went back to watching the militia camp over the sights of his FAL.

After another hour, we started to see things happening. There were disparate clumps of individuals divided through the camp, and while I couldn't be sure, I was getting the distinct impression of a decided split within the group. Pretty soon, some of those clumps started packing up their tents and hitching up their trailers.

Others weren't so inclined to skedaddle, and I started to think we were going to have to go to Plan B, at the very least. Plan B consisted of disabling their vehicles, in a rather loud and pyrotechnic manner. Plan C was going to get messier.

But as the night got older, and more and more would-be "freedom fighters" decided that this wasn't the hill to die on, the thinning ranks looked around and started to wonder about their chances of success as their numbers dwindled. More started grudgingly packing up and driving away into the night.

There were still thirty minutes left on the clock before the deadline I'd given Williamson when the last of the militia showed us their taillights. Larry and I got up off the ground, looking around carefully for any more stragglers, and then headed for our own RV point.

One crisis had been averted, at least for the moment. We could concentrate on the more immediate threat.

141

CHAPTER 16

Two days after giving Van the scare of his life, we were ready to move.

With the IED blast coming so soon after the militia's glorified drive-by, the Task Force had apparently decided that they weren't satisfied with their security at the Cody site, and moved the entire operation up to The Ranch. Which suited us just fine. Sure, our home might get a little busted up prying them out of there, but at least we only had one target to focus on instead of two.

Of course, we were still badly outnumbered and outgunned, but since when was that anything new?

We started to move down out of the hills, traveling in pairs, slowly and carefully encircling The Ranch, setting up to start whittling down their exterior security.

Naturally, the enemy always gets a vote, too.

***

"Got 'em," Jack whispered. "Three hundred meters. Right where they're supposed to be."

I peered over his shoulder. We were in the low ground, which wasn't necessarily the most ideal place to be from a tactical perspective, but there was cover down there, the only cover where we could get eyes on the choke point that we'd picked out for the ambush. Looking up the hill, I could see the two eight-wheelers he'd spotted trundling down the dirt road from the north gate.

"Somebody still hasn't learned their lesson," I said. "They're right on time."

"If they were so stupid and arrogant that they thought their drones were a good substitute for alert sentries," Jack pointed out, "then they're too stupid and arrogant to learn the lesson of varying their routine."

We lay there and waited. We hadn't gotten our ghillie suits out when we'd broken contact and fled The Ranch, but camouflage is something you do, not something you wear, so we'd adapted. We had grass and brush tied to arms and legs and stuffed in bungie cords around our torsos. Unless you were *really* looking, we'd be almost invisible until you were right on top of us.

My team was the one in the ambush position; Tim and the new guys were set up on overwatch, surveilling The Ranch itself, and Eddie had his own, similar op going on off to the south.

The two armored vehicles, their black paint gone gray with dust, continued down the road, slowly. They weren't MRAPs or MATVs, but they still had high centers of gravity, in spite of the independent suspensions for each wheel, and they had to negotiate the steep terrain carefully to avoid falling over. The CROWS turrets weren't scanning, but appeared locked forward on the lead vehicle and aft on the rear vehicle.

Jack's point notwithstanding, I was surprised. As arrogantly complacent as these fuckheads had been, I would have thought that the IED blast would have put them on their toes. But here they were, doing an exterior security patrol like they were just going through the motions.

For some reason it put my hackles up. They were playing right into my hands, and it bothered me. If anything in a combat situation seems too good to be true, it probably is.

I squinted at the lead vehicle as it got closer and closer to the dry creek bed where we were waiting. They were buttoned up; nobody was sticking his head out of a hatch, but still, they should have been scanning with that CROWS. I started to get a really, really bad feeling.

That feeling only got more intense when both vehicles stopped about a hundred fifty yards from the creek bed and sat there.

Now, an armored vehicle on a security patrol halting momentarily wasn't unheard of. Security halts are a regular part of patrolling, and especially on that terrain, it only made sense to stop and get a steadier look at the surroundings. But that CROWS stayed in place, locked forward, and nobody got out of either vehicle.

They just sat there.

Something was very, very wrong. I started to get that nasty, hollow feeling in the pit of my stomach. It was something like how I imagined a trapped animal must feel.

We didn't dare move. If we'd suspected that they'd pinged to our ambush, we could possibly have simply let them roll through without triggering the big ANFO IEDs we'd buried under the only real viable crossing across the creek bed. But without RPGs or even Logan's mutant 20mms, what the hell were we going to do if they stopped short?

The only saving grace was their weird complacency that meant they weren't scanning with the thermals in the CROWS. It was by no means certain that they'd spot us; we were well buried in the brush. But they weren't even trying, and that creeped me out more than anything else.

A fly buzzed in my ear. It was a relatively cool day, but I was sweating my ass off, lying in the dirt and rocks, feeling every bit of vegetation I'd used to cammie up that had worked its way inside my shirt and my belt chafing. And I didn't dare move a muscle.

The moment of frozen uncertainty was suddenly broken by a gunshot.

It rang out from *behind* us, northwest and up the creek bed. It was quickly followed by an intense fusillade of more fire.

The eight-wheelers still didn't move, and the CROWS turrets still didn't shift a millimeter. That was when it dawned on me. They were right on time because somebody was expecting the ambush, and wanted us in place at the right time so they could have us in a fixed position.

Find, Fix, and Finish are the three bywords of hunting High Value Targets. We'd just been Found and Fixed.

I rolled over, pulling my rifle with me, and turned toward the sound of gunfire. If those CROWS weren't engaging by then, they probably weren't going to; they would run too much of a risk of hitting their own guys, especially if they were trying to get close enough to take any of us alive.

At first all I could see was brush. Bullets were starting to *snap* overhead, a few of them clipping off branches and showering us with splinters and bits of shredded plant matter. A lot of them were the higher-pitched noise of 5.56, but there were the deeper, throatier *booms* of 7.62 rounds going the other direction. Eric, Larry, and Ben were on the six, and at least one of them was shooting back.

There were other, different-sounding shots mixed in there as well, but I didn't have time to think about trying to identify them. We had to counterattack or we were going to be fucked.

Not knowing exactly where the enemy was, and not wearing plates, I didn't get up and charge forward. That was a good way to get shot. I crawled forward as quickly as I could, looking for an opening to engage. Jack, Bryan, Derek, and Nick had also turned and came with me, all of us staying low, at least until we could get a target.

The gunfire was only intensifying. As I crawled forward, as nasty as the hornet's nest worth of rounds going over my head was, I started to realize that the opposition was throwing lead in two different directions, and some of those different-sounding reports were coming from off to the north, outside of the creek bed.

Whoever was up there wasn't shooting at us, though, at least at the moment, so I put them most of the way out of my mind, especially as I saw a muzzle flash in the brush ahead and dropped flat, the bullet going past my head so close that the *crack* of its passage was actually painful.

I squeezed off three fast shots in return, mainly just to keep his head down while I got down and tried to spot him. He was as well-camouflaged as we were, and I suddenly suspected that I knew where Baumgartner was. These had to be his hunters.

He recovered from my suppressive return fire quickly, snapping off another shot at me that was also too damned close for comfort, but I shot at the muzzle blast just as the bullet burned past my ear, and I saw him jerk and slump. I put two more shots into the lump, just to be sure.

A renewed storm of gunfire ripped through the air overhead, only to be answered by more of our own, and more from the unknowns uphill to the north. I couldn't see much; the brush down there was thick, and these guys were good at concealment. So, I was picking likely spots and putting pairs of shots into them, shooting low so as to hopefully not simply blast over their heads. If I kicked some grit in their faces or ricocheted a bullet the same way, so much the better.

Volume of fire wasn't going to do the trick with this bunch, though. A gravelly voice rose above the gunfire, shouting, "Assault through!"

Ah, fuck.

A roaring storm of automatic fire came ripping through the brush overhead, crackling through the air, shredding vegetation, and *thudding* into slender tree trunks. I pressed myself flat against the dirt as more rounds came uncomfortably close, though none nearly so close as the earlier, aimed shots.

In spite of the nearness of the flying metal death right overhead, I forced myself to look up and get behind my rifle, just in time to see a shaggy form like a sasquatch made of grass rear up from the creek bed barely fifty yards away, carbine in his shoulder, dumping his mag in our direction as he charged forward.

With so many bullets snapping and thumping overhead, the natural reaction was to get as low and as flat as possible, to curl into a tiny ball and cringe away from the bullets. Training doesn't take that impulse away; in some circumstances, it can be useful. But sometimes it needs to be overridden. Especially when there's two hundred-odd pounds of gunman coming at you from close-quarters, about to pick you out of the greenery any second and dip his muzzle to stitch you with bullets from skull to groin.

So, while every nerve screamed at me to stay down, I picked my head up, lifted my muzzle, and put two rounds just over his heart at twenty yards.

He kept moving forward, but he was dead by the time his face hit the ground. Relieved of the pressure of his fire, I was able to shift right and engage the next guy, at the same time Larry blasted him with a failure drill, two to the chest and the last one snapping his head back with a faint red spray as his momentum kept him falling forward.

Just like that, the gunfire fell silent. I almost got up to count the bodies.

Fortunately, I remembered at that moment that the hunters weren't the only ones to worry about. I still didn't know who was up to the north, and those two armored vehicles were still waiting in the wings.

If any of us had stood up, we'd have been fucked. Because right then, one of those CROWS turrets opened fire.

A hail of 7.62 rounds tore through the creek bed, smacking off rocks, thudding into trees, kicking up little fountains of grit where they hit the dirt.

We had no place to go, and nothing we could hit back with. We'd been banking on the IEDs to take them out, and they were too far away.

We were fucked.

I almost didn't hear it. The firestorm roaring down around our ears was too loud. But there was the faint suggestion of another sound, a deeper, heavier sound, and then suddenly the machine gun fire lifted.

Three more shots rang out. They were definitely something heavier than 7.62; they sounded vaguely like a big-bore magnum round.

The last shot's report echoed down the valley, and then the only sound was my own harsh breathing, the pounding of blood in my ears, and the rumble of engines receding to the south.

And Derek's tooth-gritted groans of pain.

Still not trusting that we were in the clear, I started crawling toward the sound. Along the way, I came across Ben.

He was clearly dead. He'd taken three rounds to the head and upper torso, and was lying face down in a pool of his own blood. I could see his brain.

It wasn't the time to mourn, or even try to retrieve his body. I kept going, heading for Derek.

The rest of the team was forming a perimeter, guns out. I got to Derek and found him tightening a tourniquet around his own leg.

A glance told me that his femur was shattered. He'd taken a bullet in the thigh, presumably one of the machine gun rounds from the armored vehicles, given the angles involved. His pantleg was soaked in blood, and his leg was lying at a weird angle. He'd gotten the tourniquet on quick, but I wasn't feeling particularly good about his femoral, just looking at what I could see of the wound. He needed surgery, and quick.

A footstep crunched nearby and I froze. Looking over, I saw Eric getting on his rifle's sights, but a voice rang out from the trees.

"Friendlies!" Old Man Harrick called out. "Coming in!"

Rifle muzzles lowered, and the crusty old rancher stepped through the brush. He was dressed in his hunting cammies, which actually blended into the vegetation better than most of the "tactical" camouflage patterns I'd seen. He had a chest rig on and an AR-10 in his hands.

Dave Harrick was a Vietnam vet, and looked it. His hair had gone white years ago, but it was still plenty thick, as was his mustache. Tall and barrel-chested, he was burned brown by the sun, and his eyes were flint-hard flecks of steely gray within a mass of squint lines. He looked hard as woodpecker lips, and having gotten to know the man over the last few years, he was harder than he looked. It would have been tough to make it as a rancher otherwise.

"We're clear for the moment, but we need to move," he said. "They'll be back once they start to figure out what the hell just happened."

147

"What the hell did just happen?" Eric asked as he got to his feet.

"CROWS ain't worth much if you shoot out the cameras," Harrick replied. "Dennis likes to play with that Omen of his."

I knew the rifle he was talking about. Dennis Harrick had been proud as a peacock of his .458 Magnum AR, and I knew the younger Harrick well enough to know that he probably could pick off a CROWS sensor with it.

"Derek's Urgent Surgical," I told him. "We've got to move him quick but careful."

Harrick jerked his chin toward the north. "I've got a truck on the far side of the hill. We can load him up and they'll get him into town. We'll head back to the house on horseback."

I didn't argue with him. Arguing with Dave Harrick was rarely a good idea under the best of circumstances. Having heard a few stories about his actions in Laos and Cambodia, I was pretty sure it was a worse idea under these circumstances. If he said we were clear, we were clear. I also agreed with his assessment of the need for haste.

Standing up, I did a quick scan of the area. Ben and Derek were our only casualties. However, there were only three other bodies on the ground. When they were turned over, though, none of them was Baumgartner. If he'd been there, the man had disappeared like a ghost as soon as things had started to turn.

Which meant he was still out there, somewhere. We needed to move quick. If there was anyone I expected to be fast on the turnaround, it was Baumgartner.

Larry supported Derek, who was looking more than a little pale, and started hauling him up out of the creek bed, following Harrick. I slung my rifle and picked up Ben's body. I was his team leader. I'd carry him out.

There were half a dozen men on horseback at the treeline, all in various camouflage patterns and carrying a hodge-podge of rifles, ranging from ARs to M1As to even a couple of lever actions. I didn't see Dennis, but imagined he was still on overwatch somewhere.

Frank Wagner kicked his horse forward as we came out of the trees and approached Larry and Derek. "I can get him to the truck quicker," he offered. "It might hurt more, but it'll take less time."

"Sorry, buddy," Larry said. "This is gonna suck, but we need to get you medevaced." Derek just nodded, his teeth gritted. Larry squatted down, got his big mitts under Derek's armpits, and hoisted him. Frank grabbed him by the back of his chest rig and got him over the saddle in front of him before kicking the horse into a quick walk. Derek couldn't hold back the groan of pain as he bounced against the saddle, but kept it under a scream.

Another horseman I didn't recognize sidled his mount up beside me. "I'll take him," he offered, but I shook my head.

148

"He's my guy," I said. He just nodded and jerked a thumb toward the horse he was leading behind him.

It took some doing to get Ben's body up on the horse in front of me, but we did it. Most of the rest were scanning the hills around us, hands never straying far from rifles. I recognized a few of them, others were strangers. But they were quiet and alert, and had just pulled our asses out of an ambush that should have killed us all.

Once we were all mounted, Harrick nodded curtly, swung into his own saddle, and led out.

***

To my complete lack of surprise, we headed north, quickly heading up into rough country, back into the Beartooths, though a part that we hadn't gotten into. We were still on Harrick's ranch, which was at least twice the size of ours, but we were getting up into some rough, wild parts of it, where the cattle didn't go.

Nobody said much of anything. We knew we were being watched; there was the buzz of a drone overhead, and we had quite a bit of open ground to cover. They were going to know where we were going, but aside from Baumgartner's hunters, the Task Force had not shown a great deal of ability when it came to mountain warfare, and unless I missed my guess, we were going high again.

We were. After a few miles, we turned west and went over the ridge, into a high, forested valley. In another half an hour we were under the trees and heading uphill again. I hadn't even known that Old Man Harrick ever came up this far.

I looked around at the men who'd pulled our asses out of the crack we'd gotten into. Most of them were older; I recognized two other local ranchers. Tom O'Reilly I knew had been in Desert Storm. I didn't know if Orrin Ketchum had been in the military.

A couple of others I recognized as more recent vets. Brad Lewis was a former Army grunt who had tried out for Praetorian and failed the indoc. TJ Taylor had been a Marine, and in and out of trouble with the law ever since he'd gotten out and returned home to Wyoming. I mainly knew him through Brett's bitching about him. But, troublemaker or not, right at the moment he was sitting his horse easily, his rifle held ready and his eyes alert as he scanned the woods and the surrounding mountains.

After another hour, we rode into the wide bowl of a high valley. A low, stone house had been built against the side of the mountain, and I got the distinct impression that it actually went back into the hillside. It looked relatively innocuous to the untrained eye, but a brief examination belied the idea that it was just a little mountain cabin. That place was a fortress. I could get some idea of how thick the walls were by studying the deep recesses of the narrow windows.

Old Man Harrick rode up to the stone-fenced corral beside the cabin and swung down out of the saddle. He opened the gate and led the horse in, and the rest of us followed. It was only then that I saw that the corral actually extended back into a deep stable under a massive shelf of rock.

A lot of planning had gone into this place. Of course, I shouldn't have been surprised, knowing what I knew about the old man. He had been one of those who had come back from Vietnam, found no place for themselves in society, thoroughly disliked where society had been going, and had headed for the hills.

TJ dismounted and moved forward to help me get Ben's body off the saddle, but Eric shouldered him out of the way. Ben was one of ours, and we were going to see to him ourselves.

Larry was at Eric's side quickly, and we eased our teammate's corpse to the ground before I swung down from the saddle myself. As my boots hit the stony floor of the corral, Dave Harrick loomed out of the shadow of the rocky shelf and jerked a thumb back inside the stable.

"There's a root cellar back there where we can keep him until we've got time to bury him," he said. I nodded my thanks, and we lifted Ben and carried him back into the shadows.

The root cellar was a narrow cave blasted into the rock and shored up with heavy timbers. There were a *lot* of supplies stacked on shelves against the walls, and it was chilly enough that we could probably leave Ben's body there for most of a day. A proper funeral was probably going to be some time in the future, if ever.

He wouldn't be the first Praetorian to go without a proper funeral. We never had been able to go back to Djibouti to dig up Colton's remains.

We laid Ben down on the floor, composed his limbs, and closed his eyes. We took his mags; the ammo would need to be distributed later.

Harrick, O'Reilly, and Ketchum were waiting inside the cabin when we left Ben and went in the open door in the back. As I'd suspected, most of the "cabin" had been blasted out of the mountainside. There had been a ton of work put into this little hideaway, and from the main room I couldn't see how far back it went. A solid-looking door set in a frame of heavy shoring timbers led back into the mountainside.

The main room itself was Spartan but comfortable, most of the furniture being rough, rustic pieces likely built from local timber. The floor was stone. There was no stove, only a deep, stone fireplace with several iron hooks and a spit, that could easily have been hauled up on a pack horse. The lights were either battery-powered or propane lanterns.

The rest of the team and the three ranchers were standing across the main room from each other. Ketchum looked nervous, O'Reilly was composed, and Harrick was as stone-faced as ever. My guys just looked tired and wary.

150

"We owe you a thank you, Mr. Harrick," I said. "We'd have been finished if you gents hadn't showed up." Harrick inclined his head silently in response. "But you shouldn't have gotten involved," I continued. "Now you guys are going to be targets, too."

"Bullshit," Harrick replied bluntly. "We live here, too. Who else was going to step in?"

"We've got a genuine quarrel with these guys," I said. "I already sent Van Williamson and his little 'Constitutional Defense Force' packing over this."

"And we don't?" Harrick snapped. "These little bastards have driven their armored vehicles around with abandon, scared and scattered our cows with their damned drones, and landed a helicopter in my damned hay field without bothering to ask. They've got Brett all but a prisoner in his own home, and they've been interfering with the local law every chance they get. I think we've got plenty of quarrel with 'em."

He squinted at me. "And I'll thank you not to lump the rest of us in with that limp-wristed little poser, Williamson."

"The lower profile we can keep this, the better for everybody," I protested. "We can handle this."

His gaze hardened still further. "Bullshit," he said again. "If you could handle it, you wouldn't be hiding out in the Beartooths while those jackasses are squatting in your house. As for keeping a low profile, I know more than one reason as to *why* you sent Williamson packing, and I agree. A few of us have been some of the same places you have, and we don't want that shit here, either." He looked like he wanted to spit, but there was no place to do it but the floor. "But there's only so far you can let yourself be backed up against the wall, and I'm pretty sure you know that as well as I do."

When I raised an eyebrow at how thorough his apparent understanding of the situation was, he grinned humorlessly.

"And if you're surprised that I know so much about what's going on, the day something happens in this county and I *don't* know about it, that's when you need to start worrying. That'll be the day I start to die."

I couldn't argue with him. Running off a poser ideologue with guns like Van Williamson was one thing. Dave Harrick had seen the elephant, quite possibly in a worse way than I had. Most of the stories I'd heard were second- or third-hand; he rarely talked about it. But I'd heard enough to know that he knew the cost of what he was embarking on.

"Hell, if we do this the way I'd like to," he continued, "they'll never know we were involved. They'll blame you for all of it. We're all hunters, after all, and a deer's a lot harder to sneak up on than a man." The faint echo of a smile under that snowy mustache faded. "Face it, Jeff, this *is* our fight. It became our fight when they attacked our neighbors and locked up our sheriff. We can do what we can to keep it from escalating, though from what I'm hearing it may be too late for that. But we've got no other recourse but to fight, now, and you're in no position to do it alone."

I looked to my left and right. Larry shrugged. Eric was nodding. Jack was stony-faced. Nick gave me a look that told me he thought that I was an idiot if I didn't take Harrick up on his offer. Bryan echoed Larry and shrugged. It was in my court.

Technically, I probably should have taken it up with Eddie, Tom, and Tim. But I was the man on the spot, and, frankly, Old Man Harrick was right. Turning down and running off a bunch of loose cannons who didn't know or care the consequences of their actions was one thing. These guys were different.

Grimly, I nodded my surrender and held out my hand. Harrick shook it, his rock-hard palm and crushing grip promising that I'd made the right decision.

I still wasn't entirely sure, but the decision was made. Whether I liked it or not, the Beartooth Mountain War was about to enter another phase.

CHAPTER 17

Our first move wasn't against the Task Force itself, not as such. While Tim's team, accompanied by Dennis and a few other local sharpshooters, stayed on overwatch above The Ranch, taking the occasional pot-shot when the opportunity presented itself and keeping an increasingly nervous and wary eye out for Baumgartner, the rest of us piled into several of the ranchers' trucks and headed south, for Cody.

* * *

Even professionals get complacent, if things stay quiet long enough. Baumgartner might be a different matter; the guy was, at least by reputation, barely human, and he worried me. But these guys weren't Baumgartner, and nothing had happened near Cody since the IED blast and the exodus of Van Williamson's Threepers.

So, I wasn't too worried about getting made as we closed in on the two Expeditions that were still stationed outside Brett's house. Cody was quiet and they had no reason to expect us, especially not when their buddies up north at The Ranch were taking fire every so often. They figured we were still running in the hills, soon to be hunted down by Baumgartner.

It helped that Jason O'Reilly, his brother Doug, who was barely eighteen and looked like a fresh-faced kid to me, and their girlfriends, Katie and Sami, were doing the initial approach. I'd been against letting them do it to begin with, especially given how young Doug and Sami were, but Tom O'Reilly had stood firm, saying that he'd trained them himself, all four of them knew how to use guns, and they had to see their first action eventually. I still wasn't convinced, but I was sitting in the truck behind them, along with Larry, Bryan, and Nick, ready to bring my rifle over the dash and ventilate the shit out of the clowns in the Expedition at the drop of a hat if things went south.

Hell, I was worried enough about the kids that I was ready to drop the hat myself.

They were walking down the sidewalk, the boys with their arms around the girls, laughing and carrying on like a handful of kids just coming from a party. It was late on a Saturday night, so it was entirely plausible.

As they came abreast of the first Expedition, Jason and Katie stopped and started making out. Doug and Sami laughed and kept going, up until they came alongside the second vehicle.

153

I was impressed. We'd drilled them continuously for hours, rehearsing every step of the approach and the first contact, most of us uncomfortable enough with letting them participate at all that we'd been nearly impossible to please the entire time. I was uncomfortably aware of how close they were in age and experience to Van Williamson, though I told myself that the ranchers were right. They could at least be trusted to do what they were told.

At the exact same time, Jason and Katie drew their pistols and held them to the window of the front Expedition, even as Doug and Sami did the same. I thought I saw a bit of a tremor in Sami's grip on her M&P; actually pointing a gun at another human being for the first time can be tough.

At that same instant, Larry reached down and flipped on the truck's high beams, while the rest of us piled out, rifles in hand.

The kids backed up as we moved in on the two vehicles, keeping their weapons pointed until we stepped in front of them to take over. Their part was done; we'd just needed them to get close enough without raising suspicions to immobilize the guards for the precious few moments it would take us to move in.

Neither of the Expeditions were armored; they were regular soft-skinned vehicles. So when I reached for the door handle and found it locked, the guy behind the wheel staring at the muzzle of my SOCOM 16 through the window, I just gave him a brief look that suggested he was an idiot, smashed the window with said rifle muzzle, and told him, "Open the door."

Looking a little sheepish, keeping his hands in view, he did so. I stepped back, keeping my rifle trained on him, while Larry dragged him out, put him on his face on the ground, and dropped a knee into his back. I heard his breath go out with a groan; having Larry's two hundred seventy-five pounds, plus another fifty of gear and weapons, land on your back couldn't feel good. I could hear the grunts as Nick and Bryan did the same on the other side of the vehicle, dragging the passenger out and searching him before zip-tying his hands.

Ahead, Eddie, George, Eric, and Jack were doing the same thing with the other Expedition. I heard some scuffling and Jack snarled, shortly followed by a meaty *thud*, after which things went quiet again. "Anarchy" was living up to his reputation for belligerence again.

With the Task Force overwatch out of the picture, Larry, Eddie, and I headed for the front door. Old Man Harrick had told me that Brett was effectively a prisoner, but at the same time, I didn't want to chance that he was still armed. Busting in his front door in that case, whether we were there to break him out or not, would be a good way to get shot.

"Brett!" I called out. "It's Jeff Stone! We're coming in!"

The door swung open. Brett was standing there, fully dressed but unarmed. "I can look out the window, Jeff," he said calmly. "Which I did as soon as I heard breaking glass." He looked down at the prostrate, bound bodies of his guard detail. "Took you guys long enough. I was expecting something to happen shortly after that bomb went off."

"We've been busy," I said. "Have they got the rest of your boys and girls locked down, or just you?"

"I think they've got a detachment at the office," he said, "but I was essentially the hostage for the department's good behavior. I think they sent most of the rest home, after insisting they leave their weapons at the office."

I raised an eyebrow. "Somehow I doubt that had quite the effect they were expecting."

He chuckled humorlessly. "Oh, yeah. Miguel's got enough guns and ammo squirreled away in his garage to arm the entire department five times over. But they've been laying low because I told them to."

I nodded. It made sense. Regardless of how well-armed pretty much *everybody* up there was, one did not take on a group that was as well-equipped as the Task Force lightly. Guys with MP7s in thin-skinned vehicles was one thing. MATVs and those armored eight-wheelers were something else.

"So, what's the plan?" Brett asked, accepting the subgun that Eddie handed him.

"We do the same thing to the TF goons at the office that we did here, and get your people back in charge," I said. "Then we deal with the rest of them."

"We haven't got the firepower to do that," Brett said.

"Leave that to us," Eddie told him.

* * *

Having Brett with us made getting into the sheriff's office that much easier, as we were able to go in the back. The goons hadn't relieved him of his keys, which had been stupid on their part. The handful of Task Force shooters inside had to have seen us coming on the security cameras, but offered no resistance when we busted in on them. They were fairly relaxed, in fact. And I was pretty sure I knew why.

A few minutes after we'd secured the sheriff's department, while Brett was still busy calling the rest of his deputies in, my sat phone rang. When I answered it, Tim only said, "Five vics en route, departed three minutes ago." Then he hung up.

I shoved the phone back in its pouch. "Right on time," I said. I raised my voice. "Praetorians, out front! We've got incoming!" I turned to Tom O'Reilly, who had accompanied us with several of his own militia. "Can you guys hold this down while Brett gets his people back up to speed?"

He nodded. "No problem," he said. "These guys won't be giving us much trouble." Considering that the five Task Force shooters were now sitting on the floor, with their hands zip-tied behind their backs and three big, corn-

155

fed ranch hands with ARs watching them like hawks, I believed him. I clapped him on the shoulder and headed for the door.

We'd just killed two birds with one stone. We'd busted out the sheriff's department after these goons had usurped their place by force, and we'd baited the hook in the process. Now to set it.

***

We had to move fast, but we didn't have as far to go as our adversaries did. They had to drive clear down from The Ranch, while we'd already set up just north of Cody. We just had to get back in position and hook up the detonators.

The thing about prolonged wars is that both sides learn from each other. Sometimes, one side refuses to learn, whether because of inertia or arrogance, but even if institutional learning is stifled, there are always going to be guys in the ranks who take certain lessons away anyway. And we'd seen enough convoys ambushed from one side to have a pretty good idea of how to do it effectively.

I knew guys who hated the idea of IED ambushes. They equated them with jihadis and cowardice. I could certainly understand why; I'd been on the receiving end of a few IED blasts and coordinated, complex ambushes myself. There's something about being struck without warning, about the threat of being suddenly blown apart without ever seeing it coming, that is horrifying to the warrior, and ultimately fuels his frustration and hate. That was a large part of why My Lai happened; the pent-up frustration of getting hit over and over and over for days without ever seeing the enemy was let loose by a shitty leader.

But when it was boiled down and the emotions removed, an IED was only an expedient when you didn't have LAWs or AT-4s or RPGs. And we didn't have any better armor crackers on hand.

Lying flat on the hill overlooking the highway, I watched and waited. The terrain meant we wouldn't have a lot of warning, especially if they were moving as fast as I suspected they would be.

The night was deathly quiet out there. The lights of Cody glowed to the south, across the river. The wind whispered faintly through the grass, and, far off to the east, a pack of coyotes started yipping and howling. But everything else was still. It was almost four in the morning, and nobody was likely to be out and about. Some of the farmers and ranchers were probably getting up to feed their animals at that point, but the highway was empty.

Slowly, past the yipping of the 'yotes, I started to hear something else, a distant roar. At first it was little more than a murmur, but soon built to the growl of engines. Looking north, I couldn't see anything, but they were definitely coming.

156

They had to be driving blacked out. Even as far as sound carried in the night, I should have been able to see their headlights, or at least the glow from them. But the north was completely black.

Fortunately, there's no way to hide an armored vehicle from thermals. They were moving fast enough that I might have missed them in the dark, but my PSQ-20s picked up the brilliant thermal bloom of the lead MATV's engine from more than half a klick away as the five-vehicle convoy roared down the road toward Cody.

One MATV was rolling as the point vehicle, with another one taking up the rear and three of the eight-wheelers in between. They had to be doing sixty miles an hour, which is pretty damned speedy for an armored vehicle. I'd have to time this very, very carefully.

The guardrail on the side of the road that led off the bridge did an excellent job of concealing the shaped charge that we'd set there. As the MATV hit the south end of the bridge, I triggered the IED. The vehicle briefly disappeared in a flash and a cloud of smoke and dust, as a tooth-rattling *boom* rolled across the hills.

We'd always been good at using the resources at hand; most of us had been fighting in Third World shitholes and making do with what we could scrounge, buy, or steal for quite some time. Logan's 20mms were somewhat emblematic of our way of doing things.

But since getting forced off The Ranch and into the mountains, our resources had been rather sharply limited. So, when the local ranchers had joined the fight, it had been like Christmas.

Working with ranchers and farmers means access to all sorts of useful chemicals and scrap metal. Some of those chemicals had just ignited and propelled a molten cone of scrap metal at *extremely* high velocity at the side of the MATV.

Barely seconds behind my own charge, a second detonation echoed it at the rear of the convoy, hitting the second MATV with another explosively formed projectile.

The twin clouds of dust, smoke, and flying rocks slowly settled out, revealing the wrecks of the lead and trail vehicles, both slewed across the road and mostly blocking the bridge on either end. The resolution on my PSQ-20s wasn't great, but I could still see the hole in the lead vehicle's door, glowing faintly on thermals, where the EFP had punched through the armor. The vehicle was still running, but the cab was smoking, and there was no movement from within. It wasn't going to be pretty in there.

The convoy was halted, boxed in by terrain on either side and destroyed vehicles at point and rear. One of the eight-wheelers started to move forward, as if to try to shove the MATV out of the way and get out of the kill zone, even as the CROWS turret on top began to scan the surrounding hills.

We were under blankets to help shield our thermal signatures, and peering between rocks close enough together that we'd present one hell of a small target. None of us were interested in repeating the mistakes of over-eager jihadis who'd wanted a good view for their YouTube propaganda videos.

I hunkered down and brought the captured radio we'd taken from the shooters at the sheriff's office to my lips. There was a better than good chance that they'd changed their crypto after we'd captured their people, but on the off chance that it was still good, I keyed the mic.

"Attention, you in the eight-wheelers," I called. I didn't have callsigns, and frankly I didn't give a shit what kind of cool-guy douchebag callsigns they'd given themselves anyway. "I wouldn't try to keep pushing if I were you; you presently have a string of daisy-chained EFPs on either side. We only haven't set them off because I'm not actually all that interested in killing you all."

There was a long pause, while I waited to see if they'd even heard me. Apparently, they hadn't bothered to change crypto, because I got an answer.

"Who the hell is this?" a frustrated voice demanded.

"I'm the guy with his hand on the detonator that is going to turn the rest of you into charred meat if you don't do exactly what the hell I tell you to," I replied. "I'm giving you a chance to live. Do I need to just go ahead and say, 'fuck it' and get you out of my way permanently?"

There was another pause. "What do you want?" he asked.

"I want everyone out of the vehicles with gear off and hands on heads," I told him. "If I see a weapon, you all die. If I see one of those turrets move a millimeter, you all die. If you're not out of the vics and on your knees on the road in five minutes, starting *right now*, you all die. Am I clear?"

"How do I know you're not bluffing?" he asked. He was reaching. I can't say I blamed him; no shooter ever wants to find himself in that situation. He was utterly helpless and being forced to surrender. "Surrender" had become a curse—even more so than it had been before—after Daniel Pearl had gotten his head sawed off on the Internet, and that had kind of gotten hardwired into every gunfighter who ever set foot in the sandbox since.

"Well, if the two wrecked vehicles to your twelve and six o'clock aren't enough," I said, "by all means, try me. Run the clock out. Which, by the way, is ticking while we're speaking."

He didn't reply. But after another two minutes and twenty seconds, by my watch, the rear hatch on the lead eight-wheeler opened, and figures started to shuffle out, bent over to get through the hatch, their hands on their heads.

Slowly, the other two vehicles emptied, as well. I kept one eye on them, and the other eye on my watch, my hand on the detonator.

I hadn't been bluffing. The trouble with threats is that you've got to *mean* them. If they dawdled a second past that five-minute mark, I was going

158

to blow them all to hell. It would suck; a lot of guys who had surrendered would get shredded in the process, and I'd have more blood on my hands. But we were in no position to give them an inch. We were being more than magnanimous in trying to take them alive, rather than just blasting them to kingdom come. With the disparity of forces we had, that was as merciful as we could afford to be. Let them think that they could push, and they would. And then we'd be fucked.

At four minutes and ten seconds, the radio crackled to life again. I could see the figure holding the radio below. He was scanning the hills, looking for likely covered positions, trying to spot us.

"All right, everybody's out," he said. "Now what?"

"Turn south and start walking," I told him.

"Say again?" he asked. I didn't think he'd been expecting that.

"I didn't stutter," I told him. "Start walking toward Cody. And you might want to step it out. I'm going to blow your vehicles in place in another five minutes."

"Wait a minute…" he started to say.

"You're not in a position to argue right now," I told him. "Look down in front of you, at the guardrail." When he did, I saw him visibly flinch. He was standing only a few feet from another of the IEDs we'd emplaced. "If, by some chance, you kept gunners in the vehicles, hoping that we'd expose ourselves, you might want to get them out, now. Of course, that would mean that I'll have to kill you all, since you're past the five-minute mark, and I did say that I'd touch off the daisy chain if you weren't all out by then."

While he was too far away to tell for sure, I had the sudden impression that he swallowed, hard. But when he replied, he only said, "No, everyone's out. We'll start moving."

"Time's flying," was all I said in reply.

They got the message. In a few moments, the entire line of twenty-four men was moving down the highway at a pretty brisk pace.

No one had exited either MATV. A few heads turned to look at the smoking lead vehicle as they passed, but none of them stopped to try to get anyone out. I suspected that those guys were dead; it had been a solid hit, and I knew something of what an EFP does to the inside of a vehicle.

War is hell.

Right at the five-minute mark, I hit the detonator, as promised. The bridge briefly disappeared in a string of strobing flashes and a billowing black cloud. The overpressure hammered the hills and knocked grit into our faces where we were lying on the hill above, over eight hundred meters away. We'd used "P for Plenty" on those charges; we were not taking chances on the vehicles shrugging them off.

The idea of capturing them and using them to assault The Ranch had been brought up. It had its appeal, but I'd ultimately rejected it. There were too many ways in which trying to capture them from an ambush could go wrong, including all sorts of nasty surprises left inside that I could think of. I also wasn't entirely convinced that the CROWS couldn't still be operated remotely, even from outside the vehicle. I knew a couple guys who were working on such systems, that could control a turret from a smartphone. There was no way in hell I was going to go down there only to have somebody a few klicks away turn one of those turrets around and cut me in half.

The dust began to clear, though smoke was now billowing up from fiercely burning vehicles. The light of the fires was starting to illuminate the hills to either side of the road.

Five more of the enemy's vehicles were now out of the fight.

***

We pulled off the ambush site and started hoofing it for the rendezvous. Two long-bed F350 duallies were waiting for us; TJ was driving one of them, and another guy I didn't recognize had the second. They'd been waiting since they'd dropped us off an hour before.

"Head back down to the highway," I told TJ as I got in the passenger seat. He just nodded and started the truck trundling down the dirt track toward the road. His AR was shoved between his right leg and the center console.

Given his reputation for trouble, I hadn't known what to make of TJ. But he'd been as professional as any of us so far, and I thought I was starting to get a handle on what made him tick.

TJ was one of those guys who'd gotten out of the military and felt lost. He might not have ever been the best Marine, especially if he got out after only four years, but those four years can shape a man more than he knows. I suspected that a lot of the trouble TJ had gotten into was because he'd seen combat and never felt as alive after that.

Now that he was back in the fight, *any* fight, he was himself again. I saw it in the way he held himself, the way his eyes kept moving, the way he was ready and eager to be a part of it. It was encouraging and a little sad at the same time, that it had taken this kind of shitstorm to break him out of whatever rut he'd gotten himself into.

We came out onto the side of the highway at the same time that two big panel trucks came up from the south. The line of disarmed Task Force goons was just coming abreast of us; they'd stepped up their pace when those IEDs went off.

"Hold here," I told TJ, and piled out, while the rest of the team jumped out of the truck bed. We lifted our rifles to cover the approaching men, and waited for them to come to us.

While we were better armed, we were still outnumbered, even with the good old boys in the trucks coming up the highway. This would have to be handled carefully.

"That's far enough," I bellowed. They slowed to a stop, the slinky effect making them bunch up a bit on the side of the road. In one way, that was good for us. A smaller cone of fire could take out more of them more quickly. "Get down on the ground with your hands on your heads, fingers interlaced."

There was some hesitation and a little milling around. I lifted my rifle and flicked on the tac light. "You've got five seconds before we start shooting!" I snarled. That got them moving, and in a few moments, they were all down on the ground as instructed.

It took a while to get them individually searched, zip-tied, and thrown in the back of the panel trucks, but by the time the eastern sky was starting to lighten, we were heading back into Cody. I'd already called ahead; Brett would have cells for all of them.

CHAPTER 18

We had to move fast. We'd just taken a huge chunk of the Task Force out of action, but there was still a good-sized force sitting on The Ranch, and I was sure they were yelling for help. If we were going to kick those assholes out of our home and be ready for the next counterattack, we couldn't afford to dawdle.

"It's going to be one beast of a hump," I said, pointing to the map, "but this is going to be the best support-by-fire position. That's where I want your guys." Harrick and O'Reilly nodded; we'd already established that the locals were going to stay off the X as much as possible. The assault would be entirely Praetorian shooters; I wanted the militia to stay in the wings.

It didn't mean they'd be out of harm's way. Baumgartner was presumably still up in the mountains somewhere.

Somewhere along the line, we were going to have to deal with him. That was going to be a nightmare; I knew enough about the man to be sure of that.

I'd grilled the convoy commander, a former FBI HRT shooter named Potter, about what the rest of the Task Force still up north was likely to do. He hadn't been nearly as forthcoming as Gage, but I had gathered that losing thirty guys and five vehicles would be one hell of a shock. We'd already been a lot harder nut to crack than they'd expected, and now we'd cut their effective strength in half.

He was worried, too. That much I could see from his answers and his demeanor. There was more going on than I knew about, and while I couldn't say for sure—and he sure as hell wouldn't—I got the distinct impression that he was worried that reinforcements might *not* be coming.

Even so, I couldn't afford to assume that. We had to hurry and take the rest of them out of action before they got relieved.

It could be that the whole thing was futile. I still didn't know who exactly was behind this bunch, but their resources were considerable. We could win in the next twenty-four hours only to be overwhelmed by tanks and helicopters in a week. But like Old Man Harrick, it wasn't in me to just lie down and give up.

"Watch your rear security," I reiterated. "We know they still have manhunters in the hills, and I don't want you guys getting hit from behind and wiped out because everyone was focused on the target area." I was sure I especially didn't have to tell Dave Harrick that, but some things you say in a brief just to make damned good and sure that they don't get forgotten.

"This is going to be a daylight op, which is less than ideal," I continued, "but under the circumstances I don't think we can afford to wait until dark. So, we're going to have to move fast, then get slow and sneaky, then move fast again." I made eye contact with both Old Man Harrick and O'Reilly. "You guys are going to have the longest and hardest movement, but once you're in position, make sure you wait for the signal before opening fire. We can't afford to fuck this up."

There were more nods all around. Harrick's platoon of militia would link up with the rest of the Praetorians who were still in the mountains, the RV point having been sent by code during one of the extremely brief sat phone conversations I'd had with Tom. We still couldn't be entirely certain that somebody wasn't listening in. The bulk of the armed country boys and ranchers were staying in Cody, helping Brett prepare for a possible counterattack there. My team and Eddie's were going to be the main effort, going in to clear The Ranch.

With the last of the questions out of the way, we mounted up in the motley collection of ranch trucks and offroad 4x4s and headed north.

***

As important as speed, surprise, and violence of action are to any combat action, they are always preceded by slow, painstaking, methodical preparation. Or, in this case, slow, painful, careful movement.

The south OP was our first target, and we had to get close enough without being spotted to take it and clear it before the rest of the TF back at the main Ranch buildings knew anything was up.

That was always a tall order, even when the targets were booger-eaters in mud huts. When they were well-trained, well-equipped, and using state-of-the-art comms, it got next to impossible.

Which only meant that we had to find their weakness and exploit it. And the primary weakness of any technological force is that it tends to think that its technology makes it invincible.

Now, we'd deliberately sited that OP to minimize the amount of dead space where someone could sneak up on it. That presented its own set of problems; we were effectively trying to penetrate our own security. So, when you can't use cover and concealment to their full advantage, you've got to rely on misdirection and deceit.

That was why Eddie had feinted an attack at the North Gate, pulling a glorified drive-by before retreating across the creek and toward Old Man Harrick's hay field. Then, about fifteen minutes later, he'd brought the gate under fire with long-range rifles. It wasn't enough to do much damage, but it was enough to make them, hopefully, think that any attack was coming from the north, and that it would only consist of the usual harassing fire that Tim had been dealing out for the last couple of days.

Meanwhile, Jack, Bryan, and I were creeping on our bellies through the grass and brush, heads to the ground, skull-dragging our way inch by inch toward the OP. It was going to take us a couple of hours to cross the five hundred meters from where we'd crawled around the shoulder of the mountain to the OP. But impatience *was* going to get us killed.

It had already been one hell of a grueling movement. We'd driven up to the Harrick Ranch, then taken horses up over the mountain until we were at our final rally point, just behind the pyramidal peak that rose above the back of The Ranch itself. There we'd dismounted, cammied up, and started down.

We'd only covered a little over a mile since leaving the horses behind, but it had been a brutal mile, the first klick being downhill over rocky ground, trying to stay in the trees, though we could still catch glimpses of the OP in the distance. It was a truism that if you can see the enemy, the enemy can see you, provided he's looking. I was sincerely hoping that they weren't looking that far.

The last half a klick made the downhill hike seem like a nature walk. We had gotten down onto more open ground, where the trees and bushes were lower and farther apart, and we had to move slowly and carefully, crawling on hands and knees much of the time, which was murder on knees already battered by years of soldiering.

Across the last five hundred yards, we had to get down on our bellies and inch along, careful to watch the OP—which was well camouflaged, rather like a sandbagged, fortified deer blind—without looking directly at it. While it might seem like woo to some people, the fact is that a man can often sense a stalker watching him. So, we were careful not to stare directly at a target if we could avoid it.

Right at the moment, I was lying flat behind a low scrub spruce, sweating my ass off, feeling every single minute I'd been awake for the last forty-eight hours, along with every bruise and contusion where I'd dragged my body across the rocks and brush. Keeping my scope's objective lens shadowed inside the tree, I scanned the OP.

There was no movement. The OP looked completely undisturbed. I had the captured radio still stuffed in my belt, and had been intermittently turning it on, the volume turned up just enough that I could hear it when pressed to my ear, but either they weren't talking, or they'd smartened up and changed crypto. There was no traffic.

So far, there had been at least three times where if we'd been made, I might have expected some kind of reaction. Hell, from where we were lying, we could actually see the corner of the main ranch house; if we'd been spotted, we should have been able to see the QRF coming after us. But everything was still and quiet; even Eddie had given up shooting at the North Gate. Too much, and they might start to suspect that there was something more than harassing fire afoot.

I suddenly wondered if we were too late. What if the Task Force had mobilized and headed for Cody while we'd been working our way around to come at them sideways? What if we'd passed them going south as we'd come back north?

If that was the case, then Brett, his deputies, and the militia would have to do their damnedest to hold their own until we could regroup and go support them. Second-guessing the plan at this point was counterproductive and stood a good chance of getting us all killed. I *had* to presume that that OP was occupied, and that if we didn't approach it with every bit of care we could, we'd get shot full of holes and the alarm would be raised.

So, I stifled my impatience, buried my doubts and worries as deep as they would go, slung my rifle back over my shoulder and partway under my borrowed ghillie, positioning it so that the muzzle was up out of the dirt, and recommenced my crawl.

The closer we got, the more careful we had to be. Inch by inch, we crept through the grass, trying not to breathe too deeply, trying not to make the grass move too much ahead of us. We were keeping as many low bushes and junipers between us and the OP as possible, but that hillside was just open.

I hadn't thought of it before, but I suddenly imagined putting my hand out and hearing the telltale *buzz* of a rattler. We didn't see too many of them that high, but they were around. That would be a bad day.

But I didn't put my hand on a rattlesnake, and we got closer and closer without any sign that we'd been detected.

Finally, we were lying flat on the ground, guns up, facing the rear of the OP, which was, at least from a distance, just another grassy mound with a couple of bushes around it. Only when you got up close could you see the firing slits and the slot of an entrance on the north side.

The hillside remained quiet and still; I saw no movement, and no sound reached my ears but the wind in the grass. If there was anyone in there, they were keeping really quiet.

Just as vividly as I'd previously pictured the nonexistent rattler, I had the sudden thought that there could well be a shooter in there right at that moment, hunkered back at the corner, with his SCAR 16 pointed at the entrance, waiting. This could get really dicey, really quick.

The three of us came abreast in a short skirmish line, then carefully and quietly rose from the grass, first coming to a knee, then to a forward-leaning crouch as we rushed the OP behind our rifles.

I slowed at the entrance, carefully pieing off the opening, hoping to nail anyone inside before making entry. But the "fatal funnel" was empty, the interior dark.

Here goes nothing, I thought, and plunged inside.

There wasn't a lot of room inside the OP to hide, but that also meant that there wasn't a lot of room to maneuver once I made entry. If there was somebody crouched in the corner, I was about to get shot, get in a hand-to-hand scuffle, or both.

There was nobody in the corner that I turned to cover. Nor was I shot in the back or knocked over by somebody trying to fight Jack behind me.

The OP was empty. Either they'd cleared out, or they hadn't occupied it at all.

While it was conceivably possible, I found the idea that they'd left their entire southern flank open unlikely. Which meant they'd cleared out. Which, in turn, meant that we had to move. Things were moving without us.

Looking at my two teammates, I got nods. I had to risk it. I pulled my cell out of my rig and sent a short message.

"Move on the house. Now."

***

In an ideal world, that message would have been immediately followed by the other team and a half roaring overhead in Little Birds, swooping in on the ranch house in a hail of gunfire, with *Ride of the Valkyries* blaring on loudspeakers.

While I was sure *somebody* had *Ride of the Valkyries* on an MP3 player somewhere, we were notably lacking in Little Birds, or air assets of any kind.

The three of us still had about a klick to go, over terrain that was anything but flat, so "Now" was going to be a bit negotiable. Especially when we were the vanguard; the rest of the assault force was a terrain feature to the south, waiting for us to clear the OP.

We still had some forest to move through, which would provide some concealment, but speed was now our primary concern. Fortunately, while Jack, Bryan, and I had crept our way to our objective on foot and belly, the rest of the assault force was a little better equipped to make tracks.

In moments, the snarl of engines started to become audible, and then a rag-tag collection of four-wheelers, RZRs, and dirtbikes came over the hill.

Two of the RZRs pulled up next to the OP, and we piled on, careful to keep our muzzles pointed at the dirt. Then it was off to the races.

In a few short moments, we had rolled down the slope and into the trees. Fortunately, the woods were mostly high country pine, the trees spaced out so that we could fit an ATV between them easily in most places. We still had to slow down, as there was no riding in a straight line through those woods, and while we'd pulled a lot of the fallen stuff out for construction and firewood over the last few years, there are always logs and fallen trees on a forest floor, and they make going hard for wheeled vehicles, even offroaders.

I was gripped by a formless sense of urgency. I couldn't escape the feeling that we had to hurry, that if we didn't get close fast, they were going to be ready and waiting for us, poised to mow us down as we came out of the trees. In truth, we could only go as fast as the terrain and good tactics allowed. It just didn't feel fast enough.

In fact, there were still no indicators that they even had the faintest idea we were on The Ranch at all. The militia in their support by fire position should have opened fire if they thought we'd been made; it would have been less than ideal, but it would have given us advance warning and hopefully disrupted any defenses the Task Force had in place.

Since the only sound was the growl of our own engines under the trees, I had to assume that either they'd cleared out, or they hadn't shown the militia enough preparations to make them think we were about to roll into an ambush.

Of course, that was assuming that the militia could necessarily recognize such an ambush.

Sometimes being able to run through multiple contingencies in one's head, even while maintaining alertness and situational awareness, is more a curse than a blessing.

Fortunately, I didn't have long to woolgather over every way this could go wrong. Even weaving through the trees, we got to the assault position in short order, fortunately without running into any traps or security.

I was still thinking that there was no way they could have missed the noise the engines had been making as we got into a skirmish line and advanced toward the treeline and the house.

I dropped to a knee behind one of the last pines, and the rest did the same, spread out along the treeline and facing the barns and the back of the house.

The reason we'd gotten so close without, apparently, being detected became obvious after a moment. While the terrain and the trees had masked some of the noise, I could now hear the rumble of diesel engines out in front of the house. It sounded like all the remaining vehicles had been fired up.

I couldn't quite believe our luck. Unless I missed my guess, they were gearing up to head south, responding to our successful attacks in and around Cody.

They would never be more vulnerable, especially if they thought we were still in Cody.

That didn't mean we rushed in. I scanned the back yard and spotted a figure at one of the back windows of the house, watching the trees. He hadn't seen us yet, but they'd learned from the night we'd grabbed Gage. They were watching the back.

I made eye contact with Eddie, who was crouched a few meters away, and slowly and carefully signaled to him that I saw one sentry. He nodded ever so slightly and signaled that the part of the house he could see was clear. Then he motioned an interrogative.

I nodded. Time to kick this pig.

He pulled the radio from his rig and murmured a single word into it. A few seconds later, a storm of gunfire started from up the mountain, peppering the northwest corner of the house with bullets.

At the same time, I smoothly brought my rifle to my shoulder and centered the scope on the back window.

The guy on rear security had suddenly leaned closer to the window, trying to look up the mountain to spot where the fire was coming from. He just made my job easier. I let out my breath, took up the slack on the trigger, and squeezed.

The heavy rifle surged back into my shoulder and the suppressor spat, the report of the shot drowned out by the roar of fire from above. The window glass spiderwebbed around the single, neat hole that formed right below the man's eye. He suddenly dropped out of sight.

It was about a fifty-yard sprint to the back wall of the house. It felt like a lot longer to my tired, battered carcass, and I was sure the rest were hurting just about as bad. The biggest danger right then was that we'd do something stupid out of sheer exhaustion.

Of course, the packs full of explosives and incendiaries we were hauling didn't make matters any easier.

While Eddie and his team set security on the windows and corners, the rest of us unslung the packs and stacked them strategically around the back door, under the windows, and where they'd do the most damage to the structure, particularly the incendiaries. A couple more packs got set around the corners, even as return fire from the front and the north side started to respond to the shooting from the mountain. It seemed like most of them were out front, loading the vehicles.

Once the charges were set and primed, we turned and beat feet back toward the treeline. As we neared the barn closest to the house, though, a shot snapped past my head from behind.

I spun, dropping to my belly, bringing my rifle up, even as three more shots *crack*ed by overhead, right where my head and torso had been a second before.

I hit hard, mags digging into my ribs, but better to have a little wind knocked out of you than to get shot. I returned fire as soon as I got my sights somewhere in the vicinity of the window, though Eddie had started shooting before I'd dropped. The window shattered the rest of the way, and the shooting stopped.

Picking myself up off the ground, trying not to groan with the effort, I turned and ran for the barn, where Eric and Bryan had already set up, covering the back of the house. It felt like a lot farther to run when my back was to the house than it had running toward it.

I hit a small hillock just beyond the barn and threw myself down behind it, covering the house while I bellowed at Eric and Bryan, "Turn and go!" They spun and ran past me, even as I spotted another head in the window, trying to see without exposing much more than an eye and a rifle barrel. I cranked four fast shots through the window, and the eye vanished.

In two more bounds, we were back in the trees. A storm of shots rained down on the back of the house from up the mountain, where the secondary support by fire position had been waiting for us to fall back. That should keep them bottled up in the house for a bit.

I got on my own radio. "Rancher Four, this is Hillbilly," I called. "Have you got the front covered, as well?"

"Not all of it," was the reply. "They can get into one of those vehicles without us being able to hit them."

Not ideal, but I said, "It'll have to do. All right. Cease fire."

"Roger." A moment later, an eerie quiet settled over The Ranch, seeming deafeningly silent after all the gunfire.

I didn't want to give them time to figure out what had just happened. I stuffed the radio back in its pouch and pulled out a burner phone.

We still had a landline in the house, though it was almost never used. That was the number I had set in speed dial.

It rang a few times before a voice answered. "Who the hell is this?"

"I think you know who it is, asshole," I told him. "I'm calling to give you the same offer I made Potter. Bring all of your people out, unarmed, with your hands on your heads, or I blow the house up." I didn't let him answer right away, but plunged on. "If you've got any doubts that I'd happily burn down my own house to get you fuckers out of it, carefully take a look out the back windows. But don't try coming out the door. I've got enough boom-boom stacked back there to turn anybody who tries into pink mist, while bringing the whole roof down on the lot of you."

He probably put his hand over the handset, but I could still hear him yell at somebody in the back to check out the windows and look toward the door. I waited, then heard him start cursing. "How do I know you're not bluffing?" he demanded.

These guys were starting to sound like a broken record. "Potter asked the same question," I told him. "His vehicles are now smoking scrap metal. Like I told him, though, by all means, try me. I won't object to turning all of you into grease spots."

There was another pause, and I could hear muted arguing in the background. They didn't like it any better than Potter and his bunch had, but they had to know that I'd at least stopped the convoy. They wouldn't have been saddling up to head for Cody otherwise.

The arguing died down, but the guy on the other end of the phone still didn't say anything. Then a single shot rang out from up the mountain.

"You motherfucker," the guy snarled into the phone.

170

"You didn't really think I was going to give you assholes an easy way out, did you?" I asked. I knew what had just happened, even if I hadn't seen it. One of them had tried to make a run for one of the vehicles that the militia had covered, and had caught a bullet for it. "You must be dumber than I thought. Now, are we done fucking around? Are you going to come out quietly and surrender, or am I going to burn you down?"

He started cussing me out, but I cut him off. "Listen, asshole, if you think I'm fucking around, I can touch those charges off now. I can always rebuild my house." Granted, it wasn't *my* house; that was farther out, back in the trees. "Your situation would be something more like Humpty Dumpty, only with a lot more pieces." I paused for a second. "You've got two minutes. Then I push the button." I ended the call.

After about forty-five seconds, I was starting to think they were going to make me do it. But then the radio crackled. "I've got movement out front."

My hand was hovering over the button that was going to set off the charges. But the militiaman on the far end of the radio continued. "They're coming out. I don't see any weapons, and their hands are on their heads." He sounded relieved. So was I.

Once he confirmed that there were thirty-two men kneeling on the grass out front, their hands on their heads, we got up and flowed out of the trees, heading back to the house.

***

We kept them waiting as we swept the house, carefully clearing each room. Once confident that everyone was out, we pushed out and started processing our prisoners, though not before equally carefully confirming that all of the remaining vehicles were similarly empty.

We'd just gotten the last of them zip-tied when a distant growl caught my ear. Looking up, I scanned the horizon. After a moment, I spotted four helicopters flying at treetop level, coming in from the east. They were heading for The Ranch, and they were coming fast.

CHAPTER 19

"Friends of yours?" I asked the acting TF commander. He was kneeling only a few feet away, his hands zip-tied behind his back.

"Fuck you," was all he said.

"Well, that's just downright unfriendly," Nick said wryly.

I took a second to squint at the incoming helos, trying to get my tired brain to work right. I could think of three possibilities. Either the birds were carrying reinforcements that had been called in once we'd attacked The Ranch, they were carrying reinforcements that had been called for earlier, and didn't know we'd hit The Ranch yet, or they were somebody else who was coming for the Task Force, and likely didn't know we'd taken them down.

Either the first or third possibilities had some serious potential for disaster. I turned and raised my voice.

"Somebody get on those CROWS," I snapped, "but don't move the turrets until I give the word. I don't want them knowing what's happened." I pointed to the rest. "Everybody else, get inside."

"What about them?" Eric asked, jerking a thumb at our captives.

"Fuck 'em," I said. "If their buddies burn 'em down, oh well. They probably should have stayed home and minded their own damned business."

In short order, we had the vehicles manned and everyone else inside the house, covering the doors and windows, minus the zip-tied Task Force goons, who were still on their knees in the dirt. Jack had made ominous noises about burning the prisoners down if they tried running, and we had a clear shot at all of them from the front windows of the house. But I don't think any of us would have actually done it. After all, where the hell were they going to go, in the middle of rural Wyoming, with their hands behind their backs?

We didn't have a moment to spare before the four helos were swooping in, their side doors open and machine-gunners covering the buildings. They flared fast and hard, shooters spilling from the far sides and fanning out as soon as they settled to the ground, coming around the noses of the Sikorsky S-61s with their rifles up.

Peering through my scope, I focused on the lead shooter coming from the northernmost helo. I frowned as I recognized him. I wasn't sure what to think.

We'd worked with Joe Ventner twice before, both times under the auspices of Renton's Cicero Group. He'd backed us up in Baghdad, and then moved in to backstop our ops in Mexico once we really started wreaking havoc on the *Los Hijos de la Muerte* cartel and their various backers. Joe had a well-deserved rep as a straight shooter, a man who backed up his boys and generally didn't give a shit about political niceties.

But he was still a soldier for hire, and, as exhausted and paranoid as I was, I couldn't be sure that he hadn't been hired by our enemies to back up the Task Force.

The shooters slowed, carefully approaching the house and the armored vehicles. I saw several of them were carrying LAWs; Joe had ways of procuring and caching weaponry that we tended to improvise, at least Stateside.

That told me that they'd come ready to deal with the armored vehicles, but if they'd been called in by the TF and warned that we'd neutralized them, the anti-armor weapons might still be a contingency in case we'd captured those same vehicles.

I suddenly became aware of a buzzing in my chest rig. It took some fumbling to pick it out, but after a moment I realized it was the "Renton phone."

"I'm assuming that you're in the house and/or the vehicles right now," Renton said as soon as I answered. "Please do not shoot Joe or the helicopters."

I let out a deep breath. "We need to work on that whole, 'telling me what the fuck is going on' thing," I told him.

"Likewise," he replied dryly. "I thought you were still down in Cody."

"So did they," I answered. "Tell Joe I'm coming out."

***

When I came off the porch, Joe Ventner had let his rifle hang and was walking toward me, a wry grin on his face.

We shook hands and he clapped me on the shoulder. "That was close," he commented.

"Too close for comfort," I replied. "That would have been one hell of a note to end this on. 'Contractors on the same side murder each other in blue-on-blue frenzy after their targets are already neutralized.'"

"One set of targets, anyway," he said quietly, turning toward one of the helos.

I followed his gaze, to see Renton getting off another of the green-painted S-61s, followed by another figure, who was also vaguely familiar. After a moment, I realized who it was.

"Holy shit." I had never met General Carl Stahl in person, though I'd served under his overall command in Libya. But I knew the man on sight. Anyone who'd been a Marine within the last twenty years knew General Stahl.

A barrel-chested fireplug of a man, he had been the very image of a Marine leader, with a pugnacious, bulldog face that looked like Chesty Puller had been reborn blond. He was a cigar-chomping, foul-mouthed, hard-fisted leader of the old school, who probably would have been forced out years before he ever got stars if it hadn't been for mentors in high places. He loved his Marines, and he loved to fight.

That had finally gotten him in trouble in Libya. I'd been halfway across the country at the time, and hadn't heard any details about what had actually happened, but some of his Marines had gotten drawn into an ambush near Tripoli, and he'd jumped in with the QRF to go get them out. In many ways, he was a lot like Tom.

He'd gotten his Marines out, mostly in one piece, but at the end of the day, dozens of photos of dead women, kids, and unarmed men had surfaced in the aftermath. We'd all suspected that they'd been human shields or simply posed photos; Libya had not exactly been suffering a shortage of dead bodies at the time. But it had been just the hammer that his political enemies back home had been looking for, and he was relieved of command and forced to retire.

He strode up the yard, pulling one of his signature cigars out of his pocket and jamming it between his teeth. He spared the kneeling prisoners an appraising glance before letting his eyes scan the parked armored vehicles, then he settled his deceptively mild gaze on me.

He stuck out his hand, and I shook it. His grip was as gorilla-strong as he looked.

"Good to meet you, Stone," he said around the cigar. "Renton's told me a lot about you. Including that you were down in Al-Jawf during the late unpleasantness."

"Yes, sir, I was," I answered. "Among other places. They moved us around a lot."

He nodded. "You guys were a hell of a useful asset," he said. "From what Renton tells me, you've honed your craft over the last few years." He ran another glance over our captives, who were now being moved toward the helos by Ventner's guys. "From the looks of things, he might have undersold you somewhat."

"As good as it is to meet you, sir," I said, "it's been one hell of a long few days, my guys are tired as shit, and we've still got a wounded man missing." I might respect him, but I didn't work for Stahl anymore, and I had responsibilities of my own that I wasn't going to drop to glad-hand with a retired general.

His eyes hardened. Not threateningly, but with that tough, "Marine Corps leader with important shit to do" look. "And I wouldn't dream of taking more of your time if it wasn't important," he said. He motioned toward the house. "We need to have a talk, and time is of the essence."

175

I glanced at Renton, who was standing just behind Stahl's shoulder. He nodded gravely. I shot him a brief glare that promised lots of pointy, profane words later, and then nodded, jerking my head toward the house.

"Tom should be on his way down from the hills soon," I said. "If this is that important, he should be a part of it."

Stahl just nodded. "Of course. We can wait for him. But as soon as he gets here, we've got a lot to discuss."

***

Tom looked rougher than I felt. He wasn't exactly a spring chicken anymore, and weeks of being hunted in the mountains had taken their toll. I was pretty sure he'd run out of cigarettes a while ago, too, and had just lit up his first in what had to be days. He was gaunter than I'd ever seen him, his icy blue eyes surrounded by deep, dark circles as he took a deep drag on the cigarette.

We were presently sitting around the living room of the house, which was still mostly littered with the remains of the Task Force's TOC. Stahl was standing; the rest of us—Tom, Eddie, Tim, Larry, and George—were sitting on the couch or the equipment cases they'd scattered around the room. I had grabbed one of the storm cases; if I sat on that couch I was going to pass the fuck out.

Stahl looked us over. "Well, gents," he said, "while I'm sorry it took so long to get some reinforcements up here, I need to assure you that it was not for lack of trying. There's just a hell of a lot going on elsewhere in the country, and the Group has been trying to put out fires. Trying, and failing, as the case may be."

He handed Tom the tablet that Renton had brought in. From where I was sitting, it looked like a news page. "I know Renton told you about the riots that started after the Pueblo bloodbath." I noted that he didn't call it *our* Pueblo bloodbath. "Well, over the last week it's gotten worse. Far worse.

"The riots have only intensified across the Southwest, and sympathetic 'demonstrations' in other major cities have started up. Since then, there have been several high-profile murders and assaults in Los Angeles, Chicago, St. Louis, Boston, Seattle, and New York. This wouldn't be all that interesting, except that every one of them has had a distinct political and/or racial bent, always carefully publicized and highlighted—whether the facts are true or not—to further inflame matters. As a result, the rioting has become far more vicious and far more widespread. To make matters worse, a few places have seen bombings aimed at the rioters, which have killed a few dozen and just escalated the violence.

"None of this is happening by accident, either," he continued grimly. "We don't know exactly what triggered this, but there have been several quiet assassinations happening under cover of the riots, apparently completely unconnected to them."

176

"All the unrest and rabble-rousing of the last ten years or so has been leading up to this," Renton put in. "I'm not saying that it's all been part of some master plan; nobody's *that* foresighted. But the population's been primed for this, through social media lynch mobs, twenty-four-hour outrage-of-the-minute news, and politicians cynically willing to exploit both to advance their own agendas. Now all it takes to trigger a riot is a few inflammatory photos or carefully edited video, spread across the right social networks, and hey-presto, you've got a city in flames."

"And as I know I don't need to tell you gentlemen," Stahl said, "that kind of chaos is a fucking playground for Direct Action."

"We think that 'Sulla' moved first," Renton said. "This kind of social engineering is more their style; 'Marius' tends to work more in the backroom deals, blackmail, and direct action ops impersonating law enforcement, like this Task Force. Plus, the first target taken out that we know of was a banker who's done a lot of deals on behalf of 'Marius' personalities."

"In the last five days, there have been two dozen murders of known associates of both factions," Stahl said heavily. "The Group has tried for years to try to contain this situation, but whatever sparked it, the factions are now engaged in open warfare, and risking a general civil war to conceal it."

"You're not just telling us this to bring us up to speed on current events," I said grimly, "any more than you brought Joe and his boys in to help us out from the goodness of your hearts." My own voice was a harsh croak in my ears. If I'd had a bit more sleep and hadn't been worried about where the hell Little Bob was, I might have been a little less blunt, but my Give-A-Fuck was busted. "You want us to get involved."

"You're already involved," Stahl said, just as bluntly. "You're on so many target lists it'd make your head spin, and both factions have just made concerted attempts to take you out of the picture. They may have failed this time, but you should know that they'll try again, and next time they'll be better prepared."

"Aren't they a little preoccupied with their own little war at the moment?" Eddie asked. "Why not let 'em kill each other, then send in Ventner's boys to clean up? We've just taken a hell of a beating, and we've still got a man missing."

"The longer this goes on, the harder it's going to be to bring things back from the brink," Renton said. "You don't understand; these factions have people at every level, every branch of government, multinational corporations, non-profits, you name it. On top of that, the unrest they're spreading could easily spiral out of control; they're playing with matches in a warehouse full of dynamite. It has to be stamped out now.

"As for Ventner, he's a good dude, and his boys are better than most, but they don't have the track record that you do. If we just wanted stuff smashed and people dead, I'd definitely go to him. But you gents have demonstrated a particular aptitude for going into chaotic situations, taking out targets, and disappearing without anyone knowing what the hell just happened. That's what we need now."

"Face facts, gentlemen," Stahl said. "This is now a matter of your own survival. Take out the factions, or they will eventually take you out. Working with us is in your best interest."

"And if we were to say no?" Tom asked coldly. "We'd be left in the cold, wouldn't we?"

Stahl met his gaze just as coldly. "It's a big job ahead of us, and our assets are limited," was all he said. But the message was pretty clear.

The air in the room got thick. None of us were at our peak, and when you hit that level of exhaustion, perceptions get a bit skewed. I think we were all taking Stahl's words as a threat, and no Praetorian ever took threats lightly or kindly. There was a lot of pent-up rage and violence in that room all of a sudden.

"Help us out, and we'll help you out," Renton said, his tone suggesting that he was trying to defuse the tension, at least a little. "Have you got *any* leads at all on where Sampson is?"

Angrily, grudgingly, we shook our heads. "We've got greater intel resources than you do," he continued. "We've got a better chance of finding him than you do on your own. And General Stahl's not wrong. Both factions have a vested interest in burying you, and if you think that their preoccupation with going after each other is going to make that go away, you're kidding yourselves.

"We're not trying to blackmail you," he continued earnestly, though he was met with stony, blank stares. "But we need your particular skillset and demonstrated proficiency at this sort of operation. And I'm not being melodramatic when I say that the fate of the country is at stake."

There was a long, tense silence. Finally, Tom broke it, his voice bitter. "Whether you intend to blackmail us or not, you seem to have us over a barrel," he said. "*If* what you're describing is the full truth, of course, we'd be remiss not to lend our assistance. But you understand if we're a little reticent about dealing much with your little network, given what happened to Stone's team in Mexico."

"The individuals responsible for that little fiasco have been...chastised," Stahl growled. He pointed to me. "Stone should be able to vouch for the fact that I look after my men, and I don't take that kind of double-dealing lightly, or kindly."

I had to nod. Stahl had an earned rep for taking care of his Marines, one that had had thousands of men publicly pronouncing after his dismissal that they'd follow him into Hell, damn the politicians who had forced him out.

"All right," Tom said finally, after making eye contact with all three of the team leaders. None of us were happy, but Stahl and Renton had made a pretty strong case. "We're in."

Stahl nodded. "Good. For what it's worth, I'm sorry we had to play hardball, but Renton's not kidding. There's too much at stake here for us to be able to afford to take 'no' for an answer." He shifted the cigar around to the other side of his mouth. "Take a few days, rest up, and get ready to move. We've got a lot of work to do."

***

We had more work than I think General Stahl had imagined. Our home base was in shambles, and, regardless of Renton's assurances that the Cicero Group was going to be looking for Little Bob, I had a few other contacts outside of the Group's network. After making sure Old Man Harrick's militia were on standby but no longer out in the woods, and that Ventner's boys were heading down to Cody to backstop Brett and his deputies, I headed to my little cabin and fired up my laptop. My internet connection was through several proxies that Derek had set up; nobody who might have been snooping was going to find exactly where I was or what I was looking at.

I had just emailed an old buddy of mine, from before the Praetorian days, a former Marine who had gone into the investigator business, specializing in missing persons, when I heard someone enter the room behind me.

I spun around in my chair, to see Mia had come in behind me.

I wasn't sure what to make of her presence. I was still pretty strung out, and after Renton's and Stahl's little railroad job, I was acutely aware of our history, and how it had started. What was she doing there?

I stood up as she came closer. "Why are you still up?" she asked. She touched my arm. "You should get some rest," she said.

If I'd been a little less punch-drunk I might have considered my words more carefully. But I'd been up for a long time, through two hard fights, and I wasn't exactly at my clearest.

"Why?" I asked, a faint edge of bitterness in the word that even surprised me as I said it. "Has Renton moved up the timetable? Need me at my best to do his dirty work?"

She slapped me. I hadn't seen it coming and it kinda rocked me. Before I could react, she grabbed my face between her hands and pulled me down to look her in the eyes.

"I know you're tired," she said tightly, "which is why I'm going to let it go at that, when by rights I should make you wish you were never born for saying that. You have been doing this too long. Not everything is part of the game, not everything is part of someone's agenda, not everyone is trying to get you or get something from you. The fact that you can't see that anymore *worries* me." She looked down for a second. "I went down that road a few

179

years back," she said, her voice haunted. "I lost a lot; I almost lost myself. It was why I got out of the game, and when Renton pulled me back in, I swore I wasn't going to let it happen again." Her voice got thick for a second. "Don't you dare let it happen to you, too."

Then she kissed me, hard. I'd never really thought of the word "fiercely" as describing kissing, but that's the only way I can describe that one.

She broke the kiss and let me go suddenly, turning so quickly that her ponytail almost hit me in the face. She stalked away without looking back. I couldn't be sure, since I couldn't see her face, but I had the sudden impression that she was fighting back tears.

Even as I watched her go, I caught myself wondering if it wasn't still all an act, and I suddenly felt like an asshole for thinking it. Was she right? Was I getting lost in this crapsack of intrigue, lies, and betrayal?

I heard the door slam behind her, and I slumped back down into my chair. I thought of getting up and going after her, but my stubborn streak won out.

She was right about one thing. I needed sleep. Maybe I'd apologize in the morning.

***

I was yanked out of a deep, hard sleep by the radio blaring. "Hillbilly, Geek!" Eddie was calling. It didn't sound like it was the first time he'd called, either.

I grabbed for the radio and my rifle at the same time, succeeding in knocking the radio off the nightstand, though I managed to snag the rifle before it slid down to hit the floor. I groggily searched the floor for the radio and got my fingers around it.

"Geek, Hillbilly," I croaked. My mouth felt like a small animal had died in it. It was still dark outside. Something was wrong.

"Get to the main house, pronto," he said. "Come loaded for bear."

I acknowledged curtly, my grogginess momentarily forgotten as I switched on. I grabbed my chest rig off the chair next to the bedroom door as I slammed out into the predawn darkness, swung a leg over my four-wheeler, fired it up, and went tearing toward the main house.

***

The lights were all on, and everyone who had been close enough was up, with security set and guns out. "What the hell happened?" I demanded, as I swung down off my ATV. A few rifle muzzles lowered as I called.

"Lee's dead," Eddie said grimly as he came to the back door. "Come and see."

Lee had been on Eddie's team for years. His callsign had been "Booters" because he'd gotten all kinds of butt-hurt over the prospect of being treated as the new guy when he'd first joined up; he'd retired from the Marine

180

Corps as a Master Sergeant. He'd adapted, lost the stick up his ass, and been a top-notch shooter since.

He'd been garroted from behind, his neck black and blue from what looked like it must have been a boot lace or a length of 550 parachute cord.

"He was on security, watching the back for Baumgartner or any of his hunters," Eddie said.

"How the hell did somebody get behind him?" I asked.

Before anyone could venture a guess, though, the landline phone rang. Everyone stopped and stared at it for a second, then I took two steps over and picked it up.

"You boys must be tired," a familiar voice said. "You're slipping. Your sweep missed the attic."

"Baumgartner," I said. Every eye in the room seemed to focus a little tighter on me at the sound of that name.

"The same," he replied easily. "I considered doing some more damage on my way out, but the odds were long, even for me. You guys are good. Not in my league, but good." His bantering tone vanished. "You didn't really think this was over, did you?"

"No, I can't say that we did," I answered. "Though I could ask you the same question."

He laughed. It was a dry, dead, humorless sound. "You should see what I'm getting paid for this job," he said. "You guys are barking up the wrong tree. You're fucked. The people I work for have bottomless pockets. If you try to pull off that plan you were talking about in the living room, they'll just crush you. If you're smart, you'll forget that bullshit. Maybe you'll get lucky, and they'll offer you a job if you surrender when they send the next wave after you."

"You know, I thought you were king shit back in the day, Baumgartner," I told him. "But now, I'm going to put a bullet in your brain when I get a chance. Get fucked." I hung up.

I looked at the rest, trying to hide how shaken that exchange had left me. I'd fought jihadis, narcos, Chinese commandos, and rogue American special operations soldiers. But Baumgartner fucking *scared* me.

"We've got to find that son of a bitch," Eddie snarled.

"I think he'll come to us," I said, "eventually. But that call was a taunt. He's waiting, up there somewhere, for us to come after him. He wouldn't have called otherwise. He *wants* us to go looking, and then he's going to whittle us down, one at a time." I shook my head. "Double security for the time being, and we'll have to be on the alert at all times. When the time comes, I want to ambush *him*."

I just hoped that we were able to kill him quick when that time came. Otherwise more of us were going to be joining Lee.

CHAPTER 20

We patrolled, cautiously, for the next two days, pushing a little farther into the Beartooths to look for Baumgartner. By the end of the second day, though, no one had found any sign of him, and he hadn't sprung any ambushes. He had vanished into the mountains like a ghost.

"I suspect he was trying to draw us out just so he could bag a couple of us if we offered him the opportunity," Tom said. "Good call, Jeff, on holding back. My guess is that he only killed Lee on the way out, instead of trying to wreak more havoc, because he figured he was too outnumbered. Even someone like Baumgartner can calculate odds, and whatever kind of Delta superman he might have been, he's still a survivor."

I just nodded. I was glad that nobody else had gotten killed, but I wanted to see Baumgartner's cold corpse, and sooner rather than later. After that little display the other night, I would be sleeping with one eye open until he was in the dirt.

At any rate, while I was certain we hadn't heard or seen the last of Baumgartner, we had work to do. Our rest and recovery time, as brief as it had been, was coming to an end. We'd spent a good bit of it refitting and cleaning up after the Task Force, as well as lending what help and advice we could to the militia, Ventner's contractors, and Brett and his deputies, but we'd gotten a bit of rest in there, as well.

Mia had avoided speaking to me or looking at me for the first day, which I didn't have too much of a problem with, since I still didn't know what to make of our little encounter in my cabin the other night. She'd warmed back up as time had gone on, though the confrontation was never brought up.

But the chaos tearing the country apart wasn't getting any better, and we had missions to plan. So, while it didn't feel like we'd gotten much rest and recuperation at all, we sat down with Renton's target packages and got to work.

***

I'd never been a fan of Northern Virginia.

I'd been there off and on a few times, though not nearly as often as some guys I knew who worked the contract business, mostly doing guard work or close protection for various government agencies that were either based in DC or various surrounding areas in Northern Virginia itself. Overall, it always struck me as too built up, too pretentious, and too full of its own importance, being so close to the center of government. This was where the bureaucracy lived, and you could smell it on the too-humid air.

In keeping with my warning to Renton after the Mexican fiasco, we'd kept our use of Cicero Group assets to a minimum, and arranged our own flights out to Virginia. A lot of the gear had been purchased with cash at various hole-in-the-wall stores nearby, and we'd brought the weapons in ourselves. We weren't getting burned inadvertently because we'd locally purchased weapons used in a hit. Politicians' frothing bullshit about "ghost guns" aside, you've got to present ID and get a background check to buy a gun *anywhere* but the black market, and given the assholes who run the black market Stateside, that was a non-starter.

We had taken Renton's advice and prioritized the guy on the top of the target deck he'd given us. If his information was right, this was the guy to start with.

***

"This asshole has eaten out for every fucking meal for the last three days," Eric grumbled. "You'd think he never learned how to cook."

"You've seen him," I replied. "Does he look to you like somebody who ever bothered to learn any real-life skills that don't involve a computer?"

He snorted. Eric prided himself on his skill in the kitchen, a fact that the rest of the team had taken advantage of at one time or another. He might have made a decent living as a chef somewhere, if he hadn't been doing this, instead. But with the economy in the shape it had been for years, killing people and breaking their shit paid a hell of a lot better than feeding them.

I turned my attention back across the street. "At any rate, it's one more indicator that Renton's info's good. If he's throwing that kind of money around, he's too loaded to just be a tech consultant."

Damien Chu was presently sitting in the Majestic Café, presumably enjoying a very pricey dinner in a restaurant that catered to presidents. Obviously, POTUS was nowhere near the place at the moment; otherwise Eric and I could not have been sitting in a rental sedan across the street. But it said something about Damien's tastes, and, as I'd said, it suggested that we were on the right track.

Chu was a pudgy, baby-faced young man with glasses and a shitty haircut, who dressed like a slob, but drove a *very* expensive car and patronized expensive restaurants and entertainments. Not only was he always eating out or going to "important people" bars, but we'd seen a different escort show up to his apartment every night so far. The dude had money to burn, and no problem letting everyone around him know it.

When you're supposed to be a lowly tech consultant living in a very expensive part of the country, however, that's not necessarily a good idea.

Renton's target package said that Chu's sideline—or, perhaps more accurately, his primary source of income, judging by what I'd seen—was that of facilitator. He was the guy who discreetly connected very important and high-profile people with very seedy, illegal, and immoral services.

He wasn't thought to be a part of "Marius," "Sulla," or any other faction, but what Renton and his people wanted was what he knew. And if their suspicions were correct, he knew a lot.

So, there we were, sitting in a sedan in an upscale part of Alexandria, Virginia, that didn't look like it had suffered from the Greater Depression at all, watching well-dressed young professionals walking along the sidewalks, staring at their smartphones and chatting, as if there was nothing whatsoever wrong with the world, aside from whatever petty little problems they were blowing out of proportion that day.

I usually tried to avoid that kind of cynicism regarding my fellow man. There were too many veterans of the wars who puffed themselves up as loudly and publicly as possible with their own moral superiority, apparently believing that having been to horrible places, endured hardships, and maybe even having had to do and receive violence made them inherently better than anyone around them. I didn't want to be one of those guys.

But there's a certain unavoidable culture shock that comes from being thrown from a combat situation straight into affluent, comfortable surroundings. A week before, I'd been fighting for my home, dragging my ass over rocks and brush to either kill or be killed. Now here I was, showered, clean, sitting in a comfortable car, but still in combat mode, hunting a man while everyone around me acted like my world of spooks, criminals, mercenaries, and terrorists didn't exist.

Because to them, it didn't. None of them had ever been shot at. The riots threatening to spin out of control were distant things on the news, even if the nearest was only a half an hour's drive away. Riots don't move quickly, so these people really had nothing to worry about, not for a while, anyway. So, they could concentrate on the petty little inconveniences of their day, having no other real hardships or obstacles to compare them to.

At the very least, it lent a weird sense of unreality to running surveillance in that environment. Add in the fact that there's always too much time to woolgather while on surveillance, and it makes it worse.

We had eyes on Chu's apartment, which apparently doubled as his workplace. While he had a website for his public business, he seemed to do very little actual tech consulting. All the pieces were lining up to confirm that he was just what the Cicero Group suspected he was.

My phone buzzed. It was a new smartphone; Derek had been working on a set of them for secure comms for a while, fitted with text, voice, and video apps with solid end-to-end encryption and VPNs from hell. He'd assured us that *nobody* was going to be cracking them anytime soon. In a way, it was simpler and more convenient than juggling half a dozen burner phones.

It was from Derek, though the screen just said, "Hippy." "Dude, I finished going over the dump for the last 24 and just...DAMN," the message read.

Derek was presently sitting in the hospital in Powell, having come through the first of what promised to be several surgeries for his shattered femur all right, and was working remotely. Fortunately, his cyber-war wizardry didn't require him to be on the ground, though it did require *somebody* to be.

The night before, once we'd been confident enough that Chu would be occupied at his watering hole of the night, Eddie had broken into his apartment and installed a micro-USB keylogger on his computer. He had evidently not spotted it, probably because he hadn't been looking. Eddie was *very* good at the clandestine entry game, and could come and go like a ghost, given enough time. Bryan and Jack had been poised to interrupt Chu's evening in a particularly unpleasant way, to ensure he had that time, but such had not proven necessary. Chu liked the night life, and he had enough money to flash around that, as pathetic as he looked and dressed, he had enough female attention to keep him busy for a while.

Once Chu had gotten home, every keystroke he made on that computer had gotten dumped by wifi onto a little Raspberry Pi that Eddie had stashed in the bushes outside the apartment building. That was what Derek was accessing, from his terminal halfway across the country.

"He's careful," Derek continued. "He's Tor'ed up like a mofo, every message is in code, and he scrubs everything after its been sent. Not all of his clients are that careful, though, and I've already hooked two of 'em the easy way." The "easy way" was a phishing attack via their email. Knowing Derek's twisted sense of humor, I expected that he'd disguised his attacks as juicy opportunities from Chu himself.

"This guy's dirty as hell, broheim," he concluded.

"Roger," I sent back. "We'll pay him a visit tonight. Wish you could be here for it."

"Me too, bro, me too," he replied. "Give him an extra love-tap for me."

"No problem," I answered, before putting the phone away and turning my attention back toward the Café. I checked my watch.

"Taking his time, isn't he?" I muttered.

"Relax, man," Eric said. "The later he goes, the later we break in and take him, and the less likely we get spotted doing it. You know this."

"True enough," I grumbled. "Just not looking forward to spending the next six hours following his pudgy ass around to every bar and nightclub he decides to visit tonight."

"You're getting impatient in your old age," he replied, his faint grin audible in his voice. "Isn't it supposed to be the other way around?"

I gave him a half-hearted glare. He just chuckled.

I sighed. It was going to be a long night.

***

It actually wasn't as bad as I'd expected. Maybe he'd gotten bored. It had to be kind of samey, really, as decadent as his lifestyle was. Or maybe there weren't any chicks out that night who were willing to overlook how pathetic he looked for the sake of money.

Whatever the case, he came out of his chosen bar, in Arlington, before midnight. Bar hopping didn't fit his pattern of life, so it was a good bet that he was heading home. I called ahead, letting the overwatch on his apartment know, and getting acknowledgements along with status reports that confirmed that the place was quiet, and there wasn't any law enforcement nearby. We'd still have to do this as quickly and quietly as possible.

We'd briefly considered drugging him in the bar and transporting him to a secluded spot for interrogation, but if he had intel materials in his apartment, we didn't want to have to go back for them.

Chu was clearly a little drunk as he walked out to his car. He wasn't staggering, falling down, or puking on himself, but he was moving more slowly than usual and appeared to be completely oblivious to his surroundings. Not that that was something new; we hadn't seen much in his behavior that suggested he was the most *aware* of people. He was confident in his cyber security, and thus figured that no one knew exactly who he was.

Either that, or he was confident that he had enough blackmail material on enough people in high places that he was untouchable. Frankly, from what I'd seen of the guy for the last three days, my money was on Option B.

He was about to have a very rude awakening.

He got the car unlocked and slid in behind the wheel. Even as he opened the door, I was already heading across the street.

I reached in before he could close the driver's side door, and made sure the back door was unlocked. He hadn't noticed me until I reached in past his head, and he started rather badly, even as I pulled the back door open and slid into the seat behind him.

"What the fuck?" he started to say, then stopped abruptly as I placed the cold metal of my Gemtech suppressor behind his ear. He was just sober enough to realize what that was.

"Close the door, shut your mouth, and drive," I told him. I'd thought about doing this differently, letting him get home and settle in, then breaking in and taking things from there. Either course of action had the potential to go badly. This way seemed to present a better chance of keeping control of the situation.

Chu's hands were shaking, but he did what he was told. I think the shock kept him from doing or saying anything else. If I'd read him right, and after three days of near-continuous surveillance, I should have, he'd always

187

been well-insulated from any potential consequences of his actions. The idea that somebody might come after him had been essentially unthinkable. He probably hadn't ever gamed this situation through in his head, or if he had, he hadn't exactly lived up to his idea of how he'd deal with it. Shortly after he shut the door, I started to smell piss. I wrinkled my nose but didn't roll down the window. It wasn't my car, I'd smelled far worse in my day, and I didn't need anyone happening to peer through an open window and seeing a suppressed .45 pressed to the back of Damien's fat head.

We'd already gone a block before he realized that I hadn't specified where to drive *to*. "Where are we going?" he asked. He sounded like he was about to be sick.

"Your place," I told him calmly. "Don't worry, as long as you stay calm and cooperative, nothing's going to happen to you." *Yet.* "We've got a lot to talk about, Damien."

"Wait a minute," he said, his voice getting shakier. "I've seen your face. Doesn't that mean…"

I couldn't resist. "Where you're going after tonight," I told him, "I'm not that worried about it."

I probably should have restrained myself, since he started shaking even more violently, and puked all over himself. The stink drowned out the urine smell, and I just about gagged. Fortunately, I'm not a sympathetic puker.

"Calm down," I told him. "Like I said, cooperate and there's no reason to be afraid. You're far more useful alive than dead."

He steadied a little bit, took a deep breath, gagged on his own vomit fumes, and barfed again. I kept my teeth together, as much as I wanted to start cussing him out. Weak little shit. *Shouldn't have gotten involved in shit that gets people like me interested in you, fucker.*

To my relief, the ride was a short one; the bar was less than eight miles from his apartment. He parked in the little carport behind the small, gray row-house. Behind us, Eric parked our car on the street. The rest of the team was already spread out on overwatch throughout the neighborhood.

"Just try to keep things nice and calm and casual, Damien," I told him. "You had a bit too much to drink, and I drove you home. That's all this is, and that's why you've got puke all over your front. Got it?"

He nodded, and I noted that the nod was somewhat steadier than it had been before. Either he was taking my advice to heart, or he had had time to think on the drive, and was now trying to calculate how he could get out of this. I hoped it was the former; the latter could mean more trouble than we wanted to deal with.

He opened the door and led the way inside. The row-house was apparently divided up into four or five apartments, with a short hallway through the center, which was fortuitously empty. Chu led the way toward his door, unlocked it, and stepped inside.

I was close behind him, still holding my suppressed 1911 under my jacket. It was awkward, but as long as I didn't let him get the door between him and me, I could still shoot him if I had to.

Of course, so could Eddie, who was standing in the kitchen with a black duffel bag on the counter and one of Logan's scratchbuilt subguns in his hands.

Now that we were inside, I shut the door behind us and locked it, then pointed toward an empty chair in the little living room with my pistol. "Have a seat, Damien."

He complied, though he was somewhat more composed now. He looked back and forth between us. "Do you two fuckwits have any idea who you're fucking with?" he demanded. "Do you have any idea the world of shit you just jumped into?"

Before he could get going, blustering about his friends—or blackmail victims—in high places, I cut him off. "Oh, we know full well who you are and what you do, Damien. That's why we're here. And don't bother threatening us with your client list. They're the entire reason we came in the first place."

He looked like he was about to say something, when Eddie's phone buzzed. He looked down at it. "We've got company," he said, frowning.

Even as he spoke, the door, that I'd just locked, started to open. I turned, pivoting away from Chu but never turning my back on him, my 1911 coming up in both hands and centering on the door.

The Broker, apparently utterly unconcerned that Eddie and I were each about a pound of trigger pressure short of spattering his brains all over the hallway, stepped inside, closed and locked the door behind him, and took off his hat.

He completely ignored the two men with guns and turned his vague, cold-eyed smile on Chu. "Hello, Damien," he said. "It's been such a long time."

I spared a glance from The Broker to Chu, who was staring at him with wide eyes behind his glasses, his face gone a particularly yellowish shade of green. I flicked my eyes back to The Broker, who was still watching Chu, that dangerous little smile on his face.

Chu swallowed. "What—what are you doing here, Tailor?" he asked hoarsely.

He'd gone from arrogant and abusive to even more terrified than he had been when I'd first put a gun to his head in the space of about thirty seconds. He knew who The Broker was, or at least who The Broker wanted him to think he was, and he was scared shitless of him.

"I'm here to back these gentlemen up," The Broker said. "I assume you've tried threatening them with the things and people you know. I'm afraid that your blackmail files will not intimidate these two men in the slightest, but

I thought you really needed to hear that from someone you know would not lie to you about it. And you know I would not lie about such things, don't you, Damien?"

Chu nodded jerkily, but couldn't seem to find his voice again.

"Where are the files, Damien?" The Broker asked, almost gently. "You know the ones I'm talking about. The ones that you were oh, so confident you could keep hidden even from these men with guns."

Chu swallowed again. "Those files are my insurance," he said. "If I give them up…"

"If you don't, then certain people who may or may not have already granted you legal favors because of the contents of those files will be provided with your exact location and general pattern of life," The Broker said, still in that strange, gentle tone of voice. "You may trust that these are the sorts of people who will find a way to take advantage of that information, and do so far more brutally than the generally honorable men who presently have you at gunpoint. I think you know exactly who I have in mind."

Chu must have already emptied his guts and his bladder, because he just pointed with a shaking finger toward a cupboard above the sink. "In the sugar jar," he sobbed. "There's a false bottom…"

I glanced at Eddie, who nodded. He placed the submachine gun on the counter, well outside The Broker's reach, and opened the cupboard.

He took down the indicated jar, a heavy stoneware job, and dumped the contents into the sink. When he looked in after the cascade of sugar had finished going into the sink, he reached inside and pulled.

A rubber circle came out, and he dumped a dozen flash drives on the counter.

"I believe that you will find all the intel you came here for on those, gentlemen," The Broker said. "Though his computer should be available to double-check."

Eddie took the handful of flash drives and went to Chu's computer. When he logged in without difficulty, Chu went even greener. He was watching his entire world fall apart around his ears.

"Holy fuck," Eddie said after a moment of going through the first drive. "There's a fucking cornucopia of fucked up shit on here. All with names and dates attached, too."

He yanked that drive and plugged in the next one. Even Eddie, who had once described himself as a borderline functioning sociopath, was looking a little green around the gills after the second one. "I really don't want to look at any more of this," he said, pulling the drive and turning away from the computer. "I think it's a safe bet that we've found our treasure trove."

"Is that it, Damien?" The Broker asked quietly. "I know you know better than to lie to me."

Chu nodded frantically, as he started to cry. "That's all, I swear, that's all the files, please…"

"Good." Before he could blubber anything else, The Broker drew a shortened Maxim 9 from beneath his coat and shot Chu twice in the head.

The twin *clap*s probably weren't audible far outside of the apartment, but they were startling in their abruptness. Before the brass had hit the carpet, I had my own pistol centered on The Broker's head.

"What the fuck?" I demanded. I was surprisingly calm, considering that he'd just murdered the asset we'd gone in to grab.

"Trust me, Mr. Stone," The Broker said as he lowered the integrally suppressed pistol, "it's better this way. Regardless of what you found on those drives, regardless of the crimes he has been a direct accessory to, someone would make the case that Chu was more useful alive than dead. Then he would be useful in other ways, and eventually, he would be plying his old trade the same as ever." He turned to me, cool and composed, as if we were having a conversation over coffee, instead of over the barrel of a .45.

"As extensive as those files undoubtedly are," he said gravely, "they constitute only a fraction of the human misery that Damien Chu has helped to facilitate. I simply ensured that he wouldn't be turned into an instrument of even more of it. He was a weasel who would have walked away from this scot-free. Now he won't. And you still have all the intel that you came for; probably more than you can even possibly use."

As much as he'd pissed me off, I couldn't argue with his reasoning. Anything that made Eddie green around the gills had to be bad. I glanced at Damien, who was presently leaking blood and brain matter all over his plush chair. The Broker had probably been merciful, relatively speaking.

"How did you know we'd be here?" I asked as I lowered my gun. That was the other part that bothered me. We'd kept even *Renton* in the dark on the specifics of this op.

"I haven't been monitoring you, at least not closely, if that's what you're asking," he said with a chuckle. The man was fucking unflappable. "No, this was simply a matter of some analysis of my own intel and knowing how both you and Renton think. I had Damien Chu pretty high on my own target list, and deduced that he'd be the same on the Cicero Group's, and, therefore, yours. After that, it was simply a matter of timing."

I didn't know that I believed him all the way; it was suspiciously good timing. We hadn't seen any sign of anyone else surveilling Chu, not in three days. But I let it go. "We should probably get the hell out of here," I said.

"Agreed," The Broker replied. "And we should probably leave by different routes. Keep your comms open; I'll be in touch." He turned, unlocked the door, and vanished out into the hall.

I looked at Eddie. "We need to have a talk about that guy," he said. "He's a bit too sharp for my comfort, if you know what I mean. But I'd rather do it somewhere else."

In five minutes, Damien was assuming room temperature alone, and none of us were within three blocks of the scene.

CHAPTER 21

When we got to the rendezvous with Renton, two states away in the woods outside of Southpoint, Ohio, he didn't look happy. Given that Damien Chu's murder had been on the nightly news in Alexandria the night before, doubtless followed by a flurry of panic among the well-connected, unconvicted felon set, he had to know why we didn't have a zip-tied, bagged detainee in tow. There was no way the Cicero Group had missed that swarming anthill.

He was leaning against the blank-sided utility van he'd come in, his arms crossed and a frown on his face as Eddie and I got out of the rental Jeep and walked toward him. We weren't likely to be observed; we were surrounded by woods and the local cops had no reason to consider us suspicious.

"I can't help but notice," he said as we approached, "the absence of the very scumbag I asked you to retrieve."

"That would be because he's the centerpiece of a crime scene investigation right now," Eddie said easily.

"I know," Renton said, sounding as close to monumentally pissed off as I'd ever heard him. "Somehow, that killing made it past all the chaos and havoc in DC and the Beltway to make the nightly news, probably because the station manager had been one of Chu's clients, or was friends with one of them. So, yeah. It was kind of hard to miss that part." He straightened and glared at us. "You were supposed to snatch Chu, not kill him."

"And *we* didn't kill him," I snapped. "The Broker crashed the party and double-tapped him."

That stopped his rant cold. He froze for a moment, then swallowed. "Wait a minute. Back up. *Who* killed him?"

"The Broker," I replied. "The same guy I asked you about in Mexico, whether he was El Duque or not, the same guy who enlightened us about the scam going on down there."

"He was there?" There was a new light in Renton's eyes, Chu's death momentarily lost in the fact that the underworld shadow facilitator had surfaced. "He was actually in the room?" He paused, and his eyes narrowed. "How can you be sure it was him?"

"I'm sure because this isn't the first time we've met him," I said.

I'd kept our interactions with The Broker pretty hush-hush; I knew that Renton's organization was leaky, and I'd wanted to keep that hole card up my sleeve for when I needed it. He'd saved our asses a couple of times now.

But I didn't know what his agenda was, and he'd just put me in one hell of a bind by murdering a "capture" target. No matter what I owed him, I wasn't taking the fall for a killing he'd dropped in my lap.

So, I told Renton about how he'd snapped up Serena Olivarez ahead of our hit in Honduras, then told us to meet him in Panama City. I told him about the meet where The Broker had laid out the facts behind the illusion of El Duque, the number one High Value Target in the Western Hemisphere, an imaginary bogeyman designed from the get-go as a lure to send the hitters chasing after ghosts. I told him how all of The Broker's intel, most of which had to have come from one hell of an extensive network of underworld contacts, had panned out, leading us to bad actor after bad actor, as we'd systematically taken *Los Hijos de la Muerte* and the Fusang Group apart.

"A couple of us wondered how you were hitting every target perfectly," Renton admitted, "but you'd gone so dark that we couldn't be sure what was going on until after the fact. Not that I blame you; having every heavy hitter in Latin America gunning for you can't have made anything easier."

"He beat you to the punch on the latest unpleasantness, too," Eddie said. "He warned us about the Task Force's intel, and provided a fair bit of material support, including transpo, explosives, and comms."

"Do you realize what this means?" Renton asked, finally focusing on me directly. "You sons of bitches are the only ones to have laid eyes on this guy and *known* it. You're the only ones with a single verifiable clue as to who he is."

"Who the hell is he?" I asked. "You talk about him as if he's the spider in the web—which I can't help but remember was the legend behind El Duque, too—but he's a complete cypher to us, regardless of how much we've interacted with him. Who the hell is he, and what does he want?"

"He *is* a cypher," Renton replied. "Rumors about somebody known only as 'The Broker' started circulating a little over a decade and a half ago. Nobody knew who he was, if he even was a 'he,' or even just one individual. He started making a name for himself as a 'shadow facilitator,' a dealer in primarily information, but also material resources, doing business throughout the global underworld. Word was that he had nearly bottomless resources, and he was very picky about security and who he'd do business with. But nobody ever had a clue as to who he was. He's a ghost, even more elusive than El Duque was presumed to be."

"Well, I assure you he's a very real human being," I told him. "And a very dangerous one, from what I've seen."

"No shit," Renton replied. "There have been several task forces that have been quietly put together to try to investigate him. The first two couldn't find jack shit. Rumor has it the third one started to make progress, until the head of the task force was found electrocuted in his apartment. No sign of forced entry, no sign that anyone else was ever there. The task force dissolved a few days later, and the case files were buried."

Given what I'd seen of The Broker's capabilities and ruthlessness, that didn't surprise me at all. I was sure several less subtle messages had accompanied the discovery of the task force head's body.

"Can you describe him?" Renton asked after another moment.

I gave him a look like he'd just asked if I could speak English. Reconnaissance was part of our stock in trade, and if I hadn't been able to describe a man I'd been in the same room with, I should have probably gotten out of the business long before.

So, I described the slightly pudgy, vaguely mousy, entirely non-threatening little man in as much detail as I could bring to mind. As I did, Renton's frown deepened, and I could almost see the wheels turning.

When I finished, he was slightly pale, if still looking thoughtful. His eyes were far away, and for a moment it didn't even seem like he was aware of either of us. "I need to track some things down," he said distractedly. "I'll be in touch."

"Hold on a damned minute," Eddie snapped, holding out the briefcase full of flash drives. They were the originals, though we had their collective contents on two larger external drives squirrelled safely away. The shit on those drives was poison, and we weren't going to let it fly out on its own without having *some* kind of control over that particular weapon. We didn't trust Renton and his Cicero Group *that* far. "Isn't this what you came for in the first place?"

Renton seemed to shake himself, and reached for the briefcase. "Right," he said. "Sorry. Got a bit distracted." He took the case, and finally looked directly at both of us. "As important as these files are—though having Chu himself would have been better—The Broker's involvement just made this even bigger. Like I said, I need to check up on some things. Keep your phones close, and be ready to move quickly. And for fuck's sake, if he contacts you again, *call me*."

I just nodded, unsure exactly what I was going to do if Mr. Gray showed up again. He was an unknown variable, and a dangerous one, at that. At the same time, he'd helped us out in a big way a couple of times, and as I'd already contemplated more than once, Renton's organization was not exactly one hundred percent trustworthy. While The Broker might have murdered our target, he hadn't leaked our identities to every hitter, terrorist, and gangster on the Dark Web.

I suddenly felt deeply weary as I watched Renton climb into his van and shut the door. It was a tiredness that went clear down to my bones.

I'd gotten into the business to make some money and stay "in the fight." I'd been, admittedly, a little addicted to the lifestyle of a shooter, and there hadn't been much else available in terms of work Stateside, at least not anything I'd had the patience to pursue. It had seemed easy; make money using my background and skillsets, maybe get a chance to put some lead in some pirates or jihadis, get paid to work out and shoot.

Instead, I had found myself in a poisonous snake-pit of politics, intrigue, conflicting agendas, and more and more dead bodies, including those of my friends and teammates. At that point, I didn't know for sure who to trust.

And there were too many people involved to just kill all of them.

***

We didn't have long to wait. We'd started going over the contents of the drives, as much as we could stomach, to start building our own target deck. The Broker's warning about what might have happened had Chu lived were resonating with both Eddie and me. Contingencies needed to be in place, in case our sponsors decided that some of these scumbags were "valuable" enough to let them get away with some of the truly heinous shit that Chu had first facilitated, and then documented.

I had stepped outside of the tent we had pitched in the backwoods of Kentucky. I needed some air. Damn, I had known some twisted fucks in the military, but even the most depraved infantryman or special operations soldier I'd ever known hadn't gotten quite as low as some of these politicians and captains of industry who had done business with Chu.

The Renton phone buzzed. I'd been expecting it.

"I'm sending you an address in Martinsburg, West Virginia," Renton said as soon as I'd answered it. "The meet is there in eighteen hours."

"What's the deal?" I asked.

"Not over the phone," he replied. "Eighteen hours. Don't be late."

I just sighed as he hung up and the phone vibrated in my hand to announce the text message with the location for the meeting. I had a feeling that if he was trying to keep The Broker from finding out about it, he was barking up the wrong tree.

But I stuck my head back inside the tent. "Hey," I said. "We can put the electronic sewer away for a bit. We've got a meeting in West Virginia in the wee hours of tomorrow morning."

Eddie snapped the laptop shut. "Good. This shit's bad even for me. I'm about to just start skimming for names and putting a bullseye on them just for being in the mix. Fuck what they did; if they're on here, they're dirty and need to die."

196

"No argument from me," I replied. "But let's get going. I want to have the meeting site scoped out before Renton or his cronies show up."

The address turned out to be an old red-brick factory right on the railroad tracks. The place was locked up tighter than a drum, which apparently didn't deter most teenagers, judging by what we could see. The chain link fence surrounding the complex was bent and twisted in several places where someone had evidently climbed it, and many of the windows in the buildings were broken, smashed thoroughly enough that someone could easily climb through.

It wasn't going to deter us much, either. Of course, sneaking into a locked up local landmark in broad daylight was probably ill-advised, so we settled for spreading out nearby and observing.

The locals didn't pay the place much mind. It was, after all, a constant fixture of their daily existence. Frankly, it was likely that the only people who cared much about the old brick structure were the local cops, who had to try to keep the teenagers out.

After several hours of careful observation, comparing notes via Derek's secure, encrypted messaging app, we couldn't see any signs of surveillance on the train station, or on us. We were clean, as far as we knew.

The day crept to a close, and darkness descended. The streetlights came on slowly, bathing the street and the empty, fenced-in parking lot in front of the factory buildings in dim, orange light.

That part of Martinsburg really didn't have much of a night life. The tire shop, paint store, and auto parts store had all closed just after seven. There was a diner on the far side of the factory complex, but it was well masked from the rest of the factory itself, which looked properly ominous and haunted in the sodium light of the streetlights.

We faded back into the shadows and maintained our vigil.

Shortly after midnight, a car pulled up next to the auto parts store just south of the tracks and parked. A few minutes later, a pickup parked on the street in front of the paint store. No one got out of either vehicle.

"I think the party's here," I muttered. Next to me, in the passenger seat, Larry just nodded.

For about ten minutes, everyone just sat there, watching and waiting. I couldn't see the guys in the truck, since they'd carefully parked in the shadows, but I was pretty sure they were doing what we'd been doing for the last several hours.

Finally, an old, beat-up Chevy Suburban, its white paint job peeling and rusting along the bottom, pulled up to the gate that stretched across the entrance to the parking lot. A figure got out, unlocked the gate, and swung it open, allowing the Sub to roll inside and park next to the building.

Once it was parked, three more men got out, scanning the surrounding buildings, then went inside. The light was bad, but unless I missed my guess, they were all packing some kind of short-barreled weapons, either subguns or SBRs.

We just waited. After a few more minutes, the door opened again, and then two more figures got out of the sub and went inside. It must have been crowded in that vehicle.

Larry glanced at me after we'd sat there for a couple more minutes. I glanced down at the phone in my lap, saying nothing. Finally, the screen lit dimly as the phone buzzed.

"Mars and Spooky confirmed," the message said. "No LOS on their position in the building. No other movement." "Mars" had been General Stahl's callsign in Libya. Renton had gotten the terribly original nickname "Spooky" because he was a spook. It was a callsign that probably fit The Broker better, but he already kind of had a nickname, as it were.

Jack and Eric were up on the roof of the auto parts store, with their long guns. Full-length sniper rifles were superfluous at those distances, so they'd just carried up their ACE 52s.

One hundred percent overwatch on a building complex that big, with the numbers we had, was impossible. But if we had to break out of there in a hurry, we at least knew that we had the parking lot covered.

Even so, I still waited. Let Renton stew a bit.

Finally, the Renton phone buzzed. "Where are you?" he asked.

"Outside," I replied calmly. "Making sure nobody else is coming to crash the party."

He apparently didn't know what to say to that, as the phone went quiet. But then another voice came on. "The building's clear, Hillbilly," Stahl said. "Come on in. We can't afford to stay in one place too long right now."

That told me a lot all by itself. If Stahl was concerned about staying in one place for long, even in a small town in West Virginia, it meant that whoever had gone after us was just as hot after him.

"We'll be in momentarily," I told him, and ended the call. Then I sent a mass text to the rest. "Green."

As soon as I put the phone down, I put the car in gear and rolled toward the open gate in the fence.

I could feel the guys in the pickup on the corner watching us as we went by. I got the distinct impression we'd surprised them; they hadn't spotted us until we'd moved.

As we rolled through the gate, an old Ford Bronco, just as beat-up as Stahl's Suburban, followed us from the direction of the auto-parts store. That would be Eddie and George. The rest of both our teams were scattered around the neighborhood, on overwatch.

We parked on either side of Stahl's vehicle and proceeded, carefully, inside. We each had one of Logan's homemade 9mm subguns hanging on tension slings under our jackets, in addition to pistols. They stayed hidden, but our hands were never more than a few inches from the weapons as we went in the door.

It wasn't that we didn't trust Renton or Stahl. It was that we didn't trust *anybody*.

George grabbed the door and pulled it open swiftly, and Larry and I stepped inside. We kept it as casual as possible, but each of us turned as we entered, clearing the corners on either side of the door with our eyes, even if we didn't cover them with our muzzles. It wasn't time to go guns-up, yet, but we were fractions of a second away, if that time came.

The inside of the factory had been pretty well stripped down to the rafters and the bare, brick walls. The concrete floor was dusty and littered with broken glass and bits of tile and crumbled brick. Aside from the dirty orange glow coming through the dingy windows, the only source of light was a single flashlight aimed at the floor.

There were four men situated around the room, each giving us a glance as we entered, but primarily keeping their attention focused out the windows. They were all carrying slung SIG MPXs. I thought I recognized one of them from a long time back; he looked like another Marine I'd known in Libya.

"Hey, Stone," he said, giving me the nod. "Long time."

I squinted at him briefly. "Stewart?" I asked.

"The same," he replied. The big machinegunner had aged a lot since Libya, though I imagined I wasn't exactly looking like the fresh-faced young Marine I'd been all those years ago, either. "Good to see you again. We'll have to catch up over a beer later."

I just nodded. Stewart had been with our QRF down in Al Jawf. We'd bullshitted and played far too many games of Spades in between missions and the occasional jihadi attack on the FOB. We'd fallen out of contact in the years since, but he'd been a damned good dude when I'd known him.

Stahl and Renton were standing in the middle of the enormous room, waiting. Stahl was holding the flashlight in one hand, with the other one buried in a pocket, a lit cigar clamped between his teeth, wreathing his head with clouds of smoke that glowed in the backsplash of the flashlight's illumination.

Renton was holding a tablet, the combination of pale, bluish light from the screen and the flashlight beam bouncing off the floor making him look a little like a corpse. As we approached, he turned the tablet around to show me the screen.

The man on the screen was unmistakably The Broker, though he was far younger in the photo. "Is this The Broker?" he asked.

I nodded. "I take it you've figured out who he is," I remarked.

Renton blew out a deep breath. "Yeah, you just confirmed it." He looked at Stahl. "Ryan Bates is alive."

"That's interesting," Stahl said dryly, around the cigar. "Who the hell is Ryan Bates?"

"Sorry," Renton said, putting the tablet back in the case at his feet. "I sometimes forget that that story isn't well known outside the intelligence community. Hell, it's kind of a taboo subject *within* the IC.

"Ryan Bates was an up-and-coming legend in the Clandestine Service," he explained. "He had a knack for finding information and putting seemingly disparate pieces together on the fly. He wasn't an analyst, but he considered most of the analysts to be morons. He wasn't popular, but he was usually right. He was my mentor for a few months at the beginning of my own career, during his last desk job, where he'd been stuck to try to keep him out of trouble.

"He wasn't ever the kind of guy who would 'stay in his lane.' He'd get curious about things and start digging. He uncovered a couple of nasty terrorist plots doing that, and found some connections between seemingly disparate groups that would have been missed without him.

"Well, eventually he started getting interested in Yuri Bezmenov and Anatoly Golitsyn."

When he paused, as if we were supposed to know who those two characters were, Stahl stared at him along with the rest of us. "More names I don't know," he growled. "Get to the point."

"They were both Soviet defectors," Renton explained. "Bezmenov had been KGB, and shed a lot of light on Soviet information and influence operations; the way that they carefully shaped perceptions outside of the Soviet Union. Golitsyn was also KGB, but whereas Bezmenov had been a glorified PR guy, Golitsyn was in the strategic planning office.

"Golitsyn made the case that Perestroika, Glasnost, and the eventual fall of the Soviet Union were all carefully orchestrated, by design, starting with Andropov. He said that it was all a radical restructuring of the Soviet Union, effectively bringing it under KGB control, only in disguise."

Stahl frowned. "Given the way the Russian economy and government got split up among mostly former Party and former KGB oligarchs, it doesn't sound to me to be all that far-fetched."

"The rise of the *siloviki* under Putin lends it some more credence," Renton agreed. "But the powers that be didn't want to hear it. The Soviet Union was dead, and at the time, history was over. Later, the big threat was the jihad. Russians were our friends, at least until they became a useful political bogeyman again.

"But Bates never let it go. He wasn't a ranter; it wasn't his style. But occasionally he'd talk about it, and talk about what he thought needed to be done about it. He was afraid that we were going to find ourselves blindsided by an underground KGB, undermined and weakened before being pushed aside by a resurgent Soviet Union.

"He'd given it a lot of thought. He knew just how to get inside the networks, some of which went back clear to the Cold War. He liked to quote Jim Morris in *Soldier of Fortune*, saying, 'They're all wearing the same uniforms, using the same weapons, and getting the same training.'

"Then, about eighteen years ago, his house burned down. There were human remains inside, though the roof had collapsed and mangled what was left, so there was no way to check dental records. But Bates had disappeared, and it was easier to think that he'd died in the fire than that he'd pulled a disappearing act.

"He was smart; not a word was breathed about The Broker until almost three years later. Even I never put the two together. I figured Bates was dead. But here he is, surfaced again, as the very shadowy underworld facilitator he said somebody needed to become."

"So, how does this affect our operations?" Stahl asked.

"In the most salutary way," The Broker said from the shadows.

Ten guns were immediately leveled at the sound of his voice, even Stahl drawing a 1911 and bracing his gun hand with the flashlight.

"No need for any violence, gentlemen," the man who apparently was born Ryan Bates said as he stepped deeper into the room. "I'm alone, and have no hostile intentions toward any of you."

"How the hell did you get in here?" Stewart demanded.

"There's a tunnel leading into the yard," Bates explained calmly, that same vague half-smile on his lips. "It's not the most pleasant avenue of approach, but it has the advantage of being well-shielded from view." He looked around at all of us. "Well, are we going to talk business, or are you going to shoot me and get it over with?"

Stahl lowered his gun first. "What kind of business?"

"My kind of business," Bates answered. "Information, resources, penetration of networks. As Clancy said, I've spent the last eighteen years worming my way into the global underground. I wouldn't have been nearly as helpful with the El Duque business otherwise."

I had never known Renton's first name. Now that I found out it was Clancy, I understood why not.

"Are you offering your services?" Stahl asked. "Because, given what little Renton has told me, I'm not entirely sure I trust you."

"And in your position, that is entirely reasonable," Bates replied smoothly. "I am, after all, a transnational criminal. But I am also more than that. As Mr. Stone can attest, when I offer information, it is good, and I have aided him and his company a great deal both materially and informationally." He smiled somewhat more widely. "I'm not asking you to make me one of your staff, General. I'm simply offering my network to help achieve your goals."

"Why?" Stahl asked, his eyes hard glints through the cigar smoke.

"Because I am still an American," Bates said gravely. "And I can see what is happening, perhaps more clearly than you can." He pinned Renton with a stare. "What I was warning about eighteen years ago is happening, only it's far more distributed and chaotic than I expected it to be." He turned back to Stahl. "The factions which are your primary concern are only a part of the problem. The chaos they have set in motion will not be easy to reverse, and *will* be used by other powers that they haven't even considered in their short-sightedness. I can tell you with certainty that there are agents of multiple foreign powers, powers inimical to the United States, presently within our borders and already taking steps to take advantage of the unrest and violence that is happening across the country. If we want to have *anything* left when the dust settles, you are going to need my resources and the information that I can provide, General."

Stahl studied him for a long moment, his eyes narrowed. Then he turned to me, the glowing coal of his cigar like a red spotlight. "What do you think, Stone?" he asked. "You've apparently worked with him before."

I studied Bates' calm, composed face for a moment. "I don't trust him," I began, "but that doesn't say too much; I don't even trust you all that far, sir." Renton looked like he was going to protest, but I saw Stahl's face tighten into a brief, fierce grin, that of a tough father proud of his equally scrappy son. I took a deep breath, then plunged onward. "He hasn't played us false, he's telling that much of the truth. And our asses would be in a hell of a sling if not for him. Hell, we'd probably all be dead in Mexico or Honduras if he hadn't intervened. And if he hadn't gotten involved more recently, we'd have been rolled up by those 'Marius' assholes weeks before you could bring Joe Ventner in to relieve us."

I narrowed my own eyes as I studied Bates, who returned my gaze with guileless eyes. "He called it his 'business,'" I pointed out. "And from what Renton told us when I first asked about The Broker, he said that The Broker had a reputation for being purely mercenary. He's a businessman, whatever else he is. Even if his pitch about being an American first and foremost is bullshit, I think that it's in his best interest as a businessman to maintain that reputation and be sure that his information is reliable, at least."

Stahl holstered his pistol and folded his arms across his chest, looking from me to Bates, shifting the cigar from one corner of his mouth to the other. I could see the wheels turning; for all his bluff, tough-guy demeanor, I knew "Mars" was a thinker, more than he usually let his subordinates know.

He finally faced Bates. "Well, Mr. Bates," he said, "I'm going to take you up on your offer. Mainly because if your resources are half as extensive as what you say, I can definitely use them. But also because Stone here vouched for you. He doesn't really know me, except by reputation; I was his distant commander half a country away, and that was a lot of years ago. But I know enough about him to trust his judgment, and the fact that you helped him out tends to make me somewhat more kindly disposed toward you."

He held out a hand, and Bates stepped forward and shook it. "You won't regret this, General," he said. "But right now, I suggest that we make ourselves scarce. There are people looking intently for you and for Mr. Stone and his associates, and having all of us in one place for an extended period of time would be unwise." I don't know if he knew he was echoing Stahl's earlier comment or not, but I suspected he did. He was spooky that way.

"We have a great deal of work to do," he said, stepping back toward the side door he'd entered through. "Mr. Stone knows how to contact me, and I know how to contact the rest of you. I'll be in touch."

Then he was gone.

CHAPTER 22

Denver was a wreck.

We could see the smoke from the fires on our way down I-25. A great, gray and black pall hung over the city, visible even before the skyline itself rose above the relatively flat plateau.

"Fucking hell," Bryan said next to me. He was originally from Colorado, and had lived there for a little while after he'd gotten out of the military. "I don't know whether to laugh or cry."

"I thought you didn't cry," I pointed out dryly. "Least of all for a bunch of Denver hippies."

"Nah, I don't give a shit about them," he replied. "Most of 'em are the same idiots who decided to Californicate the whole fucking state. I got Mom and Dad out of here years ago. Fuck 'em. Let 'em tear each other apart. No, I'm just not looking forward to going into that."

"Well, we're not going into the thick of it right away," I pointed out. I checked the directions Raoul had sent against the map. I wasn't going to use electronic navigation any more than I absolutely had to. Knowing the kinds of resources either of the factions could call upon, I was paranoid as shit about electronic eavesdropping. "If we get off the 25 in Thornton, we should be able to get around to the safehouse without running into any of the mobs."

"What?" he protested. "You didn't say anything about *avoiding* the trouble spots! That's where the action is! How am I ever going to get on top of you and Larry on the scorecard if I don't get to run some rioters over? I even picked the truck with the reinforced bumper just for this!"

I glared at him. He kept his eyes on the road, but couldn't keep a straight face. The corner of his mouth was raised in a faint smirk.

"Funny," I growled. "Just stick to the fucking route."

"Come on, admit it," he said, "I had you going for a second."

"No, you didn't."

"Just for a second?" He was flat-out grinning now, though he still kept his eyes on the road. "Come on, don't tread on my dreams."

"I've known you too damned long," I said. "I always know your fucked-up sense of humor, even when you think you're hiding it."

"Damn it," he said, mock-angrily, even as he turned onto the Thornton exit.

I ignored him. It was an old, old game. Bryan liked to think up the most outrageous shit he could, just to see if I'd buy it, even for a second. This was actually pretty tame, by his standards, but then, we were all a little ragged by that point. He could hardly be expected to be on top of his game.

I considered saying something to that effect, as we went over the overpass and headed east. He'd be dramatically offended, and turn his considerable mind to coming up with something that he hoped would break my brain. It would be amusing, if slightly annoying, but I had been sitting in the truck with him for hours already, and was a little too punchy to really want to play the game anymore. I held my peace.

I kept an eye out, one hand never all that far from the rifle next to my leg. As far as we knew, Thornton was a relatively safe area, affluent enough and far enough away from the major metropolitan area of Denver to have, so far, avoided the rioters' attention. But you never knew, so I kept my eyes peeled and watched our surroundings carefully for any signs of impending trouble.

It's a weird thing, to see the smoke from a city tearing its guts out on the horizon while driving past immaculately groomed parks and seeing people coming and going about their business as if everything was normal. It was even weirder to see it Stateside. The Middle East and even Mexico had had time to develop a sick sort of new normal, where people went about their lives and jobs in spite of the violence and chaos around them, but somehow that seemed less freaky in countries that were already Third World shitholes, like Iraq. There was a creeping sense of unreality to seeing it at home. It was like a particularly eerie nightmare.

In a matter of minutes, we were out of town and among the farms again, the looming pall of smoke still on the horizon to the south. If not for that, there wouldn't have been any sign that anything bad was going on at all.

* * *

The same eerie calm continued all the way down to the suburbs of Denver, even though the pall of smoke got thicker, and it became more evident that it was rising from several different places. We were going to have to do some careful reconnaissance to make sure that we didn't get tangled in one of the real trouble spots.

Some of the illusion of normality began to dissipate as we entered the suburbs. Oh, there weren't blockades set up, or mobs walking the streets. The ticky-tack houses were still fronted by impeccably groomed landscaping, and nice cars still sat on the street or in driveways. But the neighborhood watch organizations were out in force, or what passed for force in suburban Colorado, anyway.

It hadn't been obvious at first. But after we'd gotten to the safehouse, a kind of bland, gray-and-white two-story residential home that Raoul had rented for us, we noticed we were getting some looks. And when the same

206

expensive SUV with a group of three men and a woman rolled past us for the third time, it was obvious they were trying to patrol.

"What the fuck are these idiots doing?" Bryan asked, as he pulled the duffel full of his gear and weapons out of the back of the truck.

"They're protecting their neighborhood, of course," I said. I might have been a bit more sarcastic than I perhaps should have, but it was hard not to be, when you're looking at a bunch of wide-eyed yuppies trying to play neighborhood militia.

"With what?" he said incredulously. "Baseball bats and tennis rackets?"

"Don't forget golf clubs," I pointed out, following him inside as Raoul opened the door. "Neighborhood like this, you know there's got to be ten golfers per block."

He snorted derisively as he looked for a spot for the duffel.

Of course these people were scared and worried. Their entire world was threatening to come unraveled. Most of them probably *cared* so much about the plight of the "oppressed" that they'd "understood" the first riots. But now the inevitable loss of control was threatening their precious lifestyles. I couldn't be too sympathetic, especially given how many of the same people who were watching us suspiciously would probably get a case of the vapors if they saw the kind of firepower we were toting inside. And Bryan and I didn't even have any of the belt-feds.

The living room was dark, as Raoul had the blinds drawn to keep curious eyes away. The floor was presently crammed with gear bags, ammo cans, rifles, shotguns, scratchbuilt submachine guns, a couple of medium machine guns, explosives, comms, surveillance gear, urban hide kits, and personal gear. It looked like a complete gear bomb, but there was actually some order to it, once you looked a little more closely.

Bryan and I found spots for our shit, and started our own setup, but I was interrupted by Raoul. "Hey, Jeff?" he called from the kitchen, "can you come in here a minute?"

I left my rifle and kit behind and followed him in. The kitchen was cheap but bright, with most everything made of white plastic or enamel. The white veneer on the cabinets had been worn away in a few places, showing the crumbling particle board underneath. Like the rest of the house, it was unfurnished; we didn't plan on staying long enough to need furniture.

A young Hispanic man with a shaved head and pencil mustache was waiting in the kitchen. He was short and wiry, and could easily have passed for a gang-banger, except that he was presently dressed in a dark gray t-shirt with an American flag on the sleeve, cargo pants, and a rigger's belt. I pegged him for a grunt, and Raoul quickly confirmed my impression.

207

"Jeff, this is Gabriel," he said. "We were squadmates in the infantry, long time ago. He moved up here, and he's been getting me up to speed on what's been going on."

Gabriel stuck out his hand, and I shook it. He shook his head. "Never thought I'd see this shit here, man," he said. "Grew up in Chihuahua, then went to Libya. This is fucking *Denver*, man. This fucking place ain't supposed to be a war zone."

"Preaching to the choir," I told him. "Any sign of our targets?"

He shook his head again. "They're laying low for now, if they're even here," he said. "There's certainly enough chaos going on to hide them. Entire sections of the city are no-go zones if you're the wrong color, or not wearing the right colors. If the Aztlanistas and the Black Supremacy types don't go after you, the Black Bloc fucks will. Unless you're in one of the gang neighborhoods, where they've pretty much taken over, and even a lot of the radicals won't go there."

"Daggett and his hitters probably won't blend in to that bunch very well," I mused, scratching my beard. "If Daggett's still the same cocky asshole he used to be, he won't want to lower himself to blend in with gangbangers and anarchist rioters."

It hadn't entirely surprised me to see Kevin Daggett on the target deck. I'd known the former SEAL a long time ago, during my first ventures into the contracting world before Alek, Larry, Mike, and I had started Praetorian. He was an arrogant prick who saw the world in black and white, but not the same way some of us did. We saw good guys and bad guys. He saw strong and weak. He was in it for the money and the thrills. It only made sense that he'd go to work for a group like "Marius." A chance to kill people and get paid? Sign him up. If anything, I was sure he would be pissed at having missed out on The Project. Those guys had to have gotten some serious violence on in Iraq and Syria.

According to The Broker—*Bates*, rather; I was going to have to get used to thinking of him by his real name—Daggett and company were working as a hit squad for "Marius," going after their political enemies Stateside now that the riots had kicked off this little shadow civil war. And we were in Denver to go after them.

Of course, as much as I didn't expect Daggett to bother trying to infiltrate the POCRF mobs or the anarchist Black Bloc, that didn't mean he wasn't as good at clandestine movement as we were. I might hate the guy's guts for the amoral predator he was, but I wasn't going to make the mistake of underestimating his prowess because of it. If he was in Denver, he was keeping his head down, carefully surveilling his targets, and getting ready to move while all eyes were focused on the riots.

"He's here," Raoul said. "We know that much. Derek and the intel cell have picked up some hits that confirm it, comms back to his bosses. Well, his middlemen, anyway." The factions were far too decentralized and compartmented for operational orders to come from anyone who was really calling the shots.

"It's a hell of a big city to search, though," Gabriel said, "especially with all these assholes running around ready to bust heads just for the hell of it."

I thought for a moment. "We don't look for Daggett," I said after a long pause. The idea was slowly coalescing in my head, but it made sense. "We look for his target."

Raoul was nodding, already reaching for the laptop that we kept as isolated and secure as possible to review the intel data we'd copied from Chu's stash on it. "Of course," he said. "We can probably narrow down the list of possibilities." He opened the laptop, then stared at the screen for a moment. "That's still going to be a pretty long list."

But I was still thinking, the gears still turning. "They wouldn't have sent Daggett for just any old hit," I said. "He's a prick, but he's an asset. They've got lots of low-level thugs they can contract for the little hits, the functionaries and the go-betweens that they've been hitting so far." I'd seen the lists of murders, and the analysis of their significance. Most of the victims had been relative small fry, at least going by what we had in the way of network maps for both factions. The assassinations were more pinpricks; little, lethal "Fuck You"s to the opposing faction. It seemed as if, as much as their machinations were already beginning to spiral out of control, they were still avoiding all-out war with each other.

They were just content to let the little people tear each other to pieces while they dithered, unsure whether they should fully commit to the war they'd started.

"If Daggett's here," I continued, my eyes a little unfocused as I let the wheels turn, "then they've got to have their eyes on a harder target than the usual little people who've been getting squashed. That should narrow the list down some more."

Raoul had been scrolling through lists as I'd been talking. "This is still going to take a while," he commented. But it didn't take all that long before he frowned and leaned in closer to the screen.

"What is it?" I asked.

He pulled back, frowning uncertainly. "It's a possibility," he said, "but no more than that. Seems kinda like a long shot, to be honest."

"What?"

He turned the laptop around so that I could see. The dossier on the screen was for one Congressman Dwayne Hicks, representing Colorado's 7th Congressional District. Pictured was a younger man, his blond hair as impeccable as his gleaming smile. I disliked him on sight.

"Congressman Hicks, here," Raoul said, "appears on at least three lists. He apparently has a reputation for loudly condemning cronyism and corporatism, while he has controlling interests in at least two government contractors, both of which Bates believes got their most recent contracts at extremely high bids because of his influence. Bates thinks he's dirty, the Cicero Group points out that he is close personal friends with a known member of 'Sulla,' Roberto Concri, and Chu's files include several deals for drugs and underage prostitutes while in the DC area. There is also apparently an ongoing investigation into selling negotiation points to the Chinese and compromising several classified operations while in the company of foreign dignitaries. Bates informs us that the investigation is not going anywhere because of Concri."

I nodded. "If he's pals with Concri, and he's that dirty, he'd be a prime target for a 'Marius' hit squad." Concri wasn't an active politician, being a retired court judge and Senator, but by all accounts, he wielded enormous power in and around DC. He was a "godfather," a don in the gilded underworld of current politics.

"It would certainly be an escalation," Raoul agreed, "but it would account for a heavy hitter like Daggett being around. Hicks' house is in Lakewood."

"Even better," I mused. "If they keep to the more affluent, crime-free parts of town, they've got less of a chance of local law enforcement getting in their way. The cops will be across town, trying to deal with the rioters." I nodded again, making a decision. "Get me Hicks' address. We need to go see if we can spot some surveillance."

***

Urban reconnaissance in an American suburban neighborhood is a bitch. No two ways about it. There's not a lot of traffic during the day, and unless you're set up to look like a believable repairman, you're going to get looks if you don't belong there. It's as bad as a small village in Iraq, if not worse. The small village might have an insurgent cell; these rich fuckers will call the cops if they think you're casing their house for a robbery, even if the cops are up to their assholes in, well, assholes.

When you're trying to case a house belonging to a sitting US Congressman, it gets even worse.

Hicks had a detail in a pair of Level 7 armored vehicles out front at all times. It seemed a bit conspicuous to me, but he was home not too many miles from mobs of people committing arson, destruction of public property, assault, battery, and even murder *en masse* on a daily basis. He couldn't be too careful, especially when the taxpayers were paying for his security.

We had to get in and get eyes on without compromising ourselves to either Hicks' security, the neighbors, or Daggett's recon element, if it was there. The fact that we were looking for Daggett, not Hicks, wasn't going to matter to Hicks' detail one iota. Nor was it going to matter to the neighbors if they found a dude in a ghillie suit hanging out in their bushes.

Fortunately, there was a nearby park, surrounding a small lake, with running paths that intersected with the nearby suburban streets. So, the majority of our reconnaissance took the shape of early morning, late morning, afternoon, and evening joggers. Sure, most of us might have stretched credibility a little bit, being generally big, hard-looking dudes who didn't exactly fit in with the skinny suburban women who made up most of the local joggers during the day. But aside from a few odd looks, we never got interfered with.

And we apparently weren't the only ones who thought of it, either.

"Great minds think alike," Jack said, coming back in from his morning run. "That's the third time I've seen the same jogger in the last couple of days, and he looks like one of us. Daggett's guys are doing the runner bit, too."

"It makes sense," Larry said. Larry had not joined the reconnaissance mission because Larry is not a jogger, and no one who saw the six-foot-five, bald, two-hundred-seventy-five-pound Monster would ever mistake him for one. Powerlifter? Maybe. Jogger? Not a chance. "There aren't too many other ways to do it, unless you're going to break into one of the neighbors' houses and hold them hostage for however many days you've got the stakeout in place."

"Which is something I wouldn't put past Daggett," I said. "Fucker'd probably like to do it just for shits and giggles."

"It does make our job a little simpler, though," Larry pointed out mildly. "Now we just have to have surveillance on the park, and spot them coming and going. It'll be easier than trying to set up in the neighborhood."

"Good point," I said. "One less potential point of failure."

That gave me a twinge. Jim had always been the one to point out how simple was better, because the more complex an operation was, the more potential points of failure were present, and the more likely failure then became. It was one of his words of wisdom that we'd all heard a thousand times, and now would never hear again.

Damn, I was getting tired of putting friends in the ground before their time.

"Eric!" I yelled, pushing the depressing thoughts to the back of my mind. Eric and Nick were the next two up. I knew Nick wasn't going to complain about ditching the jogger disguise; he wasn't as bad as Larry, but Nick despised running. As we got older, a lot of gunfighters I knew had come to dislike it, claiming it "breeds cowardice."

"Yeah?" Eric said, sticking his head through the door from the back room where he'd staked out his patch of floor.

"Change of plans," I told him. "We're switching to vehicle-borne recon, based on the park. The opposition is using the same jogger gambit we are, so we just need to look for them."

"Roger," he replied, disappearing back into his hole.

"We're going to have to get them pinned down quick," Larry said. "They're not going to dawdle and just watch Hicks forever. Now that they've got eyes on, they're going to move soon."

"I know," I said, but some of my misgivings must have made it into my voice.

Larry raised an eyebrow. "Having second thoughts about it?" he asked.

"You've seen Hicks' files," I replied. "Would it really be that bad to let Daggett do his job, then take him out afterward?"

The big man winced a little. "Yeah, I can see the problem." He sighed, folding his arms over his chest. His mouth quirked thoughtfully under his goatee. "I guess we've got to gauge whether the damage done by letting Hicks get killed outweighs the potential good of seeing him taken out of the picture."

"You know he's never going to see the inside of a cell, regardless of the vile shit he had Chu acquire for him," I pointed out. "Not with Concri backstopping him. I know, we're trying to stop this little civil war from going any farther, but fuck."

Neither of us had an answer.

***

We weren't going to get a chance to think of one, either. Less than two hours after Eric and Nick had gotten on-site and gotten eyes on a possible target vehicle, all hell broke loose.

I'd been catching a catnap; I'd done two three-mile runs in the last eight hours, and hadn't exactly been well-rested since before those gangbangers had showed up in Powell.

When a rolling *boom* like thunder sounded in the distance, though, I sat straight up, reaching for my rifle. "What the fuck just blew up?" I asked no one in particular.

"I don't know," Raoul replied. He was heading for the window. "It sounded close, though."

"Or really big and far away," I said, with a sudden ominous feeling in my gut. It wouldn't be the first time I'd been in some proximity to a *really* big IED going off, and it never boded well.

"Oh, fuck," Raoul said from the window. He was looking to the southwest. "There's a fucking *mushroom cloud* over Denver, man!"

I looked. Sure enough, there was a roiling, mushroom-topped cloud of smoke, dust, and flying debris rising above the city, some ten miles away.

"Oh, fuck," Raoul repeated. "This is bad."

212

"How big, do you think?" I asked. I was strangely calm and clinical as I watched the tower of destruction rising into the sky. Someone less knowledgeable and more prone to panic might equate a mushroom cloud like that with a nuke, but a nuke would have been a lot bigger, and we probably would have been fried by the initial thermal pulse, anyway.

He shook his head, getting a handle on the shock. "Pack a box truck full of explosives, maybe," he said. "That's a *big* IED."

"And right smack dab in the middle of the trouble zone," I pointed out. "Things must not be bad enough yet for somebody."

They were going to get that way, though, and pretty damned quickly.

CHAPTER 23

Almost inevitably, every comms line we had started going nuts.

It took a second of filtering through the noise to pick out the phone that was showing Eric's number. I swept it up and answered. "Talk to me."

"Shit is happening," he said. "Our targets just packed up and started moving. We're tailing them, but they're moving fast, and appear to be pursuing Hicks' detail. We've caught glimpses of those Level Sevens."

Well, it sounded like we were about to get into it. Whether Hicks went down or not, this was probably going to be our only shot at Daggett until and unless he popped up somewhere else. "Where are they going?" I asked, even as I reached for my chest rig.

"Generally east, and they're *moving*," he replied. "Best guess is, they're heading for the airport, but they're going to have to swing around the trouble zones to get there."

I was already staring at the photomap of Denver in the living room, as the rest of the team, who weren't out on surveillance duties or en route, gathered around. Everything else had gone quiet, as it became evident that we had a live one.

If we'd just been after Hicks, then it would have been easy. There really were only two viable approaches to the airport, so we'd just have to set up a team on each of them and ambush his motorcade on the way through. But we weren't just after Hicks, and Daggett had a lot of ground to choose from to set up an ambush between Lakewood and the airport. If he nailed Hicks before we could catch up, he might disappear before we could pin him down.

"Everybody get saddled up," I snapped, loudly enough to be heard throughout the house. "Game time." Turning back to the phone, I told Eric, "We're on the move. Keep on 'em and keep me updated."

"Roger," he replied. "We just turned south on the 95, passing the Sheridan Plaza."

That took a second to locate, especially since I was cramming myself into the passenger seat of a truck, my rifle covered—poorly—with a jacket, at the time. They were still quite some distance away, heading generally toward Sheridan. It looked like Hicks' detail was trying to go around to the south of Denver and the riots. And the bombings.

Larry was driving, and in minutes we were screaming down I-225 toward Aurora. If Hicks came our way, we might have to overshoot, turn around, and catch up, but Larry can have a hell of a lead foot when he needs to, and with Denver in utter chaos, especially given the mass casualties that were probably the result of that bombing, getting pulled over was unlikely, at best.

Eric was keeping up a running commentary. It sounded like Hicks' detail had figured out that they were being followed, and were trying to evade their pursuers. They had broken away from the main roads and were taking multiple, high-speed stair-steps through residential neighborhoods. From what I could hear, Nick was having a hell of a time keeping up.

Larry suddenly stomped on the brake. I was thrown against my seatbelt and almost lost my grip on the phone, but I didn't say anything. I could see why he'd stopped easily enough.

One thing we hadn't quite counted on, being in such a hurry, was that having a big-ass bomb go off in the middle of Denver was going to send a *lot* of people into a panic. And when people panic, they start trying to get away from whatever scared them, preferably by the line of least resistance. When you cram everybody possible onto that line of least resistance, it turns into a bottleneck.

The 225 just south of Aurora was a fucking mess. It would have been bad enough if it had just been hordes of car-borne refugees desperately trying to get away from the mobs and the bombs. But it looked like there was also a multiple-car pileup blocking half the freeway.

"Dammit!" Larry was looking for an escape route, but we were already blocked in by at least a dozen vehicles behind us. And meanwhile, things to the south were getting hairier, judging by Eric's continuing running commentary over the phone.

"These guys are getting more performance out of those Level Sevens than I've ever seen," Eric commented. He was trying to keep his voice even and dry, though I could hear the engine roaring and Nick cussing in the background. "When this is over, I really should find out who built those for 'em."

I thought I heard Nick yell something like, "Are you seriously talking cars right now?"

I couldn't hear Eric's rejoinder because we needed to move. "Everybody out and off the freeway," I said. "We're carjacking."

It felt weird, saying that in the States. It had long been standard procedure if pinned in hostile environments, but Stateside was supposed to be permissive. We weren't supposed to steal cars at gunpoint from *Americans*.

But that mushroom cloud that was still dissipating above Denver put the lie to this being a permissive environment. We *were* downrange, and we had to act like it.

Guns came out and we piled out of the vehicle, Larry and Bryan coming around to join me and Raoul on the passenger side. From there, it was a short zig-zag run through stationary traffic to the side of the freeway, over the concrete barriers, and up the shallow, grassy embankment.

We were getting a lot of looks, and I was sure there were several calls to an utterly swamped 911 operator about the men in military gear with rifles running along the side of the freeway, but we didn't have much in the way of options left. If we were going to catch Daggett, we had to move.

We ran along the cyclone fence, between the aspens or whatever the trees were, toward the overpass that crossed the freeway ahead. From there, it got risky.

Larry, being the biggest and objectively scariest of us, probably would have made the logical choice for the carjacker, but he was also the slowest. Raoul, somewhat to my surprise, beat all of us to the street, stepped out onto the asphalt, and leveled his Mk. 17.

There wasn't a lot of traffic out on the street, particularly not going west. But the one SUV visible screeched to a halt, the overweight woman behind the wheel staring at the gaunt Hispanic man pointing a rifle at her face with wide, terrified eyes.

Raoul ran forward before she could have second thoughts about stopping, yelling at her to get out of the car. While Raoul was, really, an intel guy, he could be a scary motherfucker when he wanted to be, and he was in full *barrio* mode at the moment.

The woman was too terrified to object, or even think of locking the door when Raoul ran up and yanked it open. I caught the tail end of her pleas for her life as she got out of the vehicle under Raoul's gun.

"He won't kill you," I told her as we caught up. Larry probably could have been nicer about it, but he was huffing a bit from the run. We hadn't been jogging. "We just need your car. We'll leave it somewhere the cops can find it." I wasn't sure she'd heard me. She was quaking with fear, staring not at Raoul, but at his rifle.

"*Vamonos!*" Raoul snapped, pointing to the side of the road. She scurried away, her head down like she was expecting him to change his mind and shoot her on a whim.

I felt like an asshole, but I left her to her own limited devices and piled into the passenger seat while Raoul took the wheel.

"What the hell was she doing driving *into* Denver right now?" Larry wondered as the doors closed and Raoul threw the vehicle into gear. "She wouldn't stand a chance in there."

"I doubt she understood what the hell is going on," Bryan said acidly, as Raoul threw the SUV around the next corner and started us flying south. "She probably had something she 'really needed,' and thought that everything would just stop, just for her. Trust me, there are thousands of those people around here."

217

"Doesn't matter," I said, pulling out the phone again. Good; I hadn't accidentally hung up on Eric, though he was calling out, wondering what the hell was going on. "We needed wheels, and she was in the wrong place at the wrong time."

"Jeff?" Eric was saying, as I put the phone back to my ear.

"Yeah, I'm here," I told him. "Sorry. We got jammed up on the 225 and had to 'borrow' some new transpo."

"Well, we're coming your way, fast," he said. "Hicks' guys apparently decided that trying to lose Daggett's hitters in the residential areas wasn't working, so they just hopped on the 225 North and are running for all they're worth."

"Fuck!" The northbound part had been jammed up with traffic, but still moving. They had a good chance of getting past us before we could get back on the freeway. "Don't lose 'em," I said. "We'll catch up as fast as we can. Eddie's out on the 70, trying to see if he can cut them off there."

"I think he's going to be too far away," Eric started to say, then I heard Nick yell an inarticulate string of mashed-together profanities.

"What just happened?" I half-yelled over the roar of the SUV's engine, as Raoul put the pedal on the floor.

It took a moment before I got an answer. "Two vehicles just busted through the fence and onto the freeway, and they're forcing the motorcade against the barriers on the median, right next to the reservoir," he said. "I think this is it. Daggett's here."

"Don't tackle 'em alone," I told him. "Let Hicks get smoked if you have to. We're on our way."

"We may not have much choice—Fuck!" The line went dead.

My blood went cold. Dammit, not Nick and Eric too. Raoul had the engine almost redlining, though he had to slow down to negotiate corners. The dude was a hell of a driver, too.

"Are there any emergency turnouts to cross the freeway," he asked, "or do I have to go down to the entrance ramp south of 'em?"

I peered at the map. "No, it looks like there are train tracks between the northbound and southbound lanes," I said. "I think we're going to have to go down to South Yosemite." That was going to make it even longer until we could get on-scene.

Raoul was muttering Spanish profanity, some of which even I hadn't heard, under his breath. He was thinking the same thing.

He kept to main thoroughfares, weaving in and out of what traffic there was, bouncing over the median once to counter-flow when the traffic going the same direction we were got too thick. Once again, if the cops hadn't had their hands full in Denver, we'd have been in trouble.

We were a quarter mile from the freeway when the phone buzzed in my hand. I answered it, to hear gunfire in the background.

218

"We just had to go to ground," Eric said. "They hit the lead and rear vehicles, hard enough to flip the lead, and they're suppressing the rear vehicle while they try to pry the principal out of his. You guys might want to hurry up."

"We'll be there in two minutes," I told him. "We're two miles out."

"Make it one," Eric replied. "I don't think Hicks' detail has that much time."

"If they get Hicks and bug out, don't wait for us," I said, grabbing the handle next to the door. Raoul had just almost tipped us over making the turn onto the ramp. "Stay on those assholes and *do not lose them!*"

"Roger that," Eric replied. "Just hurry up."

Traffic on the freeway, such as it was, had come to a screeching halt. None of the local drivers wanted to get near the violence up ahead. Unfortunately, that meant a bumper-to-bumper traffic jam across all five lanes. And there was a concrete wall against the side of the ramp.

"Hang on!" Raoul yelled, aimed for the narrow gap of the shoulder between the concrete wall and the outside lane, and floored it.

There was a *bang* as we clipped another vehicle's side mirror, and then another as our own got torn off. A horrific scraping sound, followed by a ripping *crunch* announced the death of the other side mirror, followed by an even louder scrape and buffet as we bounced off the concrete wall. Then we were clear and weaving through the traffic ahead.

"That ain't gonna buff out," Bryan commented, raising his voice to be heard over the scream of the engine.

We had to weave through several more vehicles that had turned off to the sides of the freeway, before we were totally in the clear and racing down an all but empty road toward the shitstorm ahead.

The scene looked pretty much the way Eric had described it. Eric's vehicle was about five hundred meters short, among a few others that had swerved off onto the shoulder, trying to stay clear of the line of fire.

Hicks' motorcade was made up of three armored Mercedes GL550s. The rear vehicle had been crushed against the median and pinned there by a dump truck. The lead vehicle was visible, on its roof and smoking, blocking two lanes of traffic. And the principal's vehicle, in the center, was hemmed in by two big F450s.

Two men with Mk48s were in the bed of the rear pickup, pouring fire into the rear vehicle. The armor had to be degrading fast by that point; even Level 7 armor can only take so many bullets before it breaks down. They were blocking the view of the principal vehicle, but they didn't appear to be taking any fire from Hicks' detail. They had complete fire superiority, which meant they had complete freedom of action.

Time to change that. "Let's get some fire on those machine gunners," I said. "Raoul and Larry are base of fire, Bryan and I will move up, link up with Eric and Nick, and maneuver on 'em."

I got terse acknowledgements, and then we were moving, bailing out of the vehicle behind our rifles. I ducked behind the passenger side wheel, putting the engine block of the otherwise paper-thin SUV between me and the enemy, leveled my rifle over the hood, and lined up one of the gunners. I didn't want to just start spraying rounds; better to knock them both out of the fight with well-placed shots before they even knew we were there.

But just as my finger tightened on the trigger, he went dry and ducked down into the bed to reload, spoiling my shot. I started to shift to his buddy, when the two duallies suddenly surged away from the stricken motorcade, accelerating down the freeway, even as the Mk48 gunners, braced in the bed of the rear vehicle, continued to pour fire at the two Mercedes that were still on their wheels.

"Mount up!" I yelled, suiting actions to words as I yanked the passenger door open again. Raoul was *moving*; he was already behind the wheel by the time I got my door shut, and he'd had farther to go.

Nick and Eric's vehicle was starting to roll when Hicks' Mercedes blew up.

The vehicle momentarily disappeared in an evil black cloud with a bone-jarring *wham*. The dump truck, which had been left behind, rocked on its shocks, and the pinned rear vehicle was shoved backward a couple of feet. The overpressure hammered us, rocking the SUV on its suspension and shattering the windshield and the driver's side window. Raoul cursed as broken glass rained down on us, his airbag deployed, and the car alarm started wailing.

My head already aching from the tooth-rattling blast, even attenuated by five hundred meters, I helped Raoul get the airbag out of his face, yelling at him to hit the gas and get us moving. If we lost Daggett then, we'd never catch him.

Hicks was dead; I had no doubts about that. No matter how good his Mercedes' armor was, that blast had to have turned anyone inside into red mush. The flames that were steadily eating away at the vehicle's remains would have signed their death warrants even if any of them had survived.

Raoul was still cussing, though his voice sounded thick. His nose was probably broken from the airbag, judging by the blood flowing and bubbling out of it, and he was going to be sporting a couple of good shiners in an hour. But he was hitting the accelerator and moving us forward.

He slowed as we came alongside Eric's vehicle, even without me saying so, but it was already rolling. Nick looked out his own shattered window, bleeding but apparently coherent.

"I'm all right!" he yelled. "Let's go!"

Reassured that we had everybody, Raoul stomped on the gas. The engine screamed, and it sounded like all was not well with it after that blast, but he got us around the gaping crater in the asphalt and the fiercely burning funeral pyre that had been Hicks' vehicle without too much trouble. The engine screamed louder as he got us on open road and after the two duallies.

They were already moving fast, but they were heavy diesels, and presumably weighed down with some armor and reinforcement for the sake of the hit. Otherwise, they probably wouldn't have been able to block in an armored Mercedes as well as they did. We were in lighter vehicles, which would give us some speed and acceleration advantage, as long as we could keep eyes on them, but would also present some troubles if we started taking fire from those two Mk48s.

With that in mind, I hauled my SOCOM 16 up and laid it over the dash, sweeping the last bits of the shattered windshield out of the way with the barrel.

Not a moment too soon, either. One of the Mk48 gunners noticed us as the two trucks jumped on Highway 83 and headed south. After a moment, I could see the light gray puffs of the gun's muzzle blast; there's usually no visible flame in broad daylight. A second later, three rounds hit the SUV's frame with ear-splitting *bang*s.

I returned fire immediately, though I had little hope of actually hitting the asshole, given how much both our vehicles were moving. But if I could at least get enough lead flying at him to keep his head down, he might not core our own vehicle out with that fucking belt-fed.

I had no idea where the first three shots went, but the fourth must have gotten close enough, because he ducked down into the bed. I was somewhat gratified to see, as we closed the distance, that the shot spiderwebbed the back window; the glass, at least, wasn't armored. That gave me an idea.

Raoul had flinched when I'd fired; he'd caught some of my not-inconsiderable muzzle blast. The SOCOM's 16-inch barrel didn't usually burn up all the powder in the 7.62 NATO cartridge, so there was a *lot* of blast out front of the muzzle. He flinched even more, and so did I, when Larry stuck his FAL between us and opened fire. He was leaning far enough forward that his muzzle brake was ahead of both of us, but not by much.

Still, Raoul flinched away from the bruising overpressure from Larry's muzzle, jerking the wheel and swerving the SUV halfway across the road. While it spoiled my own aim, it also had the added bonus of getting us out of the line of fire for a moment. Tracers skipped off the road beside us, but missed the SUV altogether.

We were speeding past residential neighborhoods on either side of the highway. We had to end this soon.

Bryan was yelling something behind me, but I couldn't really hear over the increasingly wounded scream of the engine, which was running rougher by the minute, and the thunder of our own gunfire. Then he was yelling in my ear, "Eddie's heading for Foxfield, to try to cut them off!"

"Great!" I yelled, but then I had to get back to fighting. Another long burst flailed overhead, a few rounds flying through the non-existent windshield to smack holes through the roof.

There was more traffic on the highway down this way, almost all of it heading south, just like we were, probably made up entirely of people trying to get away from the chaos in Denver. This was not their lucky day. I was taking fewer shots as the traffic got thicker; I didn't want to scrag some innocent bystander in a Prius, regardless of how stupid they were to keep driving when there was a running firefight in their rear-view.

Our targets didn't have the same scruples. The lead truck had to slow, as traffic got thicker, and all three lanes were momentarily blocked. In response, the lead driver proceeded to PIT the vehicle ahead of him into the next two lanes.

The Precision Immobilization Technique was developed for cops to end high-speed chases, by striking the rear quarter-panel of a fleeing vehicle, causing the driver to lose control and go into a skid. Done properly, it could stop a vehicle with minimal damage and risk to anyone around.

Daggett's lead driver wasn't interested in minimizing risk. He hit the car hard, savagely putting into the next two lanes of traffic. Within moments, there was a multi-car pileup skidding onto the concrete median and into oncoming traffic—not that there was a lot of that, thankfully—with a cacophony of tearing metal and honking horns.

I was pretty sure there were some dead people in that shitstorm, but we had our own targets. And they'd just made our job a little bit easier.

The rear vehicle had had to slow just enough that for a split second, I had a solid shot at the Mk48 gunner who was just bringing his gun back on-line from the last swerve. Leaning into the rifle to mitigate as much of the recoil as possible, I double-tapped him in the face from about a hundred yards.

I'm fairly certain the second shot missed, since he rocked backwards under the hammer blow of the first and vanished into the bottom of the truck's bed. As he did so, his Mk48 fell against his buddy, who flinched away from the hot barrel. I shifted my aim to him.

Larry and I both hit him within a split second. He went down in a heap, leaving a spray of red droplets across the truck's rear window.

With the machine guns out of action, Raoul stomped on the gas, trying to close the distance as the two trucks roared down the highway, halfway onto the shoulder. We were almost out of Foxfield already, getting back out into the open. The risk to bystanders was going to be less, but with our SUV sounding increasingly wounded, the risk of losing our quarry was getting higher. From the looks of things, Nick's and Eric's wasn't doing much better; they were lagging behind.

222

The guys in the cab obviously had figured out that their rear security was gone, and they didn't fuck around with trying to open the sliding back window. They just smashed the entire rear window out with their rifle barrels.

They didn't have time to start shooting though, since Larry and I already had a bead on the cab, while they had to turn around. We raked the back of the cab with fire, dumping a mag a piece into the shattered window.

One of us must have hit the driver. The truck suddenly swerved sharply, as if a dead weight had dragged the wheel over, plowed through the guardrail and went down the embankment. It rolled once, then came to a stop on its cab, still partially pointed down the slope.

While I knew that we needed to make sure we accounted for all of them, I also knew we didn't dare let the pressure off the lead truck to check the one we'd just disabled. It was pulling ahead, almost to the intersection a quarter mile ahead.

Even as I tried to line up a shot, while the SUV's engine started to emit a loud grinding noise and began to lose power, and smoke started to come from the hood, a long burst of machine gun fire caught the lead truck broadside as it entered the intersection.

Glass shattered, flecks of paint and puffs of dust were blasted off the side by the hammering impacts, and in moments the truck had swerved off the road and plowed into the guardrail. This one didn't go through, but fetched up against a splintered post and stopped.

I didn't know how Eddie had caught up, but he had. With his truck providing some cover from oncoming traffic, he and his team advanced on the stricken vehicle, guns up.

Raoul brought the SUV to a stop, only about fifty yards ahead of where the rear truck had gone through the guardrail, and we piled out. None of us looked very good; we'd been hammered by a blast, cut by flying glass, and knocked around by our own muzzle blast. Raoul had blood all over his front. Still, we advanced on the wreck with guns up, spread out into a wedge, while Eric and Nick came down the embankment on the far side of the crashed truck, similarly alert and armed.

The truck was a mess. The dead Mk48 gunners had been thrown clear when it went through the guardrail; I could see one of them lying face down in the field. The cab hadn't done too well with the rollover, either; they'd been going too fast. It looked like the passenger side had been compressed at least a foot.

A quick check confirmed my initial assessment. No one who might have survived the gunfire had survived the crash. All four men still in the cab were dead.

When we clambered achingly back up the embankment, I noticed quite a few vehicles pulled over on the side of the road, and there were some wide eyes watching us. Probably also more than a few cell phone cameras, too. We needed to get the hell out of there.

Eddie's two vehicles were rolling back toward us, against the flow of traffic, but any southbound traffic had stopped a few hundred yards back when the shooting had started. None of them appeared all that interested in coming closer, at least at the moment, though I could hear honking, suggesting someone hadn't gotten the memo and wanted to know why everybody was stopped.

The vehicles stopped even with us, and Eddie leaned out of his window. He drew a finger across his throat. "Nobody left," he called. He jerked a thumb at the truck bed behind him. "Jump in. It'll be tight, but it looks like your vehicles have had it." He peered at the SUV. "Not sure where you got that one, but I don't think you're getting the deposit back."

Looking at the smoking SUV that was noticeably lacking windows, I also noticed just how many bullet holes were in it. We'd gotten lucky. On impulse, I jogged over to it, reached in, and pried open the glove compartment. A little rummaging turned up the registration, which had Fat Lady's address on it. I stuffed it in a pocket. I'd lean on Renton later to make sure she got the price of a new vehicle. Bad enough we'd traumatized her for life and stolen her car. I didn't want to leave her hanging after that. I'm not that much of an asshole.

We clambered into the bed, which was awfully crowded with six of us in there, even with a little guy like Raoul, and then I banged on the roof of the cab. Eddie stuck a thumbs-up out of the window, and we turned around and headed south.

The job was done. It was time to get the fuck out of Dodge. No matter how bad things were in Denver, the local law wasn't going to be able to ignore this mess.

224

CHAPTER 24

I just wanted to sleep for a week. We'd had little time to rest, going after Daggett, and the fight itself, while much of it had been on the move in vehicles, had left us all battered and bruised, ears ringing and heads pounding.

But it wasn't going to happen. Too much was already going on, and we couldn't afford to take a week off.

The vehicles were definitely burned, and it took some careful doing and most of the rest of the day to replace them. Most of us had to hang out where we were dumping the old ones, in a gully north of Highway 194, until Johnny, Sid, and Gabriel came with new trucks.

While the vehicles had been burned, the safehouse had not been, as far as we knew. Sure, we were making some of the locals nervous, but there were bigger fish to fry, and we hadn't done anything to any of them, as opposed to the mob that had left the increasingly hostile-to-everyone zone in downtown Denver to start smashing windows and setting cars on fire as far east as Monaco Parkway. It seemed that everyone was blaming everyone else for the bombing; several militia sites were blaming the POCRF, the POCRF was blaming white people, cops, and militias.

But when the phone rang, half an hour after we got back to the safehouse, it quickly became evident that there was more going on than just clashing mobs in Denver.

It was Mia calling. "I know you guys just got done with one party," she said, "but something else has come up."

I rubbed my aching, gritty eyes. "Where?"

"Westminster, Colorado, of all places," she said. "The invitation is in the usual inbox." That meant that the target package had actually been saved in the draft folder of a common email account that had been cooked up beforehand. With a muffled groan, I pried myself up off the floor and went to the nearest laptop that was connected to the internet, though it was on the same VPN from hell that Derek had on the phones.

I logged in and checked the folder. Sure enough, there was a fairly complete target package there. My eyebrows climbed as I read. "Where the hell did all this come from?" I asked. What I was looking at was a pretty extensive dossier on several college- and graduate-school-age activists, all of whom at least had some ties to the POCRF. Not only that, but there was a detailed survey of their "operations center," in a coffee shop north of Westminster itself.

"I followed up on some of their posts, especially after the bombings," she said. I could hear the satisfied smile in her voice. "Derek's not the only one who knows the cyber magic, you know. Besides, it was easy. They're sloppier than they think. Tracking their IPs down was child's play."

"You are a woman of many talents," I said, as I continued to scroll through the targeting info.

"Why, Jeff, was that a compliment?" she laughed. "I might faint."

If she'd been there, I could have glowered at her, though I was sure she just would have laughed. As it was, I was just kind of stuck, unable to come up with a witty rejoinder to her teasing.

"Jeff? You still there?" she asked.

"Yeah," I grumbled.

"How are you holding up?" she asked. "You sound exhausted."

"It was a rough party," I said, "and things haven't exactly been calm around here, since somebody decided to blow up half of downtown."

"About that," she said, her tone turning businesslike again. "Denver wasn't the only place that happened."

That got my attention. "Where else?"

"Seattle, San Francisco, San Diego, Detroit, Baltimore, Boston, DC, Atlanta, Charlotte, Chicago, Dallas…" she took a breath. "There were twenty-four in all. Do you really want the whole list?"

"Holy hell." I ran a hand over my face. "This wasn't random."

"Not even close," she confirmed. "And I don't think it was anyone domestic, either."

"Any ideas?" I asked.

"Several," she replied. "Many of them have us on their target deck as well. Especially you."

"You're thinking Caliphate or Iran?" I asked.

"The Caliphate is still about as disorganized as Al Qaeda or ISIS," she said. "I don't see this kind of coordination happening. AQ never managed to repeat 9/11, and they still only managed to hit two out of three targets then. Twenty-four? I doubt it. The Iranians? Possible."

"But you don't think so." I didn't make it a question.

"I have a mental list of suspects," she temporized, "but it's still mostly speculation for now. We'll keep looking into it. The fact that no one has claimed responsibility suggests that it wasn't typical terrorism, trying to make a point. It was intended to stoke the fires. Notice how everyone's blaming everyone else? I think that was deliberate."

I could think of a couple of possibilities just based on that. Neither of which were encouraging. "*Somebody*'s going to take credit for it, sooner or later," I pointed out.

226

"Sure," she said. "I'm expecting some imam from the Caliphate to pop up with declarations of how it was a demonstration of why the infidels need to be terrified any minute now. But that doesn't mean they did it. Taking credit for somebody else's attack has been SOP for the Sunni Salafists since ISIS first popped up on everyone's radar. Probably before them, actually."

I changed the subject. "Has there been any progress on finding Little Bob?" I asked.

Her pause told me everything. "Nothing yet," she said, sounding genuinely upset. "I'm sorry, Jeff. We're really looking. It's like he just fell off the face of the planet."

Which told me almost as much as her earlier hesitation had. It took someone with some serious resources to make somebody disappear that thoroughly. Whoever had him, they were well-funded and well-prepared. It wasn't going to be easy to get him back once we found him.

"I know that finding him is a priority," she continued, when I didn't say anything. "Renton knows it, too, though he's not happy about it. He's not looking forward to pausing operations while you guys go after Little Bob, but he knows better than to try to stop you."

I didn't have much to say to that. I knew Renton was a big-picture thinker, and as much as he'd worked to be on "our side" as much as anyone was, I knew we were still assets to him. Expendable ones, if necessary. He would probably think of our rescue of Little Bob as a "personal" mission as opposed to the major ones he had in mind. I didn't give a shit. Little Bob mattered more to me than the Cicero Group or anything else that was going on, as bad as it was. If we sacrificed him for the sake of "the mission," when we had a chance to get him back, we'd never be able to live with ourselves afterward.

"I should probably let you go," she said after a moment, when I didn't comment. "Be careful, okay?" There was sincere concern in her voice.

"You too," I told her, and was somewhat surprised to find how much I meant it. As suspicious as I'd been of her motives from time to time, the fact remained that Mia had come through for us time and again, and, somewhat in spite of myself, I found that I liked her.

There was a hint of a rueful smile in her voice when she answered. "I'm far away from any targets or likely riots," she said. "I'm a lot more worried about you than I am about me." She paused a moment, then said quietly, "Take care, Jeff." Then the call ended.

I started to read the target package in more detail, then realized that we weren't going to get it taken care of that night, anyway. We still needed to reset. I hauled myself back over to my patch of floor, lay down, and promptly passed out.

***

227

Overall, the entire setup was too easy. Our targets met regularly in a coffee shop in its own building, in the middle of a parking lot, across the street from a brewery and a movie theater. The nearest building was fifty meters away.

The target package pointed out their usual patterns, and they were definitely creatures of habit. Judging by the pattern of IP hits, they could be found at that particular coffee shop during certain set windows during the day: about thirty minutes in the morning, about ninety minutes around noon, and then for a good three to four hours in the late afternoon, early evening. Of course, they were generally plugged in via mobile devices during the other hours of the day, but those were their coffee shop hours, and therefore when they were all together and vulnerable.

Somebody should have told these kids that if you're trying to be a revolutionary, there are going to be people who are willing to use force to shut you down. If you want to keep being a revolutionary, it helps to have good security habits.

Of course, I was sure that every one of these little fucktards was a rich suburbanite with many years of university bubble-think, who'd probably never even really been punched in the face, and certainly didn't expect that they'd ever face retaliation for their activities. Force was for other people. They were important. They did the thinky stuff that made *Zee Revolushun!* happen.

Well, they were about to learn the hard way that in Fourth Generation Warfare, there are no "front lines," and if you can be found, you can be hit.

The hours they kept were right during the, presumably, busiest hours of the day for the coffee shop. That was going to complicate matters, since there were probably going to be a lot of bystanders, but their information security was sloppy enough that we had photos of all of them.

At four o'clock in the afternoon, after Mia had confirmed remotely that all five targets were on-site, two big pickups and a white-painted, windowless van pulled up in an L-shape around the coffee shop.

Eddie and his boys were in the pickups. Most of my considerably reduced team was in the back of the van. Jack was the only exception, having arrived at the coffee shop an hour earlier. He would be in the back, fussing around on a smartphone. He was lean enough that he didn't stand out from the hipsters too much, something which he would doubtless get a lot of grief for, later.

As soon as the van lurched to a stop, right in front of the coffee shop entrance, Larry threw the back doors open and we piled out. We weren't as heavily kitted out or moving as explosively as we had the last time we'd pulled a raid like this, against the *Los Hijos* nightclub "*Los Valientes*," in Culiacan. We'd expected heavy resistance there. Here, we wanted to keep things as calm and low-key as possible while we secured our targets and got the hell out.

Didn't mean we weren't still ready for a fight; every one of us had a scratchbuilt 9mm bullet hose slung under his jacket.

The five of us walked casually inside. The place wasn't as crowded as I'd been afraid it would be; there were about a dozen people scattered around the tables by themselves, and a couple more knots of college-age men and women chattering to each other.

Jack looked up from where he was sitting in the back, and nodded toward the fireplace.

There were three men and two young women sitting in the black and red easy chairs drawn up around the fire. They had an array of laptops and tablets across their laps, a couple of small tables, and the arms of the chairs, and were talking excitedly, none of them looking up from their screens.

I recognized two of them right away. Sheila Marquez was, despite her name, a platinum blond, wearing a black beret and a red scarf. The pudgy kid next to her, wearing a pink beanie over his blue-dyed hair and a black turtleneck, would be Pierce Fallon. The rest of them had their backs to us, but it was pretty obvious that this was the bunch.

We fanned out carefully, getting a couple of glances from the other patrons, but not attracting the notice of our targets at all. They were focused on their "work," and Fallon was talking quickly.

"It looks like there's a police barricade forming at Arapahoe and Fourteenth," he said. "Let's spread the word; if they can get there quickly enough, they might be able to break it up before the pigs get their shit together." I was behind him by then, and saw the post he was typing up. He had close to a dozen tabs open, with multiple conversations going, along with a couple of videoconferencing calls open in different windows. He was typing, *"Pigs r on Arapahoe! Disrupt..."*

Before he could finish typing, Jack reached into his backpack, pulled out a nine-banger, yanked out the pin, and tossed it into the center of the coffee shop.

It was far enough from the windows that it didn't break any of them, but the series of reports was still deafening in the enclosed space of the shop. We all had earplugs in, since this had been part of the plan, but the rest of the shop's clientele most certainly did not.

People were screaming and diving for the floor, thinking that either another mass shooting like Aurora or Columbine was happening, or that a bomb had just gone off. In the meantime, the rest of us, who'd been braced for the noise, flash, and concussion, moved.

As Fallon flinched violently, ducking away from the blast, I wrapped my arm around his throat and hauled him bodily over the back of his chair.

The other four targets were getting the same treatment at the same time. Fallon's laptop went over backwards off his knees as I dragged him over

229

the back of the chair, hitting the floor with a crash that sounded muted after the explosion of the nine-banger.

Before anyone could gather their wits enough to react, still dazzled and rattled by the nine-banger, we were dragging our captives toward the door and the waiting van. Even if that hadn't been the plan, I'd seen enough of their little command and control operation not to want to stick around for long. All it would take would be one person on one of those live video calls getting the word out, and we'd be surrounded by a mob in a matter of minutes. While we'd avoided most of the rioting happening deeper in Denver, Renton and Mia had been keeping us abreast of things enough that we'd seen how fast these things could develop.

Jack had been moving as soon as the nine-banger had gone off, and was forcibly clearing the way to the door, shouldering people, chairs, and tables out of the way. He had his own subgun in his hands, so anyone who was recovered enough to try to resist had sudden second thoughts as soon as that 9mm bore was pointed at their faces.

It wasn't like there was a lot of distance to cover. In seconds, we had our bewildered, choking, weakly struggling charges to the door and were dragging them out into the light rain outside and the open doors of the van.

One by one, they were shoved into the back. Eddie's boys were up in the backs of the pickups, guns in evidence, providing security. I tossed Fallon in on top of Marquez, then we were piling in on top of them and I was banging on the wall. "GO!" I bellowed, as Eric yanked the doors shut. We almost all got piled against the doors before they latched, as Sid stomped on the gas. A moment later, everyone in the stark, stripped-down back of the van was thrown against the side wall, as we took a sharp turn out of the parking lot and onto the highway.

The oldest of the five, Tommy DuChamp, was starting to protest. "What the fuck, man!" he slurred. "You can't do this! We've got rights!"

"Shut up," Bryan snarled, stepping over Fallon and Marquez to reach for DuChamp. When the thirty-something activist tried to bat his hands away, Bryan just grabbed his wrist and twisted, flipping him over on his back with a yelp. In seconds, he was zip-tied.

The rest quickly got the same treatment. Since we were in a windowless van, I decided to forgo the black bags over their heads. For the moment.

"Listen up, fucksticks," I said, over the roar of the engine. "You've got a choice. You can lie there, nice and quiet, and not get roughed up anymore, at least until you get where you're going. Or, you can be mouthy little assholes, in which case you get gagged and blindfolded. Got it?"

"The people are going to figure out what happened to us," DuChamp insisted. I wondered if he'd hit his head, or if he was just chemically enhanced. In Colorado, there was no telling. "This will not stand!"

230

"Bryan, he's all yours," I said, since Bryan had a knee planted between DuChamp's shoulder blades anyway.

"With pleasure," he replied. We had rags to use for gags, but Bryan apparently thought it was funnier to take DuChamp's scarf and stuff it in his mouth behind a strip of duct tape, instead.

"We've seen your faces," Marquez said. "Do you really think you're going to get away with this?"

That prompted a chorus of dry, humorless laughter. "Worry about yourself, Sheila," Eric said. "You've got a lot bigger things to worry about now than what's going to happen to us."

That shut her up. I suddenly smelled piss, and grimaced. Why were so many of the players in this little clusterfuck a bunch of incontinent cowards?

***

A guy I knew only as Ollie, one of Renton's "associates," was waiting at the rendezvous outside of Boulder. The RV point itself was on a stretch of narrow dirt road well outside of town. It was easy enough to see that we were clean as we approached.

Ollie was a heavyset guy, who always managed to look like a mobster from *Goodfellas* or *Casino*. If he'd been one of us, he probably would have had the callsign "Guido." He was wearing a leather jacket and leaning against the box truck parked on the grass beside the road. He grinned as we pulled up and I climbed down from the back.

"You boys sure stirred some shit up," he said. He might look like an East Coast goombah, but Ollie talked with a distinct Midwestern twang. "There's a mob around that coffee shop right now, demanding justice for The Five. They're not sure what happened, but they're sure that they're pissed off."

"Any violence, or just a lot of yelling?" I asked.

"Just chanting and broken glass, so far," he replied. "From what I've seen online, it's mostly a bunch of millennial hipsters, so they haven't got a lot of intelligence or stomach for violence. The hard-core Black Bloc, gangbangers, and racial supremacists are still setting shit on fire and shooting at cops in Denver proper."

I jerked a thumb at the van. "You need a hand with 'em?"

He grinned again. "I won't object. Can only stand so much patchouli on my hands in the first place."

***

It took a few minutes to transfer the captives. Marquez was kicking and trying to scream, but ended up just choking on the gag more. Surprisingly, the rest seemed to be in shock. Once Marquez got shoved into the back of the box truck, Ollie hauled down the back door, shook our hands, and climbed into the driver's seat. The box truck rumbled to life and trundled away down the dirt road.

We climbed back into the van and headed out. There was more work to be done.

CHAPTER 25

Hicks' assassination opened the floodgates. It was an escalation that neither side could ignore. So, that meant we were busy. While, technically speaking, we were trying to put out the brushfires, more often than not, it really didn't feel that way.

***

We'd been warned that Austin was almost as bad as Denver. The warning was wrong. Austin was worse.

Denver's violence, exacerbated by the bombing, had been primarily due to "protests" turning into mobs. Austin had seen a few protests, especially after Pueblo, but the cartels and the Aztlanista militias had quickly taken over. Most of the would-be revolutionaries and students had run for cover as soon as the real criminals and terrorists had started a shooting war with the police.

We weren't going into that mess to try to stop it. That was too much for our little company to accomplish. No, we had a couple of very specific targets.

***

Albert Eddings wasn't a politician, in the strictest sense of the word. He'd never run for or held public office. Ordinarily, that wouldn't be a bad thing, at least not to me, but the thing was, he didn't let that stop him from meddling.

Eddings didn't have a profession, not as such. He'd made a few billion in the stock market, back before the bottom had dropped out and the Greater Depression had hit. He'd also carefully diversified so that, once the global economy really had gone to hell, he'd weathered the storm better than most. That meant he had plenty of money at a time when nobody else had enough.

Now, up to that point, that just made him smart. It was what he did with the opportunity his money presented that turned matters…unpleasant.

While his public profile was generally that of a cheerful playboy who hobnobbed with politicians and celebrities, the Cicero Group's intel showed a darker side. He'd faced at least four serious felony charges, including assault and battery, complicity in human trafficking, bribery, and grand larceny. Every charge had been dismissed before even getting close to trial. Certain meetings and known connections suggested to the Group's analysts that he had financial arrangements with the judges involved.

It only got worse from there. Eddings had so much money that he'd been able to do various licit and illicit "favors" for at least half a dozen Congresscritters and a couple of Senators. Not only was he untouchable, but he had the ears of some very important people.

One of those he didn't own, but was still apparently close friends with, was one Mason Van Damme. Like Concri, Van Damme was an old hand, a retired politician and former Secretary of State. He was one of the centers of gravity around which the "Marius" network revolved, another man for whom laws and ethics were as malleable as the circumstances and the amount of money and power that could be brought to bear dictated. The Group had hundreds of gigabytes of video and photos of Eddings hobnobbing with Van Damme, and some of the video came with audio tracks that were pretty damning.

***

At 0300, two boats worked their way up the Colorado river, keeping close to the steep cliff on the west shore. Thick brush and trees overhung the water, lending plenty of shadow from the city lights and the half-moon in the clear sky above. It was chilly, since it was the middle of the night in early December, but since it was also Texas, it was still above freezing.

We couldn't see the top of the cliff; there was too much vegetation. But the southernmost point of Red Bud Island, sitting in the middle of the river, was clearly visible in the moonlight, and provided a perfect reference point. As soon as we were even with the point of the island, we were where we needed to be.

The trolling motors on the boats weren't very powerful, which was why we'd taken almost three hours to make our way up the river from where we'd launched, only about a mile and a quarter away. But they were quiet, and quiet was what we needed. We'd waited to gear up and draw out the weapons until we were well away from the launch point, and drawing any attention after that could be a problem. Two boats full of men in camouflage paint, chest rigs, and rifles weren't regular sights on the Colorado, even with the amount of violence that was already tearing Austin apart.

It was easy enough to anchor the boats; the branches of the trees hung down low enough over the water that it only took a couple of ropes and quick hitches thrown over a couple of the thicker branches. Getting up through that thicket was going to be something else.

We had a collapsible caving/maritime boarding ladder, that amounted to little more than a telescoping pole with nubs on the sides that were barely wide enough for a man's boot. But getting it through the tangle of branches was going to be tough. Eric started carefully pushing it up through the vegetation anyway. If we sat there studying it and trying to find the perfect route, this was going to take too long.

Once he got it somewhat stable against the side of the cliff, though there was still enough spring in it to suggest it was actually leaning against some of the branches instead of solid earth, Jack mounted the ladder and started up, pulling a climbing rope with him.

There was a lot of rustling and cracking going on as Jack disappeared into the shadows and branches above, and there was more coming from the rear boat. It was noisy, but unavoidable. Anyone who's ever humped a ruck through thick brush on a recon patrol can attest that part of the reason recon patrols try to stay away from people is that five to six guys with close to a hundred pounds of gear a piece sound like a herd of elephants going through the bush.

Of course, there was still enough loud music coming from Eddings' pool deck above that we probably weren't going to be compromised by a few rustling and cracking branches. Most of the rest of Austin might be hunkered down in their homes, hoping to go unnoticed as the gangs, militias, and increasingly heavily-armed, armored, and paranoid cops roved the streets, but Eddings and his hangers-on didn't give a shit. They were untouchable, after all.

Surprise, asshole.

The rope jerked, then jerked again. Jack had reached the top and secured it. I slung my rifle, grabbed hold, and started to climb. I got wet in the process; there was no way to avoid going in the water at least a little on getting out of the boat.

It was a fight getting up that cliff, regardless of what Jack had already done to clear the way. Branches grabbed at my kit or just got in the way. I had to get over a couple that were too far out from the cliff face to just step over, but too close to go under. It was a bitch.

Larry had to be having a hell of a time. He was the biggest of us by far.

I finally got to the top, where Jack had the rope securely hitched to a tree trunk that was hanging out over the edge of the cliff. Jack didn't help me over, since he was on a knee behind a bush, his rifle up, watching the yard.

We were on the edge of the property itself, though there was still plenty of landscaping casting deep enough shadows for us to hide in.

The music was coming from the brightly-lit pool, a few yards uphill from where we crouched. There was no one else in sight, at least not at first. The yard was empty, the firepit abandoned.

As I watched, though, a pair of young men came into view, pacing along the property line. They were dressed in dark fatigues and windbreakers, with glorified police belts bearing Glocks, extra mags, flashlights, and batons. As expected, Eddings had security patrolling his perimeter. There would be more inside, probably less overtly armed, discreetly ignoring the bacchanalia going on.

Eric struggled up the rope behind me, even as I got eyes on Larry, Nick, and Bryan, farther down the cliff edge. Everybody was here. We'd wait until the guards went past, then move.

But we were out of time. My earpiece crackled. "Where are you?" Eddie asked.

I hated throat mikes, but for this, we'd gone ahead and used them. With the Cicero Group once again picking up the tab, we were able to get a little fancier, gear-wise, than we had been going up against the Task Force. I pressed the mike to my larynx and murmured, "On attack pos."

"Well, you'd better move quick, then," he said. Eddie was sitting in a van down the street, there for support if we needed it, so he didn't have to worry about being as quiet as we did. "It looks like you've got company arriving. We're moving on them, but you'd better get in there and secure Albert quick, before they do."

Fuck.

Our second target in Austin wasn't technically part of either "Marius" or "Sulla." They were Mexicans, a hit squad known only as *Los Lobos Rabiosos.* They had been Mexican Marines, deserted *en masse*, and had worked for the highest bidder in the cartel wars ever since. They really didn't give a shit who was paying them, so long as they got paid. They'd reportedly worked for *Los Zetas*, the Guzman-Loera Federation, CJNG, and the Mexican government. The story went that they'd been stiffed once. They'd been hired by a small splinter cartel that had taken a bit of the Tijuana cartel after the Arellano-Felix brothers had wound up in prison, only after they'd done the job, the cartel didn't want to pay them. The hit squad had wreaked such bloody vengeance on the splinter cartel that there were rumors that the Arellano-Felix brothers wanted to offer them a reward.

We'd gotten word that *Los Lobos Rabiosos* were in Austin, on "Sulla's" payroll, and they were gunning for Eddings. In an echo of the Denver mission, Eddings was so dirty that it was sorely tempting just to let the mad dogs have him. But Eddings knew things, and he knew people, and Renton wanted to pick his brain.

And however much of a shitty human being he was, I wasn't willing to hand *anybody* over to animals like *Los Lobos Rabiosos.* I'd been in Mexico. I knew what they'd do to everybody in that mansion. While I wouldn't classify any of them as "innocent," that didn't mean I'd let them be raped, tortured, and murdered, which was what they'd get at the hands of that hit squad.

"Roger," was all I sent. Looking over at Larry, I got a thumbs-up; he'd heard it, as well. I returned the signal, then turned my attention to the target building and lifted my rifle. The time for stealth was about over. We just didn't have the time, not if *Los Lobos Rabiosos* were about to kick in the front door.

The two guards had already passed us. They didn't seem all that alert, and were bitching and complaining about all the pussy they weren't getting, out there on perimeter patrol. I gathered that there were a lot of naked girls running around the grounds.

I stepped out of the bushes, training the muzzle of my rifle on the first guard. Eric and Jack were with me, and Larry and the rest were closing from our left. "*Hsst!*" I hissed.

They turned around lazily, one of them rolling his eyes. A few of the partiers must have tried to fuck with them already that night, and they thought that was all that was going on. After all, this was *Albert Eddings'* place. Who would be stupid enough to fuck with Albert Eddings?

"Very funny, Charity," one of them started to say, but as he looked back, he saw that it wasn't Charity, whom I presumed was a stripper, or a hooker, or both, but three large men in camouflage, all pointing battle rifles at him. His eyes went wide, and his mouth started to open.

"Not a sound," Jack hissed. The guard's mouth closed with an audible *clop*. He spread his hands away from his belt. The other one followed suit as soon as he saw what was happening.

"Down on your faces, fast!" I snarled. We didn't have time to fuck around with these guys. When the second one dawdled a little, I stepped forward, intending to knock him the fuck out with my rifle butt if I had to. He got the message though, and dropped to his face faster than a recruit getting bellowed at by a drill instructor.

It was a short business to zip-tie their hands and feet, gag them, and chuck their pistols into the bushes. Then we were moving again.

We split into two elements to flow around the pool. For all the noise, the pool itself was all but abandoned, with only a few naked girls passed out on pool chairs and a couple enthusiastically going at it on another one. The chick screamed as we came into the light, but then the shooting started out front, and fucking *everybody* started screaming.

I broke into a run, sprinting for the veranda. I had to hurdle a gray-haired, pot-bellied man in a speedo, passed out in a puddle of his own vomit, to get to the door.

Fortunately, the mostly-glass door was already open. We went into the entryway and cleared it quickly, weapons tracking wherever eyeballs went, before moving deeper into the house. We had a rough floor plan, and a decent idea of where Eddings was going to be.

The volume of fire up front was intensifying. Eddie had hit *Los Lobos Rabiosos* hard, but they weren't the type to go down easily. It sounded like they were making a hell of a fight of it.

The mansion was an imitation Mediterranean villa, with everything in marble, white plaster, light-colored stone, and dark wood. The grand room's ceiling was three stories above the floor, and as big as it was, it was cluttered with expensive furniture, some of it draped with equally expensive women and rich men, many of whom had to have imbibed a lot of very expensive drugs, given that they weren't making like everyone else and running for the back, screaming.

I didn't give a shit about most of those people. They weren't the target. I'd identify hands, make sure there wasn't a weapon being pointed at us, and then shove them out of the way if they were blocking my path. Other than that, as long as they kept their distance—and most of them did, once our own weapons registered through their chemical haze—we let them be. We'd still do our damnedest to kill the hit squad, thus hopefully sparing their lives, but that was about it.

I got to the spiral staircase and pointed my muzzle up, clearing the landing above, while the rest of the team covered the other three entrances to the grand hall. Then, barking, "On me!" I started up.

One of the security guards leaned over the landing and fired a shotgun at us. I *felt* the shot pattern go past and blast chips out of the step in front of me. Stinging bits of shattered marble drew blood from my shins, through my trousers. Fortunately, he hadn't really aimed; he'd just kind of pointed the shotgun over the landing and blasted.

I, on the other hand, aimed. While I had nothing in particular against whatever poor saps were working for Eddings, you shoot at me and mine, you die. It's a simple equation. I leaned up, twisting my torso to get my rifle on-line, and put a bullet through his skull from six feet away, before he could fire again. He pitched backward and hit the landing with a *thud.*

I hurried up the rest of the steps, my rifle trained on the landing, the others right behind me. In seconds, we had three guns on the upstairs hallway, which was, fortunately, empty. I didn't know why the guard had been there by himself, but it was too late to ask him. Getting my bearings, I headed for where we were pretty sure the master bedroom was located.

The white-painted double doors yielded easily to a heavy boot, and we poured into the room, guns up and looking for targets.

There weren't any, unless one counted the half a dozen hookers on the bed and the floor, all in various stages of drug-induced stupor, and a naked Albert Eddings, hiding behind the bed and gibbering in fear.

Nick and Jack closed in on him, guns leveled, while Eric, Bryan, and Larry secured the rest of the room, and I went to the window. It only opened up onto the grounds and the pool, though, so I couldn't see any of what was going on out front.

"Hillbilly, Geek," Eddie called. "Three of them got past us and went inside. You've got company coming."

"Roger," I replied, just as a silhouette appeared in the door.

The man was wearing a ballcap pulled low over his eyes, and a skull-faced balaclava. He was dressed entirely in black, including his gloves, and had a Gilboa 9mm submachine gun in his hands.

That was about all I had time to register, before Eric and Bryan each Mozambiqued him at the same time. Suppressed or not, the 7.62 rounds ripped through the air with harsh *cracks* and sent him crashing to the floor in a welter of blood.

Eddings was down on the floor, his hands over his ears, screaming, even as the rest of the stack of Mexican killers tried to push into the room. They knew they were dead if they froze; they'd been well-trained. So, they pushed the fight, shooting as they came.

Whether it was instinct or just great minds thinking alike, we'd all dropped to a low knee as soon as the first guy appeared in the doorway. It saved our lives, too, since the hail of 9mm bullets went close overhead, blasting splinters off the bedposts, smacking holes in the plaster, shattering two of the windows, and shredding the pillows.

I was already on sights even as I hit rock-bottom, my shooting elbow almost touching the floor, and another black-clad form filled my aperture. I thumped five shots into him, even as the rest opened fire, as well. I think the last two *Los Lobos Rabiosos* killers caught something like fifteen rounds apiece, minimum. In seconds, it was all over, the bodies slumped in the doorway and leaking blood on the hardwood floor and expensive rugs.

"Hillbilly, Geek," Eddie called again. "We've secured the front; you might want to leave the boats and come with us. There's *lots* of company on the way." That had been expected. With Eddings' connections, the entire Austin PD would be his QRF, regardless of what other brushfires they had to deal with that night. And we didn't want to be on-scene when they showed up.

"Roger," I replied. "Cargo's secured, we're coming down the spiral staircase." I really did *not* want to get shot by our own guys, not for the sake of this naked sack of shit that Nick was now propelling in front of him, one arm looped through his zip-tied hands and a hand clamped to the back of his neck.

I led the way down, yelling, "FRIENDLIES!" at the top of my lungs.

"Come on!" Eddie shouted back.

As I came out into the grand entrance hall, I saw about half of Eddie's team on a knee around the room, covering the entrances and exits.

The hall was a fucking slaughterhouse. Eddie and his boys might have taken the edge off the *Los Lobos Rabiosos* assault, but they'd still gone through what had been left of Eddings' security like a buzz-saw. The scared partiers hadn't had a chance. There were bodies littering the hall, not all of them clothed. The place stank of gunpowder, blood, shit, and fear.

We didn't stick around to take it in. With the way clear, we pushed out the front door, stepping over more bullet-riddled corpses and fallen weapons, past the smoking ruin of the hit squad's van in the driveway, and onward to Eddie's van, a fifteen-pack job with the windows painted over from the inside and the seats stripped out. Eddings was propelled, none too gently, into the back, then we all piled in and Sid hit the gas, roaring away from the scene even as we heard the sirens in the distance.

We wouldn't stop until we were halfway to San Antonio. Our job in Austin was done.

It wouldn't be the last.

CHAPTER 26

Getting to Lucia Sparrow was going to be a bitch.

The lane where the Congresswoman's house was situated was presently closed off by two black, armored Suburbans. Men in khaki fatigues, plate carriers, and helmets were standing in front of the Subs, with M4s at the low ready. There were more back in the pines that lined either side of the road, and I was pretty sure there was a M240 or two back there. I could see a couple of lumps that might have been sandbagged defensive positions.

As Larry and I approached slowly, two of the riflemen leveled their weapons at our rental car, while the middle guy held up a hand for us to stop.

"Damn, these guys are not fucking around, are they?" Larry asked, lifting his eyebrows.

"They just had their principal come damned close to getting turned into pink mist two days ago," I pointed out. "We'd be a little trigger-happy after something like that, too."

I braked slowly and smoothly. The windshield wasn't armored, and any kind of quick movement was not going to be a good idea, not with Sparrow's detail as twitchy as they obviously were.

We'd actually passed the scene of the previous ambush on the way there. There was an IED crater and a *lot* of spent brass around the intersection between Highway 40 and South Woody Mountain Road, along with the bullet-riddled, burned out remains of a vehicle. Nobody knew for sure who had done it; there were certainly enough narcos running around the Southwest with an interest in smoking a Congresscritter, but a "Sulla" cutout was also suspected.

Lucia Sparrow, as it turned out, was one of the vanishingly rare politicians who had built a reputation for integrity and rock-hard principle in her five years in office. She couldn't be bribed, and she couldn't be bought, at least so went the word on the street. She'd called out corruption and lies amongst her colleagues without regard for who they were. It hadn't won her any friends, but she'd publicly proclaimed more than once, "I'm not here to make friends with other members of Congress, or the government, or even the President. I'm here to represent the people of Arizona."

Needless to say, her attitude didn't appear to have endeared her to either of the factions, either. That was why we were there.

Our problem was, we couldn't secure Sparrow if her detail was going to fight us, and they were presently paranoid as hell. And with good reason.

Whoever had pulled off the bombings in twenty-four cities, everybody and their mother was now blaming their pet bogeyman for them. There had already been enough blood spilled that most people were just looking for justification to spill more of it. The POCRF was blaming militias, the cops, and white supremacists, and calling for more "white blood" to be shed in retaliation. The Three Percenters were screaming about Federal false flags and gearing up for a war with the POCRF and their allies and the Feds at the same time. The think tanks were blaming the Russians, the Iranians, or the Caliphate. The Caliphate had claimed responsibility, though almost twelve hours late, which tended to reinforce the idea that they'd had nothing to do with it, but wanted the credit.

If the point of the bombings had been to throw gasoline on the flames, they had succeeded.

Knowing that didn't make our job any easier, staring at multiple M4 muzzles from behind an unarmored windshield. I kept both my hands on the wheel as the middle guy, who hadn't pointed his weapon, came forward.

"Sorry, gentlemen, but this street's closed," he said, his voice clipped and professional, as he came to the open window beside me. He wasn't pointing a weapon, but his hand was on his M4's firing controls, and he was a good pace back from the car, so that he wouldn't have to step back to make room to bring his carbine up if he needed to. I also noticed, out of the corner of my eye, that the two still covering us had moved to make sure he wasn't cutting off either of their fields of fire. I suspected that he'd placed himself equally carefully to give the belt-feds in the woods a clear shot, too. These guys were pros.

"Yeah, we know," I told him, keeping my hands on the wheel. "We need to have a word with your boss."

He shook his head. "I'm afraid that's not possible," he said. "The Congresswoman is not seeing anyone at the moment."

"Look, bud," I told him. "We're not here to get your principal." Well, in a way we were, but "get to safety" is different from "get dead." "We'll strip down to our skivvies if you need us to for your comfort level, but we've got to talk to your boss." Before he could answer, I pointed out, "Though I don't think seeing this big bastard here in his skivvies will make *anyone* particularly comfortable." I was hoping to ease the tension a little bit and get old boy to relax a little, but it didn't particularly work. He was probably used to douchebags trying to get by security with humor, and was probably somewhat professionally offended.

"I need you to turn around and drive away, sir," he said, in the same flat tone.

"Look," I said, "I'm going to reach for a phone. I'm not reaching for a gun, so don't shoot me."

"Do you have weapons in the vehicle?" he asked, lifting his muzzle ever so slightly.

Ah, fuck. This guy's more keyed up than I thought. This is going to suck.

"We've got your back, Hillbilly," Eddie's voice said in my earpiece. It was a little, flesh-colored Bluetooth job, in my right ear, away from the window. Eddie and I really didn't have separate teams anymore; we'd taken serious enough losses since this all kicked off back in the fall that we were essentially working as one slightly reinforced team. Fortunately, neither Eddie nor I were the kind to squabble over who was in charge.

Still, I didn't want one of us smoking this dude, who was just doing his job, if we could help it. If he got too trigger-happy, we might still have to, but that would make our job that much harder.

That didn't mean I was necessarily going to get obsequious when it came to dumb questions. This was fucking Arizona. I looked at the guy like he was stupid. "Of course we've got weapons in the vehicle," I told him, in a voice that said, without so many words, *you fucking numbnuts.* "In case you hadn't noticed, it's gotten a little dicey around here, with cars blowing up and people getting shot." He didn't look impressed, but then, I probably wouldn't in his place, either. But he didn't point the M4 at my face, so that was progress, of a sort.

Very slowly, I reached for the center console with one hand, leaning back so that he could watch every move I made. I did not want this guy getting nervous.

The phone, by design, was in easy reach. I pulled it out and showed it to him, but he tensed anyway, and the muzzle rose fractionally again.

Fuck. He's probably thinking of all the cell phones that have been used as IED initiators over the last twenty years. But we were committed, so I unlocked it and started the call before switching it to speaker. When he heard the phone ringing and nothing exploded, he relaxed a little. I held the phone out to him through the open window.

Cautiously, he stepped forward and took the phone. "Who is this?" he asked.

Renton's voice sounded tinny over the little speaker. "You can call me Baxter," he said. Even dealing with people who were supposed to be friends, the Cicero Group was being cagey. They had to be; there had been some chatter recently that suggested both factions had picked up on the fact that *somebody* was going through their assets like a chainsaw through butter. "I represent a group that has similar aims and principles to your boss. Have you heard of a man named Nelson Cuellar?"

"No," the guy said flatly. "Should I have?"

Though his voice stayed even, I could imagine the look of frustration on Renton's face. "He's the guy who killed Senator Leland," he explained, "and we believe he was the lead on the kidnapping of Judge Alitano's family. Ringing any bells now?"

A faint frown flickered across the detail lead's face. He *had* to have heard about those incidents; even with everything else going on, both had been fairly high-profile, especially as they'd happened before the bombings. "Okay, the name sounds vaguely familiar, now that you mention it," he said. "What about him?"

"We have credible information that he's been sighted in Flagstaff," Renton continued, "and reason to believe that Representative Sparrow is his next target. You've already been hit once." That got a raised eyebrow, as if our new friend was wondering how Renton already knew about it. "You are no longer secure. My associates are there to assist you in getting Ms. Sparrow to a safer location."

He eyed us skeptically. "Is that why they're armed?" he asked.

Renton chuckled. "Those boys are *always* armed, son. And they're just the two you can see. Look, do what you need to, search 'em as thoroughly as you'd like before letting them through to the Congresswoman. But you're running out of time. Cuellar's got a crew of hard-dicks that make those pussies you shot up off the 40 look like lapdogs." That wasn't strictly accurate; from what I knew, Cuellar was a bloodthirsty but generally sloppy shitbag, and his crew weren't much better. But Renton wanted to motivate Sparrow's detail to cooperate, and putting a little fear in 'em probably wouldn't hurt. "If you don't believe me, have your boss call Martin Schofield. He'll confirm everything I've said." He probably should have started with Schofield. The guy was an old FBI hand, and a personal friend of the Sparrow family. He was also one of the original Cicero Group.

The dude looked skeptical, but finally handed the phone back to me without a word. I took it, and put it back into the center console. "Out of the vehicle, please," he said, taking another long step back. "Slowly. And keep your hands where I can see them."

We complied, and he waved more of his boys over. He wasn't taking chances. I can't say I blamed him, not that it's comfortable for a man in my position to surrender himself completely to a thorough search and disarmament. I feel naked without at least a gun and two knives on me.

They didn't fuck around. They set up on opposite sides of the car, with searchers and cover men placed so that either or both of us could be shot without endangering either of the searchers or the cover men. They were pros, I'll give 'em that.

Once they were satisfied that we weren't packing concealed weapons or suicide belts—or pipe bombs up our asses; they were damned near that thorough—the detail lead just nodded down the road, past the two Suburbans. "Okay, let's go."

"Can we take the phone?" I asked.

He shook his head. "You can convince her or you can't. I'm not letting an un-screened phone into her house. Now either get moving, or get the fuck out of here."

I just nodded amicably. Fortunately, we had somewhat anticipated this possibility, which was why Martin Schofield was supposed to be keeping his phone handy.

It was almost a klick from the roadblock to Congresswoman Sparrow's house, but neither of us complained about the walk. Frankly, the only thing I was worried about was that the attack we were trying to prevent might come at any time, and I didn't want to be halfway down the road, strolling along with no weapons, when it did.

But while we didn't dare move at a rate that might make the itchy trigger fingers behind us nervous, we got to the front door in relatively good time, and all without anything blowing up.

The two-story house had red siding, including around the chimney, and a deeply shaded porch. The yard had been extensively landscaped, with leafy bushes and lots of trees. Flagstaff is a lot higher and greener than one might imagine when thinking of "Arizona." Two more black, armored Suburbans sat in the driveway, combat-parked for a fast getaway.

There were two more armed guards on the porch, and I spotted several cameras around the property. They weren't taking chances. Which was good, but a known, stationary target can always be gotten to, eventually.

The detail lead, who had still not offered his name, mounted the steps ahead of us, turning his back on us for the first time since we'd pulled up to the road block, and knocked on the door.

The man who answered the door was dressed in a suit, unlike the guys in combat gear outside. I was beginning to wonder just how big Sparrow's detail was. I knew that she'd hired Stony Creek Protection Services, since Congresscritters didn't get close protection when they were away from DC. Stony Creek had a decent rep, and they'd been pretty professional, from what I'd seen. But I'd counted at least an infantry platoon worth of guards, so far. She had to be shelling out a *lot* for this level of protection. Which meant she was scared. In a way, that was good. It could also turn out to be a liability.

The detail lead, or at least the man in charge outside, talked to the guy in the suit in a low voice, and the guy in the suit gave us a thorough, unfriendly look-over. But he finally stepped aside, and the guy with the M4 led us inside.

They must have called ahead, because Lucia Sparrow and her husband, Gary, were waiting in the living room for us. Gary was standing behind his wife, who was sitting in an armchair, straight-backed, watching us enter. The security personnel fanned out on either side of us, taking up ninety-degree offsets so that they could shoot us without shooting each other.

Lucia Sparrow was a plain, heavy-set woman, her round face looking pinched and showing growing worry lines around her eyes. One look and I could see that she was trying to stay impassive, but this was a deeply, desperately frightened woman. It was one thing to defy corruption on the floor of the House of Representatives; it was something else altogether to have someone try to blow you to smithereens less than two miles from your house.

If Lucia looked scared, Gary was positively green with terror. He was a very fat, very pasty man with a receding chin, and he was practically quaking as he watched us enter the room.

"Madam Congresswoman," I began, "I'm not going to mince words; we don't have time. We have reliable information that there are at least two groups in Flagstaff as we speak that are gunning for you. You've got good security here, but your home is known to your enemies, and that makes you vulnerable. The attack the other day was close enough; they're not going to quit. The longer you stay here, the more likely it becomes that an attack is going to succeed. You need to come with us." I glanced up at the men with guns. "We're not asking you to leave your detail behind; in fact, we'd welcome their assistance." Hopefully that helped ease a few fears.

"He says that Mr. Schofield will back him up, ma'am," the detail lead said. "I have not called Mr. Schofield to confirm that, however. I thought it best if you made that call."

"Just who are you people?" Sparrow asked. She was still trying to process everything. This could be a problem. From her reputation, I'd expected Sparrow to be made of sterner stuff.

I decided to take a chance. It might help matters along, or it might get us shot dead in Sparrow's living room. "We're with Praetorian Solutions," I said.

That had an impact. The security guys' eyes widened as one. "Holy shit," the detail lead said.

Sparrow looked up at him. "Does that mean something?"

"It does, ma'am," he said, his eyes locked on me. "Though I don't know for sure if it's good or bad. There have been whispers about Praetorian for several years now; though I've never heard of them actually operating in the United States. Their reputation is…checkered, let's put it that way."

That didn't seem to reassure her. She looked at me and Larry. "'Checkered,'" she said. "Checkered how?"

There was a wary look in his eyes. "Word is, where they go, a lot of people tend to die. They've been working in Kurdistan for the last several years, that much is public. There are stories about other jobs, though, usually really rough, action-novel stuff. Depending on who's telling the story, they're either hard bastards who get the job done without fail, or they're a pack of dangerous, off-the-leash, mad-dog killers. There are a few stories floating around to the effect that they may have taken apart a cartel down in Mexico, last year or two."

246

That must have rung a bell, because when Sparrow looked back at us, she was a little calmer, and the wheels were turning. "I'm not sure if that means we should trust them, or not," she said.

He grimaced. "Well, he's not wrong, ma'am," he said. "We're not secure enough here. If he is telling the truth, we should take him up on his offer and get you somewhere more secure." He paused, squinting at me. "Maybe you should call Mr. Schofield."

She nodded at that, and reached for the phone sitting on the lampstand beside her chair. She tapped the screen, and a moment later, it was ringing, apparently on speaker.

It rang, and rang, and rang. I started to get tense. Schofield was supposed to be ready and waiting for this call. If he'd dropped the ball, not only might we fail the mission, we might not even get out of that living room alive. Sparrow's security was *nervous*, and their fingers were awfully close to those bang switches.

Just before it went to voicemail and I decided we were fucked, trying to calculate how to close the distance and take that M4 away from old boy before he shot me, then drag Sparrow away through the woods by main force, the ringing stopped, and Schofield said, "Lucia. Good to hear from you."

"Martin, there are two men in my living room telling me that my life is in danger here, in spite of my security, and that I need to come with them," she said. "They told me to call you."

"Am I on speaker?" he asked.

Dammit, just put her damned mind at ease and let us get out of here, I thought.

"Yes," she replied.

"Stone?" Schofield called. "You there?"

"Yeah," I replied loudly. "And the clock's ticking." I was breathing a little easier, but I was still kind of pissed that he'd taken so long to answer the phone.

"I know," he answered. "Just had to make sure you were actually the ones she was talking about. Lucia," he continued, "these men are there on behalf of some of my associates. I can assure you that they are there for your protection, and you need to listen to them. There are some very dangerous people after you. Fortunately for you, these guys are even more dangerous, but you have to move quickly."

As if to punctuate his words, gunfire suddenly erupted from the woods behind the house. A moment later, the house itself was under fire, and bullets started to punch through the walls.

"*Get on the floor!*" I bellowed. Fortunately, the Stony Creek guys were on the ball, and had hauled Lucia and Gary down to the floor as soon as the first round punched through the drywall. A moment later, a long burst of machine gun fire ripped through the walls, shattering the window and sending clouds of splinters and drywall dust through the air. The lamp that Lucia had been sitting next to went dark as a bullet smashed the lightbulb.

My earpiece was still in my ear, having been overlooked by an otherwise uncomfortably thorough search, but we were way outside the range where it could link to the radio. I knew that part of the team was out in the woods behind the house, having crept there to defend against the attack that we fully expected to come from that direction, but I couldn't hear any of the chatter or get any updates. We had to wing it.

"Get to the front!" I yelled. "I've got guys in back to hold 'em off, but they won't be able to do much against that belt-fed! *MOVE!*" I looked at the detail lead. "We need rifles!"

The guy in the suit pointed toward a room off the entryway. "Ready room's in there!"

Larry and I started low-crawling that direction, even as the Sparrows' security got them moving toward the front. Any questions seemed to have been abandoned, especially as only a suicidal assassin would put himself in the middle of his own machine gun's kill zone. There were those who were crazy or fanatical enough to do that, but few, if any, of them were operating in this little shadow civil war.

The ready room was neat and professional, or would have been if there hadn't been bullets smashing through the walls. There were three equipment cases, helpfully labeled with team numbers, set against the wall, along with collapsible gear trees, some comms, and a duty roster on a white board leaning against the wall.

I got to the first gear case a few feet ahead of Larry. Low crawling sucks for big guys, too. Flipping the lid open, I saw two spare M4s, broken down, in the bottom.

Reaching in, I grabbed an upper and a lower, made sure the bolt carrier group was still in the upper, slapped 'em together, and shoved the weapon at Larry, before going diving for the other one. Fortunately, any AR-pattern rifle is pretty quick to go together, and there were stacks of loaded magazines in the next case over, so in a matter of a few moments, we were locked and loaded, spare mags jammed into pockets and belts, and heading back out the door.

Neither the Congresswoman nor her husband were crawling very fast, so we met them at the front door. Larry, having been closer to the door, led out, risking coming up to a knee and bellowing, *"Friendlies coming out!"* Neither of us wanted to get accidentally smoked by the guys on the porch.

They were, commendably, still on their posts, watching the wide swathe of open ground in front of the house, and the woods beyond. I'd known too many gunfighters turned security contractors who would have run toward the sound of the fight, and left that flank wide open.

The detail lead was yelling into his radio, and soon I heard the roar of engines. The two Subs in the driveway were ready to move, the doors open and two more armed men crouched by the passenger sides, rifles pointed toward the back, where the firefight was only getting more heated. I couldn't tell for sure, especially since I had to concentrate on getting Sparrow out of there, but it seemed like the fire coming our direction was only getting more intense. I hoped we hadn't lost anyone, but our guys were definitely getting pushed back. We were out of time.

Fortunately, the Stony Creek guys didn't fuck around. With the bulk of the house between us and the fire, they all but bodily picked Sparrow and her husband up and hurled them into the back of the closest Suburban. The detail lead pointed toward the other one. "Come on!" he yelled at us. "You can't stay here!"

Under fire, I wasn't going to argue. We stuffed ourselves in the back seat, and in moments we were flying down the road, heading back the way we'd come. The gunfire faded into the distance behind us.

The detail lead had gotten into the Sub with us. "Are they likely to come after us?" he asked.

"They might try," I said. "Between you and me, Cuellar's a shitbag, so he's probably going to throw a shit-fit when the target house is empty, and fall back to try to figure out what to try next. He probably hasn't thought much else through. But I've been wrong before." I was hoping that the boys back in the woods would have put enough of a hurting on the hitters to keep them from pursuing. While eliminating Cuellar and his team would have been an added bonus, Sparrow was our primary objective.

We got to the roadblock, to find the Subs ready to move, and the gun teams having collapsed in to the vehicles. Eddie and our other four shooters had joined them, and I could only imagine how tense that had been, before the Stony Creek guys had accepted that we weren't their enemy.

"Let us out here," I told the Stony Creek lead.

"We can't stop," he protested. "We're still less than a mile from the house."

"We need our gear, and how the hell are you going to know where to go without us along?" I pointed out.

"Go," he said. Larry and I shoved the heavy doors open and piled out.

It was a matter of moments to retrieve our weapons and vests, along with my radio. I could finally hear the radio chatter.

"Hillbilly, Albatross," Bryan was calling. He sounded winded, and he'd probably been calling for a while.

"Albatross, Hillbilly," I replied, "Just got my radio back. We're almost clear; break contact and head for the rendezvous."

"We already had to fall back," he told me. "Our boy brought a lot of firepower. I hope Sparrow has good homeowner's insurance." He paused for a moment. "Be advised; Cuellar brought his boys in on four-wheelers, and they're moving out again. They might be trying to cut you off."

"Roger," I replied. "We're moving. Get to the RV." By then we were piling back into the Sub, and the rest were following suit. "We've got pursuit coming," I announced. "Get us the hell out of here."

"Where are we going?" the detail lead asked.

"Head west, stay off the highway," I told him. "We've got an LZ set up just off the 40, about three miles away."

"Roger." The driver didn't say a word, but gunned the engine and sent us lurching down the road. The up-armored Subs might have been the best that Stony Creek could get, but anyone who's ever ridden in those damned things can attest that they are complete and total pigs. The armor gets slapped on an otherwise stock vehicle, and the engine, suspension, and transmission don't do so well with an extra ten thousand pounds of steel and composite added on.

The drivers did as I'd advised, and kept us off the highway. Soon we were bouncing down a dirt road, with pines entirely too close on either side, making for the LZ.

All too soon, the radio crackled. "We've got four wheelers behind us. About six of 'em."

The detail lead twisted around in his seat to look back at Larry and me. "Those our friends?" he asked.

"Sounds like it," I replied. "My guys said they made the approach on four wheelers, and that they were moving off the X on the same. Cuellar must really want this paycheck."

"Any ideas?" he asked. "Somehow I doubt that your bird is going to want to land with the threat that close."

"We kill them, then call the bird in," I said matter-of-factly. "Only way to be sure."

He looked a little taken aback by that, but then lifted his eyebrows a little and nodded. It had to take some getting used to, shifting into that combat mindset Stateside. But from what I knew about Stony Creek, he had to have some on-the-ground experience, so he was probably just having to slip back into old habits.

We'd never gotten out of those old habits.

He started to issue instructions to the rest of the vehicles, in a rapid, clipped tone. Larry and I listened in, internalizing our own part of the plan as we went.

We burst into the open area that had already been designated for the landing zone, and the vehicles suddenly fanned out, presenting their armored flanks to our pursuers. Ours swayed alarmingly as the driver threw the wheel over; the armor raised the vehicle's center of gravity considerably, and we almost came off one set of wheels before he brought it to a stop.

Even before the vehicle had stopped rocking on its shocks, I was heaving the door open—there was no slamming a door that weighs a hundred twenty pounds—and diving out, the borrowed M4 still on the seat, leading with my SOCOM 16.

We couldn't have timed it better if we'd tried. Almost as one, a dozen shooters leveled rifles at the pack of four-wheelers coming out of the trees from around the backs of vehicles or over the hoods, and opened fire.

The heavy *booms* of our 7.62 rifles were about matched by the lighter *cracks* of the Stony Creek M4s, just because of the sheer number of them. An unholy roar of gunfire reached out and mowed the attackers down.

It happened almost too fast to register. One moment, there were six four-wheelers, with about eight shooters on them, coming at us. The next, they were a mangled pile of wrecked ATVs and dead bodies. They'd driven right into the teeth of that wall of high-velocity metal and been torn to pieces. Two of the four-wheelers flipped over as their drivers were hit and went over backwards, twisting the throttles in their death spasms. One was still running, upside down, the wheels spinning.

The echoes were still rolling across the woods as I got on the radio again. "Dirt, Hillbilly."

"This is Dirt," Phil called. Phil was one of our primary helo pilots. He'd usually been based of the company ship, the *Frontier Rose*, but had moved his operation inland for this little fun and games. "I'm standing by."

"LZ is cold," I told him. "Bring 'er in while it stays that way. I wouldn't be surprised if we attracted some unfriendly attention with this little fireworks show."

"Roger, en route," he said. "Five minutes."

"Five minutes," I confirmed.

It took most of that time to make sure the LZ was clear and the Sparrows were ready to go. By the time we had the Congresswoman and her shaking husband out of the vehicles and ready to make the dash to the helo, Phil was already bringing the Bell 407 in, flaring hard to drop it with delicate precision right on the air panel that Eddie had put out.

"You and two others go with them," I told the detail lead. "The rest will have to stay on the ground."

"You're not going?" he asked.

I shook my head. "You're her detail," I told him. "Our job was to get them to safety, and Phil knows where to go. Now hurry up. I'm sure there are still some people around here drawn to the sound of gunfire, and not just because they're stupid and curious."

He stuck out his hand, and I shook it. Then he was herding the Congresswoman and her husband toward the helo, picking the rest of the detail to accompany them as he went.

A few moments later, the precious cargo aboard, Phil was pulling for the sky, climbing as hard as the Bell 407 would climb. Nobody'd shot any helos down yet, but comparing what was happening in the States to what had happened in Mexico, it was only a matter of time.

We were going to need to hitch a ride with the Stony Creek boys to where we'd stashed our own vehicles, but first I dug the Renton phone out of my vest. "They're on the way," I told him as soon as he answered.

"Good," he replied. "I've got another job for you, short fuse. I know you guys have been hitting it hard, but this is a pretty narrow window. Fortunately, you haven't got all that far to go."

I sighed. No rest for the wicked.

CHAPTER 27

Reconnaissance and surveillance in the desert is not fun. Not only because of the heat, the dust, and the generally inimical wildlife. But particularly on the stretch of desert around Presumidio Canyon, right on the US-Mexico border, there's just not much high ground, at least not within engagement ranges of the target site.

And from what we were seeing, the *Soldados de Unidos Chicanos* already had what overwatch positions there were sewed up.

We'd gotten the rundown on the drive south from Flagstaff. I'd grumbled about Renton's definition of "not that far to go;" it was a good three hundred miles, most of the last ninety on back roads through the desert and mountains. But it had given us time to plan that we wouldn't have had otherwise.

The tip had been pure luck. A large portion of the violence in the Southwest had already been narco-led, but as we'd discovered in Mexico on the hunt for the imaginary "El Duque," that meant a myriad of small cells working together or against each other as the situation dictated. It made tracking trends difficult. But both our own intel cell, which was getting re-situated after we'd taken the Task Force down, and the Cicero Group were trying to track what they could.

The Group had cracked into an online forum used mostly by young activists who were collaborating, often without any real understanding of the consequences, with "revolutionaries," i.e., narcos and terrorists. One of these activists in particular, a very passionate young woman named Veronica Fernandez, who apparently had been indirectly connected with just about every major Aztlanista movement that had an online presence for the last three years, though she was not an official member of any of them, had mentioned something exciting she was getting to do, down by the border. Some digging turned up that she thought that she and her friends were going to be providing transportation for some important allies in "the struggle."

That was enough to get some intel weenies digging. Pretty soon, one of her friends got spotted on a CCTV camera, meeting with a known *Soldados de Unidos Chicanos* commander.

The SUC was one of the more organized Aztlanista militias in Arizona, and had been a royal headache for what was left of Arizona law enforcement ever since the POCRF had kicked things off after Pueblo. Little was known about them; they weren't as flashy as some of the other narco and Aztlanista factions. There was no website with their goals and demands, no videos of their attacks or ultimatums delivered by masked men with digitally altered voices. They hit military and law enforcement targets, as well as major infrastructure. So far, while their attacks had been spectacular in their professionalism and effect, they had been relatively limited in scope.

The Cicero Group suspected that that was about to change.

It should have taken some doing to figure out where the meet was happening, but Fernandez and her friends, while they might be useful mules to the SUC, really, *really* sucked at OPSEC. Renton had a fucking six-digit grid coordinate for the meet, just because of those retards gushing on social media about the great things they were going to get to do for the cause.

So, there we were, creeping across the desert floor, using every bit of sagebrush and every fold in the ground as concealment as we scoped out the section of Presumidio Canyon where Fernandez and her fellow "revolutionaries" were supposed to be picking up their new allies.

With the SUC involved, we'd decided to approach cautiously, and we weren't regretting it. Nick was on point, moving slowly and silently from cover to cover through the pre-dawn gray, when he suddenly froze and held up a hand.

The rest of us were spread out in a loose wedge, similarly moving from concealment to concealment across the desert. I'd walked many a patrol in the desert that had relied on darkness and the booger-eater jihadis not having night vision, where we'd just made our way from point to point. We didn't dare take that chance with the SUC. So, we were moving carefully, stalking up to the objective as if they could see and hear in the dark. When Nick put his hand up, we all stopped where we were. I waited a second, then carefully moved up next to him.

He pointed, moving slowly. The eye is drawn to movement, with or without NVGs. For a moment, I couldn't see what he was looking at, but then the sentry shifted his position again.

There were two of them, wearing what looked like boonie hats and holding AKs, which had become the SUC's weapons of choice. They were in position on the canyon rim, overlooking the meet site. They'd be well-concealed from below by the juniper bush they were kneeling behind.

We were close; we'd gotten within two hundred yards without either seeing them or being detected. I was sure that if they'd seen us, we'd have come under fire in short order.

Unfortunately, penetrating that close meant that verbal communication was right out. I could even hear murmurs between the two sentries. Nothing that would be intelligible even if I spoke Spanish, but enough to be able to hear them. If I tried to use the radio, they'd hear it and the jig would be up.

So, instead, I went old-school, and turned to make eye contact with first Eric on my left, and then Bryan, off to the right. Careful, slow hand signals indicated that we should fan out and keep eyes peeled for more of them.

It took time, time that we didn't necessarily have. The sun was coming up fast, and the meet time was approaching. But we'd damned near been burned getting in too much of a hurry in Pueblo, and I wasn't going to repeat that particular mistake. It wouldn't do anyone any good if we blundered into the middle of things and left hostile shooters at our backs.

Slowly, we spread out along the canyon rim, keeping at least a hundred fifty meters back, and maintaining contact so that signals could be passed up and down the team. It was a strange sort of sign language that we'd developed over the years, combining conventional hand and arm signals with more detailed signs to pass more information. It was still a bitch to see some of them in the half-light of pre-dawn.

The picture got clearer. The SUC had exterior security and overwatch on the meeting site; the overwatch elements were rather more numerous and heavily armed than the external security, which amounted to four shooters with AKs, while there was a mix of AKs, PTR-91s, and two MG-3 machine guns overwatching the meet. Whoever the "new allies" were, the SUC was more worried about them than they were about anyone coming to crash the party.

They must have trusted in their useful idiot mules' discretion a bit more than they should have.

The external security was apparently only watching a couple of narrow avenues of approach, which made our job easier. It made things more difficult in a couple of spots to get past them without being spotted, but by the time the sun peeked over the horizon, we were all in position, the SUC fighters on the canyon rim had been pinpointed, and every one of them was under the gun. Even better, it didn't look like we'd been detected.

We knew, thanks to Fernandez' carelessness, that the meet was supposed to happen at 0700. More than likely, the SUC would have preferred earlier, just based on what we'd managed to find out about their professionalism from observing the aftermath of their operations, but I guessed that they couldn't guarantee a bunch of college students would get there with the vans any earlier than that. I wondered why they wanted clueless kids, but figured that whatever the reasoning, it couldn't be good. I suspected that even if we hadn't been there to interdict whatever was going to happen, the coeds would have ended up regretting their involvement in the long run.

The sun came up, and 0700 came and went. None of the SUC fighters moved, though a few started fidgeting a bit as time passed. The useful idiots were late.

Finally, about half an hour later, movement drew my eye, and I saw a plume of dust coming down from the north. Moving very carefully and very slowly, I got the plume in my scope, and made out three fifteen-pack vans trundling along a dirt road coming over the hills. It looked like the activist brigade was finally showing up.

Now timing became a little sensitive. I would have liked to have moved in on the external security, eliminated them, and been waiting in their place when the meet went down. But unfortunately, sneaking up on alert shooters and silently slaughtering them with suppressed weapons without anyone being the wiser only happens in movies. Suppressors only reduce the noise of gunshots; they don't eliminate them. As soon as the first shot was fired, it was going to be go time.

So, we watched and waited, knowing that we had no eyes on the canyon floor or the meeting site itself. We'd just have to hope we didn't wait too long.

The vans were not moving fast, and as they got closer, it looked more and more like the drivers were nervous as hell. They were driving tentatively, like little old women. They either had little or no experience driving on unimproved roads over rough terrain in the desert, or they were starting to realize just how stupid they were to go along with this little scheme. Maybe both.

I turned my attention back to the overwatch position in front of me. The SUC fighters were watching the vans, and I saw one of them mutter something to his companion. The smaller man just shook his head as he answered. I couldn't make out any words, but they looked annoyed.

I could kind of see why. They'd been out here since before the sun had come up, and there were still some Border Patrol out there, along with a few of the more hard-core militias that came down by the border, and Presumidio Canyon looked like a prime spot for some of them to look for border crossers. The longer they stayed in place, the higher the chances that somebody would stumble across this little rendezvous.

Of course, it was already too late for them to avoid it, but they were still unaware of our presence.

After what felt like forever, as the sun rose higher in the sky and started to finally banish the night chill from the desert, the vans descended into the canyon and out of our sight.

I started counting down as soon as the last one disappeared below the canyon rim. It was possible that they were waiting on whoever the students were supposed to transport, but given the mules' lateness, I doubted it. My money was on the other players already being in position; there was no other reason for the SUC overwatch to be in place.

I gave them two full minutes, plus a little change, after the last van had disappeared. The desert was quiet enough that we could hear the engines shut off and the slamming of doors, though voices were still muted by distance.

A handful of seconds after the last door slammed, I centered my reticle on the bigger of the two guys on overwatch and squeezed the trigger.

The 7.62 round caught him dead center between the shoulder blades and he fell on his face, as the supersonic *crack* of the round echoed across the canyon. I immediately shifted to his buddy, who was spinning around and bringing his AK up, and gave him a pair to the upper chest, even as the air was suddenly ripped apart by a ragged storm of suppressed gunfire. My first shot had been the signal that it was, indeed, go time.

In seconds, the SUC's exterior security died.

I heaved myself off the ground, finding that I'd stiffened up a bit after the movement, got my feet under me, and sprinted as best I could for the canyon rim. To my right and left, the rest of the team was similarly clambering to their feet and rushing forward. We had moments to take advantage of the element of surprise.

I threw myself on my belly in the dirt and rocks beside the two corpses I'd just laid out, banging my elbow painfully on a particularly jagged rock. It took a second to get back on my sights, and I leveled my rifle at the small crowd on the canyon floor.

The three vans were parked end-to-end in the dust, with three separate groups standing nearby. The kids driving the vans were immediately identifiable, as they were kind of huddled in a knot against the side of the middle van. Some of them were looking up toward the canyon rim, startled by the sudden noise of gunfire, though they looked like they were wondering what the noise was. Others were watching the group they'd met with, looking like they were starting to doubt the wisdom of some of their life choices.

The other groups had already spun around and were searching the canyon rim above them, weapons up but not shooting yet. They probably didn't quite realize yet just how fucked they were.

The SUC fighters were all in various forms of desert camouflage, ranging from MARPAT desert digis to old Desert Storm-era chocolate chip, to some British desert tiger stripes. They were also ranged about the perimeter of the site.

The guys in the middle also had their guns up, though they were dressed and equipped differently from the SUC. They were all dressed in civvies; jeans, t-shirts, and short-sleeved button-ups, with various ballcaps and even a couple of cowboy hats. But they all had skull-pattern masks over the lower halves of their faces, much like *Los Lobos Rabiosos* had worn, and they were all wearing the same low-profile chest rigs and carrying FX-05 rifles.

They also dividing their attention between the canyon rim and the SUC fighters. They were alert and wary, obviously suspecting their allies of double-crossing them.

So, I picked the one in the white cowboy hat, and shot him through the dome. His hat went flying as his head jerked backward, and he dropped into the dust with a crash.

Now, ordinarily, headshots were insurance shots. The head is a damned small target, even at that range, and we were close, barely fifty yards away. But I didn't know if he had body armor on, and I like to exploit any rifts between my enemies whenever I can find them. If shooting Cowboy in the head started the newcomers shooting at the SUC, so much the better.

Neither group opened fire immediately; apparently, they still weren't sure where the shot had come from. But one of the newcomers leveled his rifle at one of the SUC types, whom I thought I recognized as Carlos Garcia, the SUC commander whose meeting with Fernandez had started this particular ball rolling. He barked something in Spanish. He sounded agitated and suspicious.

All we needed was that momentary hesitation. Without any other signal, the entire team opened fire from the rim.

I shot the guy covering down on Garcia. He crumpled, then struggled back up to one knee and shot Garcia, before I put two more in him and one in Garcia. Garcia was still protesting when he went down hard, my round blowing a sizeable exit hole out of his side, and sucking a good chunk of his lungs out with it.

I shifted to one of the newcomers, who was now dumping rounds toward the canyon rim as he ran toward the vans, looking for some kind of cover. He got close; I had to duck down for a second as a burst ripped through the air only about six inches from my head. When I got back up, he was changing mags on the move, trying to duck around the van. I squeezed off a snap shot at him, but it only hit him in the ass cheek. He went sprawling, but he was still kicking, and now mostly occluded by the van.

The fire had slackened by then; the group had been like fish in a barrel. There was little to no cover down in that canyon, we had the high ground, and we were only around fifty yards away. The canyon floor was now littered with corpses, including a couple of the students. Who had shot them, I didn't know. I'd deal with that later. There was at least one bad guy down there still kicking.

Once the shooting stopped altogether, I cautiously rose to a knee. Nobody shot at me. "Geek!" I yelled.

"Yeah!"

"Hold your element up here and cover us!" I hollered. "I'm moving down to clear the kill zone!"

"Roger," Eddie yelled back. "We've got you!"

I led the way down, slipping and sliding down the steep wall of the canyon until I reached the bottom, my muzzle elevated to make sure I didn't bury it accidentally in the sand. I picked up some more bruises from rocks and scratches from creosote bushes as I went.

At the bottom, even as Nick and Larry came down next to me in showers of gravel and grit, I leveled my rifle at what little I could see of the one shooter I knew to still be alive, keeping an eye on the shell-shocked student activists who were staring wide-eyed at the carnage around them, frozen like bunny rabbits facing a rattlesnake, not even helping the couple of them who were bleeding and groaning on the ground.

I circled around the back of the vans, never letting my muzzle stray too far from the students' general vicinity. They might be shocked and traumatized into immobility at the moment, but there was no telling when one of them might do something stupid. That they were there at all did not speak highly of their common sense.

My boots crunching on the sandy, gravelly ground, I eased around the back of the rear van, only to duck backward as three shots *crack*ed past my face. Old boy was still back there and still had plenty of fight left in him. Another shot shattered the taillight as he tried to shoot me through the body of the van.

So, I dropped to the ground, put my rifle and my cheek against the dirt, and shot him under the van.

There wasn't a lot of him visible, even down there; he'd huddled behind the tire. But there was enough, and I dumped three rounds into what I could see, the muzzle blast throwing dust and grit into my eyes, then put two more through the tire to be on the safe side.

While I stayed in place, waiting for him to move, Larry had circled around to get a better shot at him. I kept my muzzle trained on the huddled form up until I saw Larry's boot kick the FX-05 away. He was dead.

It took only a matter of moments to check the rest of the bodies. None of us were the trusting type; we'd seen too many instances of "dead" bad guys playing possum so that they could shoot a soldier or contractor in the back, or set off a grenade. So, we started at one side and swept across, never turning our backs on an unknown corpse. Weapons were kicked away from clutching hands, eyeballs were muzzle-thumped, and corpses carefully rolled over to make sure they hadn't wedged a last minute, explosive surprise under themselves while they were dying.

Meanwhile, Bryan had broken off and herded the still-standing students around the back of the vans, while Eric checked the ones who had been shot.

One was dead. The other would probably live; he'd taken a round to the side, but it had hit a rib and skittered around to exit next to his spine. It didn't look like he'd taken any interior injuries, though he'd bled a good bit, and the rib was probably cracked, at best.

None of the SUC fighters or the civilian-clad newcomers was still breathing. Once the last corpse had been checked, I yelled, "Clear!" toward the canyon rim. A few moments later, Eddie came skidding down the side of the canyon.

"I left the rest up there on overwatch, just in case," he said. I just nodded. It was smart, especially after the firefight. Who knew who else might be out in that desert?

He looked around at the slaughter. "What have we got?" he asked. "SUC I can see. Who are these other assholes?"

I reached down and pulled down one of the skull masks. The young man was obviously Hispanic, but had none of the neck or facial tattooing that could occasionally identify narcos. "Don't know," I replied. "No insignia, and we haven't found any ID yet. They're completely sterile, near as we can tell."

"Except for those rifles," he mused. "Mexican special forces?"

"Who knows?" I answered. "It's possible; we've seen evidence of Mexican authorities and military forces working with cartels, and Mexico City can certainly act like an enemy a lot of the time. The rifles would certainly suggest Mexican Army or Marines, but then, you know as well as I do that somebody was funneling these damned things to the narcos even when we were down there."

He nodded, and smirked. "Well, whoever they were, and whatever they came across the border to do, they're bug food now." Eddie was not known for his reverence for the dead. "What do we do with the bodies?"

"Leave 'em," I said. "Let the buzzards have 'em." A few were already circling overhead. I looked toward where Bryan was still covered down on the students. "That bunch is another matter."

"I'd smoke 'em," Eddie said coldly. "Aiding and abetting."

"We're not shooting a bunch of unarmed, dumb kids," I snapped.

"It's a long hike back to our transpo," he pointed out.

"I'm not saying we're bringing them with us, either," I said. I squinted at the vans, as an evil idea started to form in my mind.

I walked around the front and joined Bryan. He had the survivors on their knees, recently joined by the guy who'd been grazed in the side, their hands on their heads. He was watching them impassively, his eyes cold, his muzzle slightly elevated. All eyes were on his pitiless stare. They probably were waiting for him to go ahead and kill them all.

Bryan wouldn't. He liked to cultivate a certain image, not unlike Eddie's actual cold-bloodedness, but he had his own moral code. I could trust him not to shoot unarmed morons, however tempted he might be.

I let my rifle dangle on its sling, though my shooting hand was still on the pistol grip. I picked out Fernandez. "So, who are the newcomers?" I asked conversationally.

She looked up at me. "I'll never tell you shit, you *pinche puto*!"

She'd barely gotten the last syllable of the insult out of her mouth when I lifted my rifle and put a round in the dirt about a foot in front of her. She flinched violently back from the report and the stinging shower of grit kicked up by the bullet. There was a risk that the round might ricochet, but it got the message across.

"Answer the question," I said, keeping my tone low and conversational. She just stared, shocked and scared.

"We don't know," the younger man next to her said, his voice high-pitched and frightened. "*Commandante* Garcia didn't tell us. He just said they were important, and that we needed to slip them in to Tucson, unnoticed."

"Well, looks like somebody noticed," Bryan drawled.

I just nodded thoughtfully, then rocked my magazine out and checked it. I'd reloaded after killing the last unknown, but I made a good show of judging the number of rounds and doing math in my head, before I rocked it back in. Then I went around the vans, putting a round in each tire and two in each radiator.

"These aren't going anywhere anytime soon," I told the students as I strolled back, making an effort to appear nonchalant. Truth be told, I wanted to get the hell out of there with a quickness. We were way too close to Mexico for my comfort. "But I wouldn't suggest sticking around."

"Wait, you're just leaving us here?" the kid who'd answered me asked. "In the middle of the desert?"

I nodded. "Sasabe's only six and a half miles from here, over those hills," I said, jerking my thumb to the southeast. "You should be able to make that. Just try to keep an eye out for the rattlers and scorpions." I lifted my muzzle slightly. "Start walking."

They weren't sure we were serious, but they didn't want to argue with the rifles, so they reluctantly complied, trying to help their wounded comrade. They didn't really succeed in doing much of anything but making him wince in more pain.

It took a while for them to get out of sight. They kept stopping and looking back as if expecting that we might relent and offer to take them with us. We didn't.

Finally, I raised a hand and circled it above my head. It was time to get moving.

***

So it went, for weeks, into months. Alek came back from Kurdistan, bringing the bulk of the company with him. We were still too busy to manage much more than a cursory hand-wave as we came and went, and the other teams went to work. We moved from city to city, state to state, barely finishing up one target before we were studying the target package from Renton for the next one. We grabbed provocateurs, took out hit squads, and made certain cogs in the factions' machines disappear.

Meanwhile, the violence ebbed and flowed, never amounting to anything but a lot of people getting hurt or killed. Every time it seemed to die down, an incident would happen to make it flare up again. The social media campaigns keeping the riots going seemed to have lives of their own. Shut down one provocateur, and another one cropped up in its place.

It was somewhat fortunate that we were so damned busy. It kept us focused on the mission at hand, and not the horror of the bigger picture. The United States wasn't coming apart at the seams. It was unraveling.

And it was becoming increasingly evident that there were players in the game, that weren't necessarily part of either faction, that were actively pulling on the threads, trying to accelerate that unraveling.

CHAPTER 28

"I still say this place looks like a Bond villain's lair," Nick murmured.

The two of us were hunkered down in the greenery, not far from the edge of the target property. We were both drenched to the skin with a combination of our own sweat and the moisture that seemed to perpetually drip off the vegetation.

"I'll be sure to keep an eye out for the faceless minions in gray coveralls," I muttered.

Sarcasm aside, if ever there was a candidate for "Bond villain" status among the factions, it was Eugene Stavros. Richer than Midas, he'd never held office, but he was the great mover and shaker in numerous political circles, mainly those that leaned left. He was suspected to be the richest man in the entire world, and he was not shy about using that money to buy influence and bankroll his preferred causes.

Unlike the likes of Eddings, however, Stavros didn't appear to be primarily driven by self-interest. Oh, he certainly profited handsomely off of his little projects, regardless of how destructive they turned out to be, but he was a pretty consistent ideologue. Unfortunately, his ideology was some kind of utopian, far-left, anarcho-communist bullshit that meant most of his bankrolling dollars went to anyone and everyone who had interests in tearing down society for the sake of "revolution." He wasn't terribly picky about their stated goals, either. As long as they were disruptive and generally leaned left, he'd give them money. Some said that he practically owned just about every Leftist political party in the States; I was personally skeptical, and apparently, so was Bates.

What none of us was skeptical about was that Stavros was one of the biggest and most central personalities in "Sulla." The more intel we gathered, the more lesser personalities we rolled up, the more it became apparent that the man had his fingers in every corner of that particular network. What his ultimate endgame was, no one could quite tell; he was on record espousing multiple conflicting agendas. If disruption was his primary aim, presumably with his weird anarcho-communist Promised Land at the end of it, it kind of made a twisted sort of sense.

His sprawling estate on the big island of Hawaii only added to his already generally sinister reputation. Twenty acres of jungle had been cleared and replaced with meticulously manicured lawn and landscaping, with a ten-thousand square foot house squatting in the middle. Personally, I thought the house was ugly as sin, but the blocky, stair-step construct of steel, glass, and white plastered concrete had just the right Frank Lloyd Wright modernist look for a Bond villain.

It also had tighter security than most government facilities. The single access road had a minimum of three hardened checkpoints on it before even reaching the main gate, which was fortified enough to withstand a truck bomb. Armed helicopter patrols circled the estate on five-mile loops, and roving foot patrols paced the perimeter of the cleared lawns, just inside a double ring of metal pylons, which the Cicero Group suspected were some sort of electric or sonic intrusion deterrent fence. It was mainly speculation; Stavros' information security was as tight as his estate's physical security.

There were also eight-rotor drones buzzing around the perimeter, augmenting the foot patrols. We'd been able to get the specs on the Arc Tech drones, though we suspected that they'd probably been modified with any number of area denial systems and weapons beyond the factory specifications.

The house itself looked like it should be somewhat vulnerable, given how much of the wall space was given up to gigantic picture windows, but there was a faint greenish tint to those windows that suggested to me that they were armored glass.

It was going to be one hell of a tough nut to crack, but the target was worth the effort.

A helicopter roared by overhead, making for the helipad on the roof. It wasn't one of Stavros' contract security patrols; this looked like a transport for somebody important. Given the line of high-end, luxury SUVs and limousines already parked in the expansive driveway, this was only the latest of several important visitors.

"This is one hell of a meet," Alek murmured. I hadn't been in the field with the big Samoan since East Africa; he'd taken over the ops chief job once we'd started operations in Kurdistan, what felt like half a lifetime ago. But once he and the rest of the boys had managed to get back Stateside, he'd insisted on falling in with what was left of our old team. Larry had effectively stepped into Jim's shoes well enough that Alek hadn't wanted to stir things up too much, and had simply filled a slot, one of several left vacant by Jim's, Ben's, Little Bob's, and Derek's absence. "You sure we're outside their detection bubble?"

"No," I whispered in reply. "But if they know we're here, they're taking their sweet time raising the alarm." Again, we didn't have reliable information as to what kind of early warning systems Stavros' estate had in place, but we were assuming the worst. Still, we'd gotten close enough through the jungle that we could get eyes on, without, apparently, being detected.

Larry's voice hissed in my earpiece. "In position. This sucks."

264

Jungle movement is some of the nastiest hiking possible, in my opinion. Between the thickness of the growth, which snags and tangles gear, weapons, and limbs equally, and the sopping heat, it is about as miserable as it gets. Add in Larry's size, and it gets worse. He had to be hurting, after the damned-near eleven klick movement to get close to Stavros' estate.

I checked my watch. Larry's was the last element to check in. All of our teams were on deck for this little party; nearly a hundred combat-hardened killers slipping through the jungle to fan out around the southern and eastern flanks of the estate. But I was less concerned about all our players being in place than I was about making sure that all the targets were there before we kicked things off.

We'd started getting wind of this little get-together about a week before, thanks both to Bates' networks and Derek's cyber snooping. We still didn't know what the occasion was, but a *lot* of "Sulla's" major personalities were flying out to Hawaii to meet with Stavros. It was too juicy a target to pass up. If the Group's analysis panned out, we could all but cripple one of the factions in one fell swoop.

Of course, I was skeptical. Decapitation strikes are rarely as effective as anyone thinks they should be. We'd found that out the hard way in Mexico, chasing the top HVT on half a dozen watch lists, only to find out he'd been a red herring. But at the very least, we would put a serious hurting on "Sulla." And at that point, that was enough.

"That looks like Senator Richardson," Nick murmured. I put my eye back to my own scope, burning through the foliage between us and the estate to watch the figures getting off the helo. Sure enough, the pantsuited woman with her blond hair pulled back behind her head certainly looked like the Senator from Vermont. A fat man in a dark suit, who had to be sweltering in the late-morning Hawaii heat, met her at the edge of the pad and shook her hand before ushering her down inside the house.

"That's got to be the last one," Bryan whispered. He was watching our rear security, but keeping tabs on what was going on at the same time.

"If everybody's on time, sure," I answered. "But we don't know for certain who all's inside."

Still, we knew we had a limited time window in which to pull this off. The meeting was set to start at two in the afternoon, and even if many of the attendees stayed around for the expensive—and quite possibly illegal for normal people—entertainment that was almost guaranteed to come later, not all of them were certain to. If we were going to crack that nut open and pry these little fucks out, we were going to have to move soon.

I was preparing to give the "go" order, which would get our diversion moving, when one of the aerial patrols went by overhead. The patrols were flying blue MD-500s, which I couldn't help but think was mainly because they wanted to imitate Special Mission Units riding around in Little Birds. They didn't have the side benches, but the side doors were open and men in cheap blue fatigues with ARs were leaning out the doors, scanning the jungle.

We hunkered down, freezing as the helo passed overhead. We were under a fair bit of concealment, but movement draws the eye, even through foliage. Getting burned at this point wouldn't necessarily be disastrous, but it never is a good idea to surrender the initiative, especially when you're looking to raid a hardened position like Stavros' manor. Not to mention that some of us had traded fire with a helicopter before, and none of us who had were in a hurry to repeat the experience.

The bird moved away, and I started to breathe a little easier. At least until a SAM *whooshed* up from somewhere below the cliff that loomed above the ocean and blew it apart.

The helo was flying low enough that the shockwave of the detonation slapped at the jungle below, and we felt the wind of it from where we were crouched. Frag whickered through the air, as the tail rotor came apart along with a good chunk of the boom, and the stricken bird spun halfway around before falling onto the lawn just over the edge of the cliff.

"I'm pretty sure that was not in the plan," Bryan said, just after the catastrophic noise of the crash ended.

Fuck. I keyed the radio. "Someone is trying to poach our targets," I sent. "Move in."

I heaved myself to my feet. In addition to the veg, the terrain, and the heat, what had made the movement so rough getting into position had been all the crap we'd needed to haul along with us. We had not expected the mansion to be any kind of a soft target, so we'd brought along any number of breaching toys, including a few that we'd never seen before, since Stavros was assumed to have enough money to have all sorts of high-tech, sci-fi security arrangements. Never mind the body armor, since we were probably going to be fighting a number of heavily-armed PSDs in close quarters. That shit adds up and gets *heavy*.

We had halted far enough back in the weeds that, while we could see, we were less likely to be seen, and were out of the presumed range of whatever effect those metal pylons on the lawn had. So, it took a good moment to get everyone up and to the edge of the vegetation.

By then, we could already hear a new snarl of helicopter rotors in the distance, even over the sirens and yelling that had erupted all over the compound after the stricken helicopter had crashed. The competition was inbound, apparently by air.

The yard was in chaos. What I could only assume were crash/fire rescue personnel were pouring out of the mansion and heading for the burning wreckage of the crashed patrol helicopter. More men with guns were spreading out on the roof and could be seen moving around the big picture windows near the visible doors. With surprise lost, this had just become an even harder target. With the number of bigwigs in there, there were going to be a *lot* of security types, all now alerted and actively looking for threats.

Well, that was why we got paid the big bucks.

I paused, just for a moment, taking a knee at the edge of the thick vegetation. With our original plan shot to shit, we were going to have to adjust, and quickly. There was no time for anything complicated; we'd have to move fast and hit hard. That meant we had to hit with overwhelming force, so we would also have to concentrate our efforts on only one breach point.

As I reached for my radio, Larry moved up with Jack and Eric, completing what was left of the team. We were the main assault team, with Tommy's team, mostly made up of new guys, backing us up.

"This is Hillbilly," I sent. "Gate team, you are now our way out. Secure the gate, prepare to support by fire, and stand by. Support by fire team, suppress those assholes on the roof, and hold position. All maneuver elements, on me, make for Breach Point Two."

As soon as I finished speaking, I was releasing the PTT and reaching for one of the bulky gadgets that I'd stuffed in a taco pouch on my rig. None of the others would fit the damned thing.

It was a black plastic box, about the size of one of the little Pelican micro cases. Small, black plastic "hockey pucks" lined front, back, and both sides. There was a simple knob next to one of the bigger pucks, on what I thought of as the "front." It was surprisingly heavy for its size, which only made it that much crappier that we needed to carry so damned many of the things.

I twisted the knob. To my right and left, Alek and Nick were doing the same to identical boxes. Then, almost as one, we lobbed them out of the bushes and toward the nearest pylons, which were only a few meters away.

We had been told that we only needed to get them within a couple of meters of the pylons, but of course, we tried to nail the metal posts themselves, anyway. None of us entirely trusted the little EMP generators, so we wanted to get them as close to their targets as possible. Mine landed about four feet from my target. Alek's overshot by a couple of feet. Nick's landed right at the base of his. He smirked, but didn't say anything or even look at us when both of us turned to look at him.

I counted to three. That should be long enough for the EMP grenades to do their thing, though there was no sound or visual indicator that anything had happened. If you were up close, you might hear a faint whine from one of the grenades, but that would have been drowned out by the cacophony of helicopters, shouting guards, and burning wreckage across the compound, anyway.

Before I'd hit "two," the support by fire element opened fire from the trees, the M60E6s' stuttering roars blending into each other in one continuous, hammering wall of noise. Dust and chips of cement were blasted off the top of the building, where the armed guards were suddenly ducking below the concrete parapet to try to keep their heads.

Coming to my feet, I ran toward the selected breach point. I could already see the specks of four incoming helicopters out over the ocean. Then there wasn't time to worry about them anymore.

I passed the metal pylons without getting shocked, or violently nauseated, or blasted back by a sonic shockwave. Whatever they did, the EMP grenades appeared to have put them out of action.

Of course, it was also possible that they didn't do anything, and were just decorations there to make Stavros feel more like a Bond villain, and we'd just wasted several thousand dollars' worth of equipment to neutralize them. But if they *had* been something nasty, then we sure would have wished we'd used the black boxes.

Besides, it was another pound and a half I didn't have to lug across that fucking lawn.

It felt like the longest sprint ever. A shot *snap*ped past my head, but was quickly answered by another long burst of machinegun fire from the trees. So far, Tim's and Ross's teams were doing a good job of keeping the shooters on the roof suppressed. They didn't have a line on the guys at the door, though.

Since they weren't taking fire, the head of the detail at the south door apparently decided they needed to move, maybe to try to maneuver on the gunners. They slid the door open, and a knot of them ran out and took a knee around the support pillars holding up the overhang.

In contrast to my sarcastic comment about faceless minions in gray coveralls, these guys were kitted out like a high-end SWAT team; Ranger Green fatigues and kit, and the by-then ubiquitous cutaway Ops-Core style helmets. They were also loaded for bear, with SCARs and at least one Mk48 visible.

I saw that Mk48 coming up to point right at my face, by then only about thirty meters away. I threw myself flat, hoping and praying that I'd get down fast enough, even though the lawn was flat as hell, and there really was no place to hide.

I probably would have been dead right there, except that right at that point, Eddie's team crashed the gate, and the helos descended on the compound.

The roaring of the armored trucks that Eddie and his boys were driving had been drowned out by the noise of the firefight and the sirens, but when a five-ton truck with another two tons of steel welded to it hit that gate at close to fifty miles per hour, there was no missing it. As solidly as the gate had been built, it still wasn't heavy enough to stop the truck. The rolling gate was smashed off its rails and twisted around by the impact. Concrete was pulverized into flying dust where the gate was ripped out of its moorings.

Even so, the gate didn't just drop flat, so the truck was almost flipped over as it bounced over the wreckage. The one behind it held back, so as not to get tangled with the first one, or repeat the experience.

I took all of that in in a split second. My focus was on that 48 gunner, who had taken his eyes off me for just a moment, as he flinched a little from the crash of the gate getting smashed in.

Just a moment was all I needed. I got my rifle in my shoulder and dumped five rounds at him as fast as I could. At least one connected solidly; he jerked and fell on his face, on top of his MG.

As I was shooting, Alek was bounding forward, sprinting another fifteen yards before dropping to a knee and opening fire. Eddie's guys rose up out of the backs of the trucks as soon as they'd stopped moving, while they were still rocking on their shocks, swinging M240Ls up on hastily bolted-on armatures, and opened fire in the same moment.

The concrete pillars provided some cover for the enemy shooters, but only some, and between us and the two 7.62 machineguns on the trucks, our opponents really had no place to hide.

Alek knocked one of the riflemen flat on his ass with a trio of shots, and I got another one high in the chest, above his plate, before two long bursts from the machinegunners tore the small knot of gunmen apart. Eddie's boys were shooting low, chopping legs and knees out from under the men so that they fell into the streams of bullets, which both gunners were playing back and forth across a pretty narrow cone. In seconds, the entryway was piled with a blood-spattered heap of torn flesh, shredded gear, and shattered bone.

We had kept moving forward while the gunners hosed down the opposition, and got under the overhang just as the first helicopter roared by overhead.

I spared a glance as it went over. It looked a lot like a Blackhawk, except that it was smaller and more angular. If I'd had the time or the energy to spare, I'd have shaken my head. Whoever these guys were, they had access to the same sort of stealth helos that DEVGRU had used on the Bin Laden raid. Except I was pretty sure these weren't JSOC; posse comitatus aside, we had people there, and if JSOC had been getting involved, we would have heard *something*.

The door gunner started shooting at the trucks. Fortunately, he wasn't shooting anything heavy enough to punch through the armor, but one of the gunners went down anyway, his 240 swiveling crazily to point at the sky. The other gunner ducked low and elevated his own gun, leaving the ground targets alone to return fire at the helo. The bird banked away, hard, as the 240 started roaring its own deadly reply.

The entire luxury compound was now a warzone. Automatic weapons were hammering in multiple directions at once, and I could barely hear myself think over the noise of gunfire and helicopter rotors. I almost missed Tim's radio call.

"We're taking heavy fire from the helos," he announced. "We're returning it, but they're going to get their shooters on the roof. The volume of fire they're putting on us is just too damned high."

I spared a glance over my shoulder to see one of the helos circling out toward the perimeter, presumably attempting to suppress the support by fire positions long enough to insert the hitters onto the roof. We hadn't humped in anti-air weaponry, so our best bet at that point was just to push through and get to Stavros and his cronies before they did. I turned back to the door, kneed Bryan hard in the ass cheek, and bellowed, "*With you!*"

My knee damned near catapulted him through the door, which hadn't been closed all the way, and was still propped open by a corpse. Actually, it would be more accurate to say it was being propped open by a helmet, which was about the only thing holding the dead man's skull together.

The entryway was, fortunately, empty, though we'd been able to see that through the armored glass of the big picture windows facing the jungle. My best guess was that the bulk of the security personnel had gotten their principals to someplace more secure, probably downstairs, while the react force had pushed to the roof and the door that hadn't been directly exposed, at the time, to machinegun fire.

We didn't have any kind of reliable blueprints for the house, so we were going to have to wing it. As soon as we'd fanned out across the entryway, rifle muzzles pointing into any corner and bit of dead space where a straggler might be crouched with a weapon, we started looking for openings.

The most obvious was the hallway leading out of the center of the room. I checked for any other doors, but there were only two ways in or out of the entryway, and one of them was already behind us and had a pile of bodies in it. I closed on the hallway, gun up and moving quickly, even as the house quivered slightly around us. Somebody had just set off a breaching charge somewhere up above. The structure was so damned heavy that it had only raised a little dust instead of shaking the entire house like it had been hit with a hammer.

The hallway was dark, though the bright light of the sun shining into the expansive living room on the far end was lighting up some of the shadows. It made for enough contrast that I almost didn't see the door open ten paces down the hall until a shotgun boomed and I felt a brutal, hammer blow to my chest.

Only years of training and conditioning kept me on my feet, answering the slug in my chest plate with a rapid series of five shots, pushing through the fiery pain. It felt like I'd been kicked in the sternum by an especially bad-tempered mule. Alek was immediately beside me, dumping more fire at the door. We'd all been trained to be precision shooters, up close and at range, but when somebody's sticking a shotgun out into the hallway and blasting away at you, it becomes a matter of survival through fire superiority. Precision can come later.

There was a yell of pain, nearly lost in the ringing in my ears and the general roar of noise, and the shotgun clattered to the floor. Alek got to the door a split second before I did. I kneed him in the thigh, wheezed, "With you!" and we flowed in, with only a bare moment's hesitation.

The shotgunner was scrabbling back from the door, holding his shattered hand, which was dripping blood all over the carpet and his cheap security guard uniform. The other guy was standing in the center of the room, his hands reaching for the ceiling as four 7.62mm carbine barrels swiveled to cover him.

There was no one else in the room. The two men weren't dressed in the shooter kits that the dead guys outside the entrance had been; they were in black slacks, duty belts, and blue, short-sleeved collared shirts with "Security Guard" badges on them. These had to be Stavros' regular security personnel, the ones that anyone of the regular public saw when they accidentally pulled up to the gate, or tried to land at the dock at the base of the cliff. One of them had tried to be a hero, and had damned near lost his life because of it.

"Down on the floor!" Alek bellowed. At the command from the towering Samoan in jungle fatigues, plate carrier, helmet, and camouflage face paint and pointing an OBR at them, both dropped on their faces instantly, the one with the shot-up hand whimpering with the pain as he did so.

They only had the one shotgun between the two of them, so Nick hastily zip-tied both of them hand and foot, while Eric checked me over. "You all right, bro?" he asked, hastily running a hand over my limbs, looking for bleeds. I was pretty sure that I'd only taken a slug to the plate, but if it had been buckshot, there was still a chance I was leaking from a hole somewhere that I hadn't noticed yet.

"Nothing like taking a sledgehammer to the chest to wake you up," I replied through gritted teeth. It hurt to breathe, but I'd been shot in the plate before. I hated to think that I was getting used to it, but it didn't seem as bad as the first time or two.

Eric stepped back, satisfied that I hadn't sprung a leak. "It's important not to get shot," he said. "So sayeth the Nigerian."

"I'll try to remember that," I replied, though the last syllable was drowned out by the hammering of gunfire out in the hallway.

Bryan and Jack were covered down on the door, with Larry looming behind Bryan's shoulder. Both Larry and Bryan were shooting out the door, returning fire at whoever had appeared in the hallway.

"More shooters coming out of the living room!" Larry shouted over the noise. "A lot of 'em!"

A moment later, both men were forced back from the door by a withering hail of gunfire that chewed at the jamb and the wall around it. More fire was roaring up and down the hallway, and after a moment, I picked out that Tommy was on the radio.

"This is Tommy Boy!" he was yelling. "We're taking heavy fire from the hallway, and can't push in any farther! We're pinned in the entryway!"

A series of heavy *thuds* shook the building. I was pretty sure that wasn't us. Whoever had decided to crash the party was using some heavy breaching charges. And meanwhile, we were pinned in a fucking closet with a couple of rent-a-cops.

We hadn't brought much in the way of frags; this had been primarily a "Capture" mission, rather than a "Kill" mission. We'd still brought a few, though, because why wouldn't we? We were Praetorians; we were always ready to wreak more havoc than anyone expected, including our employers. So, I yanked an M67 frag out of my kit, pulled the pin, cooked it for a three-count, and hucked it through the door. Everyone dropped flat.

There was a yell, a sudden slackening of the fire in the hall, and then the frag detonated with a tooth-rattling *thud*. My ears were already ringing enough from all the shooting and the low-flying helos that the noise was somewhat deadened, even though the concussion, funneled by the hallway and the door, made the impact of the slug on my chest plate feel like a love-tap.

"Tommy Boy, Hillbilly," I called. "We're coming out, watch your fire down the hallway!" As soon as he acknowledged, I yelled, "Go, go!" We had to get out there and get on top of them while the survivors were still rattled from the blast. With our competition presumably blasting their way through the house as fast as they could, we didn't have the time to spare to hunker down and play patty-cake with the "Sulla" security.

We flowed out into the hallway, which was still filled with smoke from the grenade blast. The air was thick with the stink of high explosives, blood, burned meat, and shit.

Guns up, we pushed into the living room. There were still four shooters out there, some wounded, some still crouched behind whatever furniture they'd ducked behind to avoid the blast. One of the wounded tried to lift a pistol and took a round to the dome from Alek. The guy crouched behind the sofa popped up, trying to level his MP-7, and Eric and I shot him in the face within half a second of each other. His helmet, the strap unbuckled, was thrown off as his head snapped back and he collapsed behind the furniture.

Of the other two, one was too wounded to do anything; I wasn't sure if he was even entirely cognizant that we were even there. His face was a mask of blood and shredded skin, and he was clutching shaking, bloody hands to his gut beneath his front plate. It didn't look, at first glance, like he'd been eviscerated, but he was hurting.

The other one threw his rifle on the floor and dropped on his face with his hands behind his head. Jack closed on him, kicking the rifle away, and zip-tied his hands before retrieving his pistol, unloading it, and chucking it across the room.

With half a second to observe, I could see that we had at least two different groups of shooters. Several of the dead men and the wounded guy were all in the same Ranger Green as the guys outside. The others were in the newer Storm Gray, which had been advertised primarily for law enforcement. It might have made sense in Honolulu, but out here, surrounded by jungle, I couldn't help but think that it was of limited utility.

There was more gunfire coming from downstairs. Heavy stuff, too. Whoever our unknown competitors were, they were not fucking around. We had to move.

The living room was the last room of that level. The north wall was a wide semi-circle of gigantic picture windows, through which we could see the stair-step construction of the rest of the house spreading out below us, leading toward the pool and the cliff's edge overlooking the ocean. The wreckage of the shot-down helicopter was now burning fiercely, putting a pall of black smoke over the entire scene, though the smoke was being churned into writhing whorls by the stealth helicopter that was now crouched on the lawn, the rotors still turning. Small figures in Multicam gear and helmets were on the ground, holding security around the bird.

"We've got to get downstairs," I said, as Tommy rolled into the room behind us. "I think our new friends have lapped us, just judging by the noise."

Alek had already been checking doors with Nick. "Stairs over here!" he barked.

"We'll take lead," Tommy told me. He was a beefy former SEAL, one of the few such working for Praetorian. I didn't know him well; he'd joined up while we'd been in Kurdistan, then gotten out there about the same time that Mike and I had rotated back Stateside with our teams. But he was an older guy, level-headed, and a good shooter, from what I'd seen so far. "You all right?" he asked me, noticing the still-smoking hole in my plate carrier.

I just nodded. "Took a slug. I'll be fine. Go."

He nodded, punched me on the shoulder, and headed for the stairway.

Seconds after his team started down, gunfire erupted, echoing up and down the concrete stairwell. I could see Tommy shooting up the stairs, and it sounded like there was more from down below. Our friends had secured the stairwell behind them.

Tommy suddenly grunted and dropped, his AR-10 clattering against the railing. He left a smear of red on the rail as he slid against it and slumped to the landing.

Alek ducked into the stairway and sent six fast shots up toward whoever had shot Tommy. His timing must have been good, because there was another clatter of a falling weapon, and the fire from up top ceased.

Alek pushed onto the landing, keeping his muzzle trained high, stepping over Tommy's body as he went. A quick glance confirmed that Tommy was dead; he'd been shot just above his plate, at such an angle that he probably didn't have much of a heart or lungs left.

The rest of us flowed past Alek, following Tommy's team down the steps. There was more shooting reverberating up the stairway from below, but it was shortly silenced by the bone-shaking *wham* of a grenade.

Then it all went ominously quiet.

We pushed out onto the next level, past the mangled corpses of the two shooters who had been on stairway security. It wasn't much larger than the first, and equally empty. The meeting must have been downstairs, or at least the secure room where the meeting attendees had been ushered by their protective details was.

It took moments to clear that level, and then we were heading down again.

There was no resistance as we entered the third floor down. But there had been.

The stairs opened on a round central room, with hallways branching off it. The halls we could see were strewn with bodies, mostly in plain green or gray. Aside from the one we'd killed on the stairway, I hadn't seen any corpses in Multicam yet. These guys were good. I was getting a sneaking suspicion that I knew who they were, too.

I found Tommy's number two, Daley, and tapped him on the shoulder. "Tommy's down," I told him. "You're up."

Daley wasn't a new guy, but he was considerably younger than Tommy, and I saw the brief flash of shock, horror, and sorrow cross his face as what I'd said registered. Then he got his game face back on and nodded. "How do you want to tackle this?" he asked.

"Split your team into two elements," I told him. "One goes that way," I pointed, "the other goes that way. I'll do the same with the other two hallways. Keep comms up and reconsolidate here, though situation dictates."

He nodded again, pointed out four of his guys, and soon they were flowing down the blood-splattered halls.

"Larry, you take Jack and Nick," I said. "Alek, Bryan, and Eric are with me."

On a hunch, I'd taken the hallway leading toward the back of the house and the view of the ocean. My hunch wasn't wrong.

The windows were smaller in the vast room; instead of floor-to-ceiling glass, there was a roughly two-foot, plastered concrete wall at the base. There was a gap in that wall at the center of the great, sweeping curve that faced the

274

ocean, where the pool entered the room. The floor was tiled, and the ceiling was high. Everything was very plush, very expensive, and very modern.

It was also riddled with bullet holes and blast marks, spattered with blood and offal, and littered with corpses.

The glass was obviously armored, as the bullet impacts hadn't shattered it, or even punched all the way through. There weren't that many impacts, either; most of the shots had gone into people.

They'd been thorough. This time there weren't just uniformed and armored security among the bodies, but men and women of various ages, dressed in anything from expensive dresses and suits to bikinis and speedos. Some of the latter were being sported by people who never should have worn such attire.

They'd all been ruthlessly murdered with tight groups to chests and heads. From the attitudes of a few of the bodies, they'd been shot in the head as they lay there, wounded and dying. The pool water was steadily turning red from the blood of the handful of corpses floating in it.

Stavros had been sitting in the shallows, clad in the smallest speedo possible, which was not flattering on the fat old man. Even less so was the puckered hole between his eyes and the gaping exit wound spilling blood and brain matter onto the deck behind him. Across from him, I recognized Helen Seminola, another richer-than-Midas business magnate, dressed in a one-piece swimsuit. She'd died clutching a young woman in a thong bikini to her. Both had died within moments of each other. The shooters hadn't cared who was who; everyone in the room had been marked to die as soon as the helos had landed.

Jack yelled. Looking up, I followed his eyes and his barrel to see the knot of shooters hustling toward the helo on the lawn. There were stairs leading down to the lawn from poolside, and Jack was already moving toward the door leading to the outside pool deck.

I sprinted across the room to join him. The shooters were ushering a man in business casual toward the bird. He was apparently unrestrained but tightly surrounded by men obviously ready to shoot him if he zigged when he was supposed to zag. I couldn't recognize him, but whoever he was, we didn't want them leaving with him.

Jack yanked the door open and ran out onto the deck. There was a low parapet around the pool deck, presumably to keep drunken partygoers from falling off; the lawn was a full story below. He ran to the parapet, dropped to a knee, leveled his rifle, and started shooting.

One of the Multicam-clad shooters in the back of the formation staggered as he took a round to the back plate, then dropped as the follow-up shot took him in the base of the skull. Jack shifted targets and dropped another one with three fast shots, just as I skidded to a knee beside him and got behind my own weapon.

Even before the second guy had hit the ground, the man two paces ahead of him had spun around, fast as a striking snake, whipped his SCAR to his shoulder, and fired. There was a sound like a meat cleaver hitting a melon, and Jack dropped, lifeless, to the deck. His body fell against me and knocked me aside, which probably saved my life, as two more shots *crack*ed painfully next to my ear in the next second. Then a ragged fusillade of fire started chewing up the top of the parapet, and I had to keep my head down.

But in that split second before Jack had died, I'd recognized Baumgartner as his killer, even from that distance.

The snarl of rotors began to build behind me, and I risked a glance up to see another faceted helo rising off the roof, pivoting to bring the door gun to bear on me. And I was out in the open, as exposed as a bug on a plate.

Taking a deep breath, I rolled into the pool, hoping that none of the corpses presently floating in it were carrying anything really serious and infectious. No sooner had I gone under the surface than the door gunner opened fire, blasting pits in the tile and concrete of the deck and further hammering Jack's corpse to hamburger. Rounds were smacking into the water, but I'd dived deep enough that they were spending their energy on the water, instead of on me.

I stayed down, my lungs burning, hoping and praying that Jack and I had been the only ones still on the deck, as the helo made two more passes. The darkness was starting to gather around the edges of my vision as the second pass ended, and I had to risk it. It was a choice between maybe getting shot or certainly drowning, so I broke the surface and gasped for air.

Apparently, Baumgartner had decided that getting away with their prize was more important than killing me, because even as I ducked one more desultory burst, the helos were winging away, back toward the ocean. All that was left on the ground was wreckage, fire, and death.

I dragged myself up out of the bloody pool and onto the deck, gasping for air, every fiber of my body aching. Alek grabbed me by my plate carrier, dragging me away from the pool, while the rest fanned out to set up security. It was more reflex than anything else; our targets were dead or captured, and our competition was gone.

It had not been a good day.

CHAPTER 29

We had just gotten back to the airfield and loaded the bodies onto the DC-3 when Bates called via the secure app.

I just stared at the phone for a few seconds. We'd gotten cleaned up; even at a private field, a bunch of filthy, camouflage-painted, blood-spattered shooters in kit and weapons was going to attract attention. We were getting a few looks as it was, but we were separated enough from anyone else on the field that they couldn't make out much detail, or see what we were carrying onto the plane.

We'd lost ten men in that fiasco. Jack and Tommy had died in the house. Sid had been the gunner on the trucks killed by the helo door gunner. Another seven of the newer guys, none of whom I had really known, had died when another door gunner had swept the treeline where the support by fire element had been set. A good chunk of Tim's team was simply *gone*.

After letting the phone buzz in my hand for what seemed like an eternity, I answered it. "Yeah." I was faintly surprised at how hoarse my own voice was.

"I'm sending you a photo," Bates said without preamble. "Tell me if you recognize the man in the center." A moment later, the phone dinged in my ear, indicating that a message had been delivered.

I pulled up the picture. There were three men, all in camouflage field gear, standing on a pile of rubble and grinning at the camera. From the trees in the background, I guessed it had been taken in Ukraine or one of the Baltics.

I zoomed in on the man in the center. He was older than the other two, with a squarish head and craggy, pock-marked features. He was clean-shaven and his hair was cropped short, but it was showing gray in the temples.

He looked vaguely familiar, but it took a few moments of study before it got through my fatigue- and grief-fogged brain to realize that I'd seen Baumgartner dragging that very man onto the helo on the lawn, just after he'd shot Jack in the head. "Who is he?" I asked.

"Was he there at the meeting?" Bates asked instead of replying. He must have picked the recognition out of my voice.

"He was," I answered heavily.

"Was he among the dead?"

"No," I said. "He's alive, or at least he was when Baumgartner loaded him on a stealth helo and flew away."

There was a brief pause. I had the sudden impression that Bates was rattled, and that was disturbing all by itself. If anyone in this entire clusterfuck had always remained utterly unflappable, it had been The Broker.

"His name is Dmitri Timofeyevich Sokolov," he replied finally. "And if he's meeting with faction leaders, then things have gotten worse than I'd feared."

"That still doesn't answer my question," I said. "Who the fuck is Dmitri Timofeyevich Sokolov?"

"He's MGB," Bates replied. The MGB was the agency formed by the reunion of the FSB and SVR, the Russian domestic and foreign intelligence services. It was the successor of the KGB in more ways than one. "Some members of my network have started calling him 'The Harbinger.' While he never has an official cover, where he pops up, there are usually Little Green Men in the background, and I'm not referring to the kind who come in flying saucers."

I needed no explanation of the term. "Little Green Men" had been a euphemism for Russian unconventional forces for decades. They weren't always necessarily Spetsnaz; they'd been funneling entire infantry units into target countries as "volunteers" for years. But if this guy was MGB, and in the States, then his backup probably *was* a Spetsnaz unit.

Which just made this entire nightmare oh, so much better.

"If Sokolov's in country," Bates continued, "then he's got chaos on his mind. It's what he does, not unlike your friend Xi Shang down in Mexico. The difference is, the Chinese wanted to see the chaos in Mexico continue so that they could take economic advantage, getting natural resources on the cheap. The Russians want to see the US descend into chaos in order to bring their primary geo-strategic rival to its knees."

I was about to ask what this had to do with the factions, but stopped myself. I already knew.

There hasn't been a civil war in history that hasn't been a fucking playground for outside actors, particularly those with some animosity toward the country tearing its own guts out at the time. We'd already seen it with the tide of Mexican fighters coming north across the border to join the Aztlanistas. That the Russians were joining the play was, perhaps, old news. They'd certainly fed both Right and Left with their propaganda for years, depending on who was in power at the time. I suddenly suspected I knew just who had set off the series of bombs that had really gotten the rioters stirred up.

"You're certain that Baumgartner took him?" Bates asked into the silence.

"Yeah," I answered, my throat a little tight. "I looked him in the face, just as he put a bullet through Jack's skull."

"I'm sorry," he said gravely. "I hadn't heard yet how bad the butcher's bill was."

"Bad," was all I said. Any temptation to lash out at Bates had been dispelled a long time ago, when he'd pointed out that he'd been in the game, out in the weeds of the underworld, killing and losing people, a lot longer than any of the rest of us.

"I'll let you bury your dead," he said. "But stand ready. Now that we know Sokolov is in the country, and alive, we'll have to move quickly. The fact that Baumgartner took him suggests that he hasn't made an offer to 'Marius' yet. But I imagine that even if he had made a deal with 'Sulla,' he'd be making the same offer to 'Marius.' Chaos is what he's after, not one faction coming out on top of the other." He sighed. "I take it there was no way to track Baumgartner's strike force?"

"No," I replied. "They were flying MH-Xs. Without air assets on station to track them visually, there's no way of telling where they went."

"Oh, there are ways, now that I know that," Bates replied. "Time to do some digging. We *have* to find out where Baumgartner took Sokolov and take him out of the picture. But that's my area of expertise. Stay on your toes. I'll be in touch."

***

Fifteen hours later, we landed at Southwestern Oregon Regional Airport, in North Bend. It had just rained, and the skies were clearing, though the tarmac was still wet.

Logan was waiting with half a dozen mechanics, a replacement flight crew, and a fuel truck. We weren't staying in North Bend, but crossing half the Pacific had been a long haul for the venerable old DC-3, and the bird needed a serious once-over before continuing on.

Most of us got off the plane to stretch, as well as to provide security. No place in the US was considered safe territory anymore. Our own home had become a non-permissive environment. While we might look like a handful of men just stretching their legs after a long flight, everyone had a pistol on him, and there was a lot heavier firepower close at hand, stashed in innocuous-looking duffels.

I breathed deeply of the chilly, damp air, but stared blindly at the lush greenery of the Pacific Northwest coast. My mind's eye was still on the body bags stacked in the back of the plane.

None of us had had any illusions about the dangers of our line of work. Any ideas of immortality had been beaten out of all of us long ago, when we'd worn the uniform and fought in far-off places. But burying friends never gets any easier.

Jim. Lee. Ben. Jack. Tommy. Sid. I realized that as much as I'd wanted to hold out hope, Little Bob had been missing for so long, nearly five months, that I was now assuming he was dead.

Were any of us going to survive this?

The phone buzzed and broke my reverie. It was Mia.

"Jeff, are you on the ground?" she asked, as soon as I answered. She sounded a little breathless.

"Yeah," I replied. "What's up?"

"I think I've found Little Bob," she told me. "If it's really him, he's in South Dakota. How fast can you get here?"

"It's going to be most of another day, I think," I replied. "The bird needs maintenance and fuel."

"Crap." I could almost see her bite her lip as she thought. "I'm going to go ahead and go out there and try to link up with him, or at least get some feel for the lay of the land," she said after a moment. "I'll send you a more concrete location once I know more."

"Be careful, okay?" I said, suddenly worried. I was slightly surprised at just *how* worried I was at the thought of her going into unknown territory by herself, after Little Bob had inexplicably disappeared and showed up in another state five months later. "Nowhere is safe these days."

"I know," she said. "I'm a big girl, remember? I can take care of myself. Just be ready to come running when I call, okay?"

"I'll be on my way as fast as I can," I told her.

There was a long, somewhat awkward pause, as I tried to think of something else to say. I was sure there was plenty of operational information that we needed to exchange, but right at that moment, all I could think of was the intensity of my fear of something happening to her, and I didn't know how to say it.

She didn't seem to have much to add, either. "I'm sorry about Jack and the others," she said. "I've got to go, but we'll talk when you get back, I mean, if you need to. Okay?"

"Okay," I answered. There was a lump in my throat, and I wasn't sure if it was because of our dead or because of her. "Watch yourself."

"I will." She hesitated, as if she wanted to say something else, then just said, "I'll send a location when I've got it nailed down a bit better. Bye."

I stared down at the phone after she hung up, then shoved it in my pocket and turned to see if I could help Logan and the boys get the bird reset. As tired as I was, I needed something to do.

***

We got back to Wyoming and The Ranch. It was fairly secure; Ventner had assigned some of his lower-tier contractors, mostly the newer guys with less combat zone experience, to back Brett up and keep an eye on The Ranch itself. We were a valuable asset to certain people now, and the Cicero Group was sparing no expense to make sure there wasn't a repeat of the Task Force incident.

It's nice to be appreciated.

The guys on exterior patrol had to be hating life. It was February, and while it was starting to thaw at times, we were still pretty high up, and it got damned cold. And Joe Ventner wasn't putting up with guys trying to stick to easily trafficked patrol routes, either, not after Baumgartner's demonstrated field prowess. Some of the patrols could use snowmobiles, but a lot of them were stuck snowshoeing over steep hills, often in bitter winds and blowing snow.

The static defenses on The Ranch had been noticeably beefed up, too. There were more bunkers at the gates, and more obstacles on the way in. There were fighting positions along likely avenues of approach, away from the roads. The Ranch was beginning to look like a fortress. When one considered that we were, for all intents and purposes, in the middle of a civil war, that was not inappropriate.

We got the bodies unloaded, and conducted a mass funeral for all of them. It was more than some of our fallen had gotten. And I kept worrying, because while I had a location, there had been no further word from Mia or Little Bob for the last thirty-six hours.

"I'm going to Rapid City," I told Tom. "And I'm taking the team with me."

He looked up from his desk. The retired Colonel had never looked like a spring chicken; he was older than most of us by at least a decade, and his chain-smoking didn't help, either. But he looked like he'd aged another ten years in the months since Jim had been murdered.

"Still nothing?" he asked.

I shook my head. "She should have contacted me by now. Something's up."

"Go." He didn't ask questions. There was a chance to get Little Bob back, and Mia had become one of us.

He didn't even say anything about my anxiety about her. That was to his credit. Alek had given me a little ribbing about it, though mainly to try to get me to stop brooding.

I'd barely stepped out of the room when my phone buzzed. It was Mia.

"Talk to me," I said, as soon as I'd answered.

"I know that was you in Hawaii, Stone," Baumgartner said conversationally. My blood ran cold as I stopped dead in the doorway. I could feel Tom's eyes on my back, but I didn't turn around. "You cost me some good men, and damned near fucked my mission. I figure it's only fair if I fuck you over in return.

"I'm taking good care of your buddy and your girlfriend," he continued, and I could hear the humorless grin in his voice. "You'll be happy to know that Sampson's doing pretty good, considering the shitty medical care he's gotten since he got torn up. Of course, that's a state of affairs that's not going to last, unless you come here and try to stop me." He laughed. "See you soon." Then he hung up.

Tom was on his feet behind me. "Baumgartner?" he asked. He had remarkably keen hearing, for a former infantryman.

I just nodded.

"What are you going to do?" he asked. Tom had changed over the years, becoming more of a hands-off administrator and facilitator. There had been a time when he would have taken charge and started planning right then. Instead, he was trusting me to make the call.

I couldn't help but wonder at that, just a little. Tom and I had butted heads more than once, though rarely over courses of action. It had more been a contest of wills, him being the former officer and Leader Of Men, I just a disgruntled NCO and trigger puller, but I'd refused to let him dictate shit I already knew how to do. We'd reached a truce, even a meeting of the minds and mutual trust, to the point that now he was trusting me to make the right call, despite my emotional involvement in the situation. This after the near thing that had been Pueblo.

"I'm going to Rapid City," I said quietly. "I'm going to kill him and get Mia and Little Bob back."

"It's Baumgartner," he pointed out.

"I know." I knew it was an ambush, a trap baited with the lives of my friend and a woman I realized I cared about a lot more than I'd known. And it had been laid by Baumgartner, a man who scared the living shit out of me.

"I'm calling Eddie and Ross," he said. "You go do your prep and get on the road. They'll be right behind you."

I finally turned back to look at him. His face was as cold and composed as ever.

"Taking Baumgartner out of the picture is a strategic move," he said quietly. "At least, that's what I'll tell Renton if he raises a stink over this. Between you and me, our people are more important. But Baumgartner's a bonus."

I just nodded. There wasn't much more to say. As I turned to leave, already planning the loadout and sending a mass message to the rest of the team, Tom called, "And Jeff? Watch your ass. We can't afford to lose many more shooters."

***

Baumgartner was probably hoping that we'd go in guns blazing, in a daring, kinetic, midnight raid to rescue our people. I was sure that he already had his defenses arranged to make that a losing proposition. So, I wasn't going to cater to his expectations.

If the man had a weakness, I was hoping and praying it was overconfidence. He was a preternaturally fast and accurate shot, and by his reputation, something of a physical mutant, with nearly inhuman strength, agility, and endurance. So far, he'd been utterly professional in his mission planning and preparation. But all I needed was one opening.

Baumgartner might have been in an SMU, and killed more people than cancer. But I'd slaughtered my way through pirates, terrorists, mercenaries, narcos, and special operators for the last several years. I figured he was still thinking of me as just another grunt, far below his SMU credentials. I hoped he was still thinking of me that way.

Mia had sent us the address of a farm to the southeast of Rapid City itself. Baumgartner hadn't indicated that he'd moved, and I knew that he wouldn't have. He *wanted* us to find him.

The first day's reconnaissance confirmed it. While Baumgartner didn't show his face, nor did we see sign of Mia or Little Bob, there were definitely more people around the farm than was normal, all men in their late twenties to early forties, fit and watchful, noticeably not doing farm work, and never far from what could be a concealed rifle.

We used a couple of Aeroseeker drones first. We'd first used the small quadrotors in Djibouti, and they were a useful little tool. Of course, one of them got shot down after lingering over the farm for only about ten minutes. The second one didn't last thirty seconds after it got spotted.

But we got enough of a picture to know we were on the right track. Unfortunately, we couldn't do *too* thorough a recon; they'd spot us eventually, especially given how close we'd have to get, and Baumgartner wasn't going to wait around forever. He was going to kill Mia and Little Bob sooner or later, though I figured I could count on him waiting until he contacted me first.

At least, I hoped he would. It was possible that they were already dead, and he just wanted to draw us in. It wasn't a possibility I wanted to dwell on.

He was going to expect an attack at night, probably around 0300 in the morning. Hell, there really wasn't a good time when I could expect Baumgartner's guard to be down; all times of the day or night were going to be equally dangerous.

But there are two times of the day when it's just damned hard to see, and that's what is called in the military End of Evening Nautical Twilight and Beginning of Morning Nautical Twilight. The sun has either just gone down or is just coming up, and the entire world is a sort of vague gray that is increasingly lacking in contrast. NVGs suck, the naked eye sucks, only thermals stand a chance of seeing much clearly past a few dozen yards during EENT or BMNT. I was sure they had thermals, but we had two ways of getting around that.

Unfortunately, in South Dakota in February, one of those ways meant getting dangerously uncomfortable.

It had been warm enough over the last week that most of the snow was gone, and Rapid Creek wasn't *completely* iced over. It still *felt* like it should be. Even with a wetsuit on under my cammies, the water had put icy daggers through my body as soon as I'd gotten in, and my extremities were painfully numb. It was going to make fighting interesting. But there was no other way to do it. Their security was thin along the creek. Baumgartner was too careful not to have security around the back of the farm, but they weren't necessarily expecting somebody to be nuts enough to go swimming in a farm creek in South Dakota in February.

I still got to the insertion point right on time; I'd worked hard to get there, though I'd had to temper my enthusiasm to avoid splashing around. I'd actually deliberately gotten in downstream, so that I'd have more work to get into position, thus hopefully keeping my core temperature up. My hands were still painfully cold, but I could flex my fingers, and hold onto my knife.

Right on schedule, Ross gunned the pickup out on the road, the full-throated roar of the engine echoing across the fields. Hopefully, that should get all eyes looking toward the road and away from the creek, at least for a moment.

I hauled myself out of the water, resisting the urge to hobble, as I'd essentially been low-crawling through freezing water for a quarter mile, and my muscles were stiff with cold and rubbery with exertion, grabbed the top rail of the corral in front of me, and dragged myself over, careful to lower myself to the ground rather than drop with a squelching *thud*. Then I got flat in the dead, wilted weeds next to the fence and waited.

The roar of the engine faded into the distance. There were no shouts, no movement that I could see through the early morning dimness, no gunshots, no sign that I'd been spotted at all. I still stayed put for a few moments, just to be sure.

Once I was reasonably certain that I hadn't been made, I started to creep along the fence, hugging the bottom rail, moving inches at a time. It was agonizingly slow, and I was all too aware of the morning getting brighter around me, though it was overcast enough to keep it from getting too light, too soon.

I knew roughly where the back sentries were going to be. While we hadn't had time to build much of a pattern of life, what we'd seen were pretty solid security positions, though not necessarily with eyes on the spot where I'd vaulted the fence. Still, I kept glancing through the openings in the fence, and the next one over, watching for my first target.

This was going to be dicey. I'd dragged a Compressor, an integrally suppressed .300 Blackout SBR, with me, so I wasn't so worried about firepower. It was more a matter of taking the sentries down fast enough and then moving on the house. The Blackout was quiet as hell, especially since I'd loaded subsonic rounds for it, but no firearm is ever entirely *silent*.

I spotted my target, barely ten yards away. Most of what I could see was muddy boots and Crye pants, as the fence rails occluded most of the rest of him, at least from where I lay at the moment. I'd gotten a lot closer than I'd expected.

284

Slowly, agonizingly slowly, I rolled back from the fence, the weapon in my shoulder, looking for a window that would give me a kill shot. This had to be fast and final. There was no room for fucking around.

I got a clear view of his head just as he turned and looked straight at me. I thought I recognized him for a split second, before his mouth opened and his weapon started to come up, but I had him dead to rights.

The rifle spat, sounding like a particularly quiet .22, his head jerked back with a dark, glistening spray, and he dropped like a puppet with its strings cut.

Now the game was up. Once you kill someone on an infiltration, the infiltration is over. *Somebody* is going to notice *something* wrong, even if you manage to get the body hidden without being spotted. And as quiet as it had been, a gunshot is unmistakable to the trained ear. And given that there was probably a couple centuries worth of combat experience on that farm at that moment, there would be a lot of trained ears listening.

There was, unfortunately, no way under the fence; the rails were far too close together. I had to either go over or around. The gate into the next corral was only a few feet away, though, so that was a no-brainer.

I got to my knees, then, bent double to keep my head below the top of the fence, I ran to the gate, ignoring the pained protests of my near-frozen muscles. The gate was latched, but not locked, and it was a matter of a couple of seconds to get through.

Another body was crumpled next to the hay barn, and the shaggy forms of Eric and Bryan were running forward, still in their ghillie suits. They'd been carefully crawling into position on the west flank since shortly after dark, and they'd dispatched the second sentry at the same moment I'd shot the guy next to the corral. Keeping my head down, I sprinted for the barn.

We hit the side of the hay barn at about the same time. Chests heaving, we traded a quick, "You good?" look, then got our guns up and started moving again.

Slipping around the back of the barn, we came to the backyard, which was thick with trees. It had to be deeply shaded during the summertime, though somewhat less so in February, with all the leaves off the trees. Still, there was enough concealment that we'd be able to get close to the house with less chance of being spotted, particularly if we moved fast. The clock was ticking, with those bodies on the ground.

I ran from tree to tree, trading bounds with Eric and Bryan, each of us covering the other as we moved forward. For all the urgency of the mission, this was not the time nor the place to simply rush in where angels fear to tread.

I dashed to one of the last trees before the house, a gigantic, gnarled old bastard that had probably been growing there for close to a century, and hit the trunk just as the back door opened, and a man with a rifle stepped out.

I only got a glimpse as I flattened myself against the tree, but he was short, solidly built, and wearing a chest rig and carrying a SCAR. He was alert and looking around, the door still open behind him.

I took a deep breath, visualizing exactly where I'd have to put my sights to kill him before he could get his rifle up. Then I swung around the trunk, dropping my muzzle through the Y of the lowest branches.

He was at the low ready, stepping down off the porch, looking toward my tree. He'd seen or heard something, and was looking for us.

Even as my sights came level with his head, and he started to snap his own rifle up, there was a harsh spitting noise from behind me, and his head jerked back. He dropped on his face on the dead grass of the yard, landing on top of his rifle. Fortunately, everything was still wet enough that it muffled the sound.

I came around the tree and sprinted toward the door, my rifle's sights only a bare couple of inches from my eye. I had to be ready to engage fast.

As I mounted the porch, I could hear Baumgartner's voice from inside. "What the fuck is going on out there?" he was demanding.

Another voice answered, but I couldn't make out the words.

"Well, fuck," he drawled, sounding supremely unconcerned. "I guess your boyfriend's here. Which means I'm afraid we won't have time to get any better acquainted, darlin'. Sorry. It's nothing personal."

There was a shout, a heavy *thud*, and then a series of gunshots. I went through the door behind my rifle, safety off and finger already resting lightly on the trigger.

CHAPTER 30

I knew that Eric and Bryan were behind me somewhere, but I didn't know exactly where. It was a one man clear, it was stupid, and I was probably going to die. But I knew that Mia, at least, was in there, and she might have just been murdered. If I couldn't save her, I was going to kill that son of a bitch, or die trying.

The back door opened onto a short hallway, with the kitchen immediately to the right, and the living room straight ahead. I could see one dude, a pistol in his hands, looking at something happening to the right, but hesitating, as if he was trying to get a shot at somebody, but couldn't find a clear line of fire. He saw me come through the door out of the corner of his eye, and whipped around, the Glock coming up to point at me, but I already had him, my front sight settling just above his nose even as he turned.

I double-tapped him in the face, as fast as the trigger reset would let me. The second round blew the top of his skull off as he fell.

I came around the corner, knowing I was turning my back to the second hallway that led off the living room, presumably toward the bedrooms, but there was no helping it.

There was a bearded man slumped against the exterior wall, his front awash in blood, a red smear on the wallpaper behind him. Mia was down on the floor in front of the couch.

Little Bob, almost as bloody as the corpse only a few feet away, was on top of Baumgartner amidst the wreckage of the coffee table, holding on to the killer's pistol with both hands and throwing weakening elbows into Baumgartner's face, while Baumgartner stabbed him repeatedly in the side.

It was a tricky shot, with Little Bob between us, but I put my sights on Baumgartner's head. His eyes met mine a split second before I squeezed the trigger.

I dumped five rounds into his skull from about ten feet away. The last two just bounced what was left of his shattered head around, spattering more blood and pulverized brain matter on the carpet.

Little Bob rolled off him with a groan, leaking *way* too much blood out of his side. Eric and Bryan blew past me to cover the front door and windows, while Alek, Larry, and Nick pushed in the back door.

He was hurt bad, but Little Bob was alive, at least for the moment. I turned to where Mia was lying, face-down on the carpet, my heart in my throat.

She rolled over, and I breathed a little easier. She was alive. She reached up and squeezed my hand, just to let me know she was all right, before turning to Little Bob.

There was no time for anything else. The rest of Baumgartner's shooters had heard the commotion and were coming. Alek, crouched next to the front window, over the corpse of the guy Little Bob had shot, yanked a frag out of his vest, pulled the pin, and chucked it through the already broken window. At least one of Little Bob's shots had shattered the glass.

There was a yell from outside, that was drowned out by the tooth-jarring *wham* of the detonation. Alek had put some juice into the throw, since there was no way the farmhouse walls were going to stop the buzz-saw fragments coming off the grenade. The concussion still shattered every window on the east side of the house, and blew dirt and smoke through the door and windows.

The grenade was a vital part of the plan. It wasn't just to keep the enemy's heads down and hopefully blast a few more of them to kingdom come. It was also the signal to Eddie and Ross that we had the house.

For a moment, after the echoes of the blast faded, everything went quiet. Nobody was shooting, nobody was talking. Little Bob was groaning, as Mia tried desperately to staunch the blood flowing from the dozen or more knife wounds in his side and abdomen. I wanted to help, but there were still bad guys out there, and in combat, the best medicine remains lead downrange.

An intense burst of fire hammered the front of the house, punching through walls and the remnants of window glass. We all dropped flat, and I threw myself over Mia and Little Bob, pushing Mia's head down as bullets snapped through the air overhead and the room filled with flying splinters and drywall dust.

Alek rolled onto his side, leaning out of the open front door, and hammered half a mag out the opening. The incoming fire only intensified in reply; these guys were not going to be easy to suppress, and they didn't seem to give a shit that three of their number might still be in the house. Either they figured Baumgartner and the others had to be dead for us to still be alive and kicking in there, or this bunch had selected for "functional sociopath" as much as The Project had.

If we'd been on our own, we might have been in serious trouble. But Eddie and Ross had just been waiting for that frag to go off. These were the assholes who'd hunted us in our own backyard, and they had taken two of our own hostage. The entire damn company was out for blood.

With a rattling roar, four M60s opened fire from the north, raking both the front and back yards. The fire directed at the house fell off to nothing, as Baumgartner's shooters took cover and turned to face this new threat. At least some of them did.

As I straightened from where I'd been trying to shield Mia and Little Bob from the incoming fire, I looked out the window to see three men sprinting toward the house, their weapons up. They were going to chance the fire to try to get inside and kill us.

One of them was cut down by a long burst from one of the machine guns. Alek and Nick blasted the second off his feet. I whipped my rifle to my shoulder, put the front sight post on the third one's nose, and shot him just as he saw me through the window and fired a snap shot. He missed. I didn't. He fell on his face in the dirt.

Then there was no one left to shoot. The firing died down, and Eddie's team appeared among the trees to the north, moving forward cautiously in a skirmish line, guns up, *carefully* checking the bodies. George signaled, and Herman moved over, covering the slumped but still feebly moving form of one of the opposition shooters as George carefully disarmed him and handcuffed him, searching him for backup weapons and handcuff keys. Medical treatment could come later.

"Jeff!" Mia called, a rising note of desperation in her voice. "I need help! I'm losing him!"

I spun. She was still trying to patch the wounds in Little Bob's side, but the big man was noticeably fading. His eyes were going glassy, and his breathing was getting shallow. I dropped to my knees across from Mia, ripping my own blowout kit off my gear and tearing it open frantically. We needed to patch those holes, I needed to get him covered, get an IV in him. He'd lost a lot of blood. He needed fluids, at the least.

"Dammit, Bob," I snapped, "you have got to quit getting holes in yourself."

His eyes sharpened slightly at the sound of my voice, and he searched my face. He tried to laugh, but there was a nasty gurgle in it, and he suddenly spasmed in pain.

"Take it easy, brother," I told him. "Just take it easy. We've got you."

His blood-smeared hand grabbed my wrist. Ordinarily, Little Bob had a hell of a grip, but you wouldn't know it at that point. There was no strength left in his hand. "I think he cut me up too bad, bro," he said. His voice was thin and thready, and he was having trouble breathing enough to speak. "Something…something ain't right."

"You're damned right something ain't right," I told him, past the hard, painful lump in my throat. "You're leaking." I tore another chest seal open and slapped it over one of the exposed knife wounds. Damn, but there were a lot of 'em. Baumgartner had done a number on him. "Now shut up and let us work."

But he shook his head feebly, even as his fingers slipped off my wrist and his arm fell limply to his side. "Think I've…about…had it, brother," he whispered. "At least…I didn't give…that asshole…the satisfaction."

Then he was gone.

We both saw it happen at the same time. His last breath sighed out of his lips, his muscles went limp and dead, and the light left his eyes. I just stopped, my hand still on the seal on his side. Mia let out a strangled sob, a blood-smeared hand going to her mouth.

Her other hand found mine, and squeezed, hard, as she broke down, sobbing over Little Bob's body.

I just stared down at the corpse that had been my friend and teammate, the big, friendly former Ranger who'd taken to his nickname of "Little Bob" cheerfully, taking a sort of pride in the fact that he was "Little Bob," when he topped the original Bob by three inches and sixty pounds. I could feel the tidal wave of grief coming. I wanted to fight it off, but this was too much. I could hardly breathe past the lump in my throat, and my eyes were burning. I wished I could have killed Baumgartner again. I wished I had been thirty seconds faster getting in the house. I wished…all of it futile in the face of another dead brother.

Alek knelt next to me, reaching one massive hand out to close Little Bob's eyes. His own were red-rimmed, and his mouth was tight. "We've got to go, brother," he said, his voice thick. Little Bob had come to the team after Alek had taken the ops chief position in Kurdistan, but it was a small company, and he'd been the original team leader. He knew Little Bob, and he was feeling the loss as hard as I was. In a way, it had to be worse for Alek; he'd been halfway around the world when Jim had been murdered. The two of them had been tight.

Tires crunched on the gravel of the front driveway, and vehicle doors slammed. Our extract was there.

I gave Mia's hand another squeeze, then let go, slinging my rifle. We had work to do.

It took three of us to lift Little Bob's body and carry it out to the waiting trucks. He'd lost a lot of weight since the MS-13 thugs had shot and stabbed him, but he was still a big guy. We carefully put him in the bed, covered him over with a tarp, and got ready to move out, before either law enforcement or Baumgartner's reinforcements could show up.

***

There wasn't much to do while we waited for the bird to be ready. The Rapid City Regional Airport was less than a mile from the farm we'd just shot the hell out of, so we had to have security up and early warning out, in case somebody put two and two together, between the twenty-five dirty guys with duffels that might or might not be full of gear and weapons, and the shootout that had just echoed across the farmland south of Rapid City. We'd cleaned up as best we could in the vehicles, and I'd changed out of my sopping, muddy cammies, but we still looked like we'd been in a fight. And the tarp-wrapped corpse we were toting along was not going to withstand close scrutiny for long.

Fortunately, we didn't have long to wait, since Sam had been getting the bird ready from the moment he'd touched down. We just had to load up, get final fueling finished, and get clearance. So, after a flurry of activity, I found myself in the back of the DC-3, sitting on a jump seat with nothing more to do, staring down at the tarp-wrapped form of my friend; another one I'd outlived, another one I hadn't been able to save.

Mia sat down beside me. I didn't look at her. I just kept staring down at the body. I wasn't even thinking of what I might have done better, or how I could have prevented what had happened. I didn't feel like I could think at all. My mind was a fog of grief, along with some guilt that I was so glad the woman presently sitting next to me hadn't been the one we'd lost.

She didn't say anything, though I could feel her eyes on me. Then she slid her hand across my back, before reaching over to cup my cheek with the other and pulling me close.

She buried her face in my shoulder as I wrapped my arms around her, and we wept together, wept for Little Bob and Jim and Ben and Jack and all the rest. I held her tight, silently thanking God that she was still safe, and still feeling more than a bit guilty about the thought.

We hadn't trusted her when Renton had first sent her to join us in Mexico. I'd been one of the most paranoid of the bunch. Even after everything she'd done for us, and the risks she'd taken alongside us, I'd still suspected her of ulterior motives, and I knew that it had hurt her. Now I was more than a little ashamed of that.

There was no manipulation here, no ulterior motives. Her grief was real, and I could feel that there was some of the trauma of having been Baumgartner's hostage involved in the way she clung to me even as the bird started to taxi.

***

Finally, the storm subsided somewhat. She pulled away, just a little, though she still sat close, leaning against my side. She wiped her eyes with one hand, while she reached up to hold the hand I still had wrapped around her shoulders with the other.

She looked into my eyes. She looked like hell; her eyes were red-rimmed from crying, and still a little haunted from the ordeal of the last couple of days. Her hair was dirty and disheveled, pulled back in a tight ponytail just to get it out of the way. Her face was drawn and tired. I expected I looked worse.

She was still beautiful.

A slight, hesitant smile curled her lips as she sniffled a bit. "I couldn't help but notice," she said quietly, "that, just for a moment, when I was on the floor, you seemed...rather intensely glad to see that I was all right." She searched my face, as if unsure of how I was going to react.

As for me, I didn't know what to say. There was a growing tightness in my chest as I looked in her eyes. With all the rest of the emotional turmoil roiling in my brain, I was at a loss. Her teasing I could usually grumble and growl about, to her never-ending amusement. But she wasn't teasing, now, and I was stuck.

But she must have read what I was feeling in my face, because she just smiled a little more widely, and sighed, blinking more tears out of her eyes. "If we're being honest," she said, "I've wanted you to look at me like that since Veracruz." I suddenly remembered just how convincing she'd been about being my paramour when we'd been in the public eye in that fancy, luxury hotel, along with all the flirting she'd done since, and it got me wondering. Then there wasn't anything to wonder about anymore.

She leaned in, and we kissed. I knew the rest were watching, but after everything that had happened, there wasn't any catcalling or jeering. I expected that Alek and Eddie were glowering at anyone who was looking tempted.

Once we came up for air, she reached up and touched my cheek with gentle fingertips. "If we live to see the end of this," she murmured, "you and I are going away together for a long, long time. I think we've got a lot to figure out about this relationship."

I held her close as the bird climbed into the sky. That was the shadow hanging over us. Half the team was dead or crippled at this point. Would any of us live to see the end of this nightmare?

***

Stahl was waiting for us at The Ranch, along with Renton and Bates. Renton looked a bit impatient as we escorted Little Bob's remains to the burial site that Tom had already picked out on the shoulder of the mountain above the house, but Stahl was grimly respectful, and I got the impression that he had laid down the law to Renton in no uncertain terms that Little Bob's funeral would not be interrupted nor rushed. Stahl had been a combat leader, and to him, respect for the fallen was a sacred duty.

Little Bob didn't have any family left. He'd been an only child, and his parents were long gone. We had been his family. So, aside from Stahl, Renton, and Bates, there were only Praetorians gathered around the grave. Mia stood close by my side, but she was essentially part of the family, now, too.

Mia had relayed to us what Little Bob had told her had happened. It seemed that 'Sulla' had sent a couple of minders to observe the MS-13 attack and report back. When it had gone badly, they'd gone to ground. Then, when the Task Force had shown up, one of them had listened to the Good Idea Fairy, and they'd snatched Little Bob out of the hospital and split.

Once they had him, though, they hadn't known what to do with him. Apparently, neither one of them had had the guts to just kill him; they were managers, not trigger pullers. And their handler had apparently told them to

292

hold tight and keep him secure until they could find a use for him. Presumably, they had been waiting to see what happened between us and the Task Force.

Well, their handler had gone silent, probably a victim of one or another kill- or snatch-squad. For all anyone knew, we might have killed or captured whoever it was. They hadn't known what to do without instructions, so they'd gone on with their last orders received, keeping Little Bob alive in that farmhouse and wondering what the hell they were going to do. For months.

Little Bob had bided his time, regaining some of his strength while feigning continued incapacitation, until the day he'd gotten the drop on them and killed both of them. Then he'd sent the message. Without secure comms, it had been intercepted. Baumgartner had waited until someone had showed up for him, then sprung his trap.

The funeral was short and to the point. Those of us of the praying persuasion prayed. The rest bowed their heads in silence, as we took turns shoveling the earth over what was left of another teammate.

Only after we'd trooped back down to the ranch house did Stahl and Renton approach Tom, Alek, Eddie, and me.

"It looks like we've got a target, gents," Stahl said. "Over the last twenty-four hours, no less than ten of the major 'Marius' players have flown into SeaTac. It looks like there's a major meeting going down, and we suspect that Sokolov is going to be the center of it."

"Have we gotten eyes on Sokolov himself?" I asked. "Because it was Baumgartner who took him, and he can't have had long to stash him somewhere before he flew out to Rapid City to take Mia and Little Bob hostage."

"We haven't gotten any confirmation on Sokolov's whereabouts, no," Renton put in. "But under the circumstances, nothing else makes sense. Both factions have taken huge hits to their operational resources lately; we think that 'Marius' is actually hurting worse than 'Sulla,' despite the damage the latter faction took with the Hawaii raid. 'Marius' is somewhat more centralized, and has generally relied more on direct action rather than crowdsourced violence for their immediate goals, and you guys have taken a hell of a bite out of their DA capability. 'Sulla' has been gutted, at least until the next tier steps up to take the reins of their mentors' operations, but we think that 'Marius' really isn't in a position to take advantage of the current power vacuum."

"Which would lead them right into Sokolov's arms," Tom finished.

Renton nodded. "This meet might be a chance to take the wind out of this entire shit-show," he said. "If the major players of both factions are out of the picture, we might be able to calm things down somewhat."

Eddie and I shared a look. *Where have we heard that before?* We'd seen the networked nature of this kind of irregular warfare in Mexico and Central America, and knew first-hand how hard it was to shut that sort of thing down. Furthermore, we'd seen just how decentralized the factions were. They weren't organizations; they were loose networks based on nepotism, backroom business deals, and political opportunism. Hell, I was sure there were probably going to be people at that 'Marius' meeting who were in mourning for Stavros and several others who'd gotten scragged in Hawaii.

"We've got a list of possible meeting sites," Renton continued. "Including a couple in Seattle; the riots have kind of died down for the moment, and these people tend to think they're untouchable, anyway, especially since it was their hit squad that went into Hawaii. They're going to have significant security, so they might feel safe enough to meet in the city. There are a few other possible sites, though, so we're going to have to do some advance reconnaissance."

I just nodded. I was exhausted. I felt dead. We'd already buried too many, and I was sure that even more of us weren't going to come back from hitting 'Marius' where it hurt. Sure, we'd eliminated Baumgartner, but how many other good shooters were working for these motherfuckers? There certainly was no shortage of trained soldiers running around, after damned near twenty years of continuous, low-level warfare in the Middle East and elsewhere.

But I'd do it. Because what else was I going to do?

The potential of a future with Mia was there in the background, but I couldn't let the team go after these assholes without me. Besides, these were the same fucks who had hired Baumgartner. In a strangely cold, abstract sort of way, I wanted them to pay for how they'd hurt us, never mind how they'd torn the country apart for the sake of their petty little agendas.

"There's more," Bates put in. "Half a dozen of my contacts in the Russian underworld have gone silent in the last thirty-six hours. I don't know why, though I've got my ear to the ground. But with Sokolov in play, I suspect it means something big is coming. The MGB has its claws deep in the *Mafiya*; hell, half the *Mafiya is* MGB. I'll keep digging, but we may need to move quickly."

"Great," I replied. I looked at Renton. "Any timeline for this meet?"

He shook his head. "Not yet, but given some of the targets that have already popped up, I would expect within the next forty-eight hours."

"Fucking hell," Eddie said tiredly. "No rest for the wicked, huh?"

"We're taking eight," I said. "If we try to do this with less rest than that, we're going to start making mistakes. We're strung out as it is."

Stahl nodded. "We've got assets moving to start laying the groundwork already," he said, still talking around that ever-present cigar. It had disappeared for the funeral, then reappeared between his teeth almost like magic. "The recon elements are already up there. If it comes to it, you gents will be the hitters, not the snoopers. Get some rest, and be ready to move."

On that cheerful note, we broke up and headed for the nearest place to crash.

CHAPTER 31

We'd had four days of watching and waiting to do before the meeting appeared to be finally coming together. These assholes were taking their time, most of them living larger than probably ninety-nine percent of the rest of the country could afford to at that point. The Cicero Group's recon elements tracked them through Puget Sound cruises, fine dining, and expensive parties that lasted until three in the morning. They never seemed to actually set in to do any business, and we were starting to think that we were looking at another case of rabbits sent out for the hounds to chase when things started moving.

My money had been on the venue being a coastal resort on the Sound, or a ski resort in the Cascades, but as it turned out, they converged on the Verdant Mount golf resort outside of Mount Vernon. Fucking rich people. Surrounded by mountains and woods and water, and they want manicured lawns and golf.

Of course, with all the fucking around this bunch had been doing, we couldn't be entirely certain that this was it; the initial reports had more and more of them checking into the lodge, but it could just be another party. It was immaterial to us; we had been staged at a small, private airfield outside of Arlington for the last three days, on fifteen-minute strip alert, ready to launch. While we didn't have anything like the MH-Xs that Baumgartner's strike force had used in Hawaii, the Cicero Group had managed to acquire, somehow, what appeared to be actual MH-6 Little Birds for us. Phil and Sam had been like kids in a candy store getting to know the new birds, which appeared to be brand new, as opposed to Nightstalker castoffs, which I didn't think were ever available for civilian purchase, anyway. But then, the Cicero Group had its own backchannels and connections, not entirely unlike our factional adversaries.

The phone buzzed again. We were gathered in the hangar, dressed and ready to roll, kit and weapons within arm's reach at all times. Nobody was talking much; we were all still exhausted, and the pall of the losses we'd taken was still kind of hanging over the entire team. Eric and Bryan were tossing darts at the dartboard on the office wall in the back, just for something to do. I was studying the imagery of the resort, though I as much as I stared at it, I rarely seemed to really *see* it. I'd damned near memorized the layout already, and my mind was elsewhere, though my ears were cocked for any signal that it was time to move. I was in that weird mental no-man's-land between woolgathering and switched-on.

I snatched the phone up as soon as it rattled against the tabletop. It was Carl, Renton's recon TL, via the secure app. I answered it immediately. "Yeah."

"A motorcade just pulled up to the main lodge," he reported. "And either a fireteam of meatheads just escorted Sokolov inside, or else he's got a twin running around."

"Roger, you have eyes on Sokolov," I replied, loudly enough that everyone else in the hangar could hear. Heads came up and eyes zeroed in on me.

"Confirmed," he replied. "This is it. The meeting is happening now."

"Understood. We're wheel's up," I answered, and killed the connection. If there was more information he needed to relay, he'd send it via messages. We had to move.

I spared the imagery one last glance, focusing on the lodge for a second. If I was being honest with myself, I didn't like the mission profile. Not because it was tactically unsound. No, we'd planned it out carefully. Murphy's inevitable malicious interference aside, the plan was solid.

But I wanted to call in an Arc Light and flatten that place, along with everyone in it. Failing that, I wanted to seal the exits and go through, floor by floor, killing fucking *everyone*. Just systematically murder every single one of those arrogant fucksticks whose asinine power games had gotten so many people killed already.

I turned away from the tablet, reaching up to throw my plate carrier over my head and Velcro the cummerbund around my ribs. My memory turned to the MS-13 thug I'd nearly beaten to death while he was zip-tied to a chair, and I forced the ravening, bloodthirsty beast trying to claw its way out of my chest back, shoving it back into its cave in the deepest recesses of my mind. If I gave in to that fury, I was damned, and I knew it. So, I'd keep the beast on its choke collar and do the mission as we'd planned. As I'd planned.

There was no other way. Not if I wanted to live with myself afterwards. I'd killed Baumgartner, but I knew all too well how few steps away I was from being just like him.

The rotors were already turning as we jogged out onto the tarmac, kitted up and with rifles in hand. We were all clad in identical, unmarked, plain OD green fatigues under plate carriers and wearing ATE helmets. At first glance, we'd hopefully be mistaken for a law enforcement task force. Hell, it had worked for 'Marius' for years.

I was the last one to clamber onto the side bench of my Little Bird, having made sure the other helos were up and up first. We had three teams' worth of shooters assembled, but I was the overall mission commander. Alek had maintained that he was going to be my slack man, if nothing else. As whittled down as we had been, it was still my team. He didn't want to head up another team, or take overall command of the company operations. He wanted to be with us, on the ground, and if that meant he was little more than a hired gun, that was fine with him.

Finally, I was aboard, and we were pulling for the sky.

We roared north at treetop height. I was sure local air traffic control was having an aneurism at the sudden appearance of six helicopters flying nap of the earth, without filed flight plan or airspace deconfliction. By the time they figured out what was happening, though, and were able to do anything about it, we'd be on target and going to work.

The air roared, sucking the moisture out of my eyeballs and whipping my pantlegs against my shins as we sped over the green fields below, so close that if we'd dipped much lower, we might have clipped a power line. There was no way to talk, even if any of us had had anything to say.

We climbed into the hills, and had to gain some altitude to avoid the firs and spruces that rose on the rocky flanks of the hillsides. A lake sped by beneath us. Phil's voice crackled in my headphones, which were wired into my radio.

"Two minutes, Hillbilly," he said.

I broke squelch twice, indicating that I'd heard. Game time.

The lodge was a gigantic monstrosity of a Lincoln-Log mansion, surrounded on three sides by woods, facing the golf course and Mount Baker beyond. It had a peaked roof, which precluded a top-down entry and clear, and the woods meant we had to land on the golf greens. The cordon was going to have to move fast to seal off the back side.

The first two birds swept in, flared hard, and dumped Ross's team off. They had the heaviest weaponry, since they weren't supposed to make entry, provided everything went according to plan. Half of them dropped to their bellies around the birds, covering down on the lodge with the two M60s, while the other half sprinted for the trees.

There were figures on the front porch of the lodge, presumably security personnel. Somewhat to my surprise, given everything else that had happened recently, they scrambled inside and out of sight instead of taking the guys on the ground under fire.

I took all this in as Phil banked the Little Bird in a tight circle above the lodge, giving the cordon a few seconds to get in place, and the first pair of helos time to get clear. The golf course was big, but there was limited space in front of the lodge to set us down.

Even as the birds pulled up and away, however, I looked down to see both M60s open fire, dust and bits of grass blasting away from the muzzles. I couldn't see what they were shooting at, but I guessed they'd just taken fire from some of the lodge windows.

"Dirt, bring us around so we can get some fire on those windows," I called over the radio. Phil acknowledged, and the Little Bird banked sharply to come to something close to a hover in front of the lodge.

Now only a few dozen yards from the front, we could see the shooters in several of the upper story windows. The machine guns down below were forcing them back from the windows, but from our altitude, we had clear shots.

Without a word or any other signal, Alek and I lifted our rifles and opened fire, the barks of the 7.62 reports drowned out by the roar of the helo rotors. My first pair was hasty, and missed, and the guy started to bring his MP7 up to shoot back, before I knocked him down with two more shots high in the chest. Then we were past and pulling away again, Phil starting to circle for a landing.

As Phil flared the bird hard to bring it to a hover, the skids just barely a handspan above the grass, the heavy element of Ross's team was already moving, no longer under fire from the windows, heading for the near corner of the lodge. Between them and the other element at the far corner, they had all four sides of the building covered. No one was getting in or out without getting shot.

The cordon in place, I led the assault team on a dead sprint for the front door.

We were vulnerable for that last few yards; the support by fire team couldn't do much and the entire front of the lobby was encased in now-shattered glass, including the doors. We ran with guns up, searching for targets, ready to provide our own covering fire if we had to.

We bounded up the steps to the front porch without incident, then a shotgun blast ripped through the air between me and Eric. That it missed both of us was a minor miracle.

I thudded into the heavy timber doorframe a split second before Eric did, even as Bryan and Larry dumped fire through the shattered door glass. I yanked a flashbang out of my kit, prepped it, and tossed it hard through the door. I wanted to get that sucker as close to those assholes with the guns inside as possible.

The bang went off, and Eric and I were going through the broken windows. They'd been safety glass, so there were no large fragments sticking out into the opening to get snagged on.

The lobby was surprisingly intact, given the amount of gunfire that had already been poured into it. A high-ceilinged, timber-and-stone hall, with a large stone fireplace in the center with easy chairs set around it, and a large reception desk to the right of the hallway leading back to the elevators and first floor rooms, it looked more like a ski lodge than a golf course, but since it was on Puget Sound, I guessed that it kind of fit. Bullet scars were now visible on the stones of the fireplace and pockmarking the reception desk.

The smoke from the bang was still roiling next to the side of the fireplace, so that was where we went. A dude in tan 5.11s and plate carrier was crouched behind the fireplace, having been obviously rocked by the closeness of the detonation. He was blinking at the purple spot in his vision, and probably couldn't hear our boots crunching on the broken glass all over the floor.

He saw movement, though, and brought his shotgun up. He might not be able to see, but a shotgun can still kill you if it's only pointed close enough to your center of mass. Eric shot him dead as I swiveled to cover the reception desk.

More shots sounded on the other side of the fireplace, the suppressed 7.62 sounding like harsh, echoing *claps* in the lobby. Then two more young men in the same tan fatigues as the guy Eric had shot popped up over the top of the reception desk, leveling M4s.

They were a fraction of a second too slow. I'd already had my SOCOM 16 leveled at the top of the reception desk, and only had to twitch the muzzle ever so slightly to the right to put a bullet through the rising skull of the first. A dark stain splashed against the shelves behind the desk and he dropped out of sight, as I started transitioning toward the second. Alek beat me to it. His first round smacked off the M4's optic, nearly knocking the carbine out of the man's hands, then the follow-up shot blew his eyeball backward into his brain, and he fell, his head bouncing off the desk before he collapsed to the floor.

After a brief glance to ensure that we had the lobby locked down and cleared, we swept toward the hallway.

As soon as we'd fingered Verdant Mount as a potential target, we'd studied every bit of info we could get about it, so we had a decent understanding of the layout. Granted, studying floor plans and photo imagery is no substitute for walking the ground and the hallways yourself, but we at least could be reasonably certain where the main meeting hall was on the second floor, as well as where the stairs, elevators, and most important danger areas were on all five floors.

The elevators were right out. Even if they hadn't deactivated them already, they could while we went up. Or just force the upper doors open and toss some explosives down the shaft. That meant going up the stairs to get to the conference room, which was the most likely place for the meeting to happen, unless security had moved them as soon as the shooting had started.

We got down the hall to the stairway without further incident. Apparently, security was keeping to the chokepoints, though they probably could have pinned us down in the hallway if they'd just stuck their heads out and opened fire. Hallways are death traps, which is why we tend to prefer to move from room to room in CQB.

I was beginning to think that we'd eliminated 'Marius'' A-team when I'd killed Baumgartner.

We took a handful of seconds to set up on the door to the stairway. You can't be too careful with stairways; they're nightmares.

Alek cracked the door open while I covered down on the opening, my muzzle right where I could nail anyone on the other side right about high chest. Larry tossed a flashbang in through the crack, then Alek pulled the door shut again, wrenching it closed against the resistance of the buffer.

The bang went off a split second later, and I could hear the reverberation as the stairway amplified the blast. It had to be damned painful in there for anyone covering down the stairs.

No sooner had the bang rattled the door than Alek donkey-kicked it open again and I pushed through the opening.

A burst of automatic weapons fire rattled down the stairway, even as I flattened myself against the inside wall, my muzzle pointed up between the flights, trying to get a shot at the next landing. Whoever was up there wasn't playing around, though. I ducked back as another long burst roared down at me, filling the stairway with catastrophic noise and blasting stinging chunks off the stairs and walls. It sounded like there was at least one Mk46 or some similar 5.56 light machinegun up there.

This was a problem. Charging up the stairs into the teeth of machinegun fire was a good way to get dead while accomplishing exactly dick. And time was not on our side.

I considered lobbing a frag up there, but that would mean exposing myself long enough to get the right angle, and that was a bad idea without having fire superiority. So, I got another idea.

I grabbed one of the new guys, a former Marine named Corey, who'd jumped on the assault team. "You and Billy cover down on the stairs here, and throw some fire up at them," I said in his ear, hopefully inaudibly to those up above, especially as they were still blazing away at the next landing down, trying to keep us pinned. "Keep 'em busy, but don't expose yourselves enough to get shot. You're the diversion. We're going to try to flank 'em, then call you up."

"Roger," Corey said, shuffling ahead of me along the wall. He pointed his Mk17 up between the flights and pumped a half-dozen shots up, just to give them something to think about.

Leaving Billy on the doorway, covering Corey's back, I grabbed the rest and headed back down the hall at just about a sprint.

There were two stairways, one at either end of the building. I was hoping that they'd figure we were heading up the first one, and would divert most of their forces there.

As it turned out, great minds think alike. Or at least violent minds think alike. We were halfway down the hallway to the second staircase when the door opened and five shooters poured out.

We both opened fire at the same time. I quickly ducked into the shallow alcove of a room's door as I snapped shots at the lead shooter, even as his own rounds whipped past my head with painful *snaps* that slapped the side of my head with the force of their passage.

My own shots were slightly more accurate than his. The first two hit him in the plate and staggered him. Then, braced inside the little alcove, I put the third round just below his left eye. He crashed to the floor, tripping up the guy behind him, just in time for that dude to take at least five rounds just above the plate as he fell.

For a second, the hallway was a hellstorm of flying metal and noise. Then it all fell silent, except for the dull roar of shooting from behind us, where Corey was still keeping the machinegunners on the stairway busy. All five of the hostile shooters were on the floor, and the air was thick with the smell of gunsmoke and death.

I didn't dare take my eyes or my muzzle off the hallway in front of me. I was in the lead, so that was my responsibility. "Sound off!" I barked hoarsely. My mouth and throat were as dry as the Mojave.

"Up," Alek called out.

"Up!" Nick answered.

"Up and up!" was Eric's reply.

"Up," Bryan said.

"I took a few to the plate," Larry wheezed painfully. "And my arm got trimmed, too."

"I got him," Eric called out. I could hear him move up and start checking Larry, though I still didn't turn my head to look.

"You make one hell of a meat shield, brother," I heard Eric tell Larry. "You soaked up all the rounds and left the rest of us in the clear." He paused. "Damn. Don't look now, but you took a couple to the dome-piece, too. Your helmet's tore up." After another moment's examination, I heard him clap Larry on the shoulder. "That arm's going to hurt, but you're not leaking anywhere else. Just try to keep to the back, I think it's safe to say your plate is compromised."

"No shit," Larry replied, still sounding a little pained and out of breath. I didn't know how many rounds he'd taken to the plate, but having caught a few bullets that way myself, I knew it was not comfortable. He'd be aching for a while.

"Moving," I called, and stepped out into the hallway, gliding toward the end as quickly as I knew I could shoot accurately. I stepped over the bodies, kicking weapons away from grasping hands, just in case.

I paused at the stairway, letting Alek push across and carefully crack the door open. There was still enough noise coming from the far end of the hall that I hoped anyone left up on the landing above wouldn't be expecting us, so we were staying soft for the moment. That was about to change in a second.

Letting my rifle hang, I pulled a frag out and prepped it. Then I nodded to Alek, who pushed the door the rest of the way open.

I went through the doorway, with Alek turning to enter right on my heels, his own OBR up over my shoulder. I was going to get rocked if he had to start shooting, suppressor or no, but it would be preferable to getting shot in the face.

I moved quickly to the base of the stairs, leaned back, and hucked the grenade up toward the second landing. I'd released the safety lever as Alek had pushed the door open, and the fuse was cooking before the little metal ball left my hand. There were maybe two more seconds left.

There was a yell, and then the entire stairwell seemed to explode.

It's hard to describe the overpressure of even a little M67 grenade going off in an exposed space like a stairwell. The narrow space amplifies the blast, and even though we were shielded from the frag that lashed the walls, we got hammered by the concussion. Even helmets and earpro could only somewhat mitigate the gut-punch shock.

But there wasn't time to shake it off. Alek pushed past me to take the lead, bounding up the stairs three at a time to hit the first landing and pivot around, pointing his rifle up toward the door.

Meanwhile, I grabbed my own weapon from where it dangled on its sling in front of my chest, and ran up the steps after him. Nick and Bryan pounded after me, with Eric and Larry taking up the rear. Larry wasn't moving too good; his breath had probably been knocked out, and he might be nursing a cracked rib. There was blood all the way down his left sleeve, and the front of his plate carrier was mangled from the hits he'd taken.

My aim had been good. The second landing was wreathed in smoke, the walls and doors scarred by shrapnel, and two mangled figures were slumped over similarly scarred-up and now blood-soaked Mk46s.

Alek pushed up, swiveling around to keep the next flight up covered, as the rest of us pushed past him to stack on the door into the hall for a moment.

Only for a moment. I cracked the door and Bryan threw a flashbang inside, immediately followed by a second from Nick. We were banking on anyone in the hallway expecting an entry as soon as the first went off, so we hit 'em with a second one. As soon as the second bang's concussion rattled the door, we were moving.

It had worked. There were four more shooters, dimly visible through the smoke that was now filling the hallway, staked out in front of the conference room doors. They must have been braced for the first blast but not for the second, because they couldn't see and didn't seem to have much equilibrium as we closed in on them. They must have been staring right at that second bang when it went off.

All of them still had weapons in their hands, though, and so they died in a hail of suppressed gunfire as we swept forward, Nick and I almost shoulder-to-shoulder across the hallway.

Nick pushed just past the doors to cover down the long axis of the hallway, while the rest of us set up to make entry. I tapped Bryan and pointed down the hall toward the far stairway, which was still resounding with sporadic bursts of gunfire, as the shooters there tried to keep anyone from coming up the stairs. They must have been utterly deafened by the racket, if they weren't reacting to the shitstorm behind them.

Bryan just nodded, bumped Nick, and headed down the hallway toward the stairs to relieve Corey and Billy.

Just before I kicked the door open, I heard a voice bellow something. Then the doors flew open under my boot and we were flowing in, guns up and looking for the next threats.

The conference room wasn't all that large; this was a golf resort, after all, not a convention center. It was still big enough for nearly fifty people to be seated comfortably.

My eyes immediately snapped to the guys in suits standing on the edges of the room, who were obviously PSD. My rifle swiveled to cover the first one, but he already had his hands on his head and his pistol on the floor. The other four men in similar attire were also in the same attitude.

In the center of the room stood a broad-chested, big bellied man with a round, ruddy face and thinning gray hair. He was wearing a light gray suit, and had his hands held well out to his sides, palms out and empty.

"Easy, boys, easy!" he boomed, in a pronounced West Texas accent. "I think this has gone entirely far enough. No need for anyone else to die today."

I recognized him then. This was Mason Van Damme, Stavros opposite number in "Marius."

He had the broad, open face and practiced demeanor of a big, bluff good-old-boy, but when I looked into his eyes, which were studying me intently, I could see the emotionless, shark-like cunning there. This was a dangerous man, though in a far different sense than Baumgartner and the others this son of a bitch had hired.

"I know you," he said to me, his eyes narrowing. "I've seen your picture." He nodded suddenly, as if placing my face. "You're those boys who caused all that ruckus down in Mexico a little while back," he said. "Took down an entire cartel, all by yourselves. Well, now. That's impressive. Mighty impressive." He glanced over my shoulder at the still-smoking hallway. The shooting had ceased out there, hopefully because the machinegunners in the stairway had been silenced.

"I don't know who you boys are working for," he continued, his booming voice still as firm and confident as ever. This was not a man who was easily rattled, even though he was presently staring down the still-hot rifle muzzles of the men who'd just gone through his security like a shotgun blast through tissue paper. "And I don't know what they've told you about what's going on here. I can guarantee, though, that it's only part of the story, whatever bits of it might be true.

"Now, I know you boys are patriots," he went on, his tone becoming even more conciliatory, rather like a disappointed father trying to talk sense to his wayward son. "You wouldn't have stuck your necks out in Mexico the way you did otherwise. So, I know that if you knew that what we're talking about here is saving the country, you'd be a little less quick on the trigger." He raised an eyebrow. "Hell, with everything that's happened lately, I'm sure we can make an arrangement that will benefit everybody. As it turns out, we could use people like you, son."

My eyes narrowed. "I'm sure. Baumgartner's not exactly answering your calls anymore, is he?"

He reacted. It was subtle, but his eyes flashed, just for a moment, before the practiced mask of the politician settled back in place. "You say that name with some respect, son," he said. "Gordon Baumgartner was a damned good man and an American hero."

"Gordon Baumgartner was a mad-dog killer without a conscience," I snarled, "and my one regret was that I only got to kill him once, and not before he murdered yet another friend of mine. He put too damned many in the ground as it was. That you used him the way you did tells me everything about you I need to know."

"In case you hadn't noticed, son, it's a dangerous world out there, and the country's facing threats that don't play by the old rules," Van Damme snapped. "If we're going to preserve the nation that we know and love, we've got to throw that rule book out. We've got to play the game as it is, not as we'd like it to be." His eyes narrowed. "I knew Gordon Baumgartner well. He was a good man. If he killed so many of your friends, son, maybe you need to consider your choice of friends."

I saw red. Gritting my teeth, I stepped forward suddenly, and he actually flinched, just before my buttstock crashed into his teeth and laid him out on the floor.

I leaned in and pressed my still-warm muzzle to his temple. "You should be damned glad that I'm *not* Baumgartner, you piece of shit," I hissed, "because if I was, you'd be choking on your own guts right now." I leaned on the rifle just enough to put a painful amount of pressure on his skull for a moment before straightening up.

At that very moment, the entire lodge shook with a tremendous *boom* from outside. Everyone but us flinched toward the floor.

I stared down at Van Damme, my face once again impassive. "That would be the blocking position," I said conversationally. "I hope you weren't too attached to your QRF." I keyed my radio. "Geek, Hillbilly."

"We're clear for now," Eddie replied. "German was a bit...*enthusiastic* in applying the 'P for Plenty' principle. We're going to have to go out by air, though; the road's blocked."

"We've got a few minutes, at least," I said over my shoulder. "Find Sokolov."

"That's what you're here for?" Van Damme said, though it was more of a mumble through his shattered front teeth. He laughed, a sick gurgle to the sound from the blood in his mouth. "Damn, but there's a lot of demand for ole Dmitri. Well, you're too late. He's already working for us. The phone call's already been made; things are already moving. In a few hours, the last of Concri's bunch are going to be out of the picture, and we can start to rebuild."

I stared down at him for a moment, even as Alek hauled Dmitri Sokolov to his feet and pried the cell phone out of his hands.

We had our targets, but our work, it seemed, was far from over. And now the clock was ticking.

CHAPTER 32

Presuming that time was so short as to be damned near nonexistent, the Group had moved quickly. We repaired to an abandoned Job Corps camp in the Cascades, with a shipping container lifted in to act as holding cell and interrogation room for Sokolov. The rest of the detainees from the meeting were being held nearby, in some of the camp's Quonset huts, under continual guard. The really heavy security was reserved for Sokolov.

The container was heavily insulated, making it nearly soundproof. There were no openings except for the swinging doors at one end; the other end had been welded shut. Sokolov's cell only took up half the container; that way he couldn't see daylight even when someone opened the outer doors. There was a small, two-way mirror just to the right of the heavy steel door that led into the cell.

The cell itself was barely big enough to stand up in, and was completely lacking in amenities. There was a folding cot, a wag-bag toilet, and that was it. A single, naked LED light bulb hung from the ceiling, and never went out.

I was already standing in the entryway, watching Sokolov through the two-way mirror, when Bates showed up. I was studying the little Russian, contemplating again how looks can be deceiving.

Dmitri Sokolov didn't look like an evil MGB mastermind of chaos. He didn't look like the kind of guy that Spetsnaz hard-dicks would willingly answer to. He was a balding little shrimp, with a hangdog look to his face and a receding chin, with bags under his eyes that looked like they never went away.

Fortunately, I'd learned not to judge a book by its cover a long, long time ago. Shrimp he might be, but he was calm and composed even in his confinement, never even sparing a glance at the mirror he had to know was two-way. He had exercised that morning, and while he might be small, his forearms were wiry and muscular. He had to be all whipcord sinew under his otherwise soft clothes.

Bates nodded to me as he shut the container doors behind him. There wasn't a lot of space in the "open" side of the container, either, as there was a table with several laptops for monitoring all the recording gear that the Group had crammed into the cell. Without any further comment, he entered Sokolov's cell.

He closed the door behind him, and the magnetic lock engaged with a loud *click*. He stepped over to the wall and leaned against it, his arms folded in front of his chest. "Hello, Dmitri," he said.

"Yevgeni," Sokolov replied. His cold, expressionless eyes had followed Bates ever since the man had entered, though he hadn't stirred or otherwise moved a muscle from where he sat on the edge of the cot. "Or is it Thomas? Or Emil?"

"Doesn't matter," Bates answered smoothly. "Let's talk about you."

Sokolov laughed dryly. "While I know who or what you are, Yevgeni," he said, "did you really think that your mere presence would be enough to intimidate me into talking?"

Bates just smiled that enigmatic little smile of his, that I had come find rather sinister. "My presence? Of course not. My stock in trade is information, not violence." I almost snorted at that, having watched the man murder Damien Chu without batting an eye. His voice turned frosty. "Now, what I can do with that information is something else. Would you like to know how little Alyona is doing right now?"

Sokolov just stared at him without a flicker of expression crossing his face. Finally, he said, "You expect me to place my family above my duty?"

"Isn't that what the Russian security services have been doing for the last two decades anyway?" Bates answered with a sudden chuckle. "Besides, you entered into a deal to conduct an extra-judicial killing for an extra-legal faction in the United States. It's just regular, everyday crime, isn't it? Doesn't seem like 'duty' to me. How is that more important than your daughter?"

For the first time, there might have been a flicker in Sokolov's dead-looking eyes. Bates had just caught him in a mistake, and he knew it. But he said nothing.

Bates pressed him. "Ah, but it's not just a hit on Concri, is it?" he said. "You're forgetting that I know you, Dmitri. Remember that delightful little interlude in Transnistria? I know what it is that you do. Van Damme and his cronies might have mistaken you for a thug for hire, but I know better." He tilted his head to watch Sokolov. "We are going to find your people. I would, of course, prefer it if you simply told us where to look; I'm sure little Alyona would prefer it as well. Less grief for everyone.

"But what I can't figure out is why you felt the need to make a deal with Van Damme in the first place? Or Stavros, for that matter? It's not as if you needed official cover; that's not the way you work."

His eyes narrowed. "Unless there was something you needed operationally, something that needed some kind of semi-official cover to get into the country." He shook his head pensively. "Weapons and explosives don't fit; those are obtainable anywhere. I know for a fact that *you* could find belt-fed machineguns and RPGs in London. No, my money's on personnel. Given the mess that is currently US Immigration, they must be men pretty high on somebody's watch list, or in great enough numbers that they would raise eyebrows coming in in the same place. Am I close?"

But Sokolov didn't reply. He just sat there on the cot at stared at Bates impassively.

"All right, then, have it your way," Bates said, pushing off the wall. "I'll make sure your regards are passed along to Alyona, right after she finds out that she's never going to see any of her family or loved ones ever again."

"We needed operational funding," Sokolov said, his voice flat. "The project was becoming wider in scope and taking longer than anticipated. Both of the factions were willing to pay for support, especially as their direct action assets were whittled down. So, we made a deal. We do an operation for them, and further the Kremlin's objectives in the process. Everyone wins."

"Particularly the Kremlin," Bates said wryly.

What might have been the ghost of a smile crossed Sokolov's face, though it never came near his eyes. Then it faded. "There is a safe house in Silver Spring, outside Bethesda." He rattled off an address. "The team will assemble there to strike at Concri's house in Chevy Chase." He looked up at Bates. "Are you satisfied?"

"Of course, Dmitri," Bates said. He turned and knocked on the door. I hit the release on the mag-lock, and he stepped out, pulling the door shut behind him.

"What do you think?" he asked me.

"I think he folded *way* to easily," I replied.

"He did," he replied calmly. "The safe house will be an ambush. Probably a few small-fry *brodyagi* that the MGB no longer has any particular use for."

"Or an IED," I said.

He nodded. "Entirely possible. Maybe even both. The trick with Dmitri is hearing what he *doesn't* say. You won't get a straight answer out of him otherwise."

"And we don't have enough time to break him," I muttered.

Bates shook his head. "There isn't enough time to break Dmitri Sokolov, period, end of story," he said. "No matter what you do, or what you threaten him with, he won't crack. Even the threats to his daughter were play-acting; even if we could follow through on them, it wouldn't change anything."

"Totally committed, huh?" I said, glancing back through the two-way mirror. Sokolov was still sitting on the edge of his cot, his face blank.

But Bates shook his head. "No, while the results are the same, that's not what drives Dmitri. At heart, he's still the *brodyaga* skullcracker that got recruited out of prison by Alexei Pushkin thirty years ago. While he hides it behind that flat Russian face, there is a deep vein of anger running through Dmitri, that shapes everything he does. He'd go to his grave spitting in your eye simply because you pissed him off by locking him up."

"So, what was the point of trying to interrogate him in the first place?" I asked.

"While he is very good at what he does, and cunning in his own way," Bates replied, "in many ways Dmitri is still a blunt instrument. I learned far more from what he didn't say and how he tried to redirect me than I ever did from anything he said."

"The personnel thing?"

He nodded. "The Russians have been steadily pouring gasoline on this little domestic firestorm, as much through information operations as through direct action," he said. "I think they might be preparing to turn the pressure up again, especially since some of the worst of the fires seem to be dying down, with both factions having been hurt as badly as they have. I suspect that Dmitri has a direct-action unit coming in, and Van Damme's people are supposed to get them through Customs without much scrutiny."

"So, how the hell are we supposed to find them?" I asked. "Van Damme's not talking; he's still under the misconception that we don't dare hold him long."

"Hasn't gotten used to the idea that he'll never be a free man again, has he?" Bates mused. "War is hell." He didn't sound at all broken up about it. "Fortunately, as royally balled up as everything is these days, most passenger and cargo manifests are still filed, and mostly online. I'll get some of my people looking into it. If I could borrow a few of yours, including your friend Derek? The more eyes on this, the faster we'll be able to pin down where they're coming in from."

"You've got 'em," I said. "Though Derek might not be much help; he just got out of another surgery." Trying to repair a bullet-shattered femur is a long, painful, and tricky process. "The last thing we need is Alfa Group coming in under the radar to wreak havoc along with everything else." I paused. "You think they're actually going to take a crack at Concri, anyway?"

"They might, just to be thorough," he answered. Concri was the one "Sulla" bigshot who hadn't shown up to Hawaii; apparently, he'd had to go in for minor heart surgery unexpectedly a few days before. He'd lucked out. "But if anything, he's going to be a minor target." He sighed. "This is bigger than the factions, bigger than Van Damme or Concri or any of the rest. It's a game that's been running at least since Andropov." His voice got heavy and weary. "I've spent most of my life trying to head it off. But no matter how much I've done, and how deep I got, there are too many people with short memories and shorter vision, too willing to sell their souls for a short-term advantage."

It was the most human moment I'd really ever seen from the man. He had always been preternaturally composed; cold, calculating, and dangerous, in a cheerful, debonair sort of way.

Something about the way he'd said it got the wheels turning in my own mind. "That's why you came in from the cold, isn't it?" I asked. "You got too close, and they figured out who you really are. Or at least enough of them suspected that you wound up on the MGB's target deck."

He didn't look at me, but he nodded. "I first started to think something was wrong when two of my most important contacts in Moscow went silent, about a year ago. Then I found out that they'd been snatched by the MGB on the same night, and were being held in Lefortovo Prison, without any public announcement of charges or accusations.

"Since then, large chunks of my network within the Russian underworld started getting arrested or simply disappearing. Naturally, I was careful to make that network as redundant as possible, so they haven't found all of my people, but the message was clear."

He turned to look me in the eye. "I am in similar straits with you and your company, Mr. Stone," he said. "In the immortal words of Benjamin Franklin, 'We must all hang together, or we shall surely hang separately.'"

As I met his gaze, I thought about those words, along with what Stahl had said when Bates had first "come in from the cold" in that old factory in Martinsburg. And along the way, I was suddenly struck by how true-to-life our company name, "Praetorian," might turn out to be, if things got bad enough.

I hoped they didn't. Even so, I wasn't sure I wasn't in for some serious disappointment.

***

For the next day and a half, I really didn't have much to do. We had reset; kit had been checked, mags reloaded, and everything was ready to launch for the next target. We just didn't know what the target was going to be, yet. The Cicero Group, our own intel cell, and Bates' network were all digging for something out of the ordinary, something that might indicate what Sokolov had made a deal with Van Damme for. Rumors were circulating in the makeshift team room we'd set up in the camp, ranging from the usual suspects, like IRGC Qods Force commandos to WMDs, to more exotic, even batshit insane stuff, like a geologic resonance weapon to make the Yellowstone supervolcano erupt. None of us knew, and most of the wilder speculation was more to pass the time than any sort of serious thought.

The fact of the matter was, we had too much time to think, and we were trying to avoid doing more of it than we had to. We were all feeling the losses we'd taken in the last six to seven months, and Little Bob's death had been harder than the rest, especially since the entire team had been there to see it happen, slowly and painfully. With little to do, the holes in the roster were achingly apparent, empty spaces where friends and comrades had been.

So, we worked out, cleaned weapons that didn't need cleaning, read and re-read the few books and magazines we could scrounge, and bullshitted about anything and everything besides what was happening and what had happened.

When the phone buzzed on the second day, I snatched it up as fast as I could. It was Mia.

"Derek wants to talk to you," she said as soon as I'd answered. "I just made the call myself so I could say hi." I had to admit that it was good to hear her voice. We hadn't had much time together since the flight out of South Dakota. And in my current state of mind, I couldn't help but start wondering how much of our bond had been simply shock, reaction, and grief, looking for a bit of comfort in another person. That the same warmth and affection was still in her voice when she talked to me helped.

"Hey, dude," Derek croaked. He sounded like hell; I knew he'd probably been happily working his ass off in front of two or three computers while he was still in recovery from his latest surgery. "I've had a few dozen search bots out going through every cargo manifest, passenger manifest, flight plan, and dock schedule they can worm their way into. Had to get into a couple of secure databases to do it, too. Fortunately, there are still dumbasses with access who fall for phishing attacks. It might have gotten hard, otherwise."

"You find anything?" I asked. Every eye in the team room was on me, the half-dozen random conversations stilled.

"I *think* so," he replied. "There's a freighter under Estonian registry, called the *Narva*, that's been circling out at sea off the south coast of Greenland for the last two weeks. Ostensibly, they've been having engine troubles, but they started making a beeline for Boston two days ago. They're just passing Newfoundland now."

"Have they got a cargo manifest?" I asked. That might be an indicator, if they didn't.

"Sure," he replied, "everything's aboveboard. If it is our target, I doubt the MGB would be so incompetent as to leave that detail out. But here's the catch. They've already been cleared to dock and unload, without inspection. And the signature on the clearance belongs to Marsha Westing. It took some more digging to find out who she is; she's from Senator Carlsen's office."

I nodded, though he couldn't see me. "And Senator Carlsen is a known buddy of Van Damme's."

"Got it in one, dude," he said. "It's not a smoking gun, but under the circumstances, I think it's worth checking out."

"Boston's going to be a bitch to get into," I said. Not only was Taxachusetts generally considered non-permissive territory anyway, given that in the wake of recent violence the state's law enforcement had decided to crack down even harder on gun owners, with absolutely no resulting reduction in the rampant crime and rioting, but there had just been another flare up in Boston itself. A pair of police officers had been murdered in their car, and when a young black man had thrown a rock at another cruiser, the cops, already on the warpath, had ended up killing him. Graphic video of the killing had appeared so fast that it was suspected that it had been set up, though at that point, things were already so tangled that nobody knew for sure. As a result, half of Boston was once again on fire, and the conflagration was spreading, in the name of "solidarity." It was only a repeat of what had been going on for months. I had to wonder if it hadn't been timed specifically to cover for that incoming freighter, presuming that that was, in fact, our target.

"They're still fourteen hours out from the harbor," he said. "There's still time to get up to Maine and launch from there, taking the freighter while it's still at sea. I'm sending you the full data dump."

The phone buzzed against my ear as the file came across. I thanked him and hung up. "Grab your shit," I said. "We've got a few hours to get across the country, plan a VBSS, and take down a freighter. Hopefully it's the right freighter."

I didn't have to say it twice. In seconds, gear was getting jammed into gear bags, and I was already calling Phil to tell him to get the DC-3 spooled up, and get the helos heading east. We had no time to lose. We'd plan in the air.

CHAPTER 33

It turned out not to be practical to get the Little Birds across the country on the timetable we had. So, Stahl made some calls and called in some favors, and there were six Bell 407s waiting for us when we landed, rotors already turning.

We'd gone over the data dump on the *Narva* in flight, and hammered out a hasty plan. It had taken eight and a half hours to get from Washington to Maine, including stopping in Minneapolis for fuel; the DC-3 didn't have the legs to go all the way non-stop. Considering that most of us had trained on the Maritime Special Purpose Force planning cycle, which allows six hours from Warning Order to launch, that was plenty of time. We were already in our kit—plate carriers, helmets, and weapons, with "horse collar" inflatable vests over the plate carriers—as we got off the bird and trotted toward the helos.

There wasn't a lot of room on the birds. Somebody had been busy; there were fast-ropes coiled just inside the doors. They were hooked up to what appeared to be a sort of swinging armature that had been hastily welded together and bolted inside the fuselage, presumably to make sure the ropes were clear of the skids. The 407 had not been designed with fast-roping in mind.

Sam was waiting next to the lead bird, already in his own kit, ready to fly. Since Phil had needed to fly the DC-3, Sam had taken lead for the helos, and he and his crews had gotten out by jet, provided by the Group, so they'd gotten to Maine a few hours ahead of us. I jogged up to him. "At last report, they're eighty-nine nautical miles due south," he shouted over the noise of the rotors, "doing nine knots west-southwest. It's getting a little bumpy out there, and they might have to slow down some more. I can have you on-station in about forty-five minutes, give-or-take, but we won't be able to loiter long. Weather's getting bad; it's not going to be a comfortable flight."

"Just get us there, Sam," I told him. "If you've got to drop us and come back, refuel, and re-attack, do it."

He nodded and clapped me on the shoulder before turning and climbing back into the helo's cockpit.

I looked to my left and right, making sure the teams were getting evenly spread out among the helicopters, then climbed in behind Sam and plugged my Peltors into the bird's intercom. "Head count, all birds," I sent over the radio.

One by one, I got counts from each helicopter, checking them off in my head. When we were good, I reached forward and tapped Sam on the shoulder, giving him a thumbs-up. He returned it without looking, then pulled back on the collective. With a wobble in the increasingly stiff wind off the Atlantic, the bird rose into the air, and we were on the way.

Sam hadn't been kidding; it was not a comfortable ride. It was spring, but the North Atlantic still had plenty of storms waiting to throw plenty of wind and rain around, and one of them was blowing down the coast of Nova Scotia. The sky was a leaden gray, and looking down, I could see the whitecaps on the ocean below. The bird was bouncing and rocking as we went, as if it was getting slapped around as it struggled through the turbulent air. We didn't dare get too high, either, or we might miss the ship.

"Eyes on," Sam told me over the intercom. I craned my neck over his shoulder to peer through the windscreen. It was hard to see; the storm was getting darker, and rain was starting to pelt the plexiglass, turning the outside world into a blur of grays. But when he pointed, I spotted it; a small speck of red, blue, yellow, and white. "Five minutes," he added.

"Five minutes!" I acknowledged, and passed it along the radio circuit, making sure I got acknowledgements from each bird. This was going to be dicey as it was; the more everyone was on the same page, the better.

Larry pulled back the side door and got behind the M240L that had been mounted on a scissor-mount bolted to the forward fuselage. Somebody had worked fast to get these birds fitted out for combat in less than eight hours. Pulling back the charging handle, he got ready to suppress any opposition on the deck. Without the belt-feds, any fast-ropers were potentially sitting ducks as soon as the boarding started.

The ship was wallowing a bit in the chop, but it was big enough and apparently heavy enough that it wasn't rolling *too* badly. I'd seen worse. Spray was starting to blow over the gunwales, and the rain was getting heavier. This was well and truly going to suck, even if there wasn't anyone shooting at us.

Sam led the way down, banking in a tight, slow pass around the ship, giving Larry a good long time to scan for any threats and light them up if they presented themselves. The 240 stayed quiet. Looking over Larry's shoulder, I could see that the deck beneath the towering, yellow-painted cranes was deserted.

That just meant that if they were down there, we were going to have to go in and root them out the hard way.

The cranes stood between the five covered cargo bays that formed most of the hold. They presented a serious obstacle to the birds, and reduced our options for boarding. Get too close, and between the gusts of wind and the slight, but still noticeable, rocking of the ship, we could have a devastating crash, either into one of the cranes, or into the superstructure at the stern. That pretty much left the hatch cover over the bow hold as our DZ.

The circuit completed, Sam flared the helo and brought it down toward the bow, careful to leave as close to a full rotor disc as he could between the bird and the forward crane. The way the wind was hammering the helo, I was glad to see him keeping as much distance as he could afford.

Larry stayed on the 240 while I swung the armature out, locked it, and heaved the fast-rope out the door. It was already wet from the rain blowing in, and would have been heavy as shit even dry. It took a hell of a heave to make sure it cleared the skid, and I almost didn't make it. Only the helo tipping to the side in a particularly heavy gust of wind actually kept the rope from tangling on the skid, though it almost threw me out into space, fifty feet above the deck, in the process.

Fortunately, I grabbed the edge of the door and the armature at the same time that Alek grabbed the drag handle on the back of my plate carrier. For a second, I dangled above the sickening drop, then Sam got the bird level again, and I staggered back into the cabin and got my equilibrium again. That had been too close.

If I'd had more time, I might have gotten the shakes, thinking about how close I'd just come to turning into a red smear on the deck below, before ever taking a shot at a Russian. But with Sam wrestling to keep the 407 on station, and the instinctive knowledge, come from many fights and many jumps, that to hesitate was to die, I grabbed the rope and started down.

It was a bit of a faster descent than usual; the rope was slick with moisture and even with fast-rope mitts on over my shooting gloves, it was sliding through my hands and my boots like greased lightning. I clenched hard, and felt the heat building up in my palms and the insides of my feet as I went down. I still hit hard, my knees buckling under the impact, and went sprawling on the slick, wet metal of the hold's overhead covering.

I rolled painfully away, aided by the roll of the ship, to avoid getting smashed by Alek's rapidly descending weight. I started sliding on the wet steel, only arresting myself with difficulty and struggling upright, finally getting a knee under myself and getting the Compressor SBR that I'd killed Baumgartner with up and into play.

The other three, Nick, Eric, and Larry, hit the deck quickly with heavy *thuds* that reverberated through the metal beneath me. I wasn't the only one taken by surprise by how slick the rope was; Eric didn't get clear of the rope in time, and Larry plowed into him. Fortunately, Alek and I were already up and away, holding security, so they could get untangled. That had to have hurt; Eric wasn't a small guy, but Larry was fucking *heavy*.

As soon as they got clear, Sam's copilot cut the fast-rope loose and it slithered down to the deck. Then the bird was pulling away and back into a holding pattern overhead, while the next one swooped in. I was already leading the way toward the starboard side. The wet steel was slicker than snot under my boots, but I managed to keep my footing, despite the roll of the ship.

My rifle was up in my shoulder, the red dot only inches from my eye, but so far there had been no reaction to our boarding. Some of it might have been because the weather was going to make it a bitch to engage anyone past about fifty yards. More likely, the Russkis were digging in and getting ready to make us pay for every bulkhead we passed.

There was a steep, steel-mesh ladderway leading down from the top of the hold to the decking that ran along the gunwale. Fortunately, it was only a few steps; the hold didn't rise too far above the deck. If I straightened up, I could actually look across the top of the cargo bay. Naturally, I didn't. While I wasn't exactly crouched, I glided forward on slightly bent knees, leaning forward into my weapon as I went.

I was moving fast; not only did I want to get the fuck off that exposed deck as quickly as possible, but I didn't want the rest of the assault teams getting bunched up on top of that cargo bay. If by chance there *were* Russians with, say, a PKP, up in the superstructure, and they got a good enough look through the rain and spray at what was happening, all it would take would be one long burst.

I resisted the temptation to sprint that last few meters to the hatch leading into the superstructure. If someone had popped out of the hatch as I was approaching, I stood a better chance if I could engage him before he shot me, than if I just closed the distance quickly.

Once I reached the hatch, I let the Compressor dangle and pulled a flashbang out of its pouch. It was a bit of a struggle; we were all soaked to the bone, and that made pulling anything out of the soggy Cordura a bit more of a hassle. Meanwhile, the rest of the starboard team stacked up behind me, even as Alek grabbed the dogging handles and got ready to pull the hatch open.

The hatch groaned open, I lobbed the bang in, and it was game on.

The bang went off with a sound like a sledgehammer hitting a gong, reverberating through the steel of the hull even over the roar of the wind and rain. I caught a bit of the blast through the open hatch, though I had my head down and my eyes averted. Gritting my teeth against the pain, I went in while the smoke was still swirling in the entryway.

The wraparound passageway was empty ahead as I pushed aft, only slowing to cover the next passageway that opened to my right. Another muzzle dropped down next to my shoulder to cover it as I moved across the opening, and I swiveled aft again, pushing toward the corner. There were going to be at least twenty compartments on just this deck that we'd have to clear, but unless we encountered resistance beforehand, we were going to seize the bridge and the engine room first. Once the ship was halted, there would be nowhere for the enemy to go, and we could carefully and thoroughly clear the entire ship.

The stack stayed intact behind me, with Larry, who had covered down that side passageway, turning and taking up the rear as soon as the last man passed him. We might have split the stack to clear more quickly, but the geometry of the inside of the ship would make it risky, at best. Sooner or later, somebody was going to end up in friendly sights if we did it that way.

Coming to the end of the corridor, I turned the corner and found myself up against a dead end.

The plans we had of the *Narva* suggested that there should be a narrow passage behind the galley, but it wasn't there. We might have read the plans wrong, or we'd gotten an old version from before the ship had been fitted out. Or refitted. Either way, we had to roll with the punches, so I just hooked another right and headed back forward, passing the six closed hatches of the lower-deck staterooms as I went.

As I glided forward, still having to adjust my weight to the movement of the deck beneath my feet, I kept my rifle up and watched every hatch carefully until I was passing it, and it was under another man's gun. That passageway gave me the heebie-jeebies; it would be all too easy for an enemy to suddenly pop one of those hatches open and toss a frag out into the corridor.

But they stayed shut, and after a brief pause, cheating to one side as far as possible to check the starboard side passage, leading back toward the hatch we'd just entered, I hooked around the corner and made for the hatch leading onto the ladderwell that would lead up to the bridge and down toward the machinery spaces.

I pushed past it, covering down on the port side corner, leaving just enough room for Eric to get in position on the hatch. He jostled me a little as he pulled the hatch open, I heard the bang go off, and then boots were clattering on the steel deck as the next man back went through the hatch.

I shouldn't have been able to hear it, but the sound of something heavy and metal hitting the ladderwell was different enough that it cut through any other noises. I heard Eddie yell something. There was a brief scuffling sound and a body hit the forward bulkhead, then the hatch closed with a bang.

The grenade detonation made the bangs sound like firecrackers. The overpressure hammered the hatch like a giant's fist. It felt like the entire ship shuddered.

If there had been any doubt remaining that our targets were aboard the *Narva*, there wasn't anymore. Unfortunately, the ship only had the one ladderwell, which meant that they presently had the only route to the bridge bottled up. Even if there had been another one, I found that I doubted if our flanking maneuver we'd used in Verdant Mount Lodge would have worked again.

That meant hey-diddle-diddle, straight up the middle.

I didn't have to say anything; we all knew the score, and we'd all been doing this long enough that nobody needed to talk about it in the passageway.

I heard two safety levers hit the deck, Alek counted, "One, two, three!" and Eric pulled the hatch open.

Both frags were thrown into the ladderwell; I heard at least one bounce off a bulkhead with a ringing impact, just before they blew with overlapping thunderclaps that reverberated up and down the ladderwell, some of the blast pouring through the gap still in the open hatch, though Eric had pushed the hatch most of the way closed, just long enough to shield us from most of the explosions. Then he was dragging it open again, and boots were rattling up the steps.

I could hear the *claps* of suppressed gunshots above, then Eric was hitting me on the shoulder and shouting, "Last man!"

I turned and followed him into the ladderwell. That was when I got to see what had happened with the first grenade.

Eddie hadn't made it out of the ladderwell. He'd pushed the number two man back into the passageway and hauled the door shut, closing himself in with the frag. His bloody, mangled corpse was slumped on the landing, pushed against the bulkhead by the force of the explosion.

He'd saved the whole stack, at the cost of his own life. The self-styled "borderline sociopath" had died a hero in the end.

I took it in at a glance, then I was heading up, following the sound of gunshots and pounding boots. My combat detachment had been rattled, but was still intact. It had to be.

We passed the second deck, and the third. Pairs of shooters were set at the landings on each deck, covering the hatches. We had to get to the bridge and take control of the ship, but we didn't dare leave our six-o'clock uncovered.

Finally, we hit the top deck. Nick and Herman were the first ones on the hatch leading into the bridge, Herman with his hand already on the latch, Nick holding a bang in his fist. I pushed forward, held up my own fist so they both could see it, put up two fingers, then pulled my last bang out of its pouch. I wanted maximum advantage going into this. So, we'd try the one-two punch that had worked so well against the security guarding Van Damme's conference room.

I pulled the pin and nodded to Herman. He dragged the hatch open, Nick lobbed his bang in, and even as it detonated, I tossed my own in after it.

Then we were pouring through the hatch, flooding the tiny, instrument- and control-crammed space with big, angry men with guns.

There were four men on the bridge. Three were obviously crew, dressed in orange coveralls with *Narva* stitched over the chest pockets. The fourth man was dressed in simple green fatigues and a pistol belt.

All four were down on their knees on the deck, their eyes watering from the twin blasts and the stinging smoke, hands on their heads, fingers interlaced. An AEK-971 and a PL-14 pistol were lying on the deck, about six feet away from the man in green, looking like they'd been abruptly tossed there only a moment before.

As soon as I was certain that the bridge was otherwise clear, which took a split-second scan, I moved forward, my rifle trained on the man in green's forehead, and barked, "Down on the deck! On your faces! *Lozhites!*"

The man in green complied, lowering himself to the deck and placing his hands on the back of his neck. The crew followed suit a moment later.

I slung my rifle to my back and hastily zip-tied the man in green's hands behind his back. At the same time, my radio crackled in my ear. "Hillbilly, Albatross," Bryan said. "Engine spaces are secured."

"Roger," I replied. I looked down at the man in green. "All right," I said. "Where's the rest of your team?"

"Unless they have surrendered, you have killed the rest of my team," he said, in accented but clear English. "There were only six of us. We are VALOR PMC, hired to secure freighter. I set men to secure ladder and engine spaces."

"Maritime security, huh?" I said sardonically. "Lots of pirates in the North Atlantic these days? Maybe Eskimo raiders, or French Canadians?" I let my voice turn hard. "If you wanted me to believe that bullshit, you probably shouldn't have brought weapons only issued to Spetsnaz, fucknut."

What I could see of his face remained stonily impassive.

The throb of the engines fell away to a dull background rumble. Bryan, or somebody, had backed the engines down so that we weren't going to be making much headway anytime soon. We had time to clear the ship.

"Our boy seems awfully calm," Alek said quietly.

"Yeah, he does," I replied. "Means he thinks he's got an ace up his sleeve."

He nodded. "Which means they had a contingency plan for just this eventuality, and we can expect a counterattack pretty fucking soon."

"Hey, guys," Herman called from the forward windscreen, "none of you hit the hatch cover controls for the nearest cargo bay, did you?"

Alek and I traded a look. *Here it comes.*

"Everybody get down!" I yelled, just as a long, ravening burst of machinegun fire raked the front of the bridge.

CHAPTER 34

Herman fell back from the windows in a hail of shattered glass and a spray of blood, hitting the deck heavily in front of the ship's wheel. The rest of us went flat as bullets chewed through the remains of the windows and smacked into the overhead, a few of them ricocheting off the steel to bang into consoles or the aft bulkhead.

The volume of fire was heavy enough that there had to be more than one gun. But I expected that machine gun fire from the hold was not the main effort. The PKPs or whatever was firing down there were shortly going to be the least of our worries.

"All Praetorians on first and second deck," I yelled over the radio, "get below and strongpoint on the engine room. Third deck, get your asses up to the bridge! I expect we're going to have company soon."

"This is Frodo," Shawn called over the radio. Shawn was one of the newer guys. He was solid, from what I'd seen. His five foot, four-inch stature had been what had earned him his callsign. "There are a *lot* of shooters coming out of the holds. We are *not* going to be able to hold them at the main hatch, not with only two of us!"

I couldn't see if any of the 407s were still on station; if Sam had called me and said he had to head back, I hadn't heard it, whether the radio had been blocked by the steel hull of the ship while we'd been below, or just drowned out by the noise and fury of the assault. But if the gunners in the hold weren't being taken under fire from the air, that told me that we would be without air support for at least an hour, maybe an hour and a half.

That's a long, long time in a CQB environment.

"*Friendlies!*" Ross bellowed from the other side of the still-open hatch. "Friendlies coming in!"

"Come ahead!" I yelled back. "And get low!"

Ross and Todd came through the hatch in a crouch, moving to get clear of the fatal funnel, and thus out from in front of the bristling hedge of rifle muzzles trained on the hatchway. Todd turned as soon as they were in and dogged the hatch behind him. The rest of us were already fanned out around the bridge, weapons trained on the hatch. There wasn't a lot of cover; the control console was a single unit, with two seats facing it. The rest of the bridge deck was clear, except for our captives, the shattered glass of the windows, and Herman's motionless body.

We still had a lot of firepower we could bring to bear on that hatchway, but the weight of numbers was on the enemy's side. If they flooded the bridge with enough bodies fast enough, we were going to be in trouble. And probably very dead.

We didn't have anything available to barricade the hatch, and I was starting to wish we'd brought some thermite grenades. Welding the hatch closed would have at least slowed them down, and bought us time while we waited for Sam to get back to provide some air support. Of course, that was presuming he could get back to us. The storm blowing in through the shattered windows seemed to be getting nastier.

Nick, Alek, Eric, and I were gathered near the starboard side, aimed in on the hatch. We would have the best angle on the opening when they tried to breach.

Between the howl of the wind and rain and the long bursts of machinegun fire that were still raking the front of the bridge, I couldn't hear the enemy's boots on the ladderwell or the deck outside. The first indicator that they were coming was when the dogging handle started to move.

I tucked the stock of my little Compressor into my shoulder and put the red dot right on the widening seam of the door. As soon as it had opened just about an inch, I started shooting.

I didn't have a solid target. All I could see at that point really was the seam itself. But half a dozen .300 Blackout rounds zipping through the crack in the door, one hitting the coaming and ricocheting out through the hatch with a loud *bang*, certainly got the message across. There was a yell and the hatch was yanked shut.

Todd wasn't having any of it. His own rifle slung, he took two steps from where he'd been crouched on the port side, grabbed the handle with one hand, a frag with the pin already pulled in the other, let the safety lever fly free, cooked it for a second, then yanked the hatch open about six inches, chucked the grenade through the opening, and slammed the hatch shut again.

The superstructure shook with the heavy *thud* of the explosion, and the hatch, incompletely latched, blew partway open under the pressure of the blast. We ate part of the shockwave, and got sandblasted with debris, mostly stripped flakes of paint. Fortunately, the frag was pretty much all contained in the passageway outside.

Without an update over the radio, there was no way to know how the guys down in the engine room were faring. The machinegunners out in the holds were still keeping our heads down and the storm was still howling through the windows. Gunfire wasn't going to be audible through four decks, not with that cacophony deafening us.

The hatch hung open a hand's breadth, but none of us wanted to move forward enough to close it. Besides, it gave us a clearer shot at anyone trying to come in through it.

For what felt like an eternity, we crouched behind our weapons, waiting and listening. What might have been faint screams and groans of pain came through the hatch, though, again, it was hard to tell over the rest of the noise. But the part of the hatchway we could see stayed empty.

I wasn't fooled into thinking that they'd given up. Just like we had at Verdant Mount, they were trying to think of another avenue of attack.

The first real indicator that they'd come up with something came when the machine guns went silent.

I didn't get it, not at first. It was Ross who yelled, "Watch the windows!"

At the same time he said it, I heard boots rattling on the overhead. They'd climbed up on top of the superstructure, and were going to try to make entry through the windows. It was risky, but if we stayed focused on the hatch, they stood a chance of catching us looking the wrong way.

However, the storm, the wet, and the ship's roll were more than some of them were quite ready for. There was a sudden muted *thump*, what might have been a shouted curse in Russian, and a body fell past the window, trailing a rope. Somebody had slipped.

I spared just enough of a glance back to assure myself that somebody, in this case Eric, was still covering the hatch, as the rest of us turned to address the new threat. Not a moment too soon, either, since the Russian team leader had correctly surmised that having one of his men fall off the superstructure had blown his approach, so he went live.

More ropes dropped down in front of the bridge, and at the same time, four softball-sized spheres were lobbed down through the windows. One bounced off the coaming and fell away, but the other three came in to bounce off the deck just inside the bridge.

I squeezed my eyes shut, knowing what was coming. I still saw the series of flashes through my closed eyelids, and while my Peltors mitigated the noise of the detonations, the concussions were still headache-inducing.

As soon as the last flash had flickered against my eyelids, I opened my eyes, my cheek already on my rifle's buttstock and the red dot already trained on the nearest window.

They were good; the smoke from the stun grenades was still roiling toward the overhead as the first bodies came swinging through the windows. Unfortunately for the first wave, they were swinging right into line with our muzzles, and we'd all had the presence of mind to close our eyes and keep our earpro on, thus mitigating the shock effect of the stun grenades.

My finger was already tightening on the trigger as the figure in front of me swung in through the shattered glass. The trigger broke just as his upper chest passed the red dot, and I pumped five rounds into him as fast as the trigger would reset, walking them up from his front plate into his throat and face, before he'd even gotten his boots solidly on the deck. His feet flew out from under him, the back of his head hit the coaming, and he slid down the bulkhead, leaving a red smear behind him. The rain blowing in the open window immediately started to rinse the blood away.

Across the bridge, that first wave all suffered the same fate. They had to have been worried about killing the Russian we'd captured; I couldn't imagine that they'd have held their fire coming through otherwise.

The second wave didn't.

They must have figured out that something had gone wrong. Whatever led to the decision, after another ten seconds, the second wave came through the windows with their AEK-971s tucked under their elbows, spraying down their sectors as they came.

Fortunately, we were all crouched pretty low, and mostly shielded by the control console. Bullets smacked into the console and skipped off the top, hammering into the aft bulkhead with loud *bangs*. We all did our damnedest to get really, really small, and shot right back.

I had gotten down below the far starboard corner of the control console, crammed in there against Alek's back, leaning down with my helmet damned near touching the floor as I stuck my rifle muzzle out to engage the nearest dark figure coming through the window behind the muzzle flash of his rifle. I felt a tug at my helmet, even as I shot him. He fell backward, though I couldn't tell if it was because I'd hit him, or because he'd landed on top of his buddy's corpse and lost his balance. He was still moving, so I put another round in his pelvis, which was the target that presented itself, before pivoting and shooting the next guy to my right, who had been a couple seconds behind him, in the head. I transitioned back to the first and gave him four more rounds, until he quit moving.

Everything went quiet after that. "ACE reports!" I croaked, even as I hastily reloaded. My heart was pounding and despite all the water in the air, my throat was dry as a bone. That had been about as close as I'd ever gotten to the proverbial "knife fight in a telephone booth," and I'd been in a few CQB fights before.

One by one, the rest of the guys on the bridge sounded off. We'd shot a lot of rounds, and a few guys had gotten trimmed or grazed by the storm of gunfire that our adversaries had just thrown at us, but we'd been hardpointed well enough that nobody was dead or seriously wounded. Which I thought was a miracle.

Alek turned to look at me. His eyes widened a little, and he said, "Oh, fuck!" He let his rifle hang and reached for my helmet. "Don't move!"

"What?" I didn't feel anything but the wet, the growing headache from my helmet and the exertion and stress of everything piling up, and the aches and pains of my joints from contorting into a small enough space to try to stay in cover.

"You've got a bullet hole in your helmet, brother," he said, as he ran his hands over the back of my head and neck, looking for blood. They came up clean.

Against his instructions, I reached up and tore my helmet off. Sure enough, there was a hole in it, high on the right side. I flipped it over, and found the ridge inside where the bullet had traveled through the Kevlar before stopping at the back, leaving a lump just behind my right ear. I reached up to my sopping wet hair, feeling for a wound, but my scalp was intact.

"Holy fuck, that was close," I muttered.

"Hillbilly, Monster," Larry called over the radio.

"Send it," I replied, jamming my helmet back on my head and switching places with Alek, so that he could cover the front of the bridge around the side of the console. We still weren't out of the woods yet.

"We're all green," he reported. "We've strongpointed the engine room. They've made a couple of attempts to force their way in, but haven't been all that aggressive; I think they're worried about damaging the machinery."

"They're less worried about damaging the controls," I told him. "They've tried twice up here, but we've got a lull. I think they're rethinking their strategy."

"Agreed," he said. "They've fallen back from the engine room hatches; we haven't had anything to shoot at in a couple minutes. What's the plan?"

"They've got the weight of numbers, from what we've seen," I said, "but we just hurt them pretty badly."

I was interrupted by the hatch getting blown in.

Whatever they used, it was low on frag, which saved our lives. I suspected it was a concussion charge, not unlike the makeshift ones we'd used on occasion; little more than a partial satchel of explosives wired to blow. I still felt the sting of bits of metal lashing into the backs of my legs and shoulders even as the concussion slammed me into the console.

I hadn't buckled my chin strap back up, but my helmet was still on my head, and while the impact of my gourd on the metal still hurt like hell, at least it didn't split my skull open. It had nearly knocked the helmet off my head, and I had to shove it back into position even as I pivoted to address the new threat coming from aft.

Eric was blocking my line of fire. It took a second to ID him; I'd gotten rocked. But he was facing away from me, blocking the hatch and firing through it. Brass spun rapidly away over his shoulder.

I could see him getting hit. One leg buckled underneath him, but he kept fighting, kept shooting. His rifle ran dry and he dropped it and transitioned to his pistol, emptying the SIG P220 down the passageway.

I got my feet under me and lunged toward him, my own rifle up in my shoulder. Even as I reached him and cranked a fast five shots down the corridor, his sidearm went dry and he fell.

He'd stacked half a dozen bodies in the passageway. There were two more rifle muzzles at the ladderwell, just barely sticking out far enough to shoot. They'd both flinched back from my fire just enough that they couldn't hit me. I tapped a pair of shots at one, before I somewhat more carefully shot the second shooter in the eyeball. The first one ducked back and disappeared.

Nick was already dragging Eric back from the hatchway, as Ross barricaded himself on the other side, pushing the now bent and mangled hatch itself as far against the bulkhead as he could. He almost slipped in Eric's blood. There was a wide pool of it on the deck in front of the hatch. Too wide.

Todd tapped me and I backed out of the hatchway, letting him take it. I turned to Eric.

Nick had dragged him out of the fatal funnel and was trying to strip his gear off. He was fucked up. The front of his plate carrier was shredded, two of his mags shot through, and he was bleeding like a stuck pig. He looked like he'd caught a dozen rounds from knee to collarbone.

I grabbed my knife and slit his trouser leg, where there was the most blood. More of it pumped, hard and fast but weakening, from a ragged hole in his inner thigh.

"Motherfuck," I snarled, as I yanked the tourniquet off his gear and started cranking it around his leg. It was wet and slick, and the hole was high enough up that getting the tourniquet above it without being actually on it wasn't working very well.

"And here I was," he said, "hoping that the last anyone would see of me was as I jumped into a Russian submarine with a hot bikini chick under each arm, a Desert Eagle in one hand, and a bottle of whiskey in the other."

And just like that, the blood flow from his leg slowed, stopped, and he was gone.

Maybe I was just too rocked from the blast. Maybe I'd seen too many of my teammates die. Maybe I was in shock. Or maybe my nerves were just dead. I didn't feel much of anything, just a tired, distant ache that I knew was going to get bad later. I reached down and closed his eyes. "Had to get that last one-liner out before you went, didn't you, you son of a bitch?" I asked him, before getting to my feet. There was still a fight to be won, and we were still in a bad spot. That was probably why I was so fucking calm, really. Habits of thought and action were keeping me on an even enough keel to survive.

An unfamiliar voice suddenly crackled in my ear. "Hillbilly, Hillbilly, this is Chatterbox Five Four," a woman's voice said. "Please advise your status."

330

"Chatterbox, this is Hillbilly," I answered, getting strange looks from the handful of guys who weren't covered down on a window or the hatch. "Who are you?"

"We are your backup air cover, Hillbilly," she answered. "We are three H155s with two 240 door guns apiece. The Broker sends his regards."

Bates had been busy. Not that I was complaining. "How far out are you?" I asked.

"We have eyes on the target ship now," she confirmed. "We will be within engagement range in thirty seconds."

I risked a glance out the windows, still staying low in case the machinegunners in the holds were looking to blow my head off. I couldn't see far, but after a second, squinting against the blowing rain, I thought I could make out three specks to the north. That storm was no joke; whoever this chick was, she had balls to be flying in it.

"We are hardpointed in the superstructure, Chatterbox," I sent. "Anyone out on the deck or in the open holds is a target." I no longer gave a single fuck about taking any of the Russians alive. We had the one guy we'd grabbed on the bridge; he'd do if we had to kill all the rest of them. "Be advised, there are at least two belt-feds in the aft hold, possibly more."

"Good copy, Hillbilly," she said cheerfully. "We'll clear some of that up for you. And we'll make sure we keep our fire away from the superstructure. Wouldn't want any of you boys to get hurt."

I kept bitter words behind my teeth. *It's too late for that, sister*, I thought.

Seconds later, the helos, bigger than the 407s we'd flown in on, roared overhead, turning tight circles over the ship, fire spitting from their sides as the gunners hosed down the deck and the holds with long bursts.

"Let's go," I said, hastily tac-reloading to top my SBR off. "They're going to be off balance for a couple minutes. If we can clear the superstructure, then we can deal with any left in the holds." I keyed my radio. "Monster, Hillbilly."

"Go," Larry replied.

"Hold what you've got; we're going to clear, top-down."

"Roger, holding," was all that he said. It was all that was necessary.

I bumped Todd and he flowed out, his gun still up, his sights barely more than an inch from his line of sight. This was going to be a bitch, but it had to be done. We were all dead, otherwise.

Footing was a bastard in the corridor; we had to pick our way through the heaps of dead bodies. The guy I'd shot in the eye was lying head-down on the ladderwell. The other one had retreated; there was no sign of him.

Todd moved down the ladder just far enough to get his eyes and muzzle on the next landing down, then halted, holding security while I bounded down past him, rotating around to cover the newly revealed space

331

with my own rifle, my finger just inside the trigger guard. With the Russians' illustrated tendency to substitute fully automatic fire for marksmanship, and at such close ranges, I was going to have to engage very, very quickly.

I could still hear the snarl of the helos outside, even through the metal of the hull, and the continued hammering of machinegun fire. I figured we were pretty well covered from reinforcements; we just had to worry about the Russian shooters already inside.

As I moved around the outside of the ladderwell, I suddenly came muzzle to muzzle with one of them.

He'd been waiting, but I still shot first; I'd been moving carefully, rolling my feet on the steps of the ladderwell, making as little noise as possible, so I took him by surprise, at least by a split second. Which was all I needed. As tired and worn down as I was, certain things were still hardwired from decades of training and combat experience, and my reaction time was slightly faster than his.

I blew his brains all over the inside of his helmet, then twitched my muzzle a few inches to the left to shoot his buddy. The second Russian was trying to get a shot at me while simultaneously trying to barricade himself on the hatchway, but my first round skipped off his AEK-971's receiver. He flinched, hard, and I shot him through the cheek. Blood and bits of bone and teeth were blasted out the side of his face, and he fell back against the bulkhead. Two more rounds finished him off and the rifle clattered to the deck as he slid down the metal wall to slump on top of the first corpse.

I barricaded on that hatchway, while Nick slid past behind me to cover down on the ladderwell leading down. We weren't going to leave a single danger area uncovered.

I got bumped from behind. Not a passing nudge, but a hard signal. *With you.* I pushed out into the passageway, hooking hard right to cover that way, while whoever had bumped me went left. Another bump, and I moved to the nearest hatch.

Leapfrogging by pairs, we cleared the deck, compartment by compartment. Aside from the two we'd killed on the ladderwell, and a handful of crew huddled under their bunks, the third deck was clear. We headed down to the second.

There weren't any Russians holding security on the second deck landing, and the deck was similarly clear of shooters. We found more of the crew, zip-tied them securely, and left them. They'd be interrogated thoroughly once this was over.

We found the first deck similarly unsecured. I wasn't relaxing, though; if anything, I was getting wound even tighter. There was no way that was it. There was a nasty surprise waiting somewhere. I knew it.

We found more of the crew, locked in their compartments. Most of them responded quickly enough to warning bangs on the hatches; they didn't want to endure an explosive breach. The one who didn't, hadn't dogged the hatch, so when it got abruptly slammed open he just got body-slammed on the deck instead of shot.

I had a hunch when we finally reached the galley at the stern, and signaled for a flashbang, while keeping my muzzle pointed at the seam of the hatch. There was some shuffling behind me, then a hand reached over my shoulder where I could see it, holding what had to be one of our last bangs.

Alek had ended up on the far side of the hatch, his hand on the handle, his eyes on me. I nodded, he pulled, whoever was behind me tossed the bang, and Alek slammed the hatch to for the second and a half it took the bang to detonate, before hauling the hatch wide open to let me through.

I plunged through the smoke, gun up and searching for targets.

There were half a dozen men, still in their green fatigues and chest rigs, down on the floor with their hands on their heads. Their rifles and pistols were unloaded and on the deck in front of them.

We fanned out around the room, forming a tight L-shape to cover them, alert for any suspicious movement or what might be hidden explosives or grenades. They didn't move, didn't say anything, except for one, who said in accented English, "Do not shoot. We give up."

My finger touched the trigger, my red dot on his head. After all this, *now* they were going to surrender? After Eddie, Herman, and Eric had died, and so many of their own had caught a bullet as well? I was suddenly furious, ready to murder all of them right then and there.

But I stopped, took my finger off the trigger, and lowered my weapon with a long, shuddering breath. I knew where that led. I'd killed Baumgartner for less.

One by one, under the watchful eyes and gun muzzles of the rest of us, Nick and Todd started checking and securing each of the Russian shooters, carefully rolling them over first to make sure they weren't hiding grenades under their bodies. Finally, the last of them was zip-tied to a galley chair, and we could move out to link up with Larry.

***

The main deck was a bloodbath.

There hadn't been many out in the open when the helos had started their gun runs, but with the hatch covers on the holds open, they'd had little overhead cover, and the gunners had been thorough. There were only a few Russians still gasping what was left of their lives out amidst the wreckage down there, and they were so far gone that there was nothing we could do for them.

Chatterbox was running out of loiter time, but assured that we had the ship secured, she relayed that Sam was on his way back out, and the three H155s pulled off and headed back toward land. The storm was abating a little, though looking to the northeast, I didn't think the slight clearing was going to last.

Whatever these Russian sons of bitches had had in mind, it wasn't going to happen for a while. We'd stopped this attack, at least, however much it had cost.

CHAPTER 35

The storm didn't clear up, though; it intensified. Sam had to turn back. So, under our watchful eyes and gun muzzles, the crew of the *Narva* turned the freighter north, toward the Maine coast. It was a long haul, especially since some repairs had to be made to the controls after the bridge had been shot to hell. But eventually, the ship was anchored just off one of the tiny islands east of Portland, and the engines were shut down.

The storm got worse, and we had to stay aboard until it died down, late that night. It wasn't a pleasant interlude. We'd made the Russian prisoners dispose of the bodies, except for Eddie's, Herman's, and Eric's, which we'd secured in the ship's deep freezer. They'd also had to set about cleaning up the blood and offal from the fight. Even with the bloodstains scrubbed away, though, the ship still felt stained by the violence that had just gone down inside her hull.

Fortunately, we didn't have too long to sit aboard before the weather cleared up enough for Sam to bring the helos in and take us off, ferrying the team back to the same strip that we'd staged out of. Tom had made sure that enough gear had been shipped out that we could rearm and reset, while the crew and the surviving Spetsnaz were carefully secured, sequestered, and interrogated.

We got cleaned up, made sure that the bodies were ready to be taken back to Wyoming for burial, reloaded magazines and prepped ammo belts, and then had nothing to do.

A few of the team found a couch or a clear spot on the floor and went to sleep. It had been an exhausting few days, on top of an exhausting few months.

Some of us either couldn't sleep, or didn't want to face the nightmares that were probably going to come close on the heels of passing out. We just kind of sat around the makeshift team room, silent, staring off into space, tired clear down to our bones and lost in our own thoughts. A TV was on the wall, with some flashy cable news program on, but somebody had shut the sound off in disgust a while before.

Finally, Shawn looked up and around at the rest of us who were still awake. "So, is that it?" he asked quietly. "Did we win?"

"Win?" Alek rumbled. "I doubt it. Too much has happened; taking out one Spetsnaz company isn't going to be the decisive victory to bring this all to a halt. Maybe it would have been two thousand years ago, but not in this day and age."

He glanced toward the TV. "We might have bought some breathing room, though," he mused. "It seems like some of this is starting to burn itself out; several of the cities have started to calm down a little. Maybe, if the factions have been hurt enough to stop stoking the flames, and with the Russian campaign on its back foot, cooler heads might have a chance to prevail."

"What do you think, Jeff?" Shawn asked, turning to me.

I didn't answer for a moment. Finally, I looked up at him and said, "I don't know. I've seen enough over the last few years that I'm not optimistic. I *hope* Alek's right. I really do. But you can't have mobs of people at each other's throats for months and then just have things go back to normal. I think that, best case, we've got years of low-level violence ahead as the dust settles."

"And worst case?" Todd asked.

"Worst case, the Russians had redundancies worked into their plans, and we only caught one of them," I said. "Worst case, there could be a fucking battalion of those bastards already moving into position across the country."

"And that," Alek said into the sudden silence, "is why we call him the Voice of Doom."

There was a sort of half-chuckle that went around the room. It was a much-needed moment of levity. A lot of the wisecracking had died down over the last month or so; we were just getting too tired, too strung out. Something had to give, sooner or later.

My phone buzzed, and I dragged it out of my pocket. It was Mia. I turned away from the rest and answered it. "Hey."

"Hi," she said in a quiet voice. "I was worried about you." She paused. "How bad was it?"

"We lost Eddie, Herman, and Eric," I said. My voice was low and flat, even in my own ears. I started to wonder if there was a point where the human mind simply became overloaded with the grief of losing friends, and sort of tuned the grief out. I thought I should be feeling a lot worse about it, but I just felt sort of empty.

"Dammit," she said, her voice a little choked. There was a pause, then I heard her sniffle a little. "I wish this was all over," she said. "I'm tired of losing people. I'm tired of worrying myself sick about you while you're out there. I wish I could be there with you right now, instead of across the country, talking on the phone."

I wished I had something comforting to say to her, but I couldn't think of much. Honestly, at that point I couldn't think too far past whatever had just happened and what we might be called upon to do next. But I couldn't tell her to give up hope.

"They're interrogating the Russians we captured now," I said. "Even if they don't get anything out of them, maybe showing the rest of the country that an entire company of Russian SOF tried to infiltrate and blow a bunch of stuff up will be enough of a wakeup call."

"And if it is?" she asked. There was a rather pointed tone to the question, and I thought I could tell where it was leading. "Then what?"

Meaning am I going to keep doing this? I thought. She hadn't mentioned how much she worried about me casually. *Damn, this is getting serious, isn't it?*

"I don't know yet," I told her, kind of trying to dodge the question while still being honest with her. "We're just going to have to see."

I tried not to wince at the silence over the phone. That hadn't been the answer she'd been hoping for, but I wasn't in any shape to take that step, not at the moment. She seemed to get that, though, because there wasn't any disappointment or anger in her voice when she spoke again.

"It is awfully early to be making long-term plans, isn't it?" she said. "We don't even know the extent of Sokolov's operation yet." I breathed a little bit easier, back on somewhat firmer ground. We were going to have to have the other conversation eventually, but right then wasn't quite the right time.

So, when is? that traitorous voice in the back of my mind asked. *She's asking the question because you've been at war the entire time she's known you, and time might be a damned sight shorter than you think.*

"I'll be on my way out to help the intelligence cell in the next day or two," she continued. "I'll see you then. Get some rest. You sound like you need it."

I could feel eyes on me as I hung up the phone. I really didn't feel like talking further at that point. I got up and went looking for the intel guys. I needed to know *something* about what might be coming.

***

While the Russians maintained their stubborn silence, and the Estonian crew insisted vociferously that they didn't know shit, we did manage to glean some information about what they'd been up to. They'd taken a crack at destroying their planning materials, but they hadn't completed it before Chatterbox and her wingmen had laid waste to the holds from the air.

"What a fucking nightmare." Tyler was one of our intel cell, though he looked like he could have been a shooter. Six foot five and built like a powerlifter, which he was, he had always insisted he'd gone intel because he was too big a target to be a shooter. He'd just get shot. The comment took on a certain poignancy that it hadn't before, now that Little Bob was gone. The big former Ranger had had an amazing tendency to be a bullet- and frag-magnet.

Tyler was also one of our few fluent Russian speakers in the company, which made him intensely valuable at the moment. He was sitting in the back room of the warehouse, poring over the burned and torn fragments of the Russians' plans.

"That bad?" I asked. "There was only a company of 'em."

"But a company of specially trained and prepared saboteurs and raiders, from what I can make out," Tyler replied, running both plate-sized hands over his face and ZZ-Top beard. He waved at his notes and the half-destroyed, Cyrillic-marked map in front of him. "I'm having to piece this together from fragments and vague allusions to stuff that they probably had memorized to keep it out of hard copy, but it looks like once they got into the country, they were going to split up into elements of four or five, and spread out across the Eastern seaboard to hit their targets."

"Have you got a target list?" I asked, sitting in a folding chair next to him. Holy hell, I was tired.

"Only a partial one," he said. "But that's bad enough. Power substations, reservoirs, oil and gas pipelines, telecom hubs, bridges…this wasn't going to be terrorism. This was going to be an all-out strategic strike on vital infrastructure. From what you guys found on the ship, I think they were already prepped for the first wave of targets, and then they were going to locally acquire the materials for follow-on strikes."

"And with the chaos already going on over the last six months," I put in, "nobody would be in a position to react in time."

He nodded tiredly. "And the more infrastructure they hit, the more tangled up any response would get. The entire East coast would be crippled, right when everybody's at each other's throats."

"With the endgame of the US on its knees, if not shattered outright, and the Russians the new geopolitical top dog," I sighed. "Which I am beginning to suspect was the goal all along."

"No argument from me," Tyler replied. "Russia's endgame has always been Russian security through ascendancy. No more, no less. At least we stopped this in time. We should have some breathing room."

But, unbeknownst to either of us right at that moment, while we might have stopped the knockout punch, the death of a thousand cuts was continuing apace.

CHAPTER 36

A plain white panel van pulled up beside the playground at Hayward Elementary in Birmingham at about ten in the morning. While still situated in one of the poorer communities of the city, Hayward had kept its doors open despite the unrest and violence that had wracked other parts of Birmingham off and on for months. There were still teachers watchfully patrolling the playground at recess, though some were more conscientious than others.

Amanda Jackson Jones was one of the more conscientious ones. She spotted the van immediately and felt the hackles on the back of her neck rise. She didn't know why; she only knew that there was something *off* about it. A heavier, middle-aged black woman, she was fiercely protective of the kids in her charge, especially since so many of them didn't get much in the way of parental attention when they went home.

Her fellow teacher, a younger man named Stefan, didn't notice the van; he was absorbed in his cigarette and his smartphone. When she nudged him and pointed toward the street, he just waved her off. This was his break, as far as he saw it.

Irritated by his indifference, she gave him a tongue-lashing about how dangerous the world was these days and how they were responsible for the little ones, then went striding quickly toward the fence to confront whoever was there and make sure they didn't mean any harm.

She got within ten yards of the fence before the van's side door slid open. She got a brief glimpse of two men in ski masks holding crude submachine guns in their gloved hands before they opened fire and cut her down in a hail of 9mm bullets.

The two gunmen proceeded to empty their magazines into the crowd of children on the other side of the fence, reloaded, then continued firing. Screams and wails of pain and horror rose into the morning air over the rattle of the gunfire, while Stefan stood against the red brick school building in shock, his phone still clutched in his hand.

Their second magazines empty, the gunmen pulled the door shut and the van roared away, leaving dozens of little kids bleeding, shattered, and dead on the playground.

***

Two hours later, video of the massacre was uploaded to multiple social media platforms by anonymous accounts, pledging that this was only the first stage in wiping out the "Negro menace" that was tearing the nation's cities apart.

***

Reverend Leo Haddock was tired clear down to his bones. He hadn't slept properly in weeks, spending hours and hours a day trying, *trying* to talk some sense into people. He'd been on the radio, he'd been on national TV, and he'd been on every social media outlet known to man, trying to reach people with the message that Jesus Christ loved *all* men and women, regardless of their skin color, their political party, or their economic situation, and that the rioting and violence and destruction of the last few months was only playing into the Devil's hands.

"Dear Lord," he prayed, as he slumped on the couch in his West Virginia home, "when will You turn aside Your wrath?"

As tired as he was, his head snapped up as his whole house shook with the splintering impact of his back door being kicked in. He surged to his feet, as five masked men pushed inside his living room. Two of them had pipes in their hands. A third had a machete.

"Down on yo face, whitey," the man with the machete said loudly. "Time to send a message to all them other crackers!"

Haddock tried to run toward the front door, to get out of the house, to escape. He was fifty-seven, overweight, and knew he was in no condition to fight five young men in their prime, much less when three of them were carrying weapons. He didn't own a gun; in fact, he'd never even fired one in his life.

The bigger man with the pipe vaulted the easy chair to cut him off and swung the pipe, hitting Haddock in the temple. The Reverend went over backward, hitting the hardwood floor with a *thud*.

Mercifully, the blow knocked him cold. He never woke up as the five men beat him to a pulp, crushed his skull, and then the man with the machete hacked him to pieces.

***

Gruesome photos and video of the killing spread across social networks, along with a lengthy, profane warning to any who would try to foster peace between the black people and the "So-Called White Race."

***

The demonstration was peaceful this time, at least for the moment. Officer Chad Berger had resigned himself to the idea that it wasn't going to stay that way. It was only a matter of time before the first rock or bottle was thrown, and then it was going to be game on.

The cops had been fairly hands-off at first. That had, apparently, only made matters worse. That led to him standing there, shoulder-to-shoulder with his friends, Officers Preston Hildreth and Steve Child, in full riot gear, just waiting for the day to go to hell.

340

Downtown St. Louis was already a confused madhouse. So far, the crowds weren't completely intermixed; that would come later, once the violence started. But they had black supremacists, Aztlanistas, anarchists, communists, anarcho-communists, well-meaning liberals, and "anti-fascists" on one side, and a similarly volatile mix of pissed-off law-and-order types, pissed-off professional veterans, Three Percenters, white supremacists, conservatives, anarcho-capitalists, and pissed-off libertarians on the other. And while Chad might sympathize more with a good number of the people on the latter side, he knew that at that point, anyone who was there was really just there for a fight.

Still, he was caught rather off guard by the first gunshot. While there was a lot of yelling going on out on the street, and a couple of people had gotten into shoving matches, there was usually a pattern of escalation to these riots.

It seemed like just about everyone else was similarly surprised. For a split second, everything sort of stopped, the volume dropped, and most of the demonstrators were looking around for the source of the loud *bang*.

Then a long, roaring burst of automatic weapons fire from the top floor of the nearby thirteen-story apartment building ripped through both crowds.

In seconds, everything was chaos. People were down in the street, either hit by bullets or knocked down and trampled in the panic. More were falling as the gunner played more long bursts up and down the avenue, killing as many people as possible. Even the cops fell back from that deadly hail of high-velocity metal.

By the time SWAT cordoned off the building and painstakingly cleared their way to the top, the gunner was long gone, just leaving an old RPD with the serial numbers scratched off lying on the floor. Subsequent investigation found no fingerprints, either.

***

The attack was claimed by the Islamic Council of Resistance in the Dar al Harb, an organization that no one had ever heard of before. It was immediately assumed to be a splinter group from ISIS, even though the latter organization had long since ceased to be anything but a minor action group killing at the behest of the Caliphate of the Arabian Peninsula. Whoever had done it, the usual suspects were immediately screaming over every social media network there was about "false flag attacks" and how it was *really* the work of the government, whether at the behest of the Bilderbergers, the "corporate masters" of the Right, or the Jews.

***

"Fifty-seven major incidents in the last thirty-six hours and counting," Renton said tiredly. We were still in Bangor, in the warehouse on the airstrip. Renton, Stahl, and several other major figures in the Cicero Group had come out shortly after we'd secured the freighter. This was our base of operations for the moment.

"This is coordinated," Chester Remington said. I didn't like Remington. He was still in his late twenties, with a boyish face and soft hands, wearing a suit that probably cost more than my rifle, and had made a name for himself as a think-tank strategist and commentator on war and strategy, despite having never set foot in a war zone himself. Still, as much as I disliked him, I couldn't disagree with him.

"The intensity and frequency of attacks suggest that it is," Stahl said. He looked ancient, like he'd aged another ten years just since I'd last seen him. His shoulders were hunched, and he wasn't carrying his head as high as he usually did, as if he was carrying a particularly heavy ruck. "I expect that a lot of this is the other part of the MGB's op. These attacks were supposed to spread chaos, then Sokolov's picked team would hit their targets in the confusion. If Stone and his boys hadn't taken the *Narva*, we could be looking at a far, far worse situation right now.

"But," he continued heavily, "that's not all of it. It can't be. Not after everything that's happened over the last six months to a year. Hell, longer than that. I expect that a good deal of this violence is organic."

"But the factions are crippled," Remington pointed out.

Stahl nodded. "And that's the problem," he said. "It's a hell of a lot easier to start a civil war than it is to stop it. Six months of riots, murders, and atrocities...the grudges built just in the last year are going to last for a century."

Which was about what I'd told Van Williamson in that trailer outside of Cody, what felt like half a lifetime ago. I briefly wondered if the kid was still alive, and if he'd gotten the message. Somehow, I doubted it.

"But with the factions out of the picture," Tyler said, "then we should be able to go public with this, shouldn't we? We've got the remains of a real, live Spetsnaz unit that we caught trying to get into the country with a full loadout and a comprehensive strategic sabotage and terrorism plan. I mean, let people know that we're actually under attack from the Russians, and it could throw a wet blanket over all of this. Couldn't it? People put aside their political differences after 9/11, after all. I mean, sure, it didn't last, but it happened."

Most of the Cicero Group people looked uncomfortable. Stahl just looked grim. "You'd think so, wouldn't you?" he said.

"Oh, fuck," I said. "Now what?"

A few of the softer-looking people seemed a bit shocked at my language. Stahl and Renton took it in stride. "A special task force was officially formed yesterday," Renton said, his voice low and dead. "Not to investigate the uptick in violence or the Russians. But to apprehend the shooters who raided the Verdant Mount golf course."

The words hung there in the air for a long, quiet moment.

342

"Motherfucker!" Bryan all but screamed. "We cannot catch a single fucking break, can we? 'The world's burning down around our ears, but somebody roughed up my drinking buddy just because he was selling out to the fucking Russian MGB, so let's put all our resources and energy toward that, instead!'"

"That's about the shape of it, yes," Stahl said calmly. "But don't worry, son, it's not the end of the world. We've just got to go to Plan B, that's all."

"And just what exactly is 'Plan B?'" I asked quietly.

"Essentially," Renton said, "a coup d'etat."

If it had gotten quiet after he'd announced that the government was coming after us instead of the Russians, the warehouse would have made a tomb sound festive after that. For a long moment, every one of us just stared at him.

"Just like that?" Larry asked, disbelief mixed with more than a touch of anger in his voice. Larry could be pretty libertarian, and I knew that the implications of what Renton had just said were not lost on him. "A handful of us are just going to take over?"

"Not exactly," Stahl said around his cigar. "It wouldn't work, for one thing. The bureaucracy's too big, and even if we had the manpower—which we don't—we couldn't just storm into the Capitol, hold it, and make anything better. It would only make this mess worse.

"Now, I know what you're all thinking," he continued, raising his voice a little. This wasn't the retired General speaking anymore. Mars had returned, in all his square-jawed, warrior charisma. "It wasn't supposed to work this way. We were supposed to deal with the factions, purge the poison, and the machinery of the Republic was going to set things right.

"Well, it's gone too far for that. It may have already gone too far even before the killing started. The cancer's metastasized. We got the bigwigs, but you guys of all people know how deep these networks can go. Mexico was only the tip of the iceberg. The rot goes deep, and you boys know as well as I do that the web of money and influence is too tangled to ever straighten out. Now, I'm sure there *are* plenty of people still in the government who would rather look the other way concerning our activities, and go after the Russians. That's their duty, after all. We only did what we did because *they* weren't doing it.

"But it should be pretty fucking obvious that those people still ain't calling the shots. And the ones who are, are going to keep fucking around, pursuing petty vendettas and trying to prop up their little empires, while the Russians, the Iranians, and every other motherfucker who wants a piece, who wants to see the US fall, burns the entire damned house down around our ears. They will fiddle faster and louder while Rome burns. And they'll do their damnedest to take us down first, because they know that we—that *you*—are a threat to their empires. Because you've already demonstrated that you won't stand by and get trampled on for the sake of somebody's political career or bottom line.

"Make no mistake, gents," he continued, momentarily taking the cigar out from between his teeth and looking around at all of us, including the softer Cicero Group types. Most of them didn't look back at him; few of them had been able to meet any of our eyes for long, either. "You boys have done one hell of a job, as hard as it's been." He was talking to us, the Cicero Group staff ignored. "There's more lethality packed into fewer men in this room than in most team rooms in the world. You are the nastiest bunch of hard-bitten, ruthless bastards I've ever had the pleasure to work with. Those few who know the name 'Praetorian' are rightfully afraid of you.

"But that's why you're not going to stand a chance. Don't think that the people who issued these orders are ignorant of what happened back in Wyoming a few months ago. They won't underestimate you again, and when they come, they'll come with overwhelming force and the full knowledge and approval of the Federal government, as much of a shadow of what it was that it's become. They'll steamroll you because they have no other choice.

"Which brings me to the rest of it. *We* don't have any other choice either, not anymore. The machinery of the Republic putting things back together without the factions to interfere was a dream, as much of a dream as any other revolution magically making things better. Too many of the safeguards have been dismantled, along with most of any kind of national consciousness. Neighbors consider each other mortal enemies now, whether because of politics, skin color, or some mutant combination of dumbfuckery that they've picked up from propaganda disguised as news and social media. In time, maybe it would work itself out. But you know as well as I do that we don't have that time. Sokolov's op might not have been the first, but it damned sure won't be the last. There will be a Plan B, and a Plan C, and a Plan Z One Hundred and Fifty. They're not going to leave us alone because this one failed. And that's just the Russians. We've got plenty of enemies out there besides them, too; I don't have to tell you boys that.

"So, we don't have any other recourse. We throw the dice, make our Hail Mary pass, and grab for victory, before we go down in defeat. Otherwise we all die, or spend the last days of our miserable lives in black sites as everything we fought and bled for, and everything our brothers died for, goes down in flames."

I looked around at the rest as he finished speaking, sticking the cigar back between his teeth. Mostly, I only saw expressions that I expected mirrored my own; stony, impassive, but masking a deep-running mix of anger, grief, and exhaustion.

When I looked in Stahl's eyes, past the mask of Leader of Men, I saw the same expression. He looked *old*, old and tired. Despite all the fire of his

344

words, he was a deeply weary man, and the knowledge of just what he was asking of us was plain in his eyes.

It didn't mean I was sold. "You said that we couldn't just take over by main force," I said, "which I happen to agree with. What *is* the plan, then?"

"Call it a 'Shadow Coup,'" Renton said. "There are still leaders in Congress who call a lot of the shots. We get to them, 'convince' them to cooperate, and go from there. We've got a target deck already drawn up."

I stared at him coldly. "And how long has this target list been ready?" I asked, my voice pitched low and dangerous. "Was this the endgame all along?"

He met my gaze without flinching. Renton knew me well enough to hear the warning tone in my voice. We'd been used and double-crossed before, and by this time, I think he knew all too well how badly such things could go. We'd been battered, bloodied, and lost too many friends. We were strung out, pissed off, and heavily armed. If we found out that all the pain, all the death, all the killing had just been for the sake of another power grab, things were likely to get very…intense. Very quickly.

"It's been drawn up and evolving ever since it became evident that there was no more containing the situation," he said flatly. "Remember what I told you a few years ago, on that rooftop in Erbil? This was never the ideal solution. We were trying to keep a lid on things, trying to keep cutting the fuse when one of these reckless, stupid, self-centered assholes lit it. Now it's too late for that. And I shouldn't have to tell you that there really *are* no ideal solutions in this world."

He had a point. I'd seen too much to believe in happily-ever-after, at least where war and politics are concerned.

But in a very real way, we were all looking at the death of a dream. Alek, Larry, Nick, Mike, and I had started the company with vague ideas of staying in the fight, somehow, and making something of a living in the process, in a world economy where it wasn't that easy anymore. We'd identified with a lot of the Vietnam vets who'd found themselves out of place back in The World and had gone back to Asia or to Rhodesia to fight communists somewhere else.

It had turned into more than that. We'd thrown ourselves into a shadowy, shifting war across the globe, trying to hold off the wolves that were circling what we increasingly saw as a struggling, fading society. But even while we got paid, and bent the rules we didn't outright break, we'd all remembered the oaths we'd taken to the Constitution long before. Everything we'd done, we'd ultimately done for our country. We'd hired out to fight our nation's enemies when our nation didn't have the wherewithal or the guts to do it.

And now we were being asked to effectively overthrow the government of our own country. It was a bitter pill to swallow, even as we thought back and saw how we'd come to this pass.

"I wish that I could say that if any of you wasn't feeling up to it, that you could walk, no hard feelings," Stahl said. "But it ain't that easy. The security of the op aside, they'll come for you, especially if you're on your own. It's hang together or hang separately time, gents. We need an answer."

He was right. The die had already been cast. It had been cast months ago. We had to follow through, or die. Especially with half the global underworld knowing our names and faces, and with some serious grudges attached to those names and faces, there was a decided shortage of places to run and hide. If we were outlaws in our own home, the list of hiding places would go from short to nonexistent.

I looked around at the rest of the team. It was a mix of four or five teams, now, whittled down to about a platoon's worth of shooters. A lot of old faces were gone. A lot of new ones had quickly become as old and drawn as the rest. But while I could see few without the same misgivings behind their eyes, there was an acceptance of reality in all its harshness there, too. Any kind of wishful thinking about how the world *should* be had been burned out in the gunfire, smoke, and blood of the last few years.

"Give me the list," I said, "and tell me the *whole* plan."

CHAPTER 37

It was a hell of a planning cycle. There were a couple of dozen targets, and under the circumstances, they were going to be well-protected. While Congresscritters and Senators were usually protected by DC Police while they were in Washington, most of them would have hired private security to keep them safe during the violence and unrest that had been wracking the nation, not least of all in DC itself. The PMSCs would have been hired on the taxpayers' dime, of course.

To make matters worse, we had a limited amount of time to put the plan together and move on it. We'd gotten a bit more info on the "special task force" that was coming after us. FBI, DHS, ATF, and a few other alphabet-soup agencies that I'd never even heard of were involved, and we were presently at the top of the "most wanted" list. As near as Bates knew, they didn't have our location locked down yet; they were surveilling The Ranch, but knew that most of the hitters weren't there.

Somehow it didn't surprise me that The Broker had DOJ as infiltrated as he did the global criminal underworld.

Slowly, as we worked alongside a few of Bates' people and the Cicero Group's minions to nail down our targets' movements, Larry, Tom, Alek, Nick, Bryan, and I drifted together until we were reasonably sure we had some privacy.

"I don't like this," Larry said grimly, folding his massive arms across his equally massive chest. His normally cheerful face was creased with a thunderous frown.

"There ain't much to like," I said flatly.

"Even if we do pull this off," he continued, "you do know what usually happens to the vanguard of revolutions, right?"

There were nods all around. "Even if Stahl wouldn't stand for it—and I believe he wouldn't—we still don't know for sure who all was involved in selling us out in Mexico," I said, glancing toward the Group's people, on the other side of the warehouse. "That bunch that came with him and Renton? They'd see us taken out as a threat to the regime, quietly, without troubling The General with such details."

"None of those fucksticks have the balls," Bryan growled.

"To do it themselves?" I replied. "Of course not. They're 'idea men,' they're the intellectual core, the smart people. Look at that little shit

347

Remington. He's been preaching for every intervention and power projection project for years, but he's never laced up a pair of combat boots and picked up a rifle in his life. He's too important to the cause to put his delicate hide on the line for his ideas." I was suddenly sorely tempted to spit on the floor. "At least the old Roman senatorial class had to spend time with the legions before they went into politics.

"But they wouldn't get their hands dirty, oh no. It'd be a quiet word to somebody, an exchange of cash, evidence would be found, and we'd be imprisoned or killed one by one. They already know the cost of trying to take us out all at once. And Stahl would either be too busy with other matters, or he'd be shown incontrovertible evidence that there was no other choice."

"So, what's the plan?" Nick asked.

"Believe it or not," Tom said, taking a long drag on what had to be his fifteenth cigarette of the day, "I've already gotten some contingencies in place. After The Ranch got hit, I knew we might need some bolt-holes to lay low for a while, if not permanently. I've secured a few of them, mostly in remote areas. The locals think they're prepper retreats, which isn't all that far off the mark. If worst comes to worst, we vanish and scatter to those bolt-holes. They're well-stocked, and I'm sure all of us have the skillsets to live reasonably comfortably in any of them."

"Why not just go now?" Bryan asked.

"Because Stahl still made a good point," Alek said. He'd had little to say since getting back from Kurdistan; there had been too much going on, and I'd been the primary ground commander, with more direct familiarity with the situation as it was than he had. But Alek had been one of the driving forces of Praetorian from the beginning, and we listened to him. "Our heads are on the chopping block right now. We've got too many people hunting us, and if the whole fucking country goes in the shitter, there really won't be any place to hide. As bad as this is, I think it really is the only shot we've got to preserve *something*. Otherwise, the Russians and all their little cronies are going to see this country torn apart, and we'll go down along with everybody else."

I looked around at all that was left of Praetorian's founding team. There was more weariness in the eyes, more gray in hair and beards. We'd aged what felt like a half a century just in the last few years. "So, we follow through, put Stahl and his people quietly in charge, and then break off and go dark. Sound like a plan?"

"Sounds like a plan that can go pear-shaped in about fifty different ways," Nick muttered.

"And since when have we ever had *any* op go according to plan?" Bryan countered. "A plan is just…"

"A list of shit that ain't gonna happen, I know," Nick answered. "You've been repeating that old saw for years."

"Just because it's an old saying don't mean it ain't true," Bryan retorted, in his best "Kirk Lazarus playing a black guy" voice.

"All right, knock it off," I said, glancing back toward the rest who were still planning the op. "Tom, do what you need to so we can disappear fast if we have to. Everybody else, keep your teeth together and get back to work. We've still got a lot of politicians to kidnap."

***

There were so many targets, and such a short timeframe, that Ventner's guys had been brought in to help. Joe had commented, "It's about damned time. You sons a bitches have made it damned hard to be anything but second fiddle when it comes to getting missions."

I'd stared at him coldly. "I wouldn't bitch too hard about that if I were you, Joe," I said bleakly. "Or haven't you noticed how many of the old guard are missing?"

He'd looked around at that, and there was a new look, a mix of shame and a little horror, in his eyes when he looked back at me. "Holy shit. That bad?"

"It's been a rough few months," was all I said. It was a somewhat more subdued Joe Ventner who threw himself into the planning process.

Joe and I were discussing changing up a set of targets, since the most recent information on one of them put a Senator who was on Joe's list closer to a Congressman we were slated to grab. It was going to be easier to go from one target to the next, and let Joe have the third Congresswoman, who was staying another four miles away.

"Stone?" I looked up to see Stewart walking over to us. He'd become Stahl's go-to liaison with us, since the general had found out about our time together in Libya. "Mars wants to see you," he said.

I nodded to him, got the nod from Joe that he was satisfied with the plan as we'd just laid it out, and turned to follow Stewart.

Stewart didn't have much to say on the way out of the warehouse and down to the abandoned office building that Stahl had commandeered for his temporary headquarters there in Maine. Since I wasn't feeling all that talkative, myself, I didn't complain.

Stahl was lighting up a fresh cigar as I walked into the office. There was enough of a background smell to the place to suggest that he'd been chain-smoking the things in there for the last couple of days. It wasn't a fine tobacco smell, either. Those stogies were some of the cheapest money could buy; he smoked too many of them for the fancy ones.

He looked up at me through a blue cloud of smoke as I walked in. "Change of plans," he announced, blowing another cloud toward the ceiling.

"Ah, fuck," I said. "Now what?"

He held up a hand. "It's not a bad thing, this time. It's actually going to make your life far, far easier." He took another puff and continued.

349

"Congresswoman Sparrow, whose ass you pulled out of the fire down in Arizona, has been doing work for us for a while, though not necessarily for *us*, in her mind. She just contacted me, asking for a meeting. She's got a proposal, and has about half our target list on board with it, along with the other half at least willing to listen. She wants us…me, specifically, to have a hand in it. So, there's going to be a meeting at Camp David in two days."

I frowned. "Has she explained what this proposal is?" I asked.

"She hasn't," he replied, "but one of her aides has." He pointed to the laptop in front of him. "It boils down to essentially what we already had planned, only without having to actually snatch any of the players involved. They'll come to us, instead."

"So, basically, putting the strings into your hands, declaring you the Grand Puppeteer of the US government," I said. I was tired; bluntness was all I had left.

He didn't upbraid me for the comment, though. He peered at me through the haze of cigar smoke for a moment, then nodded. "Basically," he agreed. "They're scared, and they're unprepared. Most of these clowns have played the same games that have brought us to this pass for years, never anticipating the unintended consequences of turning their countrymen against each other for their own advantage. Now they're looking for a grown-up to fix the problem, and Sparrow's offering them one. They'll posture and shout for the media and the social networks, but in the background, they just want Daddy to fix things."

"So, is the op off?" I asked.

He shook his head. "Not all of it. There's one person I still need you to grab." He handed me a packet of papers. I took it and flipped through it.

It was a target package, as I'd expected. The middle aged, immaculately groomed man looking up at me from the target photo wasn't exactly who I'd expected, though. I looked up at Stahl. "Varren?" I asked.

He nodded. "Fred Varren, media mogul, billionaire, and the President's golf buddy. Also far more of a policymaker than he's ever supposed to be, given that he's never been elected to anything in his life, or even appointed to a cabinet position. He hasn't let that stop him from calling a lot of the shots, even the ones the President *has* publicly taken credit for. And I have it on good authority that the special task force was his doing." He took a deep drag on the cigar, making the ember glow bright orange, and blew the smoke toward the ceiling again. "I want him secured. Not gently. The full instructions are in there."

"Sending a message?" I ventured, with a raised eyebrow.

"This won't work unless we can put the fear of God into a pack of people who've lived most of their lives thinking they're untouchable," he said grimly. "They have to *see* that there will be consequences for going off the reservation."

I didn't think that he was entirely aware of just how ominous those words sounded. At least, not until he took the cigar out of his mouth, leaned back in his chair, and stared at the ceiling for a long moment.

"Holy hell," he muttered. "That sounds awfully Bolshevik, doesn't it?"

"Yes, it does," I replied heavily. "But I get it. This is what lawlessness leads to, and most of these fuckers have pissed all over the law for decades, made it meaningless. And when the force of the law goes away, then force becomes the law."

He looked at me from beneath a quirked eyebrow. A small, grim smile twitched at the corner of his mouth. "And guys like you are why I always detested the academics and think-tank strategists, Stone," he said. "They think that just because you kick doors and pull triggers for a living, that you can't be a thinker. I know better."

I only nodded, looking back down at the target package in my hand. I had little to say to that. I had no doubt that he was sincere; this was Mars, after all. But knowing what we were about to do, as much as I respected the man, I still recognized that he was playing the game, trying to cement my loyalty.

Or was he? I thought of my doubts about Mia, which still lingered in the dark recesses of my mind, as hard as I tried to shut them up. Had I come to suspect *everyone* of hiding sinister, ulterior motives? *I need to get the hell out of this game, while I've still got anything left of my soul*, I thought.

But first, to deal with Fred Varren. I looked at that smug, superior face in the photo. *That smirk's not gonna last, bud,* I thought.

***

Varren's home, such as it was, was in New York. He owned several media conglomerates, and was said to own half a dozen penthouse apartments in that city alone. He also had a place in Alexandria, which brought us back to where Chu had been murdered, though we were blocks away from that incident, which had been all but forgotten in the chaos that had followed, anyway.

There weren't many penthouses in Alexandria, though prices were still high enough that there may as well have been. Even so, someone like Fred Varren couldn't stay in just any suburban house, no matter how expensive. So, he'd bought and moved into an old Civil War mansion in the middle of downtown Alexandria. I was sure the locals were fucking *thrilled*.

Of course, being situated where it was would make going in there to get him difficult. And by "difficult," I mean "a stone bitch."

Being in the middle of town as it was, there was zero screening. We'd potentially be under surveillance as soon as we pulled up. Which meant we had to go in fast. Stealth was effectively off the table.

I didn't like it in planning, and I didn't like it any more sitting in the dark in the back of the windowless cargo van that Joe Ventner himself was driving. In the middle of town, within spitting distance of DC itself, too far from any of the sporadic riots that were still going on in DC proper for them to provide any sort of smokescreen, we were more likely to run into law enforcement interference. Alexandria was big money, and with the indiscriminate and chaotic nature of the violence that was once again sweeping the nation, the rich were getting nervous.

If we'd proceeded with the rash of snatch-and-grabs that we'd initially planned for, there would have been too much chaos for the cops to zero in on any particular team. We'd stand a better chance of getting in and out before they got their shit together. Now, with only the one target, police response time was going to be a lot shorter.

It wasn't that we weren't capable of shooting our way out, and laying waste to any SWAT team that came after us. I just didn't want to. The cops weren't the bad guys.

Joe was driving because he and his boys were going to handle the transpo and outer cordon. That would leave as many of the dwindling Praetorian shooters as possible to flood the house and grounds and hopefully overwhelm whatever private security Varren had hired before anyone could get shot.

"Two minutes, Jeff!" Joe called over his shoulder.

"Roger," I answered. There was nothing else to do, really. We were packed into the back of the van, already in full kit, helmets on, rifles slung and pointed at the floor.

Two minutes later, the van lurched to a stop, and I reached out and threw the back doors open before spilling out onto the street.

"Spilling" was damned near the right word, too. Joe had parked facing uphill, so getting out the back was a bit of a drop.

We weren't on the back of the property; there was only a fence there that we'd have to climb over, wasting time and exposing ourselves for too long. But there were two gates through the brick and wrought iron fence on the north side of the property. And Joe had parked us right in front of them.

Larry was lugging the battering ram, a three-foot black pipe filled with cement with two handles on it. He hit the ground running, between me and Alek, who were similarly sprinting to either side of the gate to cover up and down the street, while the rest of the stack ran to get behind Larry.

All three hundred seventy-five pounds of man, gear, and ram hit the gate behind the six-inch head of the breaching tool. Needless to say, the gate latch had not been designed to withstand *that*. The gate nearly came apart under the assault, the splintered remains flapping aside as Nick led the way in.

Nick and the rest of the stack didn't even slow down. Neither did Larry; he wasn't done with that ram yet, and he fell in behind Bryan, huffing and puffing a little. Running never would be Larry's favorite thing to do, even if he got to smash a door open at the end of it. Alek and I swung in behind him as the Ventner shooters took up the outer cordon on the street.

It was less than forty meters from the gate to the back door, and we covered it at a dead sprint. There had been no sign of the kind of overt security that the likes of Eddings and Van Damme had employed, but I wasn't going to assume that there weren't men with guns inside. We had a little bit of concealment on the yard, between the trees and the gazebo, but that was no reason to dawdle.

Nick pushed past the door while Bryan stacked on it, and Larry stormed past Bryan to hit the door with the ram. It crashed inward, Larry rolled out of the way, and Bryan flowed inside, his suppressed ISR up and ready, with me right behind him, my own Compressor's muzzle right over his shoulder.

We were right in the central hall, with the grand staircase rising ahead of us to the right. There was a single guy in a suit at the front of the hall, who turned as the door crashed open, a pistol in his hand and a shotgun leaning against the molding that ran around the wall at about waist height.

Whatever company he worked for, he wasn't a fanatic. He took one look at us as we flooded into the hall, in green fatigues, plate carriers, and ATE helmets with suppressed SBRs pointed at his head, and he dropped the pistol to the black-and-white tile floor and put his hands in the air.

"Down on the floor!" Nick barked at him. Nick advanced on him, even as I stepped up behind him, staying back plate to back plate, my Compressor aimed up the stairs at the landing. The rest of the stack was spreading out, moving on the doors to left and right.

Bangs went through the doors as Nick secured the security guard, kicking the weapons away. I stayed on security on the stairway, along with George, until Nick said, "With you."

I led the way up the steps, pivoting as I went to keep the top of the stairs covered. It made for tricky footing, but I had no desire to get shot in the back of the head going up the stairs.

The landing was empty, but something made me pause before turning down the hallway to the left. It was a good thing I did, too, because a shotgun blast *boomed* down the hallway and blew chips of plaster off the far wall.

These guys were not the best in the business, that was for sure. Maybe we'd already killed off the cream of the crop. These guys were shaky as shit.

The other distinct possibility was that Varren had no fucking clue about security matters, and had been duped by a bunch of Z-grade rent-a-cops into hiring them.

Without much hesitation, George lobbed a flashbang past my head, bouncing it off the far wall and down the hallway. It went off with a deafening report, filling the hallway with smoke, and I was moving, with George right behind me, even as Nick posted up on the landing, facing down the opposite hallway.

The shotgunner in the hallway had been barricaded on the nearest doorway, but he hadn't had the presence of mind to pull back into the room and shut his eyes when the bang went off. He was standing half in the doorway, blinded and disoriented, as I moved on him.

The shotgun wasn't pointed at me, so I almost gave him a warning to get on the floor, but as he made out figures moving in front of him through the smoke and the green blob in his vision, he tried to bring the weapon up, so I shot him twice in the chest, then transitioned to his head, but he was already falling, his heart and lungs destroyed, as the last round blasted out the top of his skull. They weren't wearing body armor.

Since the nearest threat had come from that door, that was where we went, stepping over the corpse in the doorway with a single, long step and pivoting to clear the corner I couldn't see from the hall. He had been the only one in there.

Flowing back out into the hallway, we moved to the next room, which was accessed by a big double door. This must be the master bedroom, and more than likely where we'd find Varren, provided he didn't have a safe room that he'd been ensconced in.

The door splintered inward under George's boot, and we burst in, guns up and searching for targets.

The two contractors, in shirts, ties, and shoulder holsters, were down on their knees on the rug, their hands on their heads, their weapons well out of reach.

The safe room door was visible through the back of the partly open closet. And it had obviously been secured.

"You dumb motherfuckers," I said tiredly, as I covered the two rent-a-cops so Nick and George could close in and secure them. "Now we're going to have to risk pulping him when we pry him out of there." I keyed my radio. "This is Hillbilly," I sent. "Got the package, south side second floor. Gonna need a can opener."

"Can opener coming up," Alek replied. Larry had brought the ram; Alek had a Broco torch, just in case we ran into this eventuality. If that didn't work, well, we did have breaching charges. Varren *really* wouldn't like life if we had to use those.

"What's going on out there?" a voice called from a speaker box in the closet. That was right; sometimes these safe rooms were wired for sound, so that the person holed up in them could try to warn an intruder off by telling them they'd called the police.

"What's going on, Fred," I told him, "is that you've got thirty seconds to unseal that door, come out of there, and come with us, or we're going to cut or blast our way in and drag your ass out. I really don't think you want us to blast our way in, and cutting could get a little unpleasant, too. It's entirely up to you, though; I really don't give a half a fuck."

"The police are on their way," he said tremulously. He sure didn't sound as smug as his picture, now.

"And given their usual response time, we've got plenty of time to do violence to your safe room door," I replied. "I'm guessing that it was built standard, to keep home invaders out, home invaders who presumably don't have access to plasma torches and shaped charges." I let that sink in for a second. "Clock's ticking, Fred." Alek was already prepping the torch, fitting the copper cutting rod in place.

The truth was, I wasn't entirely sure how much time we had, and breaching that door in a way that might not kill the man inside could very well put us past our window. But he didn't need to know that.

Alek hit the end with the torch igniter, and a ferocious, spitting flame started sparking from the end of the cutting rod. "Time's up, Fred," I said, raising my voice over the snarling hiss of the torch. "You might want to step back, unless you want to kiss six thousand degrees of molten metal."

"Wait, wait, *wait!*" he almost screamed. "I'm coming out. I'm coming out!" Apparently, he didn't want to chance it.

I gave Alek a throat-cutting gesture, and he released the oxygen handle, letting the torch die. A moment later, the electronic lock *clicked*, and the door swung open.

Fred Varren was in his boxers, and looked quite a bit soggier around the midsection than in his public photos. He looked older too, the lack of gray in his brown hair notwithstanding. I suspected there was quite a bit of makeup, hair dye, and tight undergarments that went into maintaining his image.

When he didn't come out fast enough, I stepped inside, grabbed his wrist, twisted it up between his shoulder blades, and frog-marched him out into the room. "Probably should have put some more clothes on, but you'll be fine," I said. "It's a warm night."

"Who are you people?" he asked. "Do you know who I am?"

"We know exactly who you are, Fred," I told him. "As for who we are, well. We are violent people with a bit of an ax to grind with you. Now shut up, so I don't have to stuff a sock in your mouth and tape it shut."

Searching the house wasn't a priority. Fred Varren was our target, and we had him. It took only a couple more minutes to get back downstairs, out the back, and back into the vans. The cordon collapsed and we were heading out of the neighborhood moments later, even as red and white lights lit up the street and sirens wailed behind us.

CHAPTER 38

"Jeff, I'd like you to come with me," Stahl said. "You won't be able to get guns in, which I know is a problem, but that's why the rest are going to be in the trees with all the firepower we can muster."

"Why me?" I asked.

"Because whether they know it or not, you're the face of the Praetorians now," he answered. "And I need my Praetorian Guard backing me up for this." He bit the end off a fresh cigar, spat it out, and lit it. His supply seemed inexhaustible. "Like you said," he growled around the stogie, as clouds of smoke wreathed his head, "when the law is ignored, force becomes the law. These pricks need to see that, concretely, in front of their faces. And you're the emblem of that force. I'm just the retired general. You're someone who's killed people, recently, at bad breath distances. That means something."

He had a point, and antagonizing him by being an ass wasn't going to serve anyone's purposes at that point, so I just nodded, handed off my gear and weapons, and got in the Excursion with him, Mia, and Renton. Mia sat next to me and reached over to squeeze my hand. That was all. We both had our game faces on.

There were Marines manning the gate at the Presidential Retreat at Camp David. They weren't there for the sake of the usual pomp and spectacle, either. There wasn't a set of Dress Blue Alphas to be seen. These boys, and a couple of girls, were in woodland cammies, with plate carriers, full combat loads, helmets, and M27s slung and ready for combat. As the Ventner Dynamics driver paused at the gate and presented our credentials to the Corporal, who peered inside to check that faces and numbers matched up, there were four others with their rifles at the low ready, in a passable L-shape around the vehicle, watching us.

I got an extra look from the Corporal, being the only one in the vehicle not wearing a suit and tie. I was still in my greens, having expected to be out in the woods with the assault force, ready to move in and pull Stahl, Renton, and Mia out by main force if the meeting turned out to be an ambush.

Finally, the Corporal waved us by, offering Stahl a salute. That was interesting. Some of the new kids still remembered who he was.

I watched them as we rolled past. Every one of them looked about twelve years old to me. I could only imagine how young they looked to Stahl.

Camp David isn't all that big, so it was only a few more moments before the driver parked the vehicle in the lot between the arms of the big, U-shaped building where the meeting was going down, and we all got out. I stayed close behind Stahl; if I was going to be his designated attack dog, I'd play the part.

There were four Secret Service personnel waiting for us at the door. All four of us were thoroughly searched. Dressed as I was, I got a little more attention, and I considered telling the dude patting me down that he really should have bought me dinner first. But we had no weapons on us, so they had to let us through. Stahl had been asked to come, after all.

We were ushered into a large, windowless conference room with dark wood paneling along the walls, dominated by a long oak table with microphones built in. This was *the* conference room, where many a meeting of world leaders had taken place. Treaties and wars had been hashed out here.

Now the fate of the Republic itself was about to be hashed out in the same room.

The remaining leadership of the House and Senate were gathered around the table. Many of them I didn't recognize; I'd been a bit too busy trying to stay alive to pay much attention to the current circus on Capitol Hill. Unless they'd showed up on my target deck, I really hadn't given a fuck who they were.

The President, I recognized. He was hard not to know. Congressmen and Senators, for the most part, came and went, but the President was the face of the nation, so it was hard to ignore him, as much as one might want to. He was sitting at the center of the table, his suit immaculate, but his shoulders hunched and his face a mask.

As I scanned the rest of the table, I could see similar expressions all around, though some shaded more towards outrage or fear, depending on who was wearing it. None of them were comfortable with the situation, though, and certainly not with Stahl's presence.

"You're going to have to put that out, General," a young woman I pegged as an aide said into the stiff silence. "This is a government building, and there is no smoking."

Stahl just took a deeper drag on the cigar before taking it out of his teeth and blowing a cloud toward the chandelier. "*I'm* not the one here begging *you* people to fix this clusterfuck," he growled. "I'll smoke if I want."

"We called you here to ask your advice, Carl," the President corrected. He was evidently trying to sound soothing and conciliatory, but everyone present was obviously under a lot of strain. He just sounded angry, scared, and strident. "Based on your extensive experience in countries suffering from widespread unrest, several of the people in this room made a convincing case that you could offer some penetrating insight."

"Penetrating insight?" Stahl said, with a dry, humorless laugh. "That's rich." He stared coldly around the table. "But fine. I'll give you some insight." He blew another cloud of bluish tobacco smoke in the President's direction. "You lot—and those who came before you; I'm not absolving them—have spent *decades* subverting the law when you weren't ignoring it outright. Anything for an advantage, whether it made you richer or just more important. And when the law was irrelevant, you turned to populism. 'It's the will of the people!' you cried. But populism is only the mob, and the mob only works when you've got a target for its hate. A foreign enemy wasn't good enough; to too many of you, there was too much money coming from overseas to jeopardize it by calling out the Saudis—at least until they became the Caliphate, though some of you are still in their pockets, too; don't think I don't know who—or the Russians, or the Chinese, or even the Iranians.

"So, you settled for the next best thing. Other Americans. *Those* people are out to take your rights away, whatever invented rights you made up this week to get them pissed off at each other. And they played along, getting just as outraged as you needed them to be to give you all the power and all the leeway you wanted.

"Until it didn't end there. Until they started killing each other. Because that's what mobs do."

He glared around at all of them. His physical resemblance to Chesty Puller had never been quite so pronounced. "But that wasn't all. Not only did you manage to lay the groundwork for a civil war, but there hasn't been a civil war in history that wasn't capitalized on by the enemies of the nation that was tearing its own guts out. And this one's no different."

At that point, Mia stepped forward to pass out a series of stapled packets to the stony-faced or outright furious politicians sitting at the table. Some of them took them curiously, others left them sitting in front of them, apparently too affronted at Stahl's blunt speech to such important people to bother lifting a finger to examine them.

Frankly, I was surprised that they'd stayed as quiet as they had, so far. I'd been expecting shouting, cursing, and typical grandstanding and histrionics long before.

I saw a few faces turn pale, and eyes widen. I knew what was in those packets. They contained all of the Sensitive Site Exploitation photos from the *Narva*. Including the Russian corpses.

"The photos you're looking at are only a couple of days old," Stahl said into the deathly silence. "The bodies, and the captives, were a company— that's roughly a hundred men, for those of you who never served nor bothered to find out more about military matters," he added accusingly, "of Russian Spetsnaz, specially trained and equipped for sabotage and infrastructure demolition attacks. For those of you who can't read Russian, the photos of the maps on Page Five give a partial target list. The short version is, they would

359

have crippled the entire Eastern seaboard's electrical grid, communications net, and transportation, right at the same time the recent wave of violence happened."

He let that sink in for a moment. "And they ain't the only ones. The man in green, standing behind me, led the assault on the *Narva* that intercepted those Spetsnaz. He also led the team that intercepted Mexican paramilitaries coming across the Arizona border to wreak similar havoc in the name of 'Aztlan' in the Southwest." He stabbed a finger at the table. "We are under attack, an attack made possible by the same social unrest *you* encouraged for your own gain."

"I will leave aside your rather vicious accusations for the moment, General," the President said. "If this is true, then perhaps by publicizing these incidents, we can put something of a damper on the unrest. After all, shouldn't an external enemy provide some sort of unifying catalyst? It worked after 9/11."

"That was then," Stahl growled. "There have been a couple decades worth of division happening since then, and in case you forgot, that unity didn't last a year before people were playing politics with the war and the lives of the soldiers and Marines downrange. Now anything that doesn't agree with a particular faction is a lie, no matter what kind of convoluted fantasy has to take its place to kind of make sense. To make matters worse, those Spetsnaz were coming ashore at the *express invitation* of Americans, led by one Mason Van Damme."

That got a reaction. For a second, the President looked like Stahl had just slapped him in the face, though he composed himself quickly. That shot had gone home. While his expression went still, I could see in his eyes that he was starting to understand just how dangerous the situation was. He and Van Damme had been buddies, and he knew Van Damme was missing. He probably didn't know that we'd grabbed Varren yet, but he would, soon.

He also knew that if Stahl knew of Van Damme's activities, then Stahl, and presumably anyone working with him, was involved in the man's disappearance. The tension in the room ratcheted up a notch.

"That is an absurd accusation," the Speaker of the House snapped.

"It should be," Stahl replied before she could continue. "But Van Damme was caught red-handed, making a deal with Dmitri Sokolov, an officer in the Russian MGB. He even admitted to it. When personal power and factionalism take precedence, any ally is welcome, even if you're welcoming a viper into your own house. Just ask any king in history who invited a barbarian tribe into their country as mercenaries. I'm sure the story of Hengist and Horsa doesn't ring any bells to you, though it should."

So far, no mention had been made of the special task force put together to kill or capture the team that hit Van Damme's meeting. But everyone there was thinking about it. The entire dynamic of the meeting had changed.

360

But the President didn't want to go that route. Not yet. "You've given some interesting insights into how we came to this pass, General," he said stiffly. "But you have not presented any possible solutions. We invited you here to help find a solution to this crisis."

Stahl held out his hand. Mia handed him a slim manila folder. "And I have that solution right here," he said.

The President frowned. "What is that?" he asked.

"It's a couple of documents that will require your signature, along with witnesses," Stahl said. "The first is an order reinstating me to Active Duty, effective immediately, along with a promotion to a fifth star, and appointment as General of the Armed Forces." He paused for a moment. "The second is a declaration of a national state of emergency and the institution of martial law."

Now *that* got a reaction. In a moment, the room was pandemonium. Stahl's bull bellow cut through the noise. "*Shut the fuck up!*"

The Chesty Puller glare was back, amplified by the glowing cigar and halo of smoke. "*I* didn't create this pass, *you* did. *You* were the ones who fucked around and played politics while paramilitaries ran around the States, assassinating political opponents and killing anyone who stood up to them, fomenting more chaos and more death to cover their actions. *You* were the ones encouraging 'protests' that turned into riots, simply to get your faces on the news and curry favor with special interest groups. *You* were the ones fiddling while Rome burned to the ground, and now you have the *balls* to object to the *only* way to restore order while there's *anything* left of our country before the rest of our external enemies finish the job. Well, time's up. Shit or get off the pot. Sign the damned papers."

"I will not," the President said furiously. "And I should have you arrested for even suggesting such a course of action."

"Oh, you'll sign them," Stahl said, suddenly conversationally. "Because if you don't, the team that the man behind me led, that intercepted those Russians off the coast of Maine, that killed Gordon Baumgartner and his team—I believe you're all familiar with that name—that dismantled an entire cartel *and* a Chinese paramilitary operation in Mexico not long ago, that is presently staged in the woods just outside this compound, is going to come in here and kill you all."

You could have heard a pin drop. Shock and disbelief was written across the faces of men and women, most of whom had never really been threatened with true, interpersonal violence in their lives. Many of them couldn't believe what they'd just heard.

"This is one of the most secure compounds in the world," the President began, but Stahl cut him off.

"And my men will regret killing those young men and women who are only doing their duty as they see it," he said. "But they will do it. So will the teams presently covered down on your QRF and air support. Killing all of you?" He took a deep pull on the cigar. "That they probably won't regret nearly so much."

"This is insane!" the Senate Majority Leader shouted.

"No, this is the consequence of decades of governmental lawlessness and ambition, Mr. Senator," Stahl said tiredly. "The law itself came to mean only what the government said it did, and the government was made up of cliques and power-hungry politicians instead of public servants. And the law became only what the government could enforce. Well, now I'm in a position to enforce what needs to be done, and I'm enforcing it. Sign the papers, or it gets really loud and really messy in here."

It was a hard thing to watch, knowing exactly what was happening, and knowing that as awful as it was, the alternative at that point was worse.

The President just stared at him for a long moment, shock, disbelief, and anger written across his features. "This is nuts, Carl," he said. There was a pleading tone in his voice, as if he was trying to appeal to reason. "What made you think it was a good idea to come in here, after we invited you to be a part of this process, and make threats?"

"You invited me?" Stahl said. His laugh was as dry and cold as the grave. "No, Mr. President. You only spared me and my men the trouble of finding all of you and *dragging* you here."

He looked around the table again, measuring the looks that he saw. Then he nodded. "Some of you seem to think this is a bad joke, or the act of a madman. Well, to demonstrate that it is not a joke, but is, in fact, deadly serious, I would direct your attention to the screen behind me."

Renton had already consulted with an aide, and a video teleconferencing feed opened up on the big screen TV at the front of the conference room. It took a second to clear, but there were sharp intakes of breath as the image solidified.

Fred Varren was standing on the bed of a pickup truck, beneath a scaffolding made of 4x4s. There was a noose around his neck.

"The biggest mistake you made, Mr. President," Stahl continued conversationally, "was letting Mr. Varren, a man who holds no office and no authority to command any Federal law enforcement, sign the order to send the FBI and the ATF after my men. Especially after he received a mysterious infusion of cash from an offshore account, and communications from a known Russian asset immediately following Van Damme's capture. I don't take kindly to the misuse of American resources in revenge operations on the part of the MGB, Mr. President." He raised his voice. "Do it."

The truck suddenly gunned its engine and surged forward. Varren managed one strangled scream before he dropped. There was an audible *crack* as his neck broke at the bottom of the rope. His leg twitched spastically for a second, and then he was still, swinging slightly with the momentum imparted by the departing pickup. Someone in the room was violently sick on the expensive carpet.

There was a new look in the President's eyes as he looked at Stahl. There was horror there, and stark fear, along with a realization that he had never quite realized what the man was capable of. "Carl..." was all he could manage.

"Sign the papers, Mr. President," Stahl said quietly. "This has gone too far for anything else, now. If you'd listened to me five years ago, we might have headed this off. Now it's too late."

Slowly, like a man sleepwalking, the President reached for the manila folder. He read the documents carefully, then picked up a pen and signed them.

He then picked up the phone. "Yes, Ben, I know it's late," he said. "But this is important. I just recalled Carl Stahl to Active Duty." He looked briefly startled, then continued. "Yes, yes, I'm putting him in charge. You'll report to him tomorrow. There's...there's a lot happening right now, Ben." He glanced up at Stahl. "Carl will fill you in completely." He hung up the phone.

As Stahl took the papers in the shell-shocked quiet, the President said, his voice hoarse, "I hope you're satisfied."

"Satisfied?" Stahl said. "Far from it. I'd have been satisfied if we'd never gotten into this situation in the first place. If you think I *wanted* this, you're crazy." He turned, nodded to me, and led the way out of the room, leaving the civilian government of the United States of America wondering what the hell had just happened.

***

Things weren't over after that; Stahl had a lot to do to take command as quickly as possible. Most of the rest of the night was spent waking general officers up and getting him installed in the Pentagon. As word of his new status spread, nobody had the balls to object to the heavily armed and decidedly non-regulation shooters who accompanied him everywhere.

The Cicero Group had already had most of this planned out. Renton assured me that it had been an evolving contingency plan, right along with the target list for the coup, for some time. Personally, I found that just as distasteful as I'd found the rest of this business, as necessary as it had been. But I kept my teeth together. The heat was off us, at least for the moment. The declaration of martial law would be announced in the morning, and all active forces CONUS were getting their mobilization orders already. There were mutterings about the draft being necessary, which was going to be dicier than the last time it had been used, given the current social climate.

Stahl finally crashed around five in the morning, and we had a chance to get a little rest. There wouldn't be much for a while.

***

Things got ugly when the declaration of martial law went public. Extensive preparations had been made the night prior, but the Army was still spread thin, and was unable to deal with every hot spot. A lot of people died those first few days. More were going to as time went on.

The orders were simple. There were no sides. Anyone rioting, looting, placing bombs, or shooting at other Americans or the troops, died, whether they were POCRF, Three Percenters, or anyone else. Suppressing the violence was the only concern; politics came later. Stahl drummed that into his commanders, along with the implicit threat that if he got wind of any field commander taking sides, he'd send Praetorians to hang the man.

We saw little of Bates; as vital a part as he'd taken in Stahl's inner circle, his concentration was on the external threats, so he was presumably working his networks in Eastern Europe and elsewhere.

As for us, we stayed close to Stahl, those first few weeks. We suddenly found ourselves playing the part of an Executive Protection detail, rather than the special operations unit we'd acted as for years. In some ways it was a break. In other ways, it only solidified the need to cut away.

There were already steps being taken to replace us with a Marine guard detail around Stahl. After all, he was the General of the Armed Forces now; it was only fitting that his PSD be soldiers or Marines, not contractors. And as loyal to us as he professed to be, he needed to lock down the loyalty of the regular Armed Forces, now that he was running the show.

There was little sign of Tom for those first few weeks. We knew where he was; he was finishing up the details of our escape plan. So far, there hadn't been any implicit threat toward us; we were The General's boys, after all. But none of us trusted that it would last.

So, finally, during a lull in the madness, three weeks after the coup, I walked into Stahl's office at about eight in the evening. For the first time, DC had been relatively quiet for over twenty-four hours.

Stahl was sitting back in his chair, a bottle of Wild Turkey on the desk and a very full whiskey glass in his hand.

"Celebrating, General?" I asked, my voice flat.

"Celebrating?" he snapped. "No, son, this is medicating." He took a stiff swallow of the bourbon, then stared at the glass. "I rather suspect I'm not going to have much to celebrate for the rest of my life." He poured the rest of the drink down his throat, then poured another.

He stared at me with bleary eyes. If he'd looked tired before, now he appeared utterly exhausted. There were dark circles under his eyes, and there was a haunted look there that I didn't remember seeing before. "I can't forget the enormity of what we've done," he said. "What *I've* done. I took the same oath you did, Stone, only I took it quite a few years before. 'To protect and defend the Constitution of the United States against all enemies, foreign and domestic.' And yet here I sit, the military dictator of what should be a free

364

country." He took another swig. "Right now, it's a matter of drinking myself numb in the few moments of peace I have, or blowing my damned brains out." He drained the glass and poured another. "What is it?"

"I came to say goodbye," I told him.

The glass stopped halfway to his lips. "What?"

"I'm leaving," I said, "along with most of what's left of my team. Before some of the rest of the Cicero Group decide to do a more thorough job of sweeping us under the rug than they've managed so far."

He stared at me, a faint frown creasing his features. "After all this, you're just going to walk?" he demanded.

"I've got nothing left to offer you, General," I said, my own voice sounding heavy and dead in my ears. "None of us do. Do you know how many close friends we've put in the ground in the last year alone? You've got the entire US military at your beck and call now. You don't need us anymore." I met his gaze levelly. "And you know as well as I do that there are going to be those who won't forget that *we* were the ones who ultimately put the wreath on Caesar's head. That makes us a threat, and whether you want them to or not, they'll try to make us disappear, just to be sure we don't do it again." I chuckled darkly. "Remember how I said that when law loses its force, force becomes law? Well, that cuts both ways."

He shook his head in denial. "I wouldn't let that happen," he said.

"They know that, General," I replied, "which is why they'd do it without your knowledge. Your plate is full; they'll find a way to get it past you. You know history. You know I'm right."

His shoulders slumped. For a moment, the barrel-chested freedom fighter was replaced by a bent old man, alone and weary clear down to his bones. "Out of everyone who had a part in this, I hate to lose you boys worst of all. But you have taken a beating, haven't you?" He took another slug of the whiskey and looked up at me. There was something almost forlorn in his eyes. "There's nothing I can say to get you to stay?"

"No, I'm afraid not," I replied.

A faint glint came back into his eyes, and he suddenly chuckled dryly. "And knowing you, the worst mistake any man could make would be to try to force you to stay."

"You're not wrong," I said coldly.

He reached down into a desk drawer and drew out another glass. He poured some more bourbon into it, before heaving himself out of his chair and coming around the desk to hand it to me. For as much booze as I'd watched him put down, he still moved surely and steadily. The General was a practiced drinker.

"To absent comrades," was all he said as I took the glass. We raised them and drank.

"There are still a lot of bad actors who know your name and your face, Jeff," he said after a moment. "And a lot of them would be more than happy to have your scalp on their wall. I'd be a lot more comfortable with your security if you stayed."

But I shook my head. "Trust me, General, the risks outweigh the rewards. They'll have a hell of a time finding us. Rest assured of that."

He sighed. "I had to try. But now I'm out of arguments." He offered his hand, and I shook it. "Be safe, Jeff. I wish it all could have worked out otherwise."

"So do I, General," I said. "So do I."

EPILOGUE

I heard the faint rustle of cloth behind me, and Mia asked, "Another bad night?"

I turned from where I was standing on the screened-in porch of our little cabin. She was standing in the doorway, barefoot, with that black, silky robe of hers on, and her pistol in her hand.

Neither of us were ever more than an arm's length from a weapon anymore, even up there in the backwoods, miles from any other habitation. So far, there hadn't been any sign that we'd been found, but caution had become deeply ingrained in both of us.

I shook my head. "No worse than usual," I replied. I looked back out over the meadow. "Thought maybe I'd heard something." I didn't know how to describe the vague disquiet that had gotten me out of bed, and didn't really want to try.

I heard the faint sound of her putting the pistol down, then she was beside me, slipping one hand behind my back as she slid under the circle of my arm. She looked up at me searchingly. "Really?" she asked, in that tone that suggested she thought I was trying to hide from her. "Because Tiny hasn't made a sound."

I looked down at the slowly breathing mountain of fur lying on the porch next to my feet. Tiny was still really only a puppy, but when that puppy is an Ovcharka, a Caucasus Mountain Dog, it still means close to a hundred pounds of alert, distrustful meanness. Tiny didn't like people, aside from us, Larry, who was now ensconced in a cabin about twenty miles away, and Nick, who was about thirty in the opposite direction. Strangers would have had him barking as soon as they got within rifle shot.

I gave her a squeeze. "It was nothing bad," I assured her. "Just woke up and couldn't get back to sleep."

She still searched my face for a moment, before putting her head on my shoulder. We'd both had plenty of bad nights. Many times, she'd pulled me close as I lay there and shook. Some nights, it was because of soul-searing nightmares, horror shows playing themselves out in my mind as I slept. Other nights, the ghosts came back, and I woke up remembering all over again that whoever I'd just been talking to in the dream had been dead for some time. She had her own demons, as well, and there had also been plenty of nights where I'd held her close while she sobbed against my chest.

"We've taken every precaution," she pointed out. "They'd have to be wizards to find us here. Trust me, I was a HUMINTer. They're so reliant on gadgets now that they've got no real idea how to hunt for someone without them."

She was right. We were so far off the grid that it would take years of searching to pin us down. We generated our own power, and fuel for the generator was bought with cash, which had actually stabilized a bit since martial law. Water was a gravity-fed line going two miles up the mountain behind the cabin. We had a satcom rig in the back, just in case, but rarely fired it up. We had no internet connection. There was no digital way of finding us, and any other method was going to be looking for a needle in a haystack.

"I know," I assured her. "We've had this conversation before, remember?"

"We have," she agreed. "And every time you come out and stand here, scanning the sky and the treeline, even when it's still dark, I worry that you haven't quite taken it to heart. Yes, we have to be careful, but we're in a good spot."

I looked down at her. "And you say *I* worry too much," I said.

She smiled. "I married you," she said. "It comes with the job. You worry about what's out there, and I worry about you."

She put her hand to my cheek and pulled me down for a kiss. "Now, if you are quite satisfied with perimeter security, at least for the next hour," she said, "come back to bed. Mrs. Stone wants babies."

"Work, work, work," I replied, as I followed my wife back into the cabin.

THE END

STAY UP TO DATE

The American Praetorians Series is over, but there's more action to be had. Sign up for the newsletter to stay updated on my other work!

Sign up at http://americanpraetorians.com

Made in United States
Orlando, FL
08 November 2023

38716988R00225